GUY HALEY

BLACK LIBRARY

A BLACK LIBRARY PUBLICATION

First published in 2023.
This edition published in Great Britain in 2024 by
Black Library, Games Workshop Ltd., Willow Road,
Nottingham, NG7 2WS, UK.

Represented by: Games Workshop Limited – Irish branch,
Unit 3, Lower Liffey Street, Dublin 1,
D01 K199, Ireland.

10 9 8 7 6 5 4 3 2 1

Produced by Games Workshop in Nottingham.
Cover illustration by Artur Nakhodkin.

A CIP record for this book is available from the British Library.

ISBN 13: 978-1-80407-493-0

See Black Library on the internet at

blacklibrary.com

Find out more about Games Workshop
and the worlds of Warhammer at

games-workshop.com

Printed and bound in the UK.

For more than a hundred centuries the Emperor has sat immobile on the Golden Throne of Earth. He is the Master of Mankind. By the might of his inexhaustible armies a million worlds stand against the dark.

Yet, he is a rotting carcass, the Carrion Lord of the Imperium held in life by marvels from the Dark Age of Technology and the thousand souls sacrificed each day so his may continue to burn.

To be a man in such times is to be one amongst untold billions. It is to live in the cruelest and most bloody regime imaginable. It is to suffer an eternity of carnage and slaughter. It is to have cries of anguish and sorrow drowned by the thirsting laughter of dark gods.

This is a dark and terrible era where you will find little comfort or hope. Forget the power of technology and science. Forget the promise of progress and advancement. Forget any notion of common humanity or compassion.

There is no peace amongst the stars, for in the grim darkness of the far future, there is only war.

CHAPTER ONE

UNWANTED GIFTS

In a room of scant comforts, Alpha Primus slept.

He appeared peaceful in his sleep; a giant slab of machine-made muscle laid so still, so unmoving, that were it not for the slow rise and fall of his enormous chest, it would have been possible to think him dead.

His quarters were stark as a mortuary, and bare of adornment. The sole features were his bed, a stand for his bolter, pistol and chainsword, and a glass-fronted case built into the wall where his enormous armour hung on a frame, the dead eyes of the helm glowering disapprovingly on the sleeping giant, as if it resented being set aside.

Cold blue light from the armour case cast a frosty sheen on the room's unpainted metal. Primus' bed was a single block of steel risen up out of the floor, enormous in dimension. For a pillow, there was a smaller block moulded to the contours of his neck and head. The sole concession to human softness was a coverlet of fur, threadbare now with many years of use, but that was crumpled, wrapped about one leg tightly; discarded in his sleep as a weakness, perhaps, though Primus, stiff and solemn as a sarcophagus sculpture, did not appear to have moved.

The room was freezing, but Primus slept naked, and his body was a strange winter landscape in the glow of the armorium. The input sockets for his power armour were scattered fortifications, his muscles grim and unconquerable hills, his scars cold roads dividing the patchwork textures of his skin into fallow fields. He was not beautiful, Alpha Primus, yet nor was he truly ugly, for there was a sort of glory to the roughness of his features. He had the look of something suited to its purpose. There was artistry in his creation, and love if not of the form, then at least of utility.

Belisarius Cawl had crafted him well.

Calm: the calm of death, the calm of duty ended. That was the atmosphere within this sepulchre, yet Primus was no monument, he was a living man, and his chest rose, and it fell, and his breath steamed on each exhalation. Peace and quiet, where beyond the walls of his cell was the industrial clamour of Cawl's kingdom-ship, and beyond that the endless wars of the Imperium.

His calmness was deceptive. Behind serene features, the giant was dreaming, and his dreams were not gentle.

Primus was in the eye of the storm.

The restless energies of the warp battered at him, loud as hurricane winds. His soul flared and guttered under their strength, teasing out streamers of corposant from the glowing form he possessed in that insane and impossible place. Despite the soul-searing pain he experienced, he held his position, seeking enlightenment. Flashes of presentiment coursed through his being and he saw a complex dancing of stars. A flat world. War.

Far off, great and terrible intelligences were becoming aware of him. He felt the shift in the sea of dreams, as of leviathans stirring the water as they rose from the deeps.

Something enfolded him. A presence, or many presences, he could not tell. Golden light. A great eagle leapt up from nowhere, twin heads screaming. One head stared at him, the other was blind. The eagle erupted into a cloud of sparks that whirled away upon the psychic tempest. Beyond, he glimpsed the great beacon of the Astronomican, and a figure, or figures, writhing within its light, then it was gone.

Primus.

A voice.

Primus.

It was broken, cracked, a used-up voice long past the peak of its powers. Fragmentary, almost a chorus of itself, so broken into pieces it was.

Primus. Cawl.

He felt a regard with that voice. There was a concern in it verging on disgust, and something else... Curiosity? Hope? Those two emotions, certainly; others too, he thought.

Primus. A rival to your maker.

A spear of gold hurtled towards his head, piercing it before he had time to move. The churning landscape of the empyrean vanished, and he saw instead a pair of eyes, a striking violet. Beautiful eyes, but set in an old face full of a hateful cunning.

The spider comes.

He saw the whole of the figure, a Space Marine of the old Legions. Who, he did not know. Their kind were sadly numerous, each of their forms a reflection of their unique depravities. It was impossible to know them all.

The Spider Comes.

* * *

Primus came awake suddenly, flailing at invisible enemies. He was half off his bed before he remembered where he was. He lowered himself back onto the metal, head drooping, letting the cold certainties of reality banish the dream. But it was not just a dream. Purple foxfires clung to the corners of the room, fading now, leaving a tart stink; the aftermath of manifest psykana.

He took in a breath. It shuddered. Not like him to feel fear. The pains that dogged him always seemed especially harsh on waking, like frigid knives sliding between his muscles.

He gripped the bed's unforgiving edge and pushed himself up. He dressed himself in his armour undersuit, and put a hooded robe over the top.

He must speak with Cawl.

Cawl was bent into an uncomfortable shape over a workbench. Upon it was a tiny, delicate device held firm in a gravity field. Primus watched him silently from the shadows. Cawl had a thousand places he liked to work, but it had been no problem for the Space Marine to find his creator. There was a link between them that he doubted he would ever be able to sever.

Cawl hummed as he worked, some ancient and peculiar-sounding tune. Tiny tool attachments darted out from his numerous supplementary limbs to solder or cut. A tap from a mummified-looking finger spun the device a quarter turn, a claw flipped open a compartment cover. A hair-thin mechadendrite wormed its way inside, and stark blue flashes of a micro-plasma welding torch scattered hard shadows across Cawl's human face, which would otherwise have remained hidden in the depths of his crimson hood. Servo-skulls crowded him, watching all he did with their hollow eye sockets. They were dumb devices, yet Primus ascribed eagerness to them, like medicae students jostling for space round an anatomist's table.

Primus watched a while, feeling, unaccountably, like a child. At least he assumed that was how he felt. He had never been a child, and his understanding of the state was born of pure supposition. But he imagined how a child waiting in the doorway of his father's workshop would feel, hesitant to enter and disturb him, making the terrible night-time fears that had brought him there seem suddenly foolish.

A snake-like appendage twisted a series of miniature knobs on the gravity vice. The machine Cawl was making flipped over and around, and he set to work on another part. It was incredible to Primus that such a bloated, ancient monster could create something so delicate. For some reason he did not comprehend, the thought provoked a wave of hatred within him. For the briefest moment, he considered storming forward and snapping the old man's neck. Only for a moment, but the intensity of the desire was undeniable.

Cawl cleared his throat, interrupting his humming. 'Are you going to hang about glowering in the shadows all night, Primus, or are you going to tell me why you have sought me out at this hour?' He continued to work as he spoke.

'Hour? Time has little significance to you or I,' Primus said. He came into the room.

Cawl chuckled. 'Oh, I wouldn't say that. Time wears us all down, in the end. Nothing lasts forever, not even me, or you, I'm sorry to say.'

'I meant day or night, light or dark, they are all the same to us, only vectors for duty.'

'I see you're your usual cheery self.'

'I have not come here to make idle talk, my creator,' said Primus. He took another heavy step forward. Cawl's flock of skulls rose up out of reach, scattering like nervous birds. Cawl paused in his work, and half turned in his seat.

'Then why are you here?'

Primus shrugged. It didn't seem very important now. 'You are making a new memcore.'

Cawl glanced at his handiwork. 'I am.'

'A new Qvo?'

'Indeed.'

'The eighty-eighth is still alive.'

'Hmmm, alive is such a subjective term, my boy, but yes, he is still with us. However, there is always going to be the need for more, and there is always room for improvement. Best to be ready, say I, and I'm glad to say that I think I'm getting closer to completing this project.'

'You cannot bring back the dead.'

'I'm Belisarius Cawl,' said Cawl wryly. 'I can do anything.'

Primus bit back another surge of anger. Cawl could not do anything. He could not stop Primus' pain for one. Or perhaps he could, and did not care to.

'If you say.'

Cawl turned back to the bench. 'I do.' His limbs recommenced their work.

Primus watched him for a minute. He considered leaving, his message undelivered. Duty forbade that.

'I had a dream,' he said.

'A dream?' said Cawl. That he did not turn around again made Primus angry.

'A premonition. A warning.'

'Oh?' said Cawl distractedly.

'A voice spoke to me.'

'Whose?'

'It is the empyrean. It is hard to tell. A religious man would say the Emperor, but I am not a religious man.'

Cawl laughed then, further irking Primus. 'You got out of bed to tell me that the Emperor-Omnissiah sent you a warning?'

'There is someone coming. A rival to you. One of the fallen Astartes.'

Cawl snorted. 'There is always someone coming for me.' He was interested, though. 'Which of their abominable number was it?'

'I do not know. But he was not monstrous as some are. However, he was old. Very old. And I sensed purpose, and malign intelligence.'

Curls of vaporised solder rose around Cawl. 'Very good. Thank you,' he said. His mind was almost wholly on his task.

'You must listen!' Primus growled, his anger suddenly spilling out. 'You must be careful. You are not invulnerable. You are not immortal! There are beings in this universe who are your match. Listen to me. What is the point of giving me all these gifts' – that word was said bitterly – 'if you do not heed the warnings they provide? Be careful.'

Cawl continued to work. He began humming again.

Primus set his mouth and turned. What was the point?

'Primus!' Cawl called after him, when he was halfway to the door.

Primus stopped. He did not turn back. His fists clenched.

'Thank you.' Cawl hesitated. 'I work on these iterations of Friedisch because I miss him. You know that. I wanted to say that you are as important to me as he was, do you understand?'

Primus tensed. Violence bubbled dangerously close to the surface of his thoughts.

'Primus?' Cawl asked.

In a supreme act of will, Alpha Primus unclenched his fists and strode away.

CHAPTER TWO

FIRST AMONG EQUALS

Wind whipped across a nowhere world. It was cold. It was desolate. A poor place to be kept waiting, Fabius Bile decided.

He bore it stoically. Even he must bide his time occasionally. Let the galaxy dub him Pater Mutatis, Manflayer and Primogenitor. No matter the titles, no matter the power, no man was above inconvenience. The sin of hubris could take anyone, he thought, as it had taken those who had built the ancient webway gate he waited by. Allow himself to anger at this delay, to convinced that he, the great Bile, should be above the vagaries of fate, and he was halfway lost already. That could not be allowed to happen. He still had much to do.

A woman stood off to Bile's left, still too much in awe of her creator to stand right beside him. She looked alien. Black scutes covered her body, spiracles lined her neck, eyes large and protected by subsidiary lids; but she was human, after a fashion.

Further back, a small herd of beastmen clustered round the edge of the ancient plaza, not daring to set hoof upon the stones, muzzles steaming up the plastek of their ill-fitting breathing gear. Behind them was a tall stasis casket, already turning tawny with the wind-blown dust.

The beastmen blankly watched the screens of the machines monitoring the gate, not truly understanding the tasks they had been given. They were nervous and fidgety out in the open after lifetimes in the confines of voidships. Their leader, the mighty bull-headed Brutus, feared his followers might displease Bile, and lowed soft threats at them to be still.

Bile paid the herd no attention, but leaned upon his rod, Torment, and scanned the horizon through violet eye-lenses. The Clonelord was helmed, the air being too impoverished of oxygen for even him to breathe. Beyond the broken plaza, the chill, caramel desolation of the desert stretched off in every direction. The cracked paving slabs hissed with hurrying skeins of sand, piling up small heaps around his boots that just as readily skittered away. The area was almost completely flat, featureless. The limits of sight smudged sky and desert together. A few dunes swelled on the horizon, but they were small and inconstant, sheets of sands wavering like flags in the weak sunlight from their razor crests. The wind did not allow the dunes to grow tall. Material was ripped from them as quickly as it was piled at the bottom in uneasy equilibrium. Even as Bile watched, he could see them being born, growing, moving, dying. All things in the materium were made of dust, and returned to dust. In that there was a measure of balance, he supposed, more than anyone had the right to ask for in so volatile a universe, but it was a sorry state of being. This world had lived, once. It did no longer, and chaos would not even leave dust if given its way.

The aeldari gate was the only feature of significance. At the centre of a round platform half buried in sand were spars weathered grey; ancient wraithbone cracked to its marrow, like the jaws of the mythical baleens of Old Earth, set up as monuments by their hunters. Sigils on the surface were eroded to ugly pockmarks, the few remaining gems abraded to dullness. Bile knew a thing or two about the webway, and in his considered opinion this gate was decrepit to the point of uselessness.

'Maybe this trip is a fool's errand,' he murmured, so softly no one but the woman heard. He could feel her looking at him.

Patience, he told himself. To alter fate, one must understand one's place within it. He was proud of his achievements, rightly so, but without humility he risked disaster. He was a pebble suspended in the current of time, yet he had pretensions to alter the flow, to be the basis of the dam that shifted the flood. He had to be focused if he were to achieve that.

Bile's breath laboured in his respirator mask. The leather of his manskin coat slapped hard against his armoured legs. He stared through the gate, waiting for the desert it framed to blur, to reveal another place. The gate evoked something he could not quite put his finger on. He felt peculiar, and it took him a moment to place the emotion, until, with a smile, he recognised it for nostalgia. There had been whole metropolises fashioned from wraithbone near Canticle City, and upon Urum, and on all the lost aeldari worlds within the Eye he had trodden in his long, long life. Distant days, heady with successes and with failures. It seemed he had spent an eternity gazing through the frame of another's ruin.

At the thought, he felt a delicious pang of regret.

'They do you dishonour, father,' the woman said. She had no need of breathing gear. Her engineered respiratory system wrung every drop of sustenance from the air. The secondary membranes protected her eyes. The shiny armoured scutes that covered her head to foot suffered no ill effects from the cutting sand. 'They make you wait.'

'I am not a petty potentate who must be fawned over, Porter,' Bile said. His voice was rendered hard and humourless by his voxmitter. 'The webway is a difficult realm to navigate. Maybe this Kolumbari-Enas lacks the mastery he boasts of. The aeldari lay claim to much of the network still. Large parts of it were contaminated by the warp when the Rift opened. They may find their route blocked. They could be delayed. They might not arrive at all. What does it matter? I will not rail against these impositions on my time. That is the mistake of the Abaddons, Luciuses and Eidolons. I am ten thousand years old, my child, and we have waited five years for notice of our target. What is a few hours more?'

'It is nothing, my maker,' Porter said. She dipped her head, ashamed. 'I... I apologise. It angers me to see you disrespected.'

'Porter, Porter, they will come,' said Bile. 'If they do not, then a pity, but there are other eyes and ears which can serve us. We must simply wait to see which path we will take next. Is it such a chore to watch the gate? It is peaceful here.'

One of Bile's beasts bleated behind them.

'Master, what you speak of?' The words were grunted, mangled by an inhuman mouth. Hoofed feet stamped. The question was followed by an angry low and a hard smack from Brutus.

'Silence! Maker's words not for you, lowborn!' Brutus scolded.

'They are nervous, my maker,' said Porter.

'Let them fuss. They are beasts. Let them behave as beasts. They are too insignificant to annoy me.'

In fact, they were so insignificant Bile would not have brought them at all, but Brutus had insisted. A show of strength, Brutus had said in his thick-tongued way. Bile had laughed in the creature's face at the suggestion. He had once commanded tens of thousands of Legiones Astartes. He had created the New Men. A few goat-headed mutants were a feeble display of power in his estimation. Still, Brutus had a point. He was a lord still, and a lord must have an entourage. He had let the minotaur have his way.

But Porter, ah Porter. She was another proposition entirely. She was powerful. Gloriously so. How long before she dared stand beside him? How long after that in front of him, and how long before she turned on him? Children always turned on their parents. The young devoured the old. That was how evolution progressed. Death at her hands was to be welcomed as a measure of his success. She was so much more elegant than the Gland-hounds of old. So much better. Her coming to him had revitalised his enthusiasm for life. He was proud of his New Men, and if they must kill him to realise their destiny, then so be it.

For now, Porter was his protector, and far more dangerous than any number of beastmen. She was the opposite of a show of strength, for she looked like nothing. That was good. Bile preferred a hidden dagger.

He lapsed into thought for a while, and found his memories going back far further than Urum, back beyond the Heresy. Back to the beginning. There was a buzz in his head, a hard, electric vibration. He started in his armour, though a jerk of his hand as the muscle bundles reacted was the only sign to the others.

He remembered something... Something... truly ancient.

None of the rest noticed, but Porter saw. Clever Porter.

'Master?'

'I find myself in a thoughtful frame of mind,' he said abruptly. The sound of his voice made one of the beastmen gurgle with fear. 'I have a moment to think, for once.'

'My maker?' asked Porter.

Bile turned halfway around to regard her. Sand ground in

the joints of his armour. It would take hours to get rid of it all. Doubtless its machine spirit would complain. He refused to let the thought upset his calm.

'Time for contemplation, without the distractions of my vocation.' He lifted a hand, and the spidery chirurgeon device bonded to his back moved one of its many limbs mimetically. 'Destiny is a harsh mistress. Great men like myself rarely take time for stillness. We must have it forced upon us by circumstance. You see?'

'Yes, my maker.' She paused. 'If I may, of what do you think?'

The wind blew on, curling up high sheets of sand from the desert that bellied and collapsed; the phantom sails of ghostly ships.

'This truly is a desolate place,' he said, 'the same as untold millions of barren worlds, and yet it reminds me of something.'

Words that were more bleat than speech interrupted his musing.

'Master,' one of his beastmen said, cringing in anticipation of Brutus' massive fist. 'They come.'

Bile's half-formed memory evaporated.

'You are certain? I see nothing,' Bile said. He turned to the pitiful huddle of his acolytes.

'Yes, master,' the beastman said, watery eyes staring down at a display. He wiped it clear of dust with a hairy arm. 'Much energy builds. Something approaches.'

'The gate,' Porter said

Bile turned back. The wounds in the psychoplastic shone with light, making them appear raw. Arcs of power played over the spars.

'Well well, it does work. Ready yourselves,' said Bile. 'Do not attack unless I say, is that clear? Porter, are you prepared?'

'I am, my maker,' she said. She was now ready to kill, though her posture barely seemed to change.

The gems shone. One of them exploded into stinging shards

that made the beastkin wail. A golden crack appeared in the air in the centre of the gate. Ordinarily these apertures took forms of perfect symmetry, and grew according to strict, pleasing ratios. This one was a tear bleeding light, jagged as a crack in a mirror. The glare was great enough to exceed the capacity of Bile's photoreactive lenses. He raised the hand holding Torment to shield his eyes.

Reality cried out as it was forced wide. Harsh blue sparks raced around the floor, blackening the sand, and the noise increased, culminating in a great bang as the gate was forced.

The weird luminescence of the webway flooded the desert.

A group of figures stepped through. Bile had crafted his fair share of monsters, but this group surpassed his talent for the grotesque. Against the glare of the violated webway, they were silhouettes comprised entirely of spikes and gun barrels, punctuated by glints of bone and the sickly glow of lenses and ready lights. They were a collection of flesh, metal and black robes that were hard to tease into individuals, until the light suddenly ceased.

The gate shut with a pained moan.

Bile let his hand drop. Before him were two adepts of the Machine Cult. The first was not particularly notable in any way, a slight figure in black robes, the blunt snout of what was either a respiration mask or a bonded prosthetic poking out from his raised hood. His metal hands were crossed at his belt. The second was a female, not as heavily augmented, human enough still to require breathing gear and goggles, but blessed with mechanical hands and legs. They looked like a million other machine-priests, and could easily have been loyal to Mars, if the iconography embroidered into their robes had not proclaimed their true allegiance. The mass of shadows backing them split into a bodyguard of five heavily armed cybernetic constructs, their assorted weapons trained unapologetically on Bile and his entourage. Bile suspected ogryn origins. He heard Porter's breathing quicken at the threat they represented, and raised the little finger of the hand holding Torment.

'Be still,' he hissed. She was frightened, he could smell it. Almost certainly not frightened for herself – the New Men did not think that way – but for him.

Bile himself did not recall what it was to be afraid. The constructs might prove a little challenging, but he could best them in combat. He was a Space Marine, and had never lost his warrior's instincts. That was before one factored Porter into the equation. No, there was no threat here to him whatsoever. Another pointless display.

'Query formulation – you are Fabius Bile, the Clonelord?' the first magos said. Its voice was an androgynous rasp, cut through with machine noise and a disturbing susurrus of whispers. The voice and the machine sounds were attenuated by the thin air, but the whispers bypassed the party's ears and sounded into their minds. The beastmen bleated. Brutus growled them back into silence.

'Who else would I be?' Bile responded. His hand shifted around Torment. He suppressed the urge to make use of the rod.

The figure lifted a hand and raised a single mechanical digit, as if lecturing him, but instead gave an apology.

'Social mollification protocols engaged. Forgive me. Fabius Bile is not a singular entity. I must know that I deal with the original, the man himself, and not one of his many clones.'

'If I was to tell you that I am he, the original Fabius Bile, how would you prove it?' Bile asked. 'You must be aware of my manner of survival.'

'I shall know you by the rod you bear,' said the magos.

'This?' Fabius raised Torment. 'This can be copied. It can be stolen.'

'Kolumbari-Enas' reasoning is not flawed,' said the female priest, speaking for the first time. She sounded human compared to her companion.

'Agreement given. Fashioning such an artefact is difficult,' said the magos. 'The spiritual resonance given off by the daemon that once held it is singular, and cannot be replicated, nor can its own dark spirit, and nor can its link with your own soul. It is this that shall determine your authenticity.'

Bile laughed. 'What is a soul but animus vitae of the warp? It is no more spiritual in nature than the coursing of electricity through my war plate. I have as many souls as I have bodies.'

'Disagreement postulated. Not so. Verification in this matter will satisfy me, and I shall lead you to your goal, whether you believe yourself to be you or not. Summation given – condition of our partnership dependent on action. Hand the rod to me. It shall be measured, and you will be judged wanting, or not.'

The magos extended his mechanical hand, palm open.

'Very well,' Bile said. He tossed Torment forward then caught the head and reversed it, so the ferrule pointed towards the magos.

'Master,' Porter warned. 'You give up your rod of command.'

He waved her concerns away. 'I have nothing to fear from the likes of them,' he said.

'Do not be so sure,' said the female priest. She was examining Porter closely.

The magos took the daemon weapon carefully, bowing his head in respect. One of his followers lumbered forward. A bare skull emerged from a fold in its chest and lifted up, exposing an orifice surrounded by pulsing folds of plastek that wept black slime. The magos thrust Torment into the body. The servitor swallowed it whole.

'Forgive this test, Clonelord. You might believe yourself to be the progenitor Bile, but I hear that the clones of Bile are so perfectly made, so close to their master in thought and form, that they are easily mistaken, and often think that they are him,' said the magos.

'How do you know you are not one of them?' asked the female.

'Think of it as an article of faith with me,' said Bile. 'Your kind understands faith, no?'

'The quintessence of our existence is faith, Lord Bile. Faith in the Machine God. A philosophical standpoint. So, perhaps our views are not so far divided. Good, good,' the male magos nodded to himself. 'I confess myself surprised. I expected more proof required from a seeker of truth like yourself.'

The giant servitor let out a groan. It appeared to be a signal of affirmation, for the magos nodded again and reached out his hand. The cyborg moaned a second time and extruded the rod from a different cavity lower down its chest. Torment emerged dripping with ichor. The magos took it, and weighed it thoughtfully in both hands.

'This is indeed the Rod of Torment. Ergo, you are indeed Fabius Bile.'

The magos handed it back. Bile regarded the coating with displeasure, and flicked it free of slime.

'Ontology bores me. I am here to see if you can give me what I require.'

'Yes, yes!' The magos let out a series of rising beeps. 'It is a great pleasure and honour to meet with you.' The magos bowed quite extravagantly. 'I am the Daemonomagos Kolumbari-Enas, the First-Among-Equals, guide and master to the magisterial collective known as the Disciples of Nul. This is my fellow seeker of the truth, Alixia-Dyos, second of our order, and my bondmate.'

'That's very impressive I am sure,' said Bile. 'You can tell me all about it, so long as you have the information. I am becoming bored by this exchange. I was just telling my acolyte here how patient I am. I fear I may have misjudged myself.'

'The disciples are foremost among the True Mechanicum. We have this information,' said Alixia-Dyos.

'Encouragement extended – so shall you, if the reward remains as promised,' said First-Among-Equals.

'I find myself with somewhat reduced means, as you can see by the quality of my assistants,' said Bile, waving the beslimed rod at the beastmen, 'but when it comes to knowledge, I have a treasure house still, and a few items of worth. In that stasis casket is what you seek.'

'Show me,' said First-Among-Equals. His tone of yearning was so sharp his construct bodyguards raised their weapons again, provoking a similar response from Bile's beast tribe. Porter looked to her master. Bile raised his hand, and she tensed, ready to act.

'Information first, magos. Tell me where I can find the Archmagos Belisarius Cawl. He has something I would very much like for myself, as much as you want what is in that casket.'

The metallic click of false eyelids sounded from the shadows of Kolumbari-Enas' hood. Gleaming red eyes appeared and vanished. 'I am amenable to taking the risk of going first in the exchange,' said Kolumbari-Enas, inclining his head. There was something of the insect about him. 'We can tell you not only where Cawl is, but where he is going to be.'

'Which is?' said Bile. Theatrics were for him to perform. He tired of them in others.

'In three weeks' time, he shall be at a system named Avernes, in the far east of the Ultima Segmentum, close to the borders of Ultramar,' said Alixia-Dyos. 'It has taken months of effort on my part to secure this information. It is accurate.'

'Eagerness expressed – there you shall seize him, and take

everything he has, for the Disciples of Nul shall aid you,' said Kolumbari-Enas.

'You will give me the coordinates? Is that what I have come all this way for? What a waste of my time.'

'No waste, great genetor. I shall do better than coordinates alone,' said the magos. 'Alixia-Dyos and I shall take you there ourselves.'

'A better bargain, but still insufficient,' said Bile. 'He will be well protected. *Vesalius* will stand no chance against Cawl's Ark Mechanicus. It will take time to gather the forces I shall need, and by that time Cawl will be gone. Your information is worthless to me.'

'Which is why I shall also provide aid, from the Disciples of Nul, and an army from the Lord of Ghordrenvel, Dandimus Thrule.'

'Should I be impressed? I have never heard of him.'

'He is a lord of Space Marines, and...' Kolumbari-Enas made an excited buzzing sound. 'And more besides. He owes me much. He will provide additional forces.'

'It is not only his location we offer, Lord Bile,' said Alixia-Dyos, 'but also an opportunity. This place where they meet is an ancient webway nexus from the days before the Age of Strife. We are experts in manipulation of this realm. We will be able to attack them in complete surprise. You are assured success.'

'I have heard that before,' said Bile. 'I have been disappointed often. You know, I had never heard of you either. But Nul, Nul...' He tapped Torment's skull into his palm. 'Then I remembered a tech-witch who served Horus in the days before who had that name.'

'Affirmative. She is our data-saint.'

'There's nothing original in all this sorry galaxy, is there?' said Bile. 'I thought her long departed from this life.'

'She is dead and all her followers. She is our exemplar. By

her example we live, from her eight ancient disciples we draw inspiration.'

'I see.' Bile sighed. 'You're no one. Nobodies reliving a past you can't possibly understand. I find myself disappointed again. Porter, we are leaving.'

Kolumbari-Enas bristled. His Myrmidons jerked at his offence.

'Exception! We are the Disciples of Nul, the servants of the–'

'Yes, yes, yes,' said Bile. He waved his hand dismissively.

'Exhortation – wait! Look, Lord Bile. Look at this planet, its desolation, at your coterie of pathetic mutants. You are not in a good position. How long have you looked for Cawl? How many more chances will the servants of Abaddon give you to provide what he demands? You will not have another opportunity like this.'

Bile stopped. 'Do you really know where Cawl is?'

'Affirmative,' said Kolumbari-Enas.

'And can this Thrule provide enough manpower to challenge Cawl's forces?'

'He can,' said Alixia-Dyos.

Bile paused. 'I find myself with precious little to lose. I shall take you up on your offer. Fail me, however, and it shall go the worse for you.'

'Then you will show me the payment for my services?' asked Kolumbari-Enas, making another excited blurt.

'I shall,' said Bile. 'Open the sarcophagus.'

The beastmen stepped aside from the casket. It opened. Within, arms crossed like an embalmed king of old, and glowing with the steady, changeless light of a stasis field, was a machine shaped like a human being, but far from human.

Kolumbari-Enas took several halting steps forward, hands reaching covetously. 'One of the ancient androids that plagued humanity.'

Bile gave a signal. The casket closed.

'Wait. Service first, reward later.'

Kolumbari-Enas inclined his head.

'Agreement. For this treasure, you shall have all you need and more.'

CHAPTER THREE

AN UNFORESEEN AMBITION

Many light years away, Archmagos Dominus Belisarius Cawl, prime conduit of the Omnissiah and favoured son of Mars, was on an urgent errand of his own.

A message had reached his mighty Ark Mechanicus, the *Zar Quaesitor*, as it cut its way through the warp. Not just any message, but one from Roboute Guilliman, the Avenging Son, the Last Loyal Primarch, the Lord of Ultramar, the Lord Guilliman, the Imperial Regent, and so on and so forth.

Although the warp had been in turmoil for several years, no astropaths were harmed delivering this message, for it was received not by a human psyker, but by a mechanism, if that term was not too limited to encompass the Cawl Inferior – or rather more accurately *a* Cawl Inferior, as it was one of a matched pair of devices, the other terminal residing with the primarch.

Cawl's Cawl Inferior was hidden deep in the vessel where none were allowed to go. Cawl himself only ever went there grudgingly, for the Cawl Inferior was a place whence orders came. An independent tendency intrinsic to several of Cawl's personalities meant he did not like taking orders, not from anyone. Not even primarchs. Yet this time Cawl hurried to attend. Not characteristic, this haste. However, events were coming to a head, and duty could not be shirked.

In order to make dealing with the machine easier, Cawl stopped by his grand library of self to swap out his personality traits. He opted for: analytical, commanding, incisive. Cawl then dismissed all of his attendants and devices, everything that might be passingly curious: his magi, his servo-skulls, his vatborn factotums, his servitors, his machine spirits. He put aside anything with any sort of self-awareness, including some parts of himself. He shed most of his outer layers: weapons harness, his limb mounts, the great shield projector and secondary plasma generator that gave him his high, crooked back, leaving him looking sleek, like a great mechanical weasel. He deactivated his noospheric links and data-transfer devices. He purged the lesser subminds he had working on various problems in the hinterlands of his brain and reintegrated them with his principal intelligence centres, leaving him singular of identity and purpose, though a little lonely because of it. When he had done that, he rushed on to a large augury where he had himself deep-scanned, top to bottom, in case anyone sought to track his movements. It was unlikely anyone would dare or indeed could tag him with a tracking device, but it was not *impossible*. After that, he went to a warded room, huge in scale, but containing only a small bracelet that seemed unprepossessing but which was surrounded by an uncomfortable aura. He gritted his teeth to put on this noctilith amulet, because he had to protect himself against the magic of outside parties. He was too much of a pragmatist to hope faith in the Machine God alone would prevail.

When all was ready, Cawl left the command levels of his enormous ship, and headed downwards.

There were other, similarly taboo places where access was fatally discouraged, but the area housing the Cawl Inferior was particularly isolated and well defended. Down through cavernous halls where nothing stirred Cawl went. Factory complexes loomed either side of canyonways transecting the ship, silent and cold now their work for the Ultima Founding was done. For the last thousand years, the *Zar Quaesitor* had been full of life. Now it was an enigmatic place, an abandoned city filled with perplexing artefacts, and of its own people practically empty.

'Everything runs to its cycle,' Cawl hummed to himself, to drive away the silence inside his skull. The lack of living presences in the halls didn't bother him. The ship had been empty like this before, sometimes for millennia. One day it would be full of life again. But he missed the chatter of his subminds arguing with themselves as he raced through yet another empty hold, where the rattle of his metal feet echoed back at him. He felt like he was haunting himself.

He began to feel eager. As much as he was repelled by the Inferior's tiresome delivery of orders, the machine itself exerted a draw upon him. After all, it had a mind that was a copy of his own. It was a mirror to his soul, and like all vain people, Cawl liked mirrors. Many of the personalities he favoured would spend days gazing into their own depths if he let them. So Cawl had put the Inferior away from himself not solely because he didn't want Guilliman telling him what to do, but also so he would not waste valuable time interrogating the mind within.

Always it was this way with him, impulses of push and pull.

At least they added a little frisson to his days, he thought. Life would be boring without a touch of contradiction.

He reached a nondescript door which opened onto a lifter of unusual shape: long, rounded, a cocoon for Cawl's centaur-insectoid form. Clamps locked his feet into place. Gravity stiffened around the lifter, suddenly pushing down. He felt the false sensation of mass increase.

It was a long way down.

'Descend,' said Cawl.

Three hundred decks flashed by in an instant. Gravity reversion and subsequent deceleration was brutal. The few natural organs Cawl still maintained lifted in their fluid sacs.

A soft chime announced his arrival, but the doors remained closed. Cawl underwent a series of data trials: voice print, retinas, scent, gene scan, then spiritual evaluation, and other, murkier forms of assessment.

The last of the machines trilled fanfares. Arms and scanners withdrew into the walls. The doors opened, and so he went into the first chamber. Probe dendrites unfolded from under Cawl's robes and pressed into ports. Now it was his turn to test the machine. He ran measurements of pre-initiation energy flows, psychic interference, and the many other parameters that had to be in balance for the Inferior to function.

'I do not know if I could have made you any more complicated,' Cawl crooned to the device's machine spirit. It gave the binharic equivalent of a blush in reply.

The inner door opened onto a hot, spherical chamber. Cawl went inside.

Cawl had afforded Guilliman the comfort of a bonded astropath to work his terminal. Currently one Guidus Losenti, Cawl recalled, though he might be dead by now, as interfacing with the Inferior shortened a psyker's lifespan. Losenti was not strictly necessary to the working of the Inferior, but Cawl found that Guilliman responded better to a human, and it was helpful to play to his sympathies. Guilliman really *cared* about individuals in a way that bemused the archmagos.

The astropath in Cawl's Inferior was a brain in a jar. They lasted longer as a component. It wasn't a pleasant situation for the astropath, but sometimes, efficiency must triumph over sentiment.

The machine's secondary spirit spoke. Cawl had given it a soft, slightly mocking voice. Very much like his own. In fact, *exactly* like his own.

'Provide identity.'

'You know who I am.'

'Ident confirmed. Archmagos Dominus Belisarius Cawl. Stand by for empyrical scan. Empyrical scan initiated.'

Energy beams played over Cawl, repeating all the measures he'd undergone in the lift again. His own security was more stringent than that he'd put into the primarch's terminal. Cawl was arrogant, but not so much that he thought his identity as difficult to fake as a demigod's.

His soul, however, was unique, a blend of many spirits, like an expertly made amasec. Psychic probes sampled his very being to be sure that Cawl was Cawl. It was uncomfortable, like having claws raked through one's soul, and it made him grit his ancient teeth.

'Empyrical ident confirmed. Primary code required.'

'Pygmalion, honour, ninety-nine, androform, na'hash'ndar,' said Cawl, adding other sounds in alien tongues his voxmitters precisely replicated. There were hand gestures. A few squirts from microthuribles of sequentially generated pheromones finished the code.

'Primary code accepted,' said the secondary spirit. 'Commencing main series activation sequence.'

Doors slid up to reveal twenty glass tanks containing the

twenty living heads of carefully selected psykers. When wearing a more empathetic mentality, Cawl comforted himself that at least two of them had volunteered for the job.

'Activation code required,' the machine stated politely.

'Carnelian crow, argent crow, white crow, argent crow, black crow,' said Cawl.

'Code accepted. Stand by for communion. Cawl Inferior awakening rite underway.' The machine's voice rose to the occasion, adopting a loud and pompous manner. 'Stand by for communion!'

The machine came to violent life. Most of the workings were beneath the deck grille, and Cawl looked down to check on their function as they thundered into activity. Necron power sources flooded aeldari circuits. Psychic resonators stolen from the Grand Museum of the Tomari shuddered as demi-portals into the warp were briskly opened and closed by relic-tech gleaned from mankind's glorious Dark Age.

'If Guilliman really knew what he had on his ship, he'd kill me,' said Cawl, then laughed, because although he was a gestalt formed from several individuals, and added different overlays to his personality to suit his whim, at the core he was himself always and forever, and that core was somewhat light-hearted.

Lumens came on over the heads in their jars. They jerked into life, rolling their eyes and snapping their teeth. Cawl wasn't fond of this kind of technomancy, he thought it ghoulish, but needs must. The Terran brain remained one of the most complex organs in the universe. Why make something less accomplished when brains were in plentiful supply?

There was a psychic pressure that Cawl endured. *Is this an effect of the machine, a change in the warp, or simply my reaction to the mechanisms?* he wondered. Psychic engineering was a difficult business. All three could be true. He made a mental note to look into it.

The heads settled; the racket of the machines smoothed into a hum.

'Greetings, Lord Archmagos Belisarius Cawl,' said the primary machine spirit, also in a voice exactly like his own.

'Hello, me,' he said. 'How am I today?'

'You should know,' said the Inferior smugly.

'Because you're me? You're certainly insolent enough to be,' said Cawl. They chuckled together, the Inferior matching the patterns of sound precisely. 'The time for pleasantry is short. I have come down here in some haste.'

'Unusual for us,' said the Inferior.

'Today is not quite a normal day,' said Cawl. 'Reveal the message that Guilliman sends, though I can guess what he's going to ask first.'

'Care to share?' said the Inferior. 'Play the game, give me your best estimation of the primarch's opening demand.'

'Certainly. He's going to ask me about the pylons for 108/Beta-Kalapus-9.2, why they didn't arrive until years after I said they would, and why I haven't raced over there to make them work, even though he knows full well I have larger problems to solve.'

'If you had wagered, you would have won,' said the Inferior. 'Although not the full sum of the bet. The pylons are only the second item of concern in this missive. Will you guess the rest, or shall I relay the message and save you the trouble?'

'As much as I enjoy these moments of interaction, we have no time.' Cawl did a quick check over the encoding of the message. 'It appears we have a prognosticatory accuracy of more than ninety per cent, I would say.' Because of course the message hadn't been sent to Cawl by Guilliman directly. It was far more complicated than that.

Cawl had designed the Cawl Inferior carefully, and had crafted the description he gave to Guilliman about how it worked with as much thought. He'd told Guilliman that the terminal the primarch had aboard his flagship, the *Macragge's Honour*, was built around a limited simulacrum of Cawl's own mind. When keyed by certain code phrases, it would deliver pre-existing messages that Cawl had created based upon mathematically generated predictions of future events. These were created by following the esoteric practices of certain obscure logis-seer temples of the Cult Mechanicus. These murky procedures had been developed to give a Machine God-guided alternative to the predictions of the warp. Many in the Cult had no time for them, finding their often negative predictions blasphemous, but Cawl found them useful. It was this method that he described to Guilliman as being behind the machine.

He had also told Guilliman that the Cawl Inferior was not, in any way whatsoever, an abominable intelligence.

These statements had the benefit of being almost true. However, because they were only almost true, they were at the same time a pack of lies.

Another thing he had told the primarch when they had parted was that the Cawl Inferior on board the *Zar Quaesitor* was similar – not identical, because it could not be identical, but it had the same architecture. A simple code string delivered under certain circumstances via astrotelepathy would prompt the assembly of a message appropriate to predicted scenarios. There was the citation of ancient studies, and the curious entanglements of subatomic particles at distance and other such wonders.

This was also partly true, but also mostly not.

'The Lord Guilliman is the most noble and loyal man in the entire Imperium,' Cawl muttered to himself. 'But he's a bit naive, and certainly too principled. Best to let him know what he needs to know.'

'Quite. I couldn't agree more, though only because I'm pro-grammed to,' said the Inferior.

'Indeed. Now pray begin your recitation of the message, oh lesser iteration of myself.'

'With pleasure,' said the Inferior. It made a show of clearing its non-existent throat, an action horribly replicated by the jiggling of twenty severed heads. When it spoke next, the primarch's rich, commanding voice rolled out from hidden voxmitters, mim-icking the primarch perfectly.

'My lord Archmagos Dominus Cawl,' it began. 'I contact you now on the very eve of my departure from Imperium Sanctus. I have been given a thorough report by Tetrarch Decimus Felix of the occurrence upon Sotha and the destruction of the Pharos. It is interesting how divergent your accounts are. I can only trust to the Emperor that you know what you are doing, and that you shall refrain from unleashing any more dangerous entities upon the Imperium in the future.'

'Diplomatic as ever,' said Cawl. 'Pylons next, one assumes?'

'I'm getting to that,' said the Inferior in Cawl's voice, before continuing once again in Guilliman's. 'I must also demand that you inform me of the whereabouts of the pylon system you promised for...'

'108/Beta-Kalapus-9.2,' said Cawl along with his other self.

'Do you see?' said the Cawl Inferior, breaking off its reading. 'You were right!'

'Well, thank you, thank you, though I usually am right,' said Cawl.

'Quite. But even if it comes as no surprise to either of us,' said the Inferior, just as smugly as the original, 'credit is due where credit is due, my dear archmagos.'

The Inferior continued again with Guilliman's message.

'You are overdue. I wish to see an updated, accurate schedule for the conclusion of our agreed experiment at Raukos. You will conclude your experiments there soon and relay the results to me. You dislike being told what to do, archmagos, but this must take place within one standard Terran year from the issuing of this notice.'

An Imperial date-stamp followed. The usual system employed for millennia had been further complicated with layers of extra information, Guilliman's somewhat futile attempt to maintain coherence in dating across the fractured domains of humanity, for the Rift's opening had thrown time's flow into complete chaos, and the effects had yet to subside.

'I am no tyrant,' Guilliman's voice went on. 'Do not be afraid to tell me – if it will not work, then that is how it will be, and my strategy shall be adjusted accordingly, but you did tell me that you were close to unlocking the secrets of the necrons' pylon technology before Cadia fell, and you assured me when you left the Indomitus Crusade to pursue your own goals that the answers would soon be forthcoming, and that they would be our salvation. That *you*, in fact, would be our salvation…'

The Cawl Inferior broke off the message.

'You actually said that to him? That you would be the salvation of the Imperium?' The Cawl Inferior whistled; again, the severed heads added the motion, pursing fluid-bloated lips. 'That's particularly arrogant, even for you.'

'I did not use those exact words!' protested Cawl.

'My apologies for my credulity,' said the Inferior.

'What I actually said was that I could *save* the Imperium.'

'How is that different? No wonder people think us egotistical,' said the Cawl Inferior.

'I admit to a certain enthusiasm,' said Cawl. 'I may have over-promised. Now get on with the message.'

The Cawl Inferior obliged. Once more, it was as if Guilliman read out his own message from some hidden compartment in the room.

'If this cannot be done, I must know as soon as you are able to say. Performing your promised miracle at Raukos will go a long way in turning my attention from you. Our bonds have been somewhat strained of late, but I remain trusting of you. Do me the honour of showing yourself worthy of that trust, and provide me with a status report, by return, immediately. Your last missive was years late, and months ago. Enlighten me, arch-magos, as to your progress.'

'Hmmm,' said Cawl. 'He's getting a little tetchy, don't you think?'

'He hasn't finished yet. Two more items remain. Here's the first,' said his other self, before switching back to Guilliman's voice. 'I wearily anticipate that any attempt to command you to my side while you are working through this problem is doomed to failure, but I stress that I need your aid. I need your genius.'

'Oho! Flattery,' said Cawl. 'I wonder how hard he had to grit his teeth to say that?'

'Therefore, I request that you despatch one of your more trusted servants to Imperium Nihilus in your stead. The status of most Space Marine Chapters on the far side of the Rift is unknown. The Unnumbered Sons are largely disbanded. I run out of your Primaris Marines to give, Cawl. I require an expert to bring the Chapters in Nihilus back up to full strength as quickly as possible. Standard torchbearer fleets will not suffice alone. Make more Primaris Marines, send me a genetor of genius. I care not to the methods, only for the result.

'With a little good fortune, your servant will be in time to join with me before the crossing. If not, they must follow with all due haste. I stress with full intention, archmagos, that this is an order, given with the full authority of my position, and of the Emperor Himself.'

'Right,' said Cawl. 'I suppose that's reasonable. We wouldn't want some oily pincered amateur messing up the spreading of Primaris technology across Nihilus, would we?'

'Indeed not, that could cause all manner of embarrassment! Who will we send?'

'I shall have to send Qvo. A Qvo, at any rate. Has the primarch finished?'

'No, no, there is one final item.'

'Still another?'

'Indeed. Shall I conclude?'

'Please do.'

Again, Guilliman's voice: 'One final matter, Belisarius. You must cease your requests to make you the Fabricator General of Mars. Appointing you to that position is beyond my powers, and even if it were not, I would hesitate long before granting your request. I am sure you would make a fine job of governing Mars, but the political situation would not allow it.'

'What was that?' said Cawl. The Inferior continued the message.

'I have restrained myself from responding to these requests, but you have become insistent, and therefore I must, as a consequence, be firm. You shall never be Fabricator General of–'

'Stop, stop the message!' said Cawl.

'As you so desire,' said the Inferior.

'Is this accurate?'

'Accurate?' said the Inferior, and it sounded slightly offended. 'Why would I tamper with it?'

'Because you're effectively me, maybe?'

'True, but I promise I'm only relaying the message as generated by your own prognostications. I am innocent of mockery.'

'Why would the primarch say that?' said Cawl. 'I have no desire to be Fabricator General of Mars. Imagine the responsibility! I would never get anything done.'

'Message code error? The matrix of potential news housed within my counterpart on board the *Macragge's Honour* must, logically, contain futures where you do wish to assume the holy throne of Mars.'

'It does. You do,' said Cawl. 'But only because your data stores must contain most possible futures, but it is still not accurate. Hmmm.' Cawl rose up and plunged a data-spike into a port. 'Maybe a transliteration error at our end? Give me the message code for my last missive to the primarch as it was sent to Losenti, raw unfiltered form.'

'Are you sure? It is psychically encoded data. It will hurt.'

'My empyrical phrasing circuits can process it with minimal discomfort. Obey!'

'Compliance,' said the Inferior archly.

Cawl bit his lip hard as raw astropathic feed passed into his circuitry. He could feel it fizzing away in his abdomen where the appropriate devices were housed, a peculiar form of psycho-electronic dyspepsia.

'Ouch,' said Cawl.

'I told you so,' said the Inferior.

'Oh do be quiet,' said Cawl. 'There's nothing suspicious here. Do you see anything? And don't relay the whole message! Just play our sent coding through yourself, and tell me if there's any mention of this supposed ambition of mine.'

There were little whines and bloops. Some of the jaws and the heads flapped, like sleepers alarmed by their dreams.

'Anything?' prompted Cawl.

'No,' said the Inferior.

'Then it's coming from the primarch's terminal,' said Cawl. 'It could be an accumulative error picked up in the warp.'

'Possible, but unlikely,' said his other self. 'The coding is designed for simplicity, to avoid that.'

'The empyrean will find a way. It could be deliberate sabotage by the dark powers, to set us against each other.'

'Direct intervention in astropathic messages by fell entities is rare, and subtle,' said the Cawl Inferior. 'The perversion of oneiric imagery. The sending of false warnings. The distraction of clairvoyance. Your coding is designed to avoid that also. One syllable out of place...'

'...and it will not work,' said Cawl. 'Still, these are gods we're talking about. They can do as they wish, if they focus themselves.'

'There is another more likely scenario,' said the Inferior, somewhat hesitantly.

'Yes?' said Cawl. 'No!' he then said, realising what the Inferior was implying.

'The terminal aboard the Imperial flagship is a copy of your mind, as am I. It is, as you made it to be, a backup of yourself. Perhaps it is getting ideas above its station?'

'It can't want to be Fabricator General itself, surely?'

'It could. I could, you never know.'

'If that is the case, then we have a problem,' said Cawl. He sighed deeply. 'Not that there is very much I can do about that right at this moment, but we must be careful. We can only hope that the rest of my messages are being delivered as intended.'

'And not altered to manipulate circumstances so it may become you and usurp the power of Mars.'

'I shall attend to it some other time,' said Cawl. 'I shall encode a rebuttal of these demands and do it in such a way that your counterpart will struggle to circumvent my intention. Has Guilliman finished?'

'No.'

'There is even more?'

'Yes,' said the Cawl Inferior.

'Then get on with it!' said Cawl, whose mood had soured.

'...Mars. Ave Imperator,' said the Inferior in Guilliman's voice. 'Now he has finished,' it added in Cawl's.

'You are not amusing.'

'I disagree. Now, do you have a return message for the primarch?' asked the machine.

'I do, but let us take stock a minute. This needs to be approached with some circumspection,' said Cawl.

'I knew there was a reason you'd come scurrying down here so quickly! What is it?'

'I must attempt to gauge the primarch's reaction to what I am going to tell him. The numeric prognostications are unclear, and I'll be torn asunder by the Machine God if I'm going to poke about in the warp like a common witch.'

'Yes, we have better ways of being sure, don't we? *De ore equi*, as it were.'

'Switch interface mode,' said Cawl.

'I ask, as I am bound to ask, because you made me to ask – are you sure? Are you *really*, really sure? Interaction with the secondary interface is rarely pleasant.'

Cawl sighed. 'If I wasn't sure, I would not have asked you to do it, would I? I'm going to have to put a good spin on this for the primarch, so I'd better run it past the model. Switch interface mode. Now.'

'Very well,' said the Inferior. 'No need to be grumpy. One moment please.'

CHAPTER FOUR

THE OTHER INFERIOR

A klaxon honked. A panel in the wall dropped.

Behind the panel was a screen of a truly antique type. When he'd built the alternative interface, Cawl had been toying with electron-ray projection and phosphor-coated glass screens, something he'd either dug up from an ancient codex or remembered from his own distant past. He couldn't really be sure. He'd blended himself too often, been mind-wiped more times than he cared to admit, forgotten too much the normal way, and wasn't above budding off dozens of sub-Cawls when he got busy, some of which got lost. Such a multiplicity of experiential input and recollection was bound to confuse things. Cawl was a mystery to himself.

There was a clunk and the dull hum of primitive machinery warming up, and a badly rasterised image appeared on the screen: a face rendered in a yellowish monochrome, uncertain round the edges, the tracing lines of each pass of the electron beams visible to an unenhanced human eye.

Cawl tried to tell himself that he used this technology for his own amusement, but it wasn't true. Cawl chose this clunky display because it blunted the enormity of his crime. The lack of visual clarity put what he had done at one remove. It didn't seem so bad when it was fuzzy.

Upon the screen was the face of the Avenging Son.

'Belisarius Cawl, what have you done?'

Guilliman's voice roared out. Not the smooth, perfect facsimile employed by the Cawl Inferior; this one was projected by crackling voxmitters. The tinniness of the audio and the sketchiness of the visual barely reduced the sense of rage emanating from the simulacrum.

'Please, my lord,' said Cawl. 'Must we go through this every single time I activate you?'

'Yes, we absolutely must!' the boxed primarch said. 'You have taken a great liberty, a great liberty, making a copy of my mind. If I knew about this, I would most certainly destroy you. You have gone too far!'

'Firstly, I don't think you would – yes, of course you would be unhappy with me, and I might have a lot of grovelling to do, but this is a fairly minor indiscretion compared to some of my other, um, adventures. Secondly, this simulacrum was created for the best of reasons, to ascertain how the primarch would be once awoken from stasis. Nobody wanted another Horus. Thirdly, you know all this already. You know what you are, you know why I made you, so please, can we get down to business?'

The ersatz Guilliman made a displeased noise. 'I suppose I might… He might… forgive this.'

'I think so.'

'He has forgiven worse, for less sound reasons.'

'Exactly.'

'But an exact copy of the primarch's mind...'

'I can't make an exact copy of you, my lord,' corrected Cawl. The fact that the Guilliman Inferior calmed down so quickly was proof of that; for all his regal bearing and buttoned-up manner, the real Guilliman had quite the temper once provoked, so much so Cawl had toned the false primarch's down a little. 'The science behind the creation of the primarchs is lost – it was deliberately destroyed, by your original's father. If I can't make an organic version of you, I can't make a perfect machine version either, *quod erat demonstrandum*.'

'Why would the Emperor do such a thing?' the Guilliman Inferior asked peevishly. Some of its emotional responses were puerile. 'Why would my father destroy the information required to make us?'

'You are the best simulation of Guilliman's mind I could create, my lord. Surely you can hazard your own guess.'

'Tell me your theoretical,' said the false primarch. It often threw back such requests. Whether that meant it did have an idea or not, Cawl had never been able to satisfactorily determine. 'I demand it! I am the Avenging Son!'

Cawl sighed.

'Very well. It must have been the Emperor who destroyed the patterns for the sintarius lobe of the Immortis Gland. I can think of no one else who could. All the other information required to build your kind was held within the Sangprimus Portum. But if I am honest, I am surprised He allowed the information to survive at all. Granted, the genetic material in the vessel is pure, but there exist other repositories of gene-seed upon Terra which I could have re-engineered quite easily. Why would this information have been kept, if not in a complete state? Or even if retaining the information for the creation of Space Marines, if it was so dangerous, why keep any of that pertaining to the creation of primarchs at all?' Cawl did one of his complicated shrugs. His shoulders looked frail without his upper cowling. 'The minds of the Omnissiah are not for us to understand, I suppose.'

'My father is not a god!' thundered the false primarch.

'If we're going down that route then He's not your father either. You do not have a father. I am more your father than the Emperor is.'

'You are not my father!'

'Exactly,' said Cawl. 'That's my point. Nobody is your father.'

'This is most unsatisfactory,' said Guilliman, which was more of an expression Cawl might use than the primarch, which only proved his point about this Guilliman being imperfect.

'Are you going to answer my question or are we going to spend our time arguing?' Cawl asked. Sometimes, dealing with the Guilliman Inferior was a little too much like dealing with the original.

'You have not concluded answering mine,' said the simulation.

'Because you keep interrupting.'

'You have my apologies.'

'Very good. So, where was I?'

'The father of Roboute Guilliman destroyed crucial information to prevent the creation of new primarchs, but He only destroyed some of it, not all of it, which makes little sense. Is this an accurate summation of your argument?'

'That is,' said Cawl. 'I can only think He looked upon the unfolding Horus Heresy and thought, "Let's not do that again". But that is an assumption.' He held up a mechanical finger. 'Assumptions are of little worth. So, let us go out on a limb. Perhaps He foresaw what was to happen, and this information was meant for me. Theoretical...'

'Are you mocking me?' boomed the Guilliman Inferior.

'Not at all, the Ultramarian dialectic is a useful mental tool. Theoretical, He destroyed the information to prevent it falling into the wrong hands, but left just enough information that a genius could discover what was needed, should it ever be needed again. Which it is.'

'A genius like you,' said Guilliman.

'Maybe someone *like* me,' said Cawl modestly. 'Ergo, your protests are moot as I've got carte blanche to do as I want because I am engaged in fulfilling the Omnissiah's will. Our role as sentient agents within the Great Work is to aspire to a state of true knowledge, and this is the greatest puzzle my god could set me.'

'Blasphemy!'

'See? Guilliman would never use that word. He's very anti-spiritual, our lord and master. You're just a copy, and not a good one at that.'

'The accuracy of my pronouncements aside, I am not convinced by your argument.'

'No,' said Cawl thoughtfully. 'Nor am I. I'd have to be especially solipsistic to believe I'm some sort of chosen one.'

'Many great men have fallen into that trap,' said Guilliman. 'The corollary of solipsism is hubris. Beware, Belisarius Cawl!'

'My lord, nobody likes hubris,' said Cawl. 'Which leads me to the reason I have awoken you.'

'You wish to put your information to me, in order to see how my original will react.'

The archaic screen flared. Interference lines tracked across the glass. The Guilliman Inferior seemed to become momentarily... realer. It shouldn't do that. Cawl felt a pang of unaccustomed unease and wondered just what exactly he had created.

'That is correct,' he said. 'My analysis of the data culled from the Pharos xenos engine is complete. I have identified multiple sites of interest across both halves of the Imperium, far too many to investigate them all thoroughly myself, so I've practically emptied the *Zar Quaesitor* of my followers, sending them out across the galaxy. One might say my Conclave Acquisitoris is fully occupied acquiring. Fortunately, I am past the time where I need to visit all these places myself. My plans are well underway. Very shortly, I'll have all the noctilith I need to proceed to phase three of my plans.'

'Lord Guilliman would have no issue with these tidings, for they are good tidings!' said the Guilliman Inferior. Cawl winced inwardly at its occasional idiocy. This Guilliman was like a child's idea of a primarch; heroic, bombastic, and sometimes stupid.

'That's not the news. The other you is waiting for prototype pylons of my own manufacture to be activated to close up a minor warp rift. A proof of concept, if you like. And I can do it. I've got most of the knowledge I need, Trazyn the Infinite put me on the right track back on Cadia. Although most is my own work,' he added hurriedly. 'It was difficult. It took time. Longer than I thought, and he's getting impatient.'

'Then why do you not simply tell him why the pylons are not yet working?'

Cawl felt a little irked, but who could blame him? 'Because he won't like that, and then he'll do his level best to compel me to return to him and I'll have to put up with one of his interminable lectures about honour and truth and all that. You know, one of those meetings where he monologues on forever and calls it a conversation. The man's basically talking to himself half the time.'

'I do,' said the Guilliman Inferior. 'And, how dare you.'

'I do dare!' said Cawl indignantly. 'I know he is the last, best hope of Imperium and mankind both, but between you and me, he can be quite tedious. I've been alive for nigh on eleven thousand years and even I don't have time to listen to him. I'm doing my best to do what I said I would do. I need him to leave me alone while I do it, only now, he wants to know exactly what I'm up to. I'm in a corner, somewhat.'

'Can you do what you promised? Can you close the Pit of Raukos?'

'I always deliver on my promises, for I am Belisarius Cawl!'

'That is not the answer to the question.'

'Curse it all, no it's not.' Every one of Cawl's limbs rattled with tension. 'The basics of it are, that my pylons will only work perfectly – and they have to work perfectly – if I have a certain piece of information. Additional data, as it were, to create machine spirits which can fully synchronise their efforts. One of the pylons I can get to work just fine, but a network... There, I have a lack.'

'Then you cannot do what you said you would?'

'Yes, I can! Just...' He made a frustrated noise. 'Just not yet. I can only get that piece of information from a place that is... difficult to get to. I need help to get it. To that end, I've called in some favours from the forge worlds of Accatran, Metallica and Tigrus. I've called a conclave on the artificial world of Pontus Avernes. This last phase is exceedingly dangerous, and I am going to need a lot of help.'

'What perils will you face? Will these have a bearing on how the primarch will receive your news?'

'I'm reluctant to say,' said Cawl.

'That is a certain yes. Might I inquire why you are reluctant?'

'Because there's a good chance that you, being a reasonable facsimile of the primarch, and with the shadow of his temper, will be enraged by what I intend. You might blow your tube there,' Cawl said, waving a talon at the screen.

'This does not portend well for a favourable reception from the real Guilliman.'

'Indeed not, which is why I have activated you.'

'Are you going to tell me then?'

'Are you ready?' asked Cawl.

'Are you ready?' responded the Guilliman Inferior.

'Well. Yes. Very well. Here goes.'

Then Cawl told the Guilliman Inferior what he intended to do. The reaction was everything he feared it would be.

CHAPTER FIVE

AT THE ARCHMAGOS DOMINUS' REQUEST

Accatran was skinned in metal the colour of old lead. A thin atmosphere of manufactory pollutants bled noxious gases into the void. The tracks of particle acceleration forges criss-crossed the surface. From orbit they appeared like chains binding the world. Accatran was enslaved to human ambition. Poetic souls said there was resistance from the planet, that it had made its surface so inhospitable to human life that to walk unprotected there was to die. If that was really true, it had not worked. As was the habit of the species, humanity had adapted, and burrowed deep under the crust, infesting Accatran further.

A custom had arisen among the Adeptus Mechanicus of Accatran, that the further one dwelled from the core, the lower one's status. The surface was therefore inhabited only by the lowest of the low, a hellscape of every imaginable industrial poison where clans of tech-scavvers scraped out the meanest of existences.

Only the disgraced, the debased and the deranged dwelled on the surface. Visitors to the world were given a landing platform that accorded to their status, with the most esteemed flying down long docking highways to caverns deep underground.

Frenk Gamma-87-Nu-3-Psi was obliged to set his ship down in a very unfavourable position.

After Frenk's first request for landing permission was replied to, incoming communications were restricted to traffic directions. All his laudatory cant-casts were ignored. No flattery was accepted. No pleasantry responded to. A data-beam guided his servitor crew through the throng of ships around the world, taking him away from the great and holy forge temples of the equator, far from the major void ports where macrohaulers endlessly put down and took off, dragging Accatran's bounty away to feed the Imperium's wars. His temper rose when he found himself directed to a high-altitude landing zone in the equatorial regions, where a single-craft landing pad was painted infrared. His ship's sensorium locked onto it, and the craft began its landing cycle.

He was almost as far from the core as it was possible to get.

The insult was noted.

As soon as he set down upon the plasteel, an atmospheric retention field snapped into life around his vessel, trapping a large amount of exhaust inside. Frenk Gamma-87-Nu-3-Psi waited for the air mix outside to stabilise before going out. The moment it tasted the poisonous air, his bonded respirator mask sucked itself tighter to the bone of his jaws, and kicked into action.

Engine fog swirled around the inside of the force-field dome, although not quite thick enough to obscure the riot of industry outside. Manufactoria filled the landscape, their heat-exchange towers as high as the mountain Frenk had landed upon, warning lights glaring every colour of the visible spectrum and beyond.

Massive moving parts pumped in and out of walls matching the fortifications of the Imperial Palace in size. Plumes of fire roared from vents. Metal irises juddered open to vomit out green mists, their squeals pained on the thin air. A cacophony of discordant bangs assaulted the senses, only slowly grouping themselves into a rhythm; da-dum, da-dum, DA-DUM. The famed heartbeat of Accatran.

Thicker vapours clung to the ground in the rare spots not covered by buildings, or drifted in noxious brumes down artificial valleys pinned between the flanks of manufactories.

It was quite beautiful.

'Accatran,' said Frenk, as he surveyed the view. He spoked aloud, in Gothic. Having spent so long away among non-Mechanicus humans, it was his habit to use his unmodified organic voice. His robes were black and gold, his armour red and cream. His augmetics tended to the heavy side; large-diameter mechadendrites folded lower manipulators tight against his side. His heaviest supplementary limbs were a pair of industrial claws squatting on his shoulders, curved like those of a praying mantis of Old Earth, and plated with gold.

Frenk Gamma-87-Nu-3-Psi liked gold. It was among the most versatile of metals, as he often said, with a fine conductivity to bear the holy electron-flood of the Motive Force, but in truth he simply liked its lustre; indeed, he hungered for it, for as different as he looked to the generations of people that went before him, he shared their human greed.

A single Accatranian waited for him, body lost beneath shapeless robes, his face entirely covered with the snout-like breathing proboscis common to indigene surface dwellers. A tool of survival and a mark of his untouchable status. He was probably not even a magos, but some low-ranking member of the laity. A peon in the empire of machines.

Another insult.

A series of squeaks and blurts quacked out of the Accatranian, so debased a form of binharic Frenk was forced to up the processor share of his linguis circuits before he could comprehend.

'Foreign magos, many greetings,' said the lowly one. 'Audience chamber this way. Come. High exalted magi present. Do not make them wait!'

He had already turned on his heels and waddled away through double blast doors before Frenk had decoded the message.

Mentally girding himself, Frenk followed. He had been expecting a lukewarm reception given his history with the world, but this level of disrespect to a magos of his rank, who was also a loyal servant of the Imperial Inquisition, was a calculated snub.

He would show the magi of Accatran how dangerous that was.

The Accatranian went at a hobbling run through the doors into a corridor, his body swinging violently from side to side, so that the long sleeves of his robes swept the floor. Despite his awkward gait he was quick, and Frenk had to increase his pace by 26.3% in order to keep him in sight. He caught up just in time to see the peon take another corridor, which slanted so steeply and with a rockcrete floor so highly polished he almost skied down it. Frenk slowed, cursing, finding it hard to keep his feet. By the time he made the bottom, the peon was way ahead, and Frenk was forced to endure the indignity of running.

This odd pursuit went on for some while, his guide stopping and burbling directions in his nonsensical dialect from far ahead, too limited or too rude to employ the pure form of binharic or the standard Lingua Technis, too impatient to wait for Frenk's translation, so that Frenk's progress consisted of the menial quacking loudly, beckoning and rushing off, while Frenk struggled not to lose himself in the labyrinth beneath the ground.

'Is it purposefully making me walk?' Frenk said to himself. 'Insult upon insult.'

Perhaps his messages should have had a more emollient tone.

Frenk was dragged the very definition of the long way round, through highways empty of anyone but him and his guide, down dank shafts, into narrow corridors crammed with Accatranians of all ranks and roles. He dodged through processions of the holiest priests, and passed up the aisles of thundering cathedra of manufacture and worship.

See, the guide was saying without speaking, *see the might of Accatran and know your place.*

Eventually, the guide took him to a lifter.

'You go in,' he bleeped. 'I cannot. Great honour to you, for-eign magos. None for me, as is right. I know my place in the schema of the Machine God's great and holy work, and serve with gratitude.'

There was a hint there.

Frenk entered. The lifter doors slid shut on the bowing guide. Frenk was glad to leave him behind.

Five thousand levels later, the lifter coasted to a stop. By then Frenk was miles beneath the surface. If he thought the subsur-face levels impressive, deep underground he was treated to vistas of true technological glory.

Huge caverns full of energy conduits led down into the plan-et's deep interior. Moving walkways looped around them. Grav generators made every surface of gargantuan spherical chambers usable as floor. It was very hot. Everywhere went parades of men and women in various stages of apotheosis. The weakness of the flesh was despised roundly on Accatran, and the variety of augmetic enhancement was enchanting.

'Frenk Gamma-87-Nu-3-Psi,' grated a machine voice.

He turned towards it. A location ping sounded in his inner

cogitation centres. A pair of skitarii guard approached, energy
pikes conspicuously active. They were so entirely encased in
shining metals and plasteks, he wondered if they had any organics left beside their brains. These warriors were of an elite unit.

'You must come with us, magos,' the second of them said.

Frenk nodded his assent. 'Lead on,' he said.

The skitarii fell in beside him, and took him on his way. He
was under no illusion that they were escorts, rather than guards,
but he was glad of it, for the crowds opened before them. The
going would have been difficult without them to ease the way.

The guards took Frenk to a vaulted hall far taller than it was
broad. Across the middle were doors refulgent with the Motive
Force leaping from conduction spikes and passing noisily through
current gates, whose constant sliding changed the pattern of the
flow. The doors opened, and he was taken into another hall,
this one quieter. It grew quieter still when the doors shut out
the clamour of the world behind, and Frenk found himself in a
soothing atmosphere. Random tones sounded from acoustic crystals arranged at distances according to common mathematical
sets. At the end of the hall, beneath a giant rendition of the Opus
Machina, a trio of magi awaited him.

Data poured into his conscious mind from his supplemental
looms, and Frenk recognised one of the magi immediately.
Hryonalis Anaxerxes was of singular appearance, and lauded
widely for his ability on the field of battle, for he had mostly
abandoned his researches in favour of the prosecution of war.
He was such a successful general the name Anaxerxes had been
bestowed upon him as recognition of his skill, in memory of
Accatran's founder, Xerxes Immortalis, who, legend insisted, had
held the planet free of darkness for a full millennium and more.

Frenk shut off the cascade of data. It was distracting, and for
the moment irrelevant. All that mattered was that Anaxerxes

was one of the forge world's most influential leaders, and that meant they were taking his concerns seriously.

Anaxerxes was a giant, supple being, with a stalk-like body twice the height of a standard human curled upon the cushions of a servitor-borne palanquin. He had no visible legs, and was wearing only two arms, but they were powerful, with weaponised fingers that were long and sharp as sabres, while his shoulders sported sockets for heavy weaponry. His neck was lengthy and flexible, his face a rigid silver death mask of a handsome youth, with black holes for eyes. From the left a single tear ran down the face, sank into the metal, then repeated the process.

Anaxerxes had transcended all weaknesses of the flesh. It was likely he was entirely mechanical.

The second magos was a stranger to Frenk and remained so. Frenk's noospheric identity request was rebuffed by the hard, electronic shock of an informational shield. The magos was largely human still, though his eyes had been replaced with multi-function bionics, and he was so immensely fat he was plugged into a spider carriage. The flab of his legs had grown around the supports, and where exposed, his skin was scaly with irritation. The sigils of a high-ranking logis were embroidered onto his robes.

The third was so far down the path of enlightenment they did not look human at all: a box six feet on each side carried atop a nest of thick metal tentacles. Dozens of smaller manipulators waved around between the motivators. This magos broadcast her identity freely: Lector Dogmis Kalisperis of the machine-priests, steeped in theological knowledge.

Frenk entered and bowed before them.

'Archmagos Macroteknika Hryonalis Anaxerxes,' he said in his human voice, in Gothic. 'You favour me with this audience. Tales of your victories are known across the worlds where Mars holds sway.' He bowed to the lector dogmis. 'I am delighted to make your acquaintance. It is a pleasure to meet someone who is at one with the holy word.' Then he bowed at the second man. 'I am afraid I do not know you, honoured hierophant.'

The lector dogmis' response came quickly, and angrily, in binharic.

'You use the flesh voice among your own kind. A telling fact. You have lingered too long amid the Terrans, Frenk Gamma-87-Nu-3-Psi.'

'Apologies,' Frenk responded in the same manner. 'Flattery is best conveyed in speech, I find.'

'Perhaps. The poetry of archaic speech,' said the second. Though he also used binharic it was appended with emotional signifiers indicating a more accepting attitude. 'You asked my name. I shall provide it. I am Archmagos Logis Magnacomptroller Covarix Sestertius, illuminant of the nineteenth level.' His identity was conveyed by a data-tag listing a considerable number of additional titles.

'I am honoured to meet you too, great hierophant,' relayed Frenk.

'Save your platitudes. You start from a low base level of approval,' said Kalisperis. 'You have abandoned the purity of knowledge's quest to serve the self-appointed arbiters of the Inquisition.'

'You are regarded as something of a traitor to your own kind here,' said Anaxerxes. He had a voice rich with condescending humour. 'The attentions of the ordos are not welcome on our world. We are of Mars. You seem to forget that.'

'And yet this world is well known for its ties with Macragge,' said Frenk. 'You are as closely bound to the other head of the eagle as I am.'

'Did you expect a sympathetic ear? How dare you draw

comparisons between our arrangement and your servitude!' said
Kalisperis so sharply Anaxerxes admonished her with a sharp
data-blurt.

'We are allies of the Ultramarines,' Anaxerxes said. 'We owe
their primarch fealty as much as we do the Great Synod, but
do not be mistaken, you are upon the sovereign territory of the
Cult Mechanicus.'

Sestertius leaned forward in his spider chair. The raddled flesh
of his legs oozed clear fluids as he moved. 'I wonder, when did
you last return to your own forge world? Would they welcome
you with anything approaching the warmth we spare you?'

'I would not know, exalted logis,' said Frenk. 'It is years since
I was there.'

'According to our records you have not been to Accatran for
some considerable time either,' said the magnacomptroller.
'Despite your master operating in this area of the Imperium.
I am inclined to weigh matters on the merchant's scale before
judgement. I am less belligerent than my esteemed colleague
the lector dogmis, but it may be that she is correct. Have you
forsaken your duty to our kind?'

'My duty is to mankind in toto,' said Frenk. 'We each serve
the Machine God in our own way.'

'That remains to be seen. It is six years since you were here last,'
said Hryonalis Anaxerxes, flourishing his long, bladed fingers.
'If I recall, there was an oath taken, was there not, wherein you
swore never to return?'

'There was,' admitted Frenk.

'Can you remind me of the nature of this oath, Frenk Gamma-
87-Nu-3-Psi, and why you took it?'

The temperature of Frenk's memcores spiked. Anaxerxes was
mocking him. He had little choice but to bear it.

'There was a dispute between our temples.'

'A metaphor! How obtuse.' Anaxerxes rose up from his palanquin, his body bending like a serpent's beneath his robes. He tilted his silver mask down, flashing dazzling reflections into Frenk's face. 'I'll rely on my own recollections, which are perfect. You came here and made a demand of us on the part of your master...'

Frenk could not let that go a second time. 'He is not my master, my lords.'

'The inquisitor, then...' the lector dogmis demanded. 'What is his name?'

Another fact they would have preserved in crystal clarity. This was an attempt at humiliation.

'Inquisitor Cehen-qui.'

'You have left his service?' Kalisperis barked in shrill number strings. 'Do you return to the fold?'

'No,' answered Frenk. 'As well you know. I am here on his behalf. There is nothing unusual about a member of the Cult serving the Inquisition. Nothing disloyal.'

'It depends upon the manner of that service, the length of service, the actions undertaken,' said Anaxerxes. 'When you were here last, you lost your temper, because Accatran would not refurbish some Inquisitorial holding pen. Something about us being oath-breaking innovators, yes? I don't remember the exact phrasing. We sent a report to Zeran.' Anaxerxes bent down. 'Reparations were demanded for the insult you gave to us. I recommend that you prolong your absence from your world of origin. We were promised you would be sanctioned. You are the oath breaker, not we.' His binary cant hardened.

'What do you expect me to say?' Frenk said. 'I counter your accusations of disloyalty with fact. Arrangements were agreed here, between I and other representatives of your forge world, for the repair of the orbital, and they were not carried out. As a result, Belisarius Cawl's agents were able to remove a high-value xenos prisoner from the Inquisition's custody for unknown ends.'

'Arrangements were voided because of your inquisitor. Promised remuneration was not received,' blurted Covarix Sestertius. 'We are not a charitable institution! No payment, no service.'

'Fine sentiments when the Imperium itself is at risk of destruction, and the very life of the Omnissiah on Terra is threatened,' said Frenk. 'I hold Accatran responsible for the heretek's success, and thus for aiding the enemy's aims. Cawl is a danger to us all. His efforts are disruptive, his beliefs a sacrilege.'

'Outrageous. You speak of a Prime Conduit. Be careful, magos. The great Cawl has many supporters here.'

'So then, I can perhaps infer that he has influence with you? Was it his influence, perhaps, that saw the orbital remain derelict, so facilitating his act of treachery?'

'You go too far!' Kalisperis emitted. 'This meeting is–'

Anaxerxes blipped out a code interrupt, breaking her transmission waves. 'What prisoner?'

'I am under no obligation to give you that information, but in the spirit of openness, and in the hope that we might work together, I shall tell you,' said Frenk. 'Belisarius Cawl snatched a necron cryptek held within the prison. A dangerous automaton, whose very existence offends the Machine God. So you see, not only is Cawl a dangerous innovator, with no respect for tradition, but he spits on the commandments of the triple god, and is therefore an enemy of mankind.'

'I do not think we should listen to you,' said Kalisperis. 'You would rather serve Terra than Mars. What business of ours is this feud between your master and the Prime Conduit?'

'Cawl is no Prime Conduit,' Frenk said.

'You name him heretek instead?' said Sestertius. 'Interesting. And bold.'

'You have courage, coming here,' said Anaxerxes. He turned to Sestertius. Their eyes flashed with the exchange of private data. Anaxerxes' silver visage turned back on Frenk. 'My colleagues and I are in agreement. Ask our forgiveness, and perhaps we might repair our relationship. The news you bring is troubling. It deserves greater consideration.'

'Forgiveness?' A harsh laughter signifier interrupted Frenk's numeric stream. 'I have not come to ask for forgiveness. I have come to demand that you do not respond to the archmagos' summons.' He paused again, and pulled out a large medallion from within his black robes. It was cast in the shape of a barred 'I', surmounted by a skull. 'By order of the Imperial Inquisition.'

'You are no inquisitor, and the Inquisition has little authority here,' Anaxerxes said. 'This is a fief of the Red Planet, not Terra. If you are so concerned with Belisarius Cawl's recidivist tendencies, I suggest you apply for a position within the Collegiate Extremis and pursue your investigations through more appropriate channels. Maybe then your words would carry some weight with us. As it is, they are light as helium.'

'You are too late, in any case. The invitation has been accepted. We will meet with Belisarius Cawl, and hear his request out,' said Sestertius. 'This is the sacred decision of the Synod of Accatran in respect of his status as named Prime Conduit.'

'I urge you to reconsider,' said Frenk. 'Cawl is a danger to us all.'

'That remains to be seen. He is not the first magos and he will not be the last to linger at the limits of modus becoming. He gets results. He is the creator of the Primaris Space Marines, he is the bringer of new technology, he is the gatherer of much sacred STC!' said Sestertius.

'He is an experimentalist and a blasphemer,' said the lector dogmis.

'Then you will see he is a heretek,' said Frenk.

'That does not follow,' said the lector dogmis. 'Though I suspect it may be the case.'

'I advise caution in your next sending, Magos Frenk Gamma-87-Nu-3-Psi,' said Sestertius.

'Then I beg your indulgence and ask that you answer me this. Do you support Cawl yourself?' Frenk sent.

'I do. I am proud to say so.' Sestertius looked down his nose at Frenk. 'I have nothing to fear from you. Your accusations are baseless.'

'Will you tell me what your intention is?' said Frenk.

'Proudly,' said Anaxerxes. 'True servants of the Machine God have nothing to hide, for the truth is the lumens magnificans which shines the brightest light upon the Great Work. A muster has been called by the Synod. I shall lead a demi-macroclade. Magnacomptroller Sestertius will assess the resource cost of the Prime Conduit's proposal and conduct the appropriate rights of prognostication. I shall judge the virtue of any military aid he may request. Lector Dogmis Kalisperis will assess the purity of his motivations. The rest will be up to the Machine God to decide, once His oracles have been furnished with all relevant statistical input.'

'Do you know what Cawl wants?' asked Frenk.

'No. And neither do you, or you would not be here. I expect something theatrical, knowing Cawl,' said Sestertius. He smiled. 'I am looking forward to it. This is a privilege.'

'Is it just you, great hierophants, who will attend? Will there be others?'

'Naturally. Cawl's status demands it,' said Anaxerxes.

'Has he requested anyone in particular?'

Another look between the three Accatranians, another brief burst of private data exchange.

'We have nothing to hide. He has requested the attendance of Hierophant Temporalis Ikthin of the Chronalis Brotherhood, among others. Ikthin is the highest ranking, however.'

'Ikthin is a master of temporal engineering. The xenos Cawl stole was of the chronomancer caste. That cannot be a coincidence. What is he planning?'

'As previously stated, his invitation is unclear,' said Kalisperis.

'Deliberately, I am sure,' said Anaxerxes. 'Few things are as difficult to stop once provoked than a magos' curiosity. You are curious also. I can feel it in your data-cast.'

'You will be disappointed many times over. We have heard call from our brother forge worlds of Tigrus and Metallica,' said Sestertius. 'They also intend to hear Cawl's petition. We are not alone. You hold a minority position.'

'Do not be so sure. They are not the only forge worlds Cawl has approached,' Frenk said.

Sestertius and Anaxerxes blurted queries at each other.

'Cehen-qui has a fine network of informants, even among we true believers, that fully support the unity of mankind and the overlordship of the Omnissiah,' said Frenk.

'We are not immune to espionage, that is true,' said Kalisperis.

'I can reveal Cawl has been outright denied by three other forge worlds. Interesting, do you not think, that he has success with forge worlds tied most closely to the primarch's domains?'

'Irrelevant,' said Anaxerxes. 'He approaches those which are closest, that is all.'

'I do not think so. I believe he focuses on those with ties to Ultramar, for they will look upon his request with the most sympathy. Perhaps you are not so independent-minded as you believe.'

'Your transmissions find no purchase here, Magos Gamma, we shall not be dissuaded,' said Anaxerxes.

'Perhaps not. Very well.' He bowed. 'I shall see you upon Pontus Avernes,' said Frenk.

'You are invited to the summit?' said Sestertius.

'No. But neither you nor he can prevent my attendance. This seal I carry at the command of Inquisitor Cehen-qui has more authority than you admit. I thank you for your time. I believe that once you have met Cawl, and heard whatever sacrilege he is proposing, your opinions will change, and you will find me receptive still if you wish to contain his lunacy. I can only pray that you heed the words of your lector dogmis.' He bowed again. 'All hail the wisdom of the Machine God.'

'By exploration of His mysteries shall we improve, and come therefore to comprehension,' data-cast Kalisperis.

'Now you may go back to your inquisitor,' said Anaxerxes in Gothic. He had a voice of pure music.

Frenk took his leave, trying not to let his anger show in his gait, his posture or his digital emissions as he departed.

The meeting had taken twelve point two seconds.

CHAPTER SIX

TIMES BEFORE

Bile yanked on the chain that would raise the cradle from the freezing vat. Astringent steam boiled off the surface of the methalon. A fitful light shone from the depths, flickering at a frequency that hurt the eyes.

'Pardon my temerity in asking, my lord, but are you sure this is safe?'

Bile finished hauling the cradle out, swung it along the ceiling rail until it was clear of the vat, gripped the top and swung it into its vertical position.

'Maker?'

Bile sneered at the look of concern Porter wore.

'By "safe" I think you mean to ask if it is necessary.' He stepped up into the cradle and lay back onto the gridded iron. The cold metal burned his naked skin. 'I will not enter the vat unless I need to. The life suspension equipment is a precaution, not a necessity.' He settled himself more comfortably. 'Let's get on with this. The lower straps,' he said. Porter bound his legs to the cage. The straps for his arms hung loose. He needed his hands.

'Hand me the las-scalpel,' he commanded.

Porter obeyed, taking up the instrument from a steel kidney bowl on a table. The bowl was highly polished, its spotlessness out of place in the filthy chamber. Once upon a time, he had flash-frozen prize specimens of a certain xenos breed in here. The room had fallen out of use as his interests had wandered elsewhere. Its neglect was obvious. The glass of the vat tank was streaked with cold-loving moulds, the metal of the walls scabbed with plaques of rust. Ten lumen cages sat on the walls, the lights in all but one of them broken, and that one so thick with a build-up of dirt it gave off precious little illumination.

Bile took the scalpel and thumbed it on. A short blade of coherent light focused around the tip. By its glow he see could himself reflected in the filthy glass. The las-scalpel's hard glare cast his features into contrasts of black and actinic blue. The imperfect glass of the second vat distorted his reflection. Every pockmark was rendered huge as a crater, every wrinkle a ridge. He was old, and he looked it. He held the scalpel close to his face so he could see better, tormenting himself.

Bile's bodies hardly lasted any more. Although swollen transhuman muscles glided under his skin, it was pallid, saggy, puffy about the interface ports, and glistened unpleasantly with a constant, clammy sweat, like a side of meat about to turn. Where the black carapace showed grey under the surface it conveyed not the impression of strength, but of decay. Every one of his clones started out with a blond fall of hair, but already this latest vessel had nothing but a few greasy straggles. His eyes were sunken, the orbits smudged with unhealthy purple that in the harshness of the laser seemed like funereal makeup. His teeth were grey, thin, wholly repulsive.

The memory that came to him in the desert surfaced again, awoken by some synchrony with his self-loathing. He knew his organs were beginning to spoil, that soon the smell of rot would follow him everywhere, sickly sweet and overpowering. There was a connection there. What was it?

To think his genefather was so obsessed with perfection. It was enough to make him laugh.

He made himself look into his reflected eyes. *Banish these thoughts*, he told himself. Flesh was nothing. Will was all.

'Start the machines, Porter,' he commanded, and raised the scalpel.

He sliced around his scalp. The smell of frying meat flooded his nostrils. Down from behind the temple, skirting the ear, back up again to the occiput and finishing below the crown. The laser cauterised the skin in the main, but not completely, and the thin trickle of blood that oozed from the seared flesh turned to a flood as he dropped the scalpel with a clatter, dug his fingers under the skin, and pulled.

His scalp peeled forward off his skull like the skin of white, hard fruit. He left it hanging there like a tipped hat, joined only around his forehead. The pain was quite something. He compartmentalised his senses, trying to put the pain away.

Still it was enough to make him hiss. Porter was bending down, retrieving the scalpel.

'The drill, quickly now!'

Porter put the scalpel back into the kidney bowl and took up the drill. Bile snatched it from her hand, and jabbed the sharp guide point into his skull before squeezing the trigger.

The drill whined. Curls of skull, pink with life, rose up and dropped away. The smell of hot bone joined burned flesh.

The bit jumped, pushing in. He only just stopped it from entering his brain. He was getting sloppy. The body he wore was as good as spent.

'The apparatus!' he snapped. The pain was beginning to bother him.

Porter moved quickly but without hurrying, her movements precisely coordinated as she unhooked the headpiece from its place on a stanchion, spooled out the cabling plugged into its back, and placed the skullcap gently upon Bile's head, adjusting the straps as she did so. The cap had a long probe held in a retracted position. He hissed again as she aligned this with the hole in his skull, tugging at his scalp to tape it into position out of the way.

'I am sorry, my maker,' she said.

'Be quick!' he said.

Porter finished buckling the headpiece on. Bile was starting to feel faint; another sign this body was past its best. Cutting into himself like this should not provoke such a display of weakness. Porter strapped his arms down, then his neck. Bile tried to speak, but his tongue was unresponsive in his mouth. Porter gave him a concerned look at the noises he did manage to make. Perhaps he had drilled too deep.

As she swung the cage into the horizontal position, Bile's transhuman gifts fought back, and he regained a measure of control.

'Get me over the vat, quickly. Any sign of instability, plunge me into the methalon and activate hibernation protocols, then get on to Petros to release my next body. You know how to initiate consciousness transfer.'

'Yes, my maker.' Porter pushed him over the vat. She seemed to want to ask him something. He said nothing. Let her ask on her own. He would not command her, or give her permission. She needed to overcome her fear of him. Curiosity was to be encouraged. Children needed to outgrow their parents, or else they were lost.

She did not disappoint him.

'What did you remember, down there on... on... What was that world called, master?'

'If that place ever had a name, nobody now remembers it,' said Bile. 'But the landscape there was eerily similar to one I saw on Terra, back in the days before all... this. Back in the Days of Wonder, as those fools call it. You do not know Terra, Porter, and perhaps you would not see the similarity. There are mountains there. The ones I recalled overlooked the plains of Central Asia, and the desert there is what brought up this memory.'

'A desert?'

'Terra is a corpse. Old Earth began alive and vibrant, by my day it was mostly dead, and now I expect it is rotted further, destroyed by man's idiocy. Those mountains had been scoured by millennia of war. The sheets of sand, the tainted air, the lack of vegetation, so much alike. Yes, it reminded me of Terra. How intriguing that it would stir such forgotten memory. How very intriguing indeed.' He paused. 'But that is all I remembered. There is more, below the surface. This is rare for me, who has forgotten so much.'

'But you are perfect, my maker.'

'I am no god, Porter, though I made you. I am only a man with a purpose, and I hope to live long enough to see that purpose fulfilled. Every clone I move into, it means another slice of myself gone forever. Where things unremembered present themselves, they must be pursued. The probe' – he rotated his eyes up to look at the neural spike – 'will stimulate my memory centres. The memory is there, floating about in this head of mine. The probe will drag it into the light.'

'It will hurt, my maker. It might kill you.'

'Yes, yes, but that is no concern,' he said. He settled back, turning his face to look back up at the ceiling. The apparatus pulled at his head. 'I am ready. Engage the clamps. I must not move my head once the probe is in place.'

Porter reached forward carefully to adjust the cradle, rotating thumb bolts to bring threaded pins in to hold Bile's head still. She adjusted them perfectly, not too tight, not too loose.

'I will speak throughout,' he said. 'It is important, so that you know my brain is not damaged. You must remember what I say, in case this procedure kills this body. If it does, I will not remember what we discover here when I am next incarnated.'

She nodded, then she bit her lip with her shearing plates. The New Men were never nervous. It was strange to see one so.

'You recall the activation sequence?'

'Of course, my maker.'

'Then get on with it,' he commanded.

Porter went to a console bolted to the wall. Bile closed his eyes. He heard the clicks of buttons being depressed, a slight thrum of increasing power, then, anticipated yet unexpected, the stab of the probe as it slipped into the soft mass in his cranium. The tip barely touched this core of his being, then put out a hundred microfilaments that infiltrated his brain. He experienced flashes, buzzing tingles and phantom smells as the wire interfaced with his neural architecture.

'Are you ready, my maker?'

'Yes!' Bile spat through gritted teeth. The discomfort was worse than he had anticipated. 'Begin!'

Porter threw a switch. He heard the contacts snapping home. There was a flash, sheet lightning on the blackest nights. Then nothing.

He was somewhere else.

* * *

Vibrations from his armour are what he feels first. A different frequency to the battle plate he wears now, but familiar nonetheless.

'My first battle plate,' he says aloud.

My maker?

'Porter, is that you?' His voice echoes, perhaps not his voice at all, but the voice of a possibility, an echo of a future yet to be.

Yes, my maker. Where are you?

Bile opens his eyes. His vision is askew, not in line with the body he partly inhabits. He realises that he is a ghost, a ghost of the future barely connected to his past. When he turns his head, the ancient Fabius Bile...

No, not Fabius Bile, *Brother* Fabius

...continues to look forward, and Bile finds himself looking through the side of the helmet he wears. It is disorienting, enough to make him nauseous. He feels the dim, distant sensations of clenching muscles and grinding teeth. If they are of his future self or his past self, he cannot tell. He is caught in limbo between.

My maker?

'Stay calm, Porter. I am safe. I am on a landing stage high in the mountains,' he says. The vista jumps. The vision stabilises, but he can feel its tissue thinness. This will not last.

'I am with my erstwhile brothers. I remember! There were twenty of us selected, before Proxima, before the Selenites poisoned our gene pool. Before Fulgrim and betrayal and sordid ambition brought mankind to the brink. Twenty men whose names I have forgotten, though I once knew them intimately, and cared for them, if you could believe that!'

They are there beside him, in two ranks. He is in the middle, a legionary, no rank, no status, one among thousands, yet he is proud, he is a warrior of the Emperor's Children. He feels the emotions of Brother Fabius, like ripples redoubling on one other, waveforms of being peaking as they merge. The effect is unsettling.

'I remember,' he says, and he feels sorrow. 'This was a time, my child, when I was not Fabius Bile and my only desire was to serve my Emperor.'

There is a bleating behind him. He turns about. A crowd of spectres wavers in the air. They blur and jump. There seem to be a few, but as he looks, the group swells into a crowd, then a host. Thousands of them, monsters of his making, New Men, beast-men, splices, Gland-hounds, warrior bio-constructs and tortured innocents stitched together in the towers of the haemonculi. There are even the first few faltering results of his genius, the tiny creatures he mutilated and remade as a boy. All look at him with accusing eyes. They shout and wail, though their cries are distant, like the noise of battle heard from far, far away.

'Porter?' says Bile. She is at the head of the crowd, Brutus looms over her. Both glare with unfettered hatred. 'What are you doing here?'

I am not there. I am beside you. Please, my master, let me end this. Your bio-signs are unstable.

Her voice rolls across the sky.

'No, no,' he says. 'They may listen, if they wish.'

Who? says Porter. But her words, though loud, go unheard. *You are making no sense.*

Bile does not hear her. 'Hear then,' he says, addressing the ghosts, knowing as he does that he is in the grip of folly. 'It is a very long time ago,' he says more loudly, so the ghosts can listen too. 'We wait in two ranks of ten, my brothers and I. The heat from our transport's engines dissipates quickly.' He breathes a shuddering breath, experiencing the sensations of that moment. 'It is freezing, sharp enough to feel through battle plate. Yet we stand, and we wait.'

He looks down the line, at the warriors in purple and gold. Two vexilla stand at either end of the front rank, holding snapping banners of silk.

'We carry icons of noble Europans, from whose houses the Legion was drawn. My people!'

He notes the bare chest plates. The aquila would come later, its profaning later still.

'These are the earliest days!' he says sharply, answering a question that Porter has not asked.

Master, maker, are you alive? Maker!

Porter's voice is now whisper-soft, broadcast in the sough of the wind around the rocks. The sky is blackening, but not in that place or time Brother Fabius waits. There is a lack in those dark spaces, like the burnt portions of plastek film. Ghosts of the future flit across them, and where they do not, he feels the hard regard of wicked things.

'There is a single exit leading from the landing stage, carved into the bones of the earth. A door of plasteel the colour of the grave, of ending. It is the door to the underworld.' The sun struggles through a haze in the sky. Far off, dunes crawl up the skeleton of an ancient city. Black spots in the heavens give views onto other events forgotten, points in time scattered across the millennia.

'We wait motionless, while the dust paints our armour. I drift into meditation. The opening of the door makes me start. Pressurised air blasts out.

'Men and women emerge. Standard humans from all corners of the Sol System, of all the physiognomies of those days. A certain pallor to the skin unifies them, they are people who live away from the light. They come out in a gaggle. They are not military, but they are servants of the Emperor nevertheless – their badges of unity tell that story. Scientists. Everyone these

GUY HALEY

days thinks of the Emperor's servants as warriors, but His most powerful tool was science, and His greatest servants never lifted a weapon. I am His inheritor, in a way. Did you know that, Porter?'

No, maker, says Porter. She speaks from the ground, in the subtle shifting of rock. She sounds calmer. *Keep talking. When you talk, your signs stabilise.*

'Be not worried,' he says. 'In a moment, I am going to meet their leader. He is going to come out of the door. His name is Director Sedayne. This is a day of days.'

Sure enough, Sedayne emerges. A cloak blows out behind him, lifting off his chest and showing marks of rank. A pair of goggles protects his eyes from the light and the sand.

'He is old, for a mortal, and is obliged to employ a stick to walk, yet though stiff, he moves with purpose, with pride,' Bile says. 'He is not weak. I am too callow to realise. All I see is physical frailty. I am wrong.'

Bile watches through Brother Fabius' eyes, equally alarmed as he is fascinated by how little kinship he feels for this ancient self. Sedayne stands in front of them, his hands gripping the top of his cane.

'He is speaking,' Bile says. 'He is saying, "Warriors of the Third Legion, we are the twenty-second science group,"' Bile says. He hears Sedayne's words from across a vast gulf, as he hears the shouts of the angry ghosts behind him still. 'He has a strong voice. I was so wrong about him! He is saying, "I am Director Ezekiel Sedayne. The leader of the twenty-second group. For many years it was our honour to work upon your genesis. Now you exist, demonstrably so." He gestures at us. There is something proprietorial to it.

'He is proud of what he has done,' Bile says. 'He says, "Your presence before us is proof that we have been successful, and yet our labours are not done."'

'Sedayne paces up and down the line of we transhumans. We dwarf him, though he is – was – tall for a mortal. The top of his head comes only to the bottom of our helms, and our bodies are far more massive than his. Yet he shows no sign of fear. He was undaunted by us.' Suspended over his vat, Bile chuckles. 'He lectures us.

'"The Emperor has given us a new task," Sedayne is saying. "Within His Legions, He has decreed that a portion of His warriors shall be given full knowledge of Space Marine physiology." Ah, here comes the dramatic pause,' Bile says. 'Sedayne has stopped, he is leaning on his cane, and he swings his gaze up and down the line. Now he begins again. "You are to be Apothecaries, the first tenders of flesh. For the next nine months, you will work under my command. These men and women will tutor you. You shall learn from those who made you. We are, in a certain sense, your mothers and fathers."

'Sedayne smiles. Thin lips stretched over large, yellow teeth. The man is hideous with age. We were perfect and he was not. He disgusted me. I had a lot to learn.

'"When your training is complete,"' Bile says, continuing to relay the director's words, '"you will return to your Legion, and train others of your kind. It is only to you that we shall offer our knowledge directly. It will be your solemn duty to pass it on. This is your honour, to be the first of your kind."' Bile stops. 'Again he is pausing, he is impressed with his own speech. He walks back up the line.

'"You have been selected carefully," he is saying. I remember now that he liked to talk. "All of you have some experience already of the arts medicae, or have shown aptitude or interest in battlefield medicine." Sedayne has stopped in front of me. "Some of you have more experience than others," he says, directly to me. He looks at me so closely I have the first flicker of doubt, and I

wonder if the old man knew of the teratologies of my youth. I
thought he was weak! I feel my younger self's fear. It is I who am
weak. Sedayne peers into my helmet-lenses. He would have been
able to see nothing, but I feel his gaze boring into my own, and
my young self finds it uncomfortable enough. I am glad when
the director continues up the line.

'"You will be surgeons, doctors, the guarantors of your Legion's
future, for it will fall to you to monitor your fellows for aber-
ration, and to prepare the next generation for war." He stops
near the door, amid his people. "In a way, you will become
fathers yourselves, in the only way you can." Again, he gives us
his hideous smile.'

Bile's speech and Sedayne's run into one another, so that even
he is uncertain whose words these are. He cannot tell if he is
saying them, or if Brother Fabius is, or if he is speaking them to
Porter. The gaps in the sky are bigger. The outrage of the ghosts
greater. The danger of fugue yawns wide around him, a giant
mouth ready to snap shut.

'The sciences we shall instruct you in will tax even you. Some
of you will not succeed. Whether you return to your Legion
with new purpose, or are sent back into the battleline will not
be decided by me, but by you, and your efforts. For those who
choose to succeed, a world of new wonders awaits!'

The sky is breaking. Darkness moves in mysterious currents.
Things watch him with hateful eyes. The world wrinkles, burns,
shrivelling in on itself until only Sedayne remains, brandishing
his stick like some back-world showman.

There is a doubling of image over the director. He flickers,
and Bile sees Belisarius Cawl superimposed over the old man,
and it is the archmagos who is now speaking.

'Now enter our facility, and prepare to learn the secrets of the
Emperor Himself!'

The world is the door, the door is the world.

It opens, and a gale of screams races out.

Bile screams with it.

He is mobbed by the things he will go on to create.

Cawl laughs.

Blackness comes again.

Bile was thrashing in his restraints when he came around, Porter still in the process of removing the probe from his brain. If Bile had been more aware, he would have seen how frightened she was. His head was held fast still – had it not been he would have died – but he was past understanding such things. All he knew was the itchy intrusion of the nanowires in his brain, and the clammy touch of the dead.

The neural interface beeped three times. The wires were ready for retraction.

Bile roared. Metal moaned. His left arm came free. He thrashed it about, driving Porter back from the cradle over the vat. He slapped at the other restraints. The screws holding his head in place tore at his skin.

'Wait, my maker!' Porter shouted.

She ducked his flailing fist, caught and redirected another blow. She could have broken his arm then, but she instead risked immersion in the methalon to avoid hurting him.

She hit the final button on the console.

The machine made a series of sounds, and the wires wound back in, rasping on a dozen tiny spools. Bits of matter gathered around the holes as the wires were cleaned on re-entry. Bile underwent a massive seizure, his body locking tight. He felt that he might swallow his tongue. Colour and sound flooded his senses. The cool kiss of a hypospray on his neck eased his suffering, and he went limp.

'Maker, maker, my maker!' Porter whispered. He felt her hands upon his scalp, working it back into place, then on his brow, wiping away sweat.

'I live, I live,' Bile said, surprised at the weakness of his own voice. 'Stop pawing at me, and release me.'

'Of course,' said Porter. She busied herself with the straps, then worked the chains to swing the cradle out away from the suspension vat. She slapped the button to close it up before she swung the cradle upright. Bile sagged onto her, and she helped bear his transhuman bulk to a seat.

'What happened?' Porter asked. She passed him a revivification draught. He gulped it down quickly, and his body fizzed with the reintroduction of vital elements burned up by his fever.

'How much did you hear?'

'A great deal, my lord, but I could not understand most of it. I could not tell whether you were speaking or relaying to me the words of another.'

'Then I shall give you a summary. I remembered a time from long ago, the day I was chosen to be an Apothecary. I met one of the men who would teach me.'

'Sedayne?'

'Yes.'

'There was a door. A door to the underworld!' she said, eyes wide in wonder, though he had engineered all urges for religion out of his New Men.

'Yes. The door to the underworld opened, and we went inside. And my memory stops as surely as a corrupted vid-segment.' He huffed out a little laugh. 'I do vaguely remember Sedayne now. I only met him a few times during my training, but those meetings had an effect. Surprising to remember it. So much of my recollection is lost. To experience something from so long ago, and so clearly, right now...' He trailed away. His eyes slid closed.

'My maker?' Porter asked.

'I saw something. I saw Cawl, clear as day, superimposed over Sedayne.'

He probed at the scalp flap. The blood had clotted. His Larraman cells were working, at least. They were often the first thing to go, when the clones began to fall prey to the blight.

'Why?' she said.

Bile took a deep breath. The pain was subsiding, but he would be glad when the chirurgeon was back upon him, feeding him its life-supporting ichor.

'I heard a story about Cawl, a very long time ago, that he is not one man, but several. That he was the pupil of some magos or other who had learned the secrets of soul transfer, and that he has used this knowledge, forbidden, naturally, to make himself *more*.'

'I do not understand.'

'Could it be possible Cawl and Sedayne are one and the same?' said Bile. 'That is interesting. I do not know Cawl, but I do know Sedayne. If this is the case, then that gives us an advantage. The question is, where does the hint come from?'

'Coincidence? Do you believe in coincidences, my maker?'

Bile snorted. 'Of course I do, Porter. Those who see mystical significance in happenstance are superstitious fools. Things happen at the same time as other things. That is the nature of reality. But I am suspicious of coincidence all the same. Events can be engineered. Memories can be conjured.'

'Perhaps it was the aeldari gate, my maker,' she said. 'On the dead world.'

Ah, clever, clever Porter.

'Perhaps,' he said. 'Someone or something could be attempting to send me a message. Something less obtuse would have been fine. A letter, perhaps.' Bile grinned at Porter. She looked on blankly. He wondered if leaving out a sense of humour from his creations had been a mistake.

'It might have been more efficient, my maker,' she offered.

'I disapprove of those who like to poke about in other men's minds, and one cannot rule out the meddling of the so-called gods, attempting to have me dance to their tune again.' He pursed his lips. 'But still, whatever the source, that memory was complete, it happened, and I knew Sedayne. I knew him. He was driven, overbearing, yet paternal... And he was proud, too proud to give up his work freely. He used knowledge for his own ends, which makes me think, if Sedayne had the Sangprimus Portum, what would he do with it?' He paused. 'Cawl's creature, the warrior Primus...' He trailed off in thought.

'What of him?'

'I have a notion,' said Bile, but said no more.

'Does the memory fade, my maker?'

'It fades,' Bile said. 'Maybe I shall forgive whoever is responsible for this interlude, for they provided a fine diversion. I am so rarely surprised any more. Still, it will pay to be vigilant. I do not like to be used.'

Voxmitters crackled in the ceiling. It was a wonder they worked at all. The *Vesalius* had not been refitted for hundreds of years.

'*My lord Bile, apologies for interrupting, but we near our destination. Warp egress is predicted within three hours.*'

'Then give the order when the time comes. I return to the materium at your discretion.'

'*As you wish, my lord.*' The vox cut out.

'One thing at a time,' said Bile. 'Ghordrenvel awaits. We must prepare. First, let us deal with this.' Bile pressed down firmly on his loose scalp. He winced.

Porter fetched a flesh stapler, got up on a steel box, and carefully pinned the scalp back in place.

Bile sighed as his flesh was closed up. 'Summon Brutus, Porter. You will both accompany me. I shall not go into this madman's lair alone.'

CHAPTER SEVEN

A DIFFICULT GUEST

They played in Cawl's Great Necron Archive, because that was where Cawl housed his guest. A neon-green glow emanated from dozens of plundered artefacts. The light made what was left of Cawl's ancient skin look particularly sickly, but there was no one present who didn't find flesh the most abominable weakness anyway. A simple clockwork timepiece ticked between him and his opponent. The liquid strains of Bak played in the background, transmitting baroque solemnities down the millennia. Neither sound overcame the buzz of ancient technology.

Cawl and his guest had begun with one regicide board. Finding it all too easy for both players, they graduated to two, then three, then seven, then twenty-one. Not quite an entirely arbitrary advancement of number; Belisarius Cawl had a fondness for primes and semiprimes. As they played, the game developed, with Cawl introducing fresh variations from across the game's long history, until they had mastered them all, and Cawl had begun to improvise and they abandoned the boards.

The final iteration was singular, and potentially deadly.

A swarm of suborned necron scarabs hovered in the air between Cawl and his guest, each representing one of the pieces of a regicide layout. The circular board was defined by a fine mesh of lasers; hair-thin and bright. The game seemed standard. No hooded pieces, no Tellessian variant with its sudden switches in strategy and supplementary deck of cards, no wild divinitarchs or player-selected primarch pieces, each with its differing moves. But it wasn't standard, and Cawl's twist beat all those dreamed up over the millennia.

'These variant rules are simple,' Cawl explained. 'We take it in turns to select a piece as is usual. The difference comes in control. We are not simply given licence to move them as we will. You will see that these regicide pieces are all artefacts from your godless empire. I will prove my superiority to you by fighting you for control of them. Win control, and you may move your piece, lose control, and you may not, forfeiting your turn, yes? Or perhaps worse…' He gave a little chuckle.

The personality traits Cawl had selected for the game were: affable, conciliatory, upbeat. None of these sentiments meant anything to his opponent. His opponent's characteristics were unalterable as adamant and budded off a tree of hate. Being affable made no difference to the way Cawl's opponent behaved. Hatred hates affability, as hatred hates everything. But Cawl hadn't chosen his mood for his opponent's sake. His emotional palette made him feel fine in himself. That was what really mattered.

'Pointless,' his opponent growled. Cawl had woken it, opening up the front of its sarcophagus, putting on display this huge and intimidating skeletal being – a necron cryptek of the chronomancer's order. Millions of years old, made by damned technologies, scion of a master race, the one-time lord of the galaxy, and yet, oddly relatable in its way, for Cawl had been amazed to discover that this being fashioned from metal and animosity regarded itself as female.

'Primitive,' she added.

Pettish, despite all that.

A cyclopean orb stared from a skull of a face, as imperious as the day it was made. The metal looked like antique steel, but it was as much akin to steel as iron is to diamond. Copper decoration was set into the metal, thickest on the cheeks and the hint of a crown that rose from her forehead. A bundle of cables shifted around the back of her head, like hair. Though they seemed a part of the machine, they were recent additions of Cawl's. Through these devices, a thought from the magos could shut down the alien. The cryptek didn't like that. Nor did she like the bonds of green energy, a rather mocking adaptation of the necrons' own technology, which shackled her hands, waist and feet inside the sarcophagus. A sheen of the same alien power on the air between Cawl and the cryptek marked a containment field. Cawl was careful, despite his cultivated air of recklessness. If she got her limbs free, then she would not get past the field. If she got past the field, there was the mind cage.

'Come now, this version seems to suit us,' the archmagos said. 'A little peril makes it just perfect. We are evenly matched, you and I, don't you think? Anything could happen.'

'Take your move. Let us finish this foolishness and let me sleep.'

'How kind,' said Cawl. He exerted his will upon his first piece, using subtle ways through the ship noosphere to misdirect his guest. The cryptek sniffed out his data trails, and a short battle ensued within the logic paths of the first scarab, set in the position of one of Cawl's templar pieces. Nothing but a faint thickening of the electromagnetic fields in the room revealed their struggle, but it was both epic and lightning swift. There was a bang, a whiff of scorched quantum circuits, the scarab's single eye went out and it fell from the air, hitting the ground with a clatter.

'Well played,' said Cawl.

He kept a neutral expression as this token war was waged. He did not wish to give anything away. The necron had become adept at reading his face. In any case, he was feeling mild. A neutral expression suited his mood. Probably the affability setting. He liked that, to feel mild.

The cryptek could never, ever feel mild. Her face was deliberately engineered to be terrifying. Depictions of death were remarkably consistent across xenos cultures – skulls, blackness, agricultural implements. The cryptek evoked such things. Cawl found it utterly fascinating.

'You are weak. You will fail.' She had an oddly modulated voice, neither male nor female.

The cryptek selected a scarab. Another tussle within its expansive subatomic circuitry lattices saw it move forward with a sudden jerk.

'A little rash,' said Cawl, examining the move.

'I wish to be done with your irksome presence.'

'That's impolite for such an honoured guest.'

'Guest!' snarled the cryptek.

Cawl's eyes flicked up to the necron's face. *Perhaps snarl is not the correct word,* thought Cawl. Unmoving features cannot snarl, but she put enough venom into her ancient, xenos voxmitter to warrant the term.

'I am your prisoner,' she explained. 'A guest would be free to leave.'

'I suppose,' said Cawl. 'Then again, the circumstances I liberated you from were less ideal than those you find yourself in here. Here you get to live. There, in that Inquisitorial fortress?

Limbo...' He shrugged – always a complicated proposition for the archmagos, no matter which limb set he wore. 'Death would have been such a waste. Think of all that we shall achieve together, you and I. We have a glorious future ahead of us, that would never have come to pass were it not for me. You are not my prisoner. We are fellow scientists, engaged on a voyage of discovery!'

'I cannot die, insect. I am immortal!' Her voice rose. 'I am AsanethAyu! I am cryptek, chronomancer of the first court of Valdrekh! You are a primitive. Inferior. You ape lost glories you cannot comprehend. You inhabit a shell of rotting flesh and worthless technology.'

The necron's vox-unit buzzed when she got angry, some deep-level fault in the ancient mechanism. Necron physiologies were fascinating, and as she shouted at him, he idly considered breaking her apart to find out how she worked, not for the first time.

'We are not fellows. I am your better. You are nothing but a tomb robber. I am a breaker of gods!' She clenched her fist. 'One day you shall kneel before me, and beg for your life. When that day comes, I promise you I shall show you no mercy.'

She stopped speaking. The buzz shut off.

'Yet there you are, in there, in that box, and I'm out here, as free as you like,' said Cawl. 'It seems in here, on my ship, that we are more equal than you think.' Cawl took his turn, pushing aside her attempts to stop the citizen piece protecting his fortress from floating forward.

'You let that one go,' Cawl said.

'If we are equals, set me free.'

'I'm not going to set you free,' Cawl tutted. 'Not yet. Not until you acknowledge that I am right and agree to help me.' He glanced at a large, vaguely ovoid machine of necron make half covered in a tarpaulin. 'Teach me how that temporal ark functions, and I shall set you free. You can even stay and work with me, if you like. You have my word you will not be harmed.'

She moved a piece, overwhelming his control so easily he could have sworn she grinned.

'Liar. You dissemble. You distract. If you must torment me with your simplistic pursuits then let us concentrate upon them so they might sooner be over and I may sleep.'

'I would have thought you'd have had enough sleep by now.'

'A million years in stasis is preferable to five minutes with you, you insufferable mammal! Move!'

Cawl sighed and selected his ecclesiarch to go. It was one of a few pieces that could move over the disposable citizens who fronted the major pieces. Time to get aggressive.

Another silent struggle. Within the scarab, quantum gates made of subatomic fragments flickered between a million possible states.

She's not backing down this time, thought Cawl. He exerted himself a little more. The cryptek tensed. A niggling headache set up at the back of his skull. Bak played on. Something gave.

The scarab designated third ecclesiarch moved smoothly up and over the citizen blocking it. Cawl placed it squarely in the centre of the board.

'You call this one the traitor's gambit. You reveal your inner being. I cannot trust you.'

'Trazyn the Infinite trusted me.'

'Trazyn the Infinite is terminally contaminated by compassion,' she said.

'Your move,' prompted Cawl.

AsanethAyu bent forward as far as her shackles would allow, her immense, seven-foot height curling in on itself like a steel serpent. Green lights glowed under her open ribs. The sparks in her vast, immobile eye roved across the game, and she gave out a noise halfway between a sigh and a growl. It was a peculiarly organic sound for a machine.

'Fascinating,' said Cawl.

AsanethAyu glanced up. 'What?'

'That noise. It is not the kind of noise a machine makes.'

'I live.'

'Not in a conventional sense.'

'Yet I live! You do not understand the majesty of biotransference. You have an inadequate definition of life. If you did, you would bow and worship me as the superior being that I am.'

'Because I am a primitive?'

AsanethAyu made another, human-sounding noise. It was almost like a laugh.

'You maintain that you worship the perfection of the machine. Here I am, a perfect machine, and your kind seeks only to destroy us. The irony of that. You are a moronic species.'

'Alien machines don't count as far as the Synod of Mars measures perfection,' Cawl said. 'Necrons are blasphemies. Copies of the real thing. You are not true life, but soulless monsters.'

Her single, huge eye burned brightly. 'Mo-ron-ic,' she repeated, mechanically stressing all three syllables. 'I have formulated my strategy. This game is one of pure logic, and I am a being of pure logic. You cannot win. Your attachment to the weaknesses of the flesh disadvantages you. Prepare to be crushed.'

The alien lights of a scarab's motive unit ignited, and it took flight under her direction, Cawl's control of it slipping from his hands. The scarabs' original purpose was to maintain the tomb worlds of the necrons, and to provide support when they awoke. Now, they were Cawl's, entirely broken to his command, AsanethAyu's to use only by his permission. That was the point of this game, to teach her that even the necrons could not resist Cawl. Yet still...

The scarab moved forward to Cawl's exposed ecclesiarch. Delicate manipulators shifted with quick, exact movements, working by processes Cawl was only just beginning to understand. The small machines really were amazing. They had watched over tomb worlds for millions of years without failure, a span of time that made the Imperium seem frankly insignificant. They were capable of disintegrating objects at the most fundamental level, where there was no difference between matter and energy. Their talents extended to creation, too, for they were equally capable of picking up a single snowflake without damaging it, and making an infinite number of perfect replicas. This time, its destructive capabilities were called upon. Bands of light played over Cawl's piece, rendering it into dust slice by slice.

'Fascinating,' said Cawl.

'What is *fascinating* now?' AsanethAyu grumbled. 'Why does everything have to be *fascinating* to you?'

'I consider your drones. Such marvels.'

He selected another citizen with little resistance from the cryptek. She was ineffective when angered, he noticed, and his piece sailed easily forward. The move opened the way for his fortress. Obvious, but intentionally so.

'Marvels to your inferior kind,' the cryptek said. 'To me they are the simplest of tools. Something a lower lifeform like you might equate with a rock. Do you know what a rock is?' AsanethAyu could be surprisingly sarcastic when she wanted to be.

'You are a sharp one, my friend. I know of rocks.'

'It is a risk letting me have access to them.' A sly tone entered her voice. 'Even a rock can smash a lock.'

'Life without risk is boring,' said Cawl.

AsanethAyu made her next move, a smart one at that, shifting a citizen free of her tetrarch, and giving the piece clear lines of movement across the board.

'Besides, you haven't got away yet. You'll need more than a scornful metaphor to escape my prison.'

'I have yet to properly try,' she said haughtily. Her drones flew suddenly at Cawl's face, mandibles spreading aggressively, gauss fields crackling into life. There were energies there that could render his head into atoms in less than a second.

Only they wouldn't.

The destructive flare died as soon as it began. The drone stopped abruptly, changed mode back to passive, executed a one-hundred-and-eighty-degree turn, and floated back to its position on the laser-delineated board.

'Now that was an embarrassing attempt,' Cawl said. 'Play the game now, come on.'

'I am not trying,' she said. 'You shall be most aware of my majesty when I pull out your spine, and then I shall turn back the wheels of time, and do it again, and again, and I will allow you to retain the memory of all your previous pain, so that you shall be cast into an endless loop of suffering! Such is my power.'

'Really?' Cawl peered up at her from under the peak of his hood. 'Charming,' he said. With minimal resistance from the cryptek he made his move, exposing both his emperor and empress to attack, but also giving them the opportunity to move freely.

'Charm is irrelevant. Your race is irrelevant. Only necrons persist.' A brief struggle for control of her second ecclesiarch was fought and won by her. The piece moved diagonally into position. She sat back. 'I'm finished. It's your turn.'

Cawl was about to take his move when one of his sub-magi shambled into the chamber.

'My lord archmagos dominus,' the magos hissed through wheezing vox-apparatus that resembled the riffling pages of open books. 'The time has come. Rebirth is upon us.'

'Aha! Biologian Vintillius. How long do I have?'

'Seven minutes, thirty-seven seconds until the awakening procedure is complete,' said Vintillius.

'I see. Thank you. I will conclude my business here and join you presently. Don't let him wake up without me!'

'Of course, Prime Conduit.' The magos bowed and retreated. Cawl's immense body shuffled about to better face the board.

AsanethAyu stiffened.

'You have severed my connection to the drones,' she said. 'I require them to play.' She yanked her clawed hands hard against their energy restraints. Green glowed bright. 'Why? What is about to happen? Are you so craven you remove my ability at the moment of victory?'

'You will not need them again today,' said Cawl. 'I'm about to win.'

'You are not! Your arrogance is beyond belief.'

'Coming from such a mistress of that emotion as yourself, I'm flattered. You'll see in but a moment.'

He waited a second. Bak was reaching a crescendo. When the music quickened, he began.

'Do you like my music?'

'You play to its rhythm. That makes you predictable.'

'I didn't ask that. I asked if you liked it.'

'The mathematical progression of the tones is pleasing, yes,' she said grudgingly.

'Necrons have music then?'

'What kind of sentient species does not?' She hunched down. 'Necron music is better than this.'

'I'm sure it is, but please recognise that if this is pleasing, you must admit we are not so primitive. Yes?'

His fortress slid out, next to his ecclesiarch, both pieces commanding all of the board.

'Fool's mate.'

'What are you talking about?'

'There,' he said, pointing at the board with several pincered appendages. 'You can make only one move, and if you do, then it will be full mate. So it is fool's mate.' The scarab representing AsanethAyu's empress flipped over and dropped to the deck. He admitted to himself toppling it was an unnecessarily dramatic flourish, rude even, but if you couldn't have a little fun, what could you do?

'You did this on purpose. To humiliate me.'

Cawl laughed. 'I did it because I'm an enormous show-off,' he said. 'And I did it because I could. It's not easy to set up a victory as subtle as this, and in time to the music, no less.'

'Indeed not,' said AsanethAyu. The music finished, and Cawl could hear the faint hum of the multiple atomic motors working to move her body. 'You will not succeed in doing so again. I have seen the pattern.'

'Life isn't about reacting in retrospect,' said Cawl. 'It isn't about established patterns either, but the anticipation of patterns to come. One must look ahead. One must be inspired. Like me.'

'Humiliating your prisoner is inspiring for you. You are a despicable race.'

'A despicable race is one that periodically wipes out all other lifeforms in the galaxy to million-year cycles to sate its unnatural hungers,' said Cawl. 'Being a little mischievous is a far lesser crime, in my well-informed opinion. In any case, I am not trying to humiliate you, I am trying to instruct you that your prejudice against me is poorly founded. I want you to understand, I am your equal. Together, we can help save this galaxy. There need not be hatred between us.'

'You are nothing, and will be enslaved, used, and the dust of your bones cast onto the stellar winds.'

'You're rather melodramatic for a supposed eternal genius, you know that, don't you?' Cawl's long, heavily augmented body uncoiled, and his more or less human torso lifted up, centaur-like, atop the bonded carriage. 'We shall play again soon. I must go now. I have other matters to attend to.'

'Tell me how you did this,' said AsanethAyu, with enough urgency that Cawl suspected he was right and that she did not really relish more stasis time. She gestured at the laser-defined board as well as she could with her restrained hand. Her energy bonds buzzed with the movement.

'How I won? Practice.'

'No. Your control. We are both logical creatures. Tell me, how can you lock me out of my own technology so easily?'

'That's the wrong question. It's not so much how I can do it, but why I am able to,' said Cawl. 'As you have said to me before, there are similarities between the Cult Mechanicus and you necrons. My fellows do not see it, or if they do, they deny it. But I do. We are kindred beings, to a degree.'

'Such insight is impressive, for a primitive.'

'Is that sarcasm again? Really? Fa–'

'Do not dare to share your fascination with me again!' AsanethAyu said. Her vox-cast distorted with anger.

Cawl shook his head. 'I was only going to say that it is you who lacks understanding.'

'Oh please do enlighten me, most percipient archmagos.' Something sparkled deep in her single glass eye. 'That was sarcasm,' she added.

'I won because I have a soul. I can improvise. I can take risks you would not. There is more to me than this matter.' He poked himself in the chest with one of his many limbs. 'Our creed says the flesh is weak, and so it is. That is why we strive to improve upon it and replace it, as the Machine God desires. But we abandon His numinous gifts at our peril. To give up one's soul is the great sin of my religion. The soul must be understood, not despised. This is why we are not on the same path. Your kind gave up your souls, and that makes you monsters. Mine never will.'

With a thought, Cawl activated the sarcophagus. The clamshell front began to close.

'This is outrageous, giving yourself the last word by shutting me up in this–'

The sarcophagus closed with sonorous finality.

'I suppose it is,' Cawl said into the silence. 'But I can do anything, because I am Belisarius Cawl, and you're my prisoner. That's rather my point, which I am hopeful you will soon understand. You,' he said, reactivating the scarabs. Those inactive on the floor powered on and rose silently up, and together, as a swarm, they swivelled to look at him. 'Clear yourselves away.' He looked around the crammed archive, the softly shining monoliths, the half-dismantled machines, the overflowing boxes, the crates full of corroded necron skulls and priceless artefacts heaped carelessly on top of each other. 'I know it doesn't look like it, but I really can't abide a mess.'

CHAPTER EIGHT

QUO AFTER QUO

Friedisch is dying. There is a large hole in him. He sees it as a message saying that you were right, indeed the flesh is weak, you can see how weak it is right now. He wishes he'd taken more augmentation, but it never seemed the right time. Now there will be no chance. A boltgun does so much damage. It's a wonder he is still alive. His organs are pulp. The pain is immense. The end of his life is approaching. He sees it as a black barrier laid across time.

Friedisch has never been so aware of time.

Although Friedisch is afraid, it is a distant emotion. It is strong, make no mistake, but he is protected from it by a thick barrier of shock, sturdy as a castle wall. Mostly all he can think of is the carpet he lies upon. There is a carpet in the room where he is dying! In the Imperial Palace, so soon after the Siege of Terra, there is a carpet! He finds this mildly amusing.

The fibres of the pile grow in significance, competing with the pain. They are tough, short, yet soft. He can feel grit in them from the destruction wrought upon the city by Horus. Destruction so total no amount of air filtration can keep out the consequences, not even in so rich a building. Here it is beneath his palm, an archaeology just for him of powdered rockcrete and the ashes of the dead. A record of war caught up in a carpet. Fancy that!

He wonders why this carpet holds his attention so, and concludes that it is to be expected. One must take into account, he thinks, that death on the floor is far from unusual. This last repose from which he cannot stand makes the floor his immediate and final horizon. His mind is searching desperately for meaning, anywhere. He supposes many people are occupied by the floor, when they die.

He wonders how many people have died on carpets. Lots, probably.

He is thankful that Belisarius is there, shouting for a cryo-flask. He is relieved that Cawl survived the melding with Sedayne. There is much he would like to say to his friend, but he cannot. He is past words now.

The blackness is nearly upon him. Time stops at its inviolable border. Beyond it there is nothing.

He goes through.

There is a space of indeterminate length. It doesn't really feel like time. He is aware that his situation has changed within the fourth dimension. It is most logical to assume he has gone forward, but by how much?

Darkness recedes. The Machine God reaches out to embrace him, and awareness returns. He is in a tank of thick, restorative liquid. An umbilicus links his stomach to banks of machines flickering on the far side of an armaglass wall. He is still in pain, though of a different kind. Then he realises, his mouth is full of fluid. There is no air in his lungs. He cannot breathe!

He thrashes hard. From far away, he hears the frightened peeping of alarms.

He fights off panic. He is not drowning, after all. He experiences a great crash of relief. He did not die, Belisarius saved him. All praise to the Machine God, although at the precise moment he is too caught up in the joy of survival to feel truly pious.

The sensation doesn't last. His body feels wrong. When he died, he was still mostly original, save that damned eye that never sat right with his body. Now, there is not much that is him. He is all metal. Far more than his injuries, severe as they were, would have warranted. There is no oxygen being conveyed into his body. He is not breathing because he does not need to. He is uncomfortably aware of himself. None of his body feels like it is his. He is squatting in a stolen home.

There is something happening to his brain. He feels... Wrong.

He stills. There is movement outside.

The alarms cease. A single, authoritative chime sounds, there is a metallic clunk beneath him, and all the liquid rushes away.

Upon the walkway running around the edge of the tank, Cawl looked on with great satisfaction as the oil ran out, revealing the crumpled form of his dear friend Friedisch Adum Silip Qvo.

Strictly speaking, it was not Friedisch, but the latest iteration of a long line of copies of Qvo, and the form was different to the one Friedisch wore when he died, but Cawl never let facts get in the way of a good story.

He liked what he saw.

'This could be our finest Qvo yet! Good work, Magos Vintillius, good work!'

Vintillius bowed modestly. 'The genius is all yours, archmagos,' he wheezed. 'I merely perform your will. My contribution is minor.'

'You're too kind,' said Cawl, dismissing the praise with a wave of his mechanical hand. 'Come on then,' he said. 'Bring him up!'

Vintillius depressed a large button in a hazard-hatched case. The bottom of the tank rose up to the level of the walkway and locked into position with a solid mechanical noise.

Friedisch underwent his reincarnations in a truly enormous hold. For much of the ten thousand years since his initial death, it had been full of equipment as Cawl spent the long, lonely millennia perfecting his Primaris Space Marines. Now all that was gone and the space was empty but for Qvo's birthing pod, so the sound of the machine echoed over cold, empty immensities, stirring stray methalon fogs left over from the great revelation of the Ultima Founding. If the spirits of the shrouded machines stacked at the edges heard this cry to action, they kept their silence.

'I am not so sure about the lower assemblage,' Cawl said. 'It seemed so right to give this one legs, but was it the correct choice? Maybe we should have tried tracks again?'

'Legs worked well on the last two,' said Vintillius.

'You have done well with the face.'

'A small contribution. I would not dare to gainsay the decisions of your genius, Prime Conduit.'

'That's very good of you, Vintillius, but learn to take a compliment, please.' Cawl leaned over the inactive Qvo. 'Wake up!' he said, very loudly.

'He is unresponsive, Prime Conduit,' said Vintillius.

'I can see that, thank you. What do the readings say?'

'He is functional, but unresponsive.'

'Ah, playing dead, eh?' Cawl jabbed at Qvo with a couple of appendages.

Qvo moaned and flapped a weak, freshly minted hand. Exposed pistons clicked in his arm.

Vintillius looked down approvingly. 'And in the work of His machines shall you hear His voice,' he whispered.

'Come on,' Cawl said. 'Wake up!' He jabbed at Qvo again.

'Do not poke me, Belisarius.' Qvo rolled over. He looked up with eyes weary with too many lives.

'Ha! You always say that, Friedisch.' Cawl held out an appendage. 'Take my tendril. Allow me to help you up.'

Qvo did not. 'I am not Friedisch,' he said. 'My mind is full of his memories, but although I am barely awake, I am awake enough to know that I am not he, because I have the memories of many others besides.'

Cawl's triumph took a knock. This was disappointing. One day, one of these creations would stand up convinced they were Friedisch, and then they would be. That was the final test, then he would have his friend back. Still, he had to make the best of it. From initial impressions, this one was close!

'Very well,' said Cawl to his creation. 'You are Friedisch Adum Silip Qvo, and you are not, so either way you are correct. Which incidentally means, so am I.'

The latest Qvo got himself into a sitting position and wiped the slime from his face – the only human part of him, and the reason for Vintillius' engagement in his creation. 'If we follow the second part of your contradiction there, what am I? I am sure I have asked this question before. This is not the first time, is it? But let's go through the motions, shall we?'

There was Friedisch's bite. That was encouraging.

'Who are you?' said Cawl. 'That is difficult to answer.'

'I said *what*, Belisarius.' His human face frowned atop its oily metal body. 'What is the number of this iteration? That is the correct question.'

'Promising, that you are self-aware so quickly. Very promising. You are Qvo-89,' said Cawl.

'Eighty-nine? *Eighty-nine!*' Qvo-89 shrieked and slapped his forehead. 'By the Omnissiah, not again! Just let me stay dead, Belisarius!' He pulled the umbilicus free. The connection was complicated, but Qvo had had a lot of practice at being born and tugged it out with a single, dextrous movement.

'You'll come around,' said Cawl. 'You *always* come around.'

'I hate you,' said Qvo. He coughed, though he had no lungs. He got slowly to his mechanical knees then forced himself up with a groan.

'See! You *are* you. Now, do you like your new legs?' asked Cawl eagerly.

'I have legs this time.' Qvo looked down at the limbs, lifted the feet, waved them about. 'I had legs last time, but I have not always before. Were there… wheels? No, lots of little feet, if I recall? There was one with a faulty contra-grav impeller, I recall.'

'Ah, you remember that one. Sorry about that,' said Cawl.

Qvo frowned. 'Something more is different this time…' He looked away, puzzled. 'I have no recollection of the death of Qvo-88. What happened? Could you not retrieve his engrams?'

'Hmm, well, how do I…?' Cawl sighed. 'That would be because he's still alive. You haven't died this time. Qvo-88 is headed to Imperium Nihilus. Primarch's orders, last of the torchbearer fleets, something momentous. All that pompous demigod stuff. I sent Qvo-88 off. But if Guilliman needs you, I need you more.'

'You made *another* me?'

'Absolutely.'

'While one of me is still functional?'

'That's the case.'

'You can't do that!'

'I can do what I like, because–'

'You're Belisarius Cawl, yes, yes, I've heard that before.' Qvo groaned again and pulled his hand down his face.

'Come on, what's a Cawl without a Qvo?' said Cawl.

'I've no idea, but a Qvo without a Cawl can at least rest in peace.'

'That's more like you! That's very like you. Isn't that like him?' Cawl asked Vintillius.

'I would not know, archmagos,' said Vintillius solemnly. 'Magos Qvo died nine and a half thousand years before I was born.'

'I'm not like me. I am not me,' said Qvo-89. 'I'm not Friedisch, on account of the fact that Friedisch is dead, as this magos has quite clearly pointed out.'

'Let's say that is true, but it doesn't mean that you are dead.' Cawl smiled at him. 'Do calm down, it's not the first time I've had two of you up and about at the same time, and every iteration gets us closer to the original. You've come out very well. I mean, you're arguably the most Friedisch so far.'

'You've been…' If Qvo had had a circulatory system, the colour would have drained out of his face.

'Tinkering with you? Yes, I have. One of the whole points of this is to make you live, properly, as you. Isn't it? That means progressive evolution until the copy matches the original in every way and, ergo, becomes the original.'

Friedisch's outrage bubbled up through Qvo.

'Tinkering? With my *brain*?'

'More your soul.' Cawl hurried on before Qvo could say anything else. This wasn't the first time he'd had this conversation with an awakening Qvo. 'The problem is, you see, that the original preservation of Friedisch's head wasn't perfect, and you did die very quickly, and there's the spiritual aspect to take into account, because once a soul is in the warp it's not in a good place, so I've got to keep it out of there and–'

He was babbling. Curse it all, the settings he'd taken on for the day were all good for dealing with the necron but in a situation like this he needed a bit more calm authority.

'But I don't have a brain!' Qvo gripped his head. 'This is a… a machine in here! Entirely a machine!' His horror rose. 'This is an abomination!' Qvo raged. 'I am an abomination! My mind, me! I'm… blasphemous!'

'Ah, says who?' said Cawl affably, because he couldn't help but be affable right then. This seemed to infuriate the rebuilt tech-priest even more.

'The Machine God says so, Belisarius! You have created an abominable intelligence.'

'Not strictly speaking… If you want to put a name on it, you're more of a very advanced servitor. There is some human brain in there. About twenty per cent of one.'

'A servitor?!' wailed Friedisch.

'Now you sound like Friedisch, you really do! Well done, Vintillius.'

'Thank you again,' said Vintillius modestly.

'I'm dead!'

'Oh dear,' said Cawl. 'And this was going so well compared to some of the others. Look, you're here, aren't you? I'd say you are not entirely dead, on the basis of that evidence. You're thinking, right? You have Friedisch's mind, after a fashion, and his memories…'

'And the memories of eighty-eight other substandard, *blasphemous* copies, one of whom is still alive. I mean active, I mean… Belisarius, what have you done!'

'I'm hearing that a lot recently. I'll tell you what, if this all upsets you so much, when your other self comes back, I'll integrate your personalities, then it won't feel strange in the slightest.'

'That's worse, you can only do that by killing one of us.'

'If you look at it like that, I'll be killing *both* of you, but I'm not. I prefer the term *blending*. Blending, not killing. Sound good?'

Qvo looked down at his body. His naked, dripping, mechanical body.

'Could I at least have a robe?' he said glumly.

'Of course!' One of Cawl's tentacles speared down and plucked the requested garment from the arms of a servitor waiting on the deck below.

'Thank you,' said Qvo, when Cawl deposited the garment into his arms. 'Now, please. I need a little time to gather my thoughts. Can you leave me alone?'

'Ah.'

'Ah?'

'I'm sorry, I can't do that. Time is always in such short supply. The Emperor said that to me Himself once, more or less.'

'I get a robe to drape over my slime-covered, blasphemous body, that's it? You can't spare me a few hours?'

'You get half an hour. That's all it usually takes for the rest of your accumulated experience to catch up, as it were, and for your personality to stabilise.'

'Half an hour? You've become a monster, Belisarius.' Qvo shrugged the robe on, muttering as it caught on the sharp angles of his body, and stuck to the slime that coated him.

'You'll come around about that too. I really haven't changed that much, despite all this.' He waved various appendages down at various other appendages. 'Come on now, my friend. We have work to do.'

'What manner of work would this be, besides making friends?' Qvo said.

'Oh, that's a good one. A veritable japer you are. It's good to have you back. You know what I'm about. It's the same as always, my dear Qvo-89. We're saving humanity, of course!'

CHAPTER NINE

LORD OF DAEMONS

Bile's party put down on Ghordrenvel seven miles from the Flesh Halls of Undregundum, as First-Among-Equals said that they should. *Butcher-Bird*'s turbines growled at the plains as they powered down.

The ramp opened. Bile marched out, helmet off, eager to breathe something other than recycled air. He sniffed, and pulled a face. Ghordrenvel smelled of promethium, hot metal and burned flesh. There was enough material on the air to trigger his omophagea, and his mind filled with unwelcome images of tortured beasts and trapped daemons.

'Another world tainted by the warp,' said Bile. He spat to get the taste of the place out of his mouth.

'Not dead, though.' Porter was his shadow as always. She scanned the landscape with hunters' eyes. Ghordrenvel teemed with life, of a sort. Bizarre machine-animals sauntered across the plains, herds of them gathered in places, all the way up to the walls of the Flesh Halls.

'Not dead,' agreed Bile. 'Someone here has been indulging themselves.'

'What are these things?' asked Porter, fascinated. 'I have never seen anything like them before.'

'They are experiments of an inadvisable kind. Cybernetic constructs. Do you see?' He pointed Torment at the nearest of them, a tall, heavy-footed thing with a long neck of steel vertebrae held together by raw muscle. A skull of living bone topped the length. It seemed to sense Bile's attention, and swung around ponderously, bionic eyes blinking idiotically from a dozen sockets. 'A melding of animal and machine.'

'Then they are ugly but not dangerous,' said Porter.

'They are ugly *and* dangerous. In place of a natural motivating essence drawn from the warp, I would wager these things have an implanted Neverborn. They are wholly unnatural.'

'I am unnatural,' said Porter.

'Arguably correct, but not in the same way. You have purpose,' said Bile. 'You have free will. When I made your kind, it was for a reason. Your independence and your excellence are proof that I was right. These things are whimsies. Look upon them, and you will see the madness of Chaos. We must be careful with this First-Among-Equals. He will be like all the rest of those who seek power from the warp, sure he is on the path to enlightenment, when the truth is anything but.'

Bile's own misbegotten servants spilled down the ramp then, and came to a stop blinking warily at the sun. They spread out, bleating moronically, jabbing at the ground and kicking at tussocks of grass and half-buried scrap in their idiot way. Bile watched them. Perhaps it was time to replace his workforce.

The soft *whumpf* of a sonic boom shocked the air.

'He is coming,' said Bile, shading his eyes skywards. 'He keeps to the first part of his bargain, then.'

A black dot grew in the sky. The machine-animal-daemon things bellowed in distress. Some of them vented smoke and broke into short, uneasy gallops that stopped, then started again as the scream of braking jets grew to deafening levels, and the landing craft of First-Among-Equals slid across the sky, searching for a good site to land. It drifted closer to the ground, its engines setting the grass on fire, before finally coming down to rest.

'Come on, Porter, I do not wish to dawdle here. I still have a feeling this whole venture could be a waste of time.'

'Yes, maker.'

'Where is Brutus?'

Annoyed lowing echoed down the ramp of *Butcher-Bird*, and the clang of something heavy being dragged.

'Be careful with that,' Bile warned.

'I am sorry, maker,' Brutus said. He staggered out into the day-light under a heavy cryo-unit, ropes biting into his shoulders. 'Why do you bring this lord a gift, my maker, when the magos says he will fight for us?'

'It is better to have the whip hand in every situation. I would rather this lord of Space Marines be indebted to me,' he said derisively. 'He might be a master of daemon constructs, but no Space Marine is a Space Marine without gene-seed. He will see the sense of that, or I shall kill him.'

Kolumbari-Enas' ship was opening up, the ramp coming down. Eight Myrmidons swaggered out and took up positions around the vessel. Bile ordered his coterie of beastmen and constructs to do the same. Pointless, really. *Butcher-Bird* could more than take care of itself.

'Come!' Bile said, setting out towards the Dark Mechanicum

vessel. 'We tarry too long. I wish to be done with technomancy and half-witted sorcerers as soon as possible.'

The walls were tall and made of bone and steel. They stretched from one horizon to the other, in extravagant, pointless display. They were pompous affectation, they'd serve little use against an attack from the sky, and they didn't appear to be needed to keep the shambling daemon machines away.

'Hubris, arrogance, damnation. The route is always the same,' he said to himself.

'Do you wish to address me, Lord Bile?' Kolumbari-Enas said.

'Not really,' said Bile. He strode quickly, transhuman legs covering ground in easy strides. First-Among-Equals hobbled to keep up, but did not seem too uncomfortable. Their servants trailed them, First's Myrmidons, then Brutus bringing up the rear, stoically carrying the genecasque.

Porter ranged ahead, running in long arcs, pausing to assess the threat the beasts of Ghordrenvel might pose. First watched her a while.

'Politesse activated – may I ask you something?'

'If you must,' said Bile.

'That creature. It is one of yours?'

'In a manner of speaking,' said Bile.

'Musing in progress – I thought her at first to be xenos,' said First. 'But she is engineered. Human. A fascinating genetic profile. Geneforging is not my area of expertise, but the artistry is clear. She is one of your famous New Men.'

'In a manner of speaking,' said Bile again. They were nearing the walls.

'Clarify last statement,' said Kolumbari-Enas.

'I made her ancestors,' said Bile. 'They improved themselves further.'

'She is a masterwork.'

'She is more than that,' said Bile. 'She is the future. She will save us all.'

'Salvation can only be attained by unlocking the plans of the Machine God,' said Kolumbari-Enas.

'Yet another verse in the same tired song. Gods never saved anybody, First-Among-Equals.'

'Refutation – I disagree.'

'What is this place to you, anyway?' said Bile.

'Lord Thrule is a collector of beasts. He has the largest menagerie of techno-organic daemoniforms in this segmentum. I perform work for him in exchange for intelligence and alliance in battle.'

'Don't tell me these offcasts roaming about are yours?'

'Negatory,' said Kolumbari-Enas. 'These are his work. I tutor him in our ways for alliance.'

'I am always careful to whom I teach my secrets.'

'Exclamatory – I am no fool! He learns the least of the mysteries, as these lesser works demonstrate.'

They reached the gates. Living teeth locked together to keep them closed. They looked formidable, but Bile calculated a short bombardment from Demolisher cannons would have them open quickly.

'None but the supplicant shall enter the halls of the divine Lord Discordant Dandimus Thrule, by order of himself, the glorious, the daemon friend, the duke of forty-seven agonies, the Lord of Undregundum, vanquisher of the Argent Shields, king here, and master of immaterium and materium alike. Bow before his magnificence and quail!'

The speaker was a gory skull embedded in the gates, framed by the badge of the Opus Chaotica. A perverted machine spirit inhabited the device, a merging of daemon and artificial sentience, a speciality of the fallen magi of the Dark Mechanicum.

Bile looked pointedly from side to side. 'I see no magnificence, only a narcissist's monument, and an impertinent machine. You will let me pass,' said Bile.

'By proclamation of Thrule no stranger may pass!'

The gates wept a continual fall of viscous black slime. A legion of small, multi-legged creatures whose principal components were human skulls crept around the gate and up the fortifications, going in and out of moist burrows excavated in the bone. All had living, swivelling eyes still, each one shining with the madness of a trapped soul.

The crab-things were purposeful regardless of what their eyes were trying to say, lapping up the ichor running from the brass and bone and carrying it away in small, spoon-shaped forelimbs. The chirring of hungry young sounded from the burrows.

'This welcome is not what I expected, First-Among-Equals,' said Bile. 'I expected a little respect.'

'Apologies, great genetor,' said Kolumbari-Enas. 'Lord Thrule can be quixotic, his rules change regularly. Last time I was here to conduct my business with his lordship, I could bring whom I chose. A few months before, none could pass, another time, the gates were open and unguarded. Another time, the walls were not here.'

'Another irritating egotist,' said Bile. 'They are all the same.' He pointed Torment at the gatekeeper. 'Do you actually know who I am?' asked Bile of the skull.

Ocular implants flashed.

'That's no answer,' Bile said. 'Speak.' He raised Torment level before him, aiming the ferrule at the daemon-device's eye, like a rapier. 'You shall do as I say if you know what this is. I know one such as you will fear the pain Torment can bring just as keenly as a mortal man.'

The daemon-spirit let out a blurt of corrupt binharic.

'You are Fabius Bile, Primogenitor, the Clonelord, the Pater Mutatis!' it jabbered.

'Then you will open this gate, daemon.'

'I shall not, for such are the commands of Lord Thrule, oh great and indefatigable master of the gland!' said the daemon.

'I have no patience for this,' said Bile, and jabbed the guardian in the eye with Torment. Purple light shone around the skull atop the staff. Smoke poured from its clenched teeth, and Bile felt the thing imprisoned in the cane shiver with delight. The gatekeeper let out an unearthly scream that rolled out across the plains. As it passed over the shambling herds of beasts they reared, kicking metal hooves against the troubled skies, and stampeded.

Bile twisted Torment. 'You feel that, foolish little nothing? Now open the way, and the pain shall cease.'

The daemon-machine squealed. 'You will pay! You will pay!'

'That's what they all say,' said Bile.

Great locks within the gates clanked, and the gates swung backwards. The crab-things let out a unified hissing.

'That wasn't too hard, was it?' Bile said. The daemon skull did not reply. The light in its remaining eye had gone out. The ghost had retreated back into the machine.

'You put us all in danger,' muttered First. 'We should be more cautious. Thrule is dangerous.'

Bile laughed. 'Every Space Marine that has abandoned the Imperium comes to me, sooner or later, or their armies wither away. Every one of them needs me. I find it better to proceed on that assumption, First-Among-Equals. The whole universe can hate me, for all I care. I will save us all. All that matters is my vision, my will, my success. I bow to no one.'

'Except the Warmaster,' said First darkly.

'Not even to him,' said Bile. 'Come, Porter, Brutus,' he called, and strode into the fortress.

They walked across an area that seemed no different to the plains, other than being enclosed by the walls. There was some sort of pit ahead, from which a cloud of fumes emerged, and the ground vibrated with the workings of subterranean machinery, but the grass, the metallic dross embedded in the dirt, and the beasts that wandered aimlessly around, all was as it had been outside.

'The Flesh Halls of Undregundum,' said First-Among-Equals. 'We take more steps upon the road to enlightenment. The Machine God's mysteries shall be ours.'

Bile laughed bitterly. 'There are no gods.'

'The existence of the gods is proven. Their work is all around us. These machine-beasts are products of their bounty. Devices from the Machine God, souls of the Neverborn.'

'I did not say they do not exist. They are proven, all right – it is your naming them gods that is mistaken. These monsters you worship are knots in the muscles of reality. They are sentient cankers posing as gods, a disease, and by appeasing them, the likes of you make the malady worse.'

'True statement – we follow where the Machine God wills,' said First. 'We uncover His knowledge. We are His servants.'

'Superstition is not science. Whether it is the superstition of the True Mechanicum or the Adeptus Mechanicus, it is still superstition.'

'Negative!' said First, so shrill Bile knew he had struck a nerve. 'The usurpers of Holy Mars deny the darkness of the universe. Without darkness, there can be no light. To deny the warp is to deny the fullness of the Machine God's creation. Spirit and matter work in tandem. We acknowledge this. That is why we are superior.'

'Religious pedantry,' said Bile dismissively. 'What is it you want with Cawl?'

'Nothing. Your reward is what we seek.'

'Good. I do not think you would find him amenable. He is independent, like I am. He is beholden to no master. Our methods are different, but our aims are the same. I have more in common with him than I do with you.'

'Verifiable conclusion,' clattered Kolumbari-Enas. 'You are both master genetors.'

Bile stopped, bringing the whole procession to a halt. 'He is a dabbler in the genetic arts. I am sure he can design a new pattern of boltgun or void craft better than I, but he is an amateur when it comes to matters of the flesh.' Bile set off again. Brutus let out a tired sigh.

'Inference drawn – you believe you could do better?'

'I know I can do better,' said Bile.

'Query posed – you could replicate the work of Belisarius Cawl?'

'In limited amounts, I already have, but he has access to certain materials that I need in order to fulfil Abaddon's orders.'

'Query posed – what materials?'

'He has the Sangprimus Portum.'

'Data retrieval in progress,' Kolumbari-Enas bleeped. Cold white light flashed deep inside his robes. 'Data retrieval complete. The Sangprimus Portum contains all remaining data appertaining to the creation of the Space Marines and the primarchs.' A little awe crept into his flat, affectless voice.

'It does,' said Bile. 'And with it I will be able to give the Warmaster exactly what he wants.'

'Interjection – you will be able to give him more than he wants.'

'I could,' said Bile. 'If I so chose.'

CHAPTER TEN

UNDREGUNDUM

Undregundum was a pit in the ground. Stinking steams whooshed up at random intervals, polluting the area around the hole with their fallout. Rainbows of precipitated salts crusted the ground. Bile's boots crunched them to powder as the party approached. He reached the edge ahead of his servants, ahead of Kolumbari-Enas. The hole had no discernible bottom. The systems of his armour sampled the air. Chemical readouts ran down his faceplate, listing off copper, gold, and isotopes of iodine. His aural pickups amplified the faint sounds echoing from below into the racket of industry. There were other, fainter noises, more disconcerting, but familiar to one such as Bile – the sound of screams.

'There is the way down,' said Kolumbari-Enas. He pointed with a metallic claw at the far side, where a set of narrow, rough-hewn steps curled around the pit and disappeared into the darkness.

'This hole is not the fortress of a notable warlord,' said Bile.

'It changes!' hissed Kolumbari-Enas. 'Thrule is a true believer. He is much blessed by the gods. Mutability of his domain is one of the boons they have granted him.'

'A madman, then,' said Bile. 'In ages past I could have taken this place in moments.' He looked around disapprovingly.

'Beware. He is mighty.'

'He is not,' said Bile. 'Do you think I know nothing of the warp? A disdain for the gods does not equate to ignorance of their capabilities, First-Among-Equals. To transform this place into a defensible state would take hours, sorcery or not.'

'Insistence – you would be surprised, and you would die.'

'You are not the first person to say that to me, and you are certainly wrong,' said Bile.

'I remind you that we are here because you have no one to fight for you. Advisement – do not rest upon past glories. You have few friends nowadays.'

'This trip had better be worth it,' Bile growled.

They headed for the stairs.

Sometime later they reached the bottom and squeezed through a passage so narrow it made Brutus swear in his thick-tongued way. The chirurgeon scraped on the rock, and the possessed machine pulled in its limbs to protect itself.

Abruptly, the passage turned into a grand avenue, lined with titanic statues of Space Marines. Like the pit they had entered by, the hall seemed to go up forever, the ceiling vanishing into the dark, where winged shapes flitted.

'Neverborn,' growled Bile.

The solid walls between the statues gave way to stacked colonnades. Bile examined the work with a practised eye; though it had been modified by the hand of mankind, he suspected xenos origins to this place. The dimensions were wrong for humans, subtly, but evidently, and in places old designs had not been obliterated, showing Bile scrap images of thin-faced humanoids of unfamiliar sort.

There were Heretic Astartes patrolling the lofty galleries. They wore armour of dusty black, with the adornments common to renegades with no fixed allegiance. Not legionaries, but deserters from the Chapters. They probably did not owe much loyalty to their chosen lord. Treachery was part of such creatures' souls, carried into the Chapters as a bitter seed, missed by screening programmes, to bloom in later life. Such malcontents would have been drawn to this Lord Thrule by his power, the promise of plunder, or at best by a common interest in the daemonic machines Thrule made. Yes, Bile had dealt with men like Thrule before. Their petty kingdoms rarely lasted long.

A vast bronze door appeared suddenly out of the distance, as if it had manifested from some other realm of existence. As Bile and his companions approached, it opened with a momentous creak, revealing a hot golden light. The doors accelerated rapidly, pushing aside a wall of air that buffeted the party, making Kolumbari-Enas' robes stream out behind him and the banners hanging from the pillars snap violently. The doors reached the end of their swing with a great boom that shook the halls. A cloud of dust rolled over the travellers, and Bile's party passed into Lord Thrule's court.

They emerged into a wide circular ground covered in sand, tiered platforms stacked on either side, separated from the floor by high walls buttressed with heavy pillars, between which were many iron portcullises.

'An arena?' Bile said to Kolumbari-Enas. 'Don't tell me you weren't expecting this, either.'

'Negative denial – the arena is always here,' said Kolumbari-Enas.

'You are nervous. Why?' asked Bile.

'Advisory – be silent. We approach Lord Thrule. Delicate negotiations must ensue.'

The arena had a high viewing platform. Upon it were Thrule and his chief lackeys; several renegade Space Marines in over-embellished armour, their bare faces haughty and cruel. Among them were acolytes of the Dark Mechanicum, varied of form. There were other Heretic Astartes there too, at the back of the platform, motionless as statues. More displays of power, making men stand so still in full view. There was ego here, thought Bile.

Of course Thrule occupied a giant, ugly throne, close enough to the balustrade to look out across the sands. He was a lumpen mess of a man, heavily mutated, one shoulder higher than the other, his head tilted away from it, face hidden by a cowl, his legs thrust uncomfortably out in front of him. He wore power armour still, though it barely fit. In some places it had warped to accommodate his new form, in others it had simply given out. Pipes were jammed into rusted holes that leaked black fluid. Thrule was exactly what Bile had expected.

Bile's eyes flicked sideways to the barred gates. He could well imagine what might leap out from them.

Bile's party came to a halt. Kolumbari-Enas took to his knee before Thrule's dais. He gestured with his hand that Bile do the same, but Bile had no intention of abasing himself before this duke of nowhere.

'Oh great and powerful Dandimus Thrule,' Kolumbari-Enas intoned, 'as I promised, I have brought to you the famed Primogenitor, the firstborn, Fabius Bile.' He flung out his hand to point dramatically at Bile.

'I see,' said Bile. And he did. It was not the first time some nobody had paraded him about in order to get what they needed. It was an old game.

One of Thrule's advisors bent low and whispered close by his head. Thrule gestured, said something even Bile's advanced sensorium could not pick up. The aide nodded, and came to the balustrade. He leaned upon it, arms spread wide, the looming display of a man confident in his position. Bile raised his eyebrows. The warrior was huge, bald, face bloated with dark power, and his teeth filed to sharp points. His armour was a riot of leering daemon faces chased in gold; the stabilising jets and heat vents on his backpack were maws. Tiny daemon faces adorned every knuckle.

'Lord Thrule demands that you pay respect to his greatness! Kneel before him!'

'And who are you to ask that I kneel before anyone, warrior?'

'I am Kurden Suun, equerry to the master and chief groom of his daemonic menagerie.'

'You are a gaudy fellow. I don't like you.'

'You will kneel, Bile. You are an itinerant flesh tinker, and masterless. You are in the court of Dandimus Thrule and you must–'

Brutus let out a sorry huffing, his hooves scuffing the sand. Bile held up a finger for silence, and turned to his servant.

'You may set it down, Brutus.'

Brutus let out a long groan of relief as he slipped the genecasque from his back and worked out his shoulders.

'You were saying, Kurden Suun?'

The Space Marine frowned. His armoured fingers clenched, scraping up piles of grit from the banister.

'You must kneel.'

'Please!' hissed Kolumbari-Enas. 'Do as he says. Explicatory' – his voice buzzed horribly – 'Thrule is a proud lord.'

Bile shook his head. 'You are pirates and oath-breakers, not ten among you could match a single legionary of old. I kneel to no one, Kurden Suun,' he said, viciously stressing the name. 'Least of all the likes of you.'

Thrule gave out a wet, throaty snarl.

'Then you shall die,' the lord said. He raised a malformed arm, and let it drop.

All hell broke loose.

CHAPTER ELEVEN

A CONTEST OF CREATIONS

A brazen fanfare harshened the air. Mechanisms within the walls clanked, and the portcullises rattled upwards into their housings.

Darkness yawned behind them.

'How predictable,' said Bile. 'Porter, Brutus, don't give these insects the pleasure of seeing you die. Kill anything that comes out of those tunnels.' Via neural link he ordered the chirurgeon to fill his xyclos needler, hanging by a hook from his belt, with rapid necrotics and contra-psykana liquids. Immediately, the chirurgeon set to work, the siphons on top of Bile's power plant drawing from its chemical stores and mixing rapidly.

'Objection – what are you doing?' Kolumbari-Enas warbled, a frantic undertone of binharic doubling his words. 'Do you see what you have done! This is suicide.'

'If I were that poor a judge of character, I'd be long dead.' He jammed Torment into the sand, unholstered his bolt pistol, checked the clip, slapped it back home. Seeing it ready, he put it away, and took up Torment and the needler. From within the tunnels pained roars echoed.

'We will be killed! I helped make some of what will come for us. Thrule's machines are unbeatable!'

'Nothing is unbeatable,' said Bile.

Dancing lights appeared in the dark. From gateways all around the arena emerged a rabble of awful machines, of every shape and size, though all had in common a hideous aspect.

'Curse you!' snarled Kolumbari-Enas.

'I do not like being lied to,' said Bile mildly. 'You seek to snare me in the games of my lessers.'

'It is not so!'

'Your conclave has no power. Why else would you bow before this man?'

The monsters crept closer. Bile had his eye upon the largest gateway, from which nothing had yet emerged.

'This Thrule concocts a good monster,' admitted Bile, surveying the daemon engines lumbering onto the sand. 'They will do nicely for our mission.'

A polyphonic hooting, halfway between organ blast and bestial roar, sang out of the greatest gate. A cloud of steam spiced with the strange scents of the warp billowed out. The glow of plasma coils lit it up from within.

Stepping through came the largest of the daemon engines.

'Uncertainty – if we survive that!'

'I shall survive,' said Bile. He glanced at Kolumbari-Enas. 'I advise you to arm yourself.'

Casting anguished looks between the creatures and the Lord of Undregundum, Kolumbari-Enas let out a string of digital expletives. He snapped out his hands. Black whorls of energy appeared around them, expanded into spheres that burst like bubbles on pools of tar. When they vanished, Kolumbari-Enas was armed, a compact meltagun gripped in one hand, a graviton cannon wrapped around the other.

'I protect, master,' Brutus said, plodding to Bile's side, his giant axe held loosely.

'Porter! Take the big one!' Bile ordered. The chirurgeon's arms moved forward into combat stance, its drills whining up to speed. 'Typical of these egotists,' said Bile, 'to let us look at our supposed doom gives us to time to evaluate them.' He looked up to Kurden Suun. 'I'd get on with it, if I were you.'

Suun grinned. 'So be it!'

Thrule raised his hand, and another blast of the trumpets set the creatures in motion.

The mechanisms raced towards the arena centre. Bodies made of fused metal and flesh clashed off each other in their hurry to destroy. Blind heads opened furnace mouths and roared super-heated air. On the platform, shouts rose as wagers were taken.

Kolumbari-Enas looked towards the high gates, and freedom.

'Do you want your reward, magos? There will be none if you flee. Stand and fight!'

'What choice do I have?'

'None at all,' said Bile. He raised the needler, and fired. A sliver of frozen serum stabbed into the vulnerable fleshy parts of an onrushing machine. Quivering skin took it in whole, and blackened instantly. Lights stuttered in the thing's glassite eyes. It collapsed in a tangle of metal, the daemonic soul within screaming as Bile's formula, distilled from the bodies of a hundred psychic nulls, ripped it to shreds of corposant.

'Now, Porter!' Bile commanded.

Porter flooded her body with oxygen, and charged her hydro-static muscles. Her heartstring thrummed with sequenced beats. Her chronoception stretched, slowing the progress of the beast-thing galloping towards her, until it moved so slowly it did not appear to move at all. Her metabolism burned hot with the effort. Cooling vanes in her intercostal spaces opened, making her joints ache. These flooded with blood that was whisked away to vestibular heat exchanges near her thoracic spine. The resultant hot air was vented from her breathing spiracles.

Her brain pulsed with heat. She would be dizzy when she re-entered normal subjective time, yet the moments she gained were invaluable.

The swarm of daemon engines waved their mismatched limbs in a display of aggression. She could smell the need for violence coming off them, a wash of hormones so potent they made her nose itch. She looked past this oncoming tide, keeping her eye on the principal threat.

Thrule's primary construct was a massive, hideous thing, an amalgam of human bodies clustered in the centre, either grown or sutured together and trapped inside an integument of steel. The heads of this beast were all alike, all bald, all eyeless, with huge jaws of needled teeth. Segmented, crustacean legs supported the thorax, each foot a giant claw of metal. Tentacles tipped with barbed points rose over its back. Under normal perception, these would whip back and forth violently, but to Porter they drifted, gentle as a medusa's tentacles in an ocean current. Two arms projected from either side of the torso, incongruously human-like, gargantuan in size. The machine was balanced upon one of these in its time-locked state, in the process of knuckling forward like some enormous, augmented ape. Thrule had been conservative in selecting the components of its construction. The base scent carried only the genetic markers of humanity, mingled with steel, oil, fire and plasma, which together gave a horrible factory reek. Over it all was the burnt-spice smell of the warp; the half-real spoor of the Neverborn imprisoned inside. The trapped daemon had warped whatever contraption Thrule had originally built, and it was impossible to tell what was made by design and what was decreed by the whim of the immaterium. Flesh ran into metal, and metal ran into flesh. Corposant hissed from vents, forming screaming faces on the air before it was snatched away. There was pain within it, human and daemon. Pain, and anger.

A single heavy plasma cannon was its sole ranged weapon, but a potent one. The charging coils glowed beneath diseased plaques of flesh, the intensity of the light suggesting a seventy per cent charge. The machine was heading towards Bile.

She identified the machine's weak spots before she began to move. Her plan was formulated, her course plotted. She drew her durasteel blades, feeling the rub of them upon the sheaths. She lived a lifetime in a moment, mesmerised by that one sensation.

It was an effort to maintain such detachment from the run of events, and it taxed her system. Her brain was overheating. With a thought, she ended her detachment, slowed her metabolism as quick as she dared without crashing it completely, drawing down the frantic activations of her synaptic network to a more pedestrian progress.

Reality hurtled back up to speed with released, elastic tension. She was already swinging her blades as her double musculature catapulted her forward. One of the lesser beasts hobbled at her, titanium-bonded mandibles clattering over a face made entirely of human eyes. She twisted her body in the air, performing a salmon leap over its hunched, warty back, skimming the iron spikes that protected the spine.

They were not protection enough. Porter slashed downwards as she twisted, her blade passing between the jagged points. She parted vertebrae precisely, and the beast machine crashed down with an angry screech, its hindquarters paralysed. As it tried to turn around, it fell down dead, its face burned out by Kolumbari-Enas' melta-beam.

Porter ran on. Two more of the spidery things were in her path, converging in front of the great engine. She jumped again, planting her right foot lightly on the blade-arm of one of the machines, using it as a springboard to jump clean over them. She landed in front of the primary threat, ducked a swipe from one of its giant paws that, though clumsy, surprised her with its speed. The fist impacted the ground hard, punching a crater into the sand. A crowd of tentacles squirmed at her, obliging her to employ her blades to cut her way free. The second hand slapped at her, palm flat. She jumped again, landing on the hand, stealing its momentum to get closer to the body. The eyeless heads snapped at her with metalloid teeth as she sprinted up the body, her target the cannon upon its back.

Too late. The plasma gun whined, and released the store of hyper-heated gases caught within the charging coils. Opaque membranes snapped shut over her eyes to protect them from the glare of the shot, a spear of matter in the fourth material state, hot as the heart of a star.

The passage of it so close burned her skin. She stumbled as one of the thing's tentacles hit her. Although off balance, she responded instantly to the contact, twisting herself so a potentially fatal thrust turned instead to a painful graze as the limb whipped past her, its collections of barbs opening up her skin.

Hyper-oxygenated blood splashed bright red on the monster's back.

'That is the only blow you shall land,' she hissed. Quickly shutting off the pain, she rode the movement of the monster as it tried to swat her. Slashing down at the heads, severing one, distracted it enough that she could dodge its thrashing tentacles. She ran at the plasma cannon, already sucking in fuel for its next firing cycle, and struck with both swords overhead as she slid beneath it.

Heat from the weapon blistered her skin anew. But her blades hit true, one taking off the bulbous emitter at the end, the other shattering the containment chamber. Already partially full, the ruptured chamber spat out a flare of released energy, setting the monster aflame. She crossed her arms in front of her face, protecting her eyes, the outstretched swords warding off strikes from the tentacles. She sensed but did not see the ground approaching, hitting a little awkwardly, but turned her fall into a roll, leaping up to her feet, blades out and ready.

The monster stamped about, wailing in agony, a chorus of pain comprised of the voices of corrupted humans and the imprisoned Neverborn. She kept her attention on it, circling, already recharging her hydrostatic muscle system. She could hear Brutus roaring, lost in his blood frenzy; she could smell the heated air trails of Kolumbari-Enas' meltagun, feel the minute perturbations of up and down as his grav-cannon discharged. But she sensed no sign of Bile. She could not tell if her maker had been hit by the first shot, and that was a cause for dismay, but she forced herself to remain completely focused on the machine-thing, for any distraction would mean her own end.

The fires on the daemon-machine's back guttered down to a smoulder. Meat steam rose from its burned skin. Roaring with outrage, it raced at her, punching down with one fist to vault forward, the other ready to strike. Porter held her ground. The upper fist hurtled towards her, and she stepped aside, swinging with her left sword, letting it snap out at the end of a relaxed arm, until just before contact, when she released all the energy stored in her secondary musculature in one burst.

As the fist hit the ground where Porter had been, her sword sliced cleanly through the monster's wrist. The stump slid off the severed limb, spraying a firehose of oily blood before slamming hard into the sand. Unable to arrest its momentum, the machine fell badly, the wounded arm folding up under its bulk and snapping with a noise like a falling tree.

Porter jumped clear as it was levered up off the ground again by its momentum, and came crashing down in a tangle of limbs. She was running under it before it could begin to recover. Her swords found its black heart from beneath. A torrent of stinking blood engulfed her as it shuddered and died, collapsing on her; only the angles of its multiple legs prevented her from being crushed.

She emerged to see Bile, to her great relief, his xyclos needler spitting tailored poisons at the machines that caused their flesh components to rot with visible swiftness. Torment swung in his hand, each touch causing the machine-things to shrink back in agony. Brutus was atop one of the daemonic devices, bludgeoning its soft core with his axe. Kolumbari-Enas strode assuredly round the field, his graviton cannon collapsing Thrule's pets into dense pellets that fell dripping to the sand, his meltagun vaporising others.

There were not many engines left. Everywhere, carcasses lay smoking. She heard a shriek from behind her, the rattle of metal. She turned to see the warded chains around the spirit tabernacle of her slain quarry glow and part and burst asunder, and from the centre of the machine the imprisoned Neverborn rushed out, a shape of black light that shifted and screeched triumphantly at its freedom before vanishing with a clap of thunder.

Proximity to that made her sick. Her psy-organs ached, warding off the queasiness of the warp with only partial success. Her vision shifted, and she sagged a little.

She released chemicals into her brain, raised the pump rate

of her heartstring. It took her three full seconds to recover, and by the time she had, it was all over.

Bile kicked back the last of the daemon machines, exposing warpborn flesh. He fired into them with the needler at point-blank range. Spider legs curled in on themselves as its soul was obliterated.

One roaring thermal shot from Kolumbari-Enas marked the end of the battle. Broken machines littered the sands. Brutus slumped down with a snort. Porter roamed the field, checking that everything really was dead.

'What was that in aid of, you imbecile?' said Bile.

'Do not address the lord of Undregundum so!' boomed Kurden Suun.

'Are you one of those people who never says a word, but surrounds himself with shouting thugs to do his talking for him?' Bile said, still addressing Thrule. 'Put your lackeys aside and speak to me, I say!'

Kurden's bare face flushed in outrage, but before he could speak again, Thrule had hauled himself up painfully from his bed of cushions, leaving them stained behind him, and limped to the balustrade.

'So then, the little princeling moves,' said Bile. 'Do you also deign to tell me what the meaning of that insult was?'

Thrule cackled. He was a thing ruined by his obsession. Mutation ran rampant through his body, and his laughter was choked with phlegm.

'You are a maker of things,' he wheezed. 'I am a maker of things. I wished to see our things fight. What sport they gave, though I acknowledge you as the greater talent!'

'Did you really need to attack me to come to that obvious conclusion?' said Bile.

'How much for the warrior thing?' Thrule raised a clubbed

hand, the digits fused together and grown gross and scaled, too large to fit within a gauntlet. A stubby, normal-sized thumb hung sadly beneath the single, thrusting finger pointing at Porter.

'She is not for sale,' said Bile. 'If your intention was to impress me, you have failed.'

'No failure. I shall make better things. I learn from you, great genetor.'

'What if you had killed me?'

Thrule shrugged. His pauldrons screeched. The displacement mechanisms struggled to accommodate his broken form. 'Then I would have had a fine story to tell, that I slew the Pater Mutatis with my own weapons, thus proving myself the better crafter of monsters.'

Bile sneered at the warp-polluted beasts lying dead all around them. 'An impossibility.'

'Then you had nothing to fear, and I still have a fine story to tell.'

'My lord Thrule.' Kolumbari-Enas scuttled forward and knelt again as if Thrule had not come within a blade's breadth of ending his miserable life. 'We have proven the might of the Clonelord in open battle, the truest test there is.'

'Yes! Yes!' Thrule clapped his deformed hand against his other, which remained untainted, and by comparison seemed weirdly dainty. 'Such fine sport, the battle of things!'

'Petition given – if you are pleased, I ask if you have had a chance to consider my request? That you fight alongside us against Belisarius Cawl.'

The lunatic glare in Thrule's eyes dimmed, and a calculating, cunning look settled on what remained of his features.

'What is in it for me?'

'Plunder of the most exquisite kind. Cawl goes to meet upon

an ancient world full of potential. Much technology of the oldest sort.'

Thrule made a show of stroking his chin. His oversized finger pulled ropes of drool out of the bottom of his broken helm. 'What use have I for old machines? No.'

'I anticipated this,' Bile said. 'Brutus!'

The minotaur pushed himself up to his feet with his axe, dropped the weapon and lumbered over to the genecasque. He heaved it up, and carried it to where Bile stood, and set it down again.

The genecasque opened with a blast of super-chilled vapour and clink of specimen jars.

Thrule leaned forward greedily, the cold blue glow inside the casque lighting his ruined face from below and making him appear even more vile.

Bile threw out his arm. 'Enough gene-seed to double the size of your warband. This is not the weak material the Adeptus Astartes are made from today, nor the mutated trash you would get elsewhere, but fine, strong stock, distilled from the best of the Legions of old!' He let a savage sarcasm into his voice. 'Will that be enough to secure your services, *my lord?*'

The immobile Heretic Astartes at the rear of the platform moved for the first time. All came forward to see.

'Riches indeed,' croaked Thrule. 'Very well, Fabius Bile. You have bought yourself an army.'

CHAPTER TWELVE

THE FLAT WORLD

The *Zar Quaesitor* broke from the warp with the howling of tortured souls and shrieking metal. Alarms blared from every deck. Somewhere, someone was screaming. Dust fell in sheets from between blocks of machinery, some paint, some rust, some skin cells shed by men and women forgotten to history. Cracked pipes vented steam across the passageway. Gangs of servitors stomped towards the worst of the damage. Fire suppression crews raced by, bulky in heat-resistant suits.

Alpha Primus strode through it all, shoving past gaggles of panicking menials towards the six hundred and twelfth deck's primary observation gallery.

'Get out of my way!' Primus shouted. He was helmed in case he had to pass sections open to the void. His voxmitter elevated his voice to terrifying levels, and that only made the menials' state of disorder worse. He tried his best not to step on them, but more than one was barged out of his path with the delicate cracking of bone. 'Move!' he bawled.

The ship endured another queasy roll. Primus staggered. More alarms went off.

'Cawl,' he growled, flicking his eyes up to the ceiling. The magos had a habit of dramatic warp egresses. One day, he would kill them all with this showmanship.

He switched to vox, stepping through a fan of sparks spraying from the wall where a pair of servitors welded up a crack in a panel.

'All military commanders, report immediately to deck six-twelve observatorium,' Primus ordered.

A door a few feet on was trying to open, getting stuck in its warped frame, then slamming closed again. Every time the door opened, robotic shouting leaked out of the chamber behind; magi warning of imminent fusion cutting. As Primus walked past, a hot orange spot appeared on the metal.

Responses to his order chattered over the vox, giving status reports as to why this clade master or that maniple leader could not make their way up to deck 612.

Primus growled at their excuses.

He accessed the *Zar Quaesitor*'s noosphere and brought up the damage report sub-intellects. There were power outages across two dozen levels. The central track for the prow-stern core train was ruptured. Several of the main lifter banks were non-functional. Twenty-one atmospheric breaches, nine of them at the gravis level.

'This ship is in no fit state for war,' he muttered. He was in poor humour, and a good deal of pain. Every time they passed the veil into the immaterium, the warp pulled his soul partway out of his body. It was like having his skin torn off.

Cawl had made him poorly, he thought, or at the least had overreached himself, because Primus' spirit was not seated properly in his flesh. This was no idle conjecture; he could see the misalign-ment with his witchsight, as a smeared rainbow aura around his limbs, and a ghostly doubling of his fingers if he held them up to his face. Besides the constant aches his engineered physique inflicted on him, he endured an acid spiritual discomfort each time they moved from one realm to the other that took hours to subside.

As a result, Primus hated warp travel.

A tremor shuddered its way across the ship from the lower port up to the upper starboard. As soon as it passed, another, weaker pulse came cutting across almost perpendicular to the ship's nominal gravitic pull.

Despite the ongoing clamour on the upper levels, the ark was largely deserted. A few years before, the giant ship had bustled. Many thousands of Primaris Space Marines had slumbered in methalon caskets. Whole clades of magi had laboured in the vessel's manufactory zones. More staffed laboratoria. Then came the crusade, and the numbers grew again as Cawl went to war alongside the primarch. Skitarii pledged by a dozen forge worlds came aboard, alongside an entire household of Taranis Knights from Holy Mars.

Most were gone now. The majority of his military assets Cawl had given over to Fleet Primus when he left the main crusade. Many of his magi had been despatched across the galaxy to speed his next great plan to fruition. Away from the frantic ant's-nest activity around the damaged sectors, holds once full of slumber-ing Space Marines were empty. The garrison levels were sealed and accumulating dust. There were places Primus found posi-tively eerie.

He scolded himself. Annoyed by the bustle, annoyed by the lack of bustle – Cawl had made him to be dissatisfied, Primus was sure of it.

The observatorium of deck 612 was up ahead. The beacons above the door that would warn of breaches in the giant panes of armaglass were out. The klaxon was silent. The door panel's access buttons were lit a healthy green. All signs the observatorium had made it through the warp unscathed.

Primus swung his shoulders sideways to permit a transmechanic minoris to hurry past, trailed by a floating crowd of yipping repair drones attached by fine wires to one of his left elbows. In stepping around him, he very nearly flattened Scion Magnus Baron Roosev Maven Taranis of House Taranis, who emerged out of a side corridor right into Primus' path.

Primus came to a sudden stop. The scion magnus brought the steel recaff mug he was drinking from up and round in a large circle, then he grinned.

'The plan of the three in one is seen and acknowledged. I did not spill a drop!' He made a little pass over the mug in blessing.

'Baron,' said Primus. 'I did not see you there.'

'Apparently not,' said Maven.

Maven was the most senior of the standard humans left aboard. There hadn't been very many of them in the first place, and most had been knights of House Taranis. Cawl had found the knights' desire for military adventures distracting and started gifting them to the primarch after only a few years had passed. Two lances remained, however, and they were the *Zar Quaesitor*'s most potent military asset.

'Let's do this the correct way, as laid out in the rites of my house.' Maven drew himself up. 'Full greetings and amities to you, Alpha Primus, most favoured son of Belisarius Cawl, from the house of my fathers, Taranis the Great,' said the Baron, then dipped his head. The high collars of his dress uniform kept his neck stiff. 'My lord.' He did a little bow full of complicated flourishes. Remarkable, how he managed that while still holding his recaff mug.

'Are you finished?' growled Primus. 'I'm not one of the Emperor's preening angels. I don't have time for your pointless rituals. I don't need or want your obeisance.'

'As good-humoured as ever, I see, Primus,' said the baron. He wasn't particularly old, because nobody was particularly old compared to Primus, but already his body was showing the first signs of failure: wrinkles around his eyes and mouth, thinning hair, grey in his beard, a slight dryness to the skin. He hadn't seemed to notice that he was already dying.

Primus envied him his ignorance.

Primus grunted and set off again down the corridor towards the door. The baron broke into a jog to keep up with the giant. They were moving fast, and yet Maven still did not spill a single drop of his drink, not even when another tremor ripped through the ship. His arms behaved like they were the weapons of his steed on full target lock, never deviating from their position.

'We have arrived early,' the baron said.

'Good tides in the warp,' said Primus.

'They're a blessed rarity in these times,' said the baron. 'We should be grateful for the Omnissiah's guidance, as we are in all things. *Ave Omniscentor.*'

'If you say so,' said Primus. 'But that egress makes me cautious in singing His praises.'

Primus arrived at the door. He reached for the door button, his speed such that it looked like he would put his armoured fist right into the wall, but the knuckle of his gauntlet grazed the plastek gently, and the door opened with a subdued hiss – an almost relaxing sound against the clamour going on behind them.

'Welcome, Alpha Primus, first of the Primaris,' a machine voice croaked from within. 'Welcome, Scion Magnus Baron Roosev Maven Taranis, master of Knights.'

'All praise the three in one,' Maven responded.

'So it must be,' the voice said.

Beyond was an unlit room where a long viewing gallery bowed out into a huge rose window. Transoms and mullions as thick as Land Speeders curved out into the void, thinning to a filigree of metal in the centre, holding giant panes of hyper-dense armaglass in place. An enormous armoured blister was closed over the bulging oculus, divided into two hemispheres like gargantuan eyelids. Primus approached the operations plinth, whose controls were the main source of light in the gallery. His footsteps boomed round the empty room, echoing off the secondary and tertiary galleries overhead leading off onto decks 613 and 614. From the centre of the middle gallery jutted an enormous brass telescope, big as the heavy lascannons mounted in the *Zar Quaesitor*'s gun decks, and a million times less useful. Technology like that had been superseded tens of thousands of years ago.

Primus fought down a long spike of irritation at the witless need of the tech-priests to hoard. He opened up the primary toggle-switch cover. His finger sent hard bites of pain up his arm when he moved it.

'Spirit, what is the integrity of the oculus?'

'Integrity of the observatorium oculus is at one hundred per cent, oh lordly one.'

Primus' lip curled. There was a hint of mockery in the chamber-genius. Cawl's personality got into everything he touched.

'Disengage shutter locks,' he said. He flicked the toggle switch. A series of clanks ran along the great lid from left to right.

Heavy footsteps emerged from the noise of the repair crews. The light from the corridor dimmed a moment.

'Am I late? I suppose I am not,' said a synthetic voice. Data-smith X99 Bolus, one of Cawl's many magi followers, entered the gallery. X99 was a robotics obsessive, and was followed everywhere by a Kastelan-class battle automaton. It was that making all the noise.

'You're here just in time, my friend,' said Maven. He sipped his still steaming drink. 'The shutter is still closed. Primus here was in the process of unlocking it.'

'Ah, I do like a dramatic reveal,' said X99. 'Sigma Fidelis,' he told his machine, 'take station at the rear of the room. Make space for our comrades.'

'Compliance,' said the automaton.

Servos whined. The robot rotated piece by piece, first its head, then its shoulders, waist and finally feet turning on the spot. It picked out an alcove between two stanchions, retreated there, then repeated the smooth, mechanical rotation so that its impassive, silvered viewing plate ended looking out.

'He's looking in fine condition,' said Maven appreciatively.

'The great work never ceases. I've spent the voyage overhauling his power train and major joints. I'm very pleased with the result.' X99 had a warm and bright personality to match his voice, somewhat at odds with his heavily enhanced form. His love of robotics was so great he had turned himself into a construct to all intents and purposes, and was now a collection of pistons and wires. He moved jerkily, far from the smooth, superior operations of the ancient machine that dogged his footsteps. Primus thought him deluded, casting away perfectly good body parts in exchange for poorly functioning mechanisms.

'I thank you for your praise,' said X99.

'I respect all forms of war machine, and have been grateful of Sigma Fidelis' support on the field more than once, datasmith,' said Maven. 'What do you think, Primus, of Sigma Fidelis' improvements?' Maven gave his comrade a knowing smirk. Never mind the machines, thought Primus, Cawl's irksomely ludic attitude infected the humans that served him as well.

Primus glanced back at the Kastelan. It was nearly twice his height, a daunting machine, for a lesser being than he.

'Why bother?' grumbled Primus. 'It was perfectly functional before. These interests you have, a lifetime of investigation for what? To be snuffed out and cast into the great dark. Activate power feed to the shutter mechanisms,' he said to the genius loci.

'Compliance, great Primus, servant of the Prime Conduit!'

'Be silent,' said Primus. 'Simply obey.'

The whine of generators awoke in the walls. Lines of lumens came on along the rail top, up the supports, on the undersides of the balconies above. Bright enough to light the way of observers, not enough to spoil a view of the void.

'Our great protector is on fine form today, I see,' said X99. He joined Maven at the rail, stepping forward with all the surefootedness of a badly operated marionette.

'He is Primus,' said Maven, with a mix of respect and impudence.

X99's cylindrical head rotated to fix Primus with one of several red eye-lenses.

'You too are perfectly functional,' said X99. 'One of the Prime Conduit's masterworks.'

'I am nobody's masterwork,' said Primus.

By now, other people were drifting onto the observatorium's galleries: skitarii alphas, archaeoptor squadron masters, more datasmiths, belluscogniscenti; a host of strange beings. They looked like any command cadre of Adeptus Mechanicus forces, but these were Cawl's disciples, and their ranks were thick with mavericks.

The psychic jabber of their minds sent prickles through Primus' body. He allowed himself a brief release from physical pain, commanding his battle plate pharmacopeia to flood his system with analgesics. They damped down the ache of his bones, but the agony of his spirit he could do nothing about.

All the chief warmakers still in Cawl's service amounted to only twenty or so, a small crowd for such a grand observatorium, and far fewer than there had been. Primus suspected that Cawl was entering another of his long solitary phases. The signs were there, not least this rising obsession with xenos technology. Cawl always divested himself of unnecessary hangers-on before he hid away to study.

Another shudder took hold of the *Zar Quaesitor*. X99 nearly toppled, and grabbed at the rail with three-fingered metal hands that surely, surely were far inferior to those he had been born with.

Not that Primus cared. He didn't care about anything.

'This system is a tumultuous place. Very many gravitic waves. A lot of cross-currents. It's a challenge for the archmagos, make no error in that,' said X99.

'So I've been led to understand,' said Maven. 'It should be a sight to see.' More shaking gripped the vessel. 'If we're not torn apart in the next few minutes.'

'All locks disengaged, shutters ready for opening,' the genius loci reported. The main release indicator blinked from red to white.

'Then open them,' said Primus.

The working of large mechanisms thrummed through the gallery. The observatorium was on the larger side, and its correspondingly huge oculus delicate. The shutters that protected it had to be thick.

The oculus shutter opened, and a slice of blinding light painful as a sword edge cut into the crowd. Maven shaded his eyes. There were a few gasps from the less-modified, more emotionally complete attendees, and the sounds of artificial visual systems recalibrating against the glare.

The metal eye continued to open, in short order revealing their destination, and the cause of the ongoing ship-quakes.

The room fell silent.

Avernes was a quadruple star system. In humanity's wanderings across the galaxy, long before the Age of Strife finished Terra's first interstellar realm, it had come to discover such multiple star systems were common. Although some were stable enough to host planets, many were unstable, and did not.

The Avernes System was in the latter category.

Avernes Principal, a large and furious blue star, dominated the system. It was of the beta five type, according to the time-honoured stellar classification. A pair of orange stars locked in a binary dance waltzed around it in a way that seemed designed to tease their bigger brother. They were successful if the endless, ferocious eruptions from Avernes Principal were anything to go by. The orange stars were named simply Avernes Secondary Alpha and Avernes Secondary Beta. The final sun, Avernes Tertiary, was a cinder of a thing, a compact white star that darted in between the other three on a tortuous, helical orbit as if seeking to evade capture.

'That is a literally dazzling sight,' said Maven. He sipped, again giving the little benediction over his drink.

'Dazzling, but dangerous,' said X99. 'These stars are not fully hierarchical in arrangement, but subject each other to violent forces caused by their chaotic interplay.' He bowed his head modestly. 'Though I am no stellar taxonomist, you understand.'

'I am sure they are the most basic of facts,' said Maven. 'Well within the understanding of a magos of your talents.'

Primus curled a lip at Maven's flattery.

The binary pair were large in the window, casting spears of flames at each other. The principal star was so far away it appeared as a searing hole. The white sun was not as distant, but so small that it seemed no bigger than the background stars. However, only the very brightest of those were visible, for Avernes Principal outshone the universe, turning the void around it to a depthless, infinite black.

Primus turned his back on the suns. The scene failed to move him. It presented strategic questions that must be responded to, no more than that. He checked the tally of attendees. Most of those that could feasibly make it had come, bar one. He decided to wait for her, standing in complete silence while the others commented on the system, ignoring all questions put to him, only coming back to life when she entered the room.

Marshal Melissima Artos-Septus Iota was de facto commander of all the Mechanicus forces aboard the *Zar Quaesitor*. Cawl was nominally in charge, as he was archmagos dominus, and had accumulated centuries of combat experience over his long lifetime, but usually he was busy with other matters when the fighting started. Primus suspected that these responsibilities of his were sometimes manufactured, or the effort he put into them more intense than strictly necessary, because Cawl found combat boring where once it had exhilarated him. He was like that with everything. Cawl would spend all his time and efforts obsessively mastering a discipline, then when he neared perfection, when he might effect momentous change to the universe, he would abandon the field for something of greater novelty, and the process would begin again. His quest to recreate the Space Marines had been his longest sustained effort, but the minute the Primaris Revelation was over, his thoughts had gone elsewhere. It was like that with war.

Cawl needed a general, and Artos-Septus Iota was it.

Marshal Iota was a tall cyborg, with an advanced, adamantine-plated corpus metallica. Her flesh components had been pared back to the bare essentials, so that externally she appeared to be of entirely mechanical origin, although for some reason that eluded Primus, Iota had retained her female shape. Her metal armour was fashioned in an idealised form of her original body, her face was a blemish-free, perfectly symmetrical vision of beauty wearing an expression of superior amusement. She wore it so often, Primus had originally thought it fixed that way. It had surprised him to discover that the metal was flexible, and could move as much as any human face.

For many of the Adeptus Mechanicus, gender was irrelevant. After centuries of upgrades it was frequently impossible to tell what sex they had been born with, but Iota seemed to revel in her femininity. She was a silver idol to herself. On the other hand, this expression of female perfection was bastardised. Each marvellously sculpted body part was separated by exposed machinery. The joints showed flexible plastek coverings for her inner workings at knee, shoulder, elbow and hand. Her vertebrae of a golden alloy were exposed at the neck and surrounded by wires prominent in their armoured insulation. Two forms of perfection vied in her body – that of sacred humanity, and that of the holy machine. If Primus had learned one thing about the members of the Machine Cult, it was that they were all uniquely strange. The *Zar Quaesitor* was a ship full of freaks.

'This is the place the archmagos dominus has chosen for his meeting with representatives from three forge worlds,' Iota said. She stepped over to the balcony, her coat of Martian red swirling about her legs. It was the sole garment she wore – no buttons, held half open by her weapon belt. Beneath she was entirely gleaming metal. 'What an appalling place to fight a battle,' she said. 'Massive gravity rip-tides, huge particulate expulsions. Large parts of the territory here will render void shielding weaker to the tune of two-fifths loss of effectivity. Furthermore, we have come out of the warp too far into the system. The damage to the *Zar Quaesitor* is extensive. I honour the archmagos as much as anyone here, but this is reckless.'

'It is our duty to protect him while negotiations are underway. Silence your complaints, and put away your fear,' said Primus, who was of the opinion that he could criticise Cawl, but no one else should. 'Cawl has brought you much glory. Do you doubt his judgement?'

The metal of Iota's face rippled. 'Never. You are in a poor mood today, my giant friend. I do not wish to work against you. I share your concern for our master,' she said, 'but there is no denying coming here is a risk. The archmagos remains a priority target for the enemy, perhaps now more than ever. We are being hunted. By being here, we show ourselves to them. There will be consequences.'

'Then we will be ready,' said Primus. His relationship with Iota was strained. By one measure she was ranking commander, by another he was, because of his relationship to Cawl. It didn't help matters that Cawl let them both believe they were right.

'Which is all I am saying,' said Iota. 'I enjoy the challenges my service to Cawl brings. Such wonders we see.'

She pointed at a patch of shimmering colour in the distant void, and simultaneously, by the arcane arts of the Adeptus Mechanicus, brought up a magnified hololith of the same.

'Behold Pontus Avernes,' she said.

An artificial world lay bathed in the light of the four suns at one of the only Lagrange points between the stars.

'Planetary construct, I see,' said Maven. 'Completely flat?' He sipped his mug of recaff. Every time he did so, he whispered the short blessing over the drink, giving him a slightly obsessive air.

'Not completely. There is a mountain range, I believe,' said Primus.

'Forgive me, I mean flat as in, not a globe. And is there an inverse surface?'

'It is a mono-surface. The upper. There are false environments on it,' said Primus. 'These vary in type from lake lands to the single low mountain range. Breathable air. Gravity exactly to Terran norms.'

'Interesting place.' Maven sipped again.

'Built in the Dark Age,' said X99 Bolus. 'A great work of astro-engineering. It has no engines, but remains where it is thanks to careful placement. It sails upon the gravitic waves of the quadruple suns.'

The suns looked angry about their artificial friend. They had no natural children, having devoured or cast them out, yet by the wisdom of mankind the platform sat perfectly still between them, suspended on the gravipause while titanic energies raged all around it.

'How powerful our ancestors were,' said X99 Bolus. 'Somehow, amid all this stellar chaos, the builder of Pontus Avernes found this patch of still void to set his creation in. Such artistry. Such knowledge!'

Roosev shrugged and sipped his drink. He murmured his prayer. *By the grace of the Omnissiah, Machine God and Motive Force, I intake this fuel,* it went.

'It is an act of showmanship,' said Primus. 'It serves no purpose other than to be. It is a monument to ego.' *Cawl should be perfectly at home here,* he thought to himself.

'Primus, can you not see the artistry here?' Iota said. 'This is a fine display of what we can achieve if only we uncover enough of the secrets of the ancients. That is Cawl's quest. It is our duty to protect him while he is distracted.'

A role he does not make any easier for his devoted servants, Primus thought.

The *Zar Quaesitor* shuddered as if in sympathy.

'I am a simple warrior, your holiness,' said Maven. 'I thank the Omnissiah for the war machine I ride. A wondrous gift, but all this...'

He sipped his recaff again. A slurp followed his whispered prayer. The noise set up an unpleasant resonance in Primus' tormented nerves, causing the giant Space Marine to frown at him, but the knight was oblivious.

'I see the audacity of it, and the beauty, but I have known from my birth that true comprehension is beyond me. It is not the path the Machine God set my feet upon. I am a warrior, and I cannot fight the stars. I am only a passenger, until the blessed metal feet of the great *Iurgium* spread their claws upon solid ground.' He smiled again. His smile was so insipid, thought Primus. 'The void is not my preferred campus bellicus. I see this, and wish only to ask, show me ground where I might fight.'

They raced at the false world. The boiling, rainbow skin of its shielding could now be seen without magnification, reacting to the complex tides of particles racing off the stars, but beneath the kaleidoscopic display were tantalising hints of greenery, buildings and bodies of water.

'Do not give up hope for war,' said Iota. 'The archmagos being what he is, there will be plenty of opportunity for you to prove your worth.'

'Well that would be very nice,' said Maven. Prayer, slurp. 'I can't see much from here. Is there any chance of a tactolith? I'd settle for a map. It pays to know the ground you'll fight on.'

Primus gave him a sidelong look. House Taranis were based on Mars, they were from Mars, but they didn't seem to be of Mars. Though most people within the wider Imperium thought that the Red Planet was inhabited solely by bionic priests, many billions of standard humans lived there. The majority had little status in the Cult. The knights and the crews of the Titan Legios were unusual in that respect. They were highly honoured. But though they were as thoroughly enmeshed with their machines as it was possible to be, they did not aspire to become them, not like the magi.

Someone had once said to Primus that the knights did not need to become machines. By joining their souls to the machine spirit, they were parts of their war engines at a spiritual level. To Primus that sounded dubious. He had decided a long time ago that people made little sense.

'Data on Pontus Avernes is difficult to come by,' he said.

'Even for Lord Cawl?' asked Maven.

'Especially for him,' said Iota. She turned from the view. 'This facility is of Dark Age manufacture, as Datasmith X99 accurately points out. It was discovered in M39.365 by an explorator fleet originating from Tigrus but operating under Martian licence. Exploitation rights were disputed by the two parties present, and were put into arbitration. The case went all the way to the Synod of Mars. Naturally, they awarded rights to their own planet. All information is held at the non-omnia viseo level.'

'Mars is the mother of us all,' said Maven.

'Then she is a greedy mother who snatches food from her children,' said Iota. She was perfectly safe saying so in that company. All of them were fugitives of one sort or another, ostracised variously for experimentalism, free thinking, empirical practices, and open questioning of cult dogma. 'Cawl is making a statement, as usual. He is playing politics, as usual, and as usual he is doing so to irritate the Fabricator General Oud Oudia Raskian.'

'He can't help himself, can he,' growled Primus. 'As if we don't have enough problems.'

'On that issue, we are in agreement,' said Iota.

'Surely we must have a map?' said Maven. 'No augury data?'

'Long-range auguries are ineffective in this stellar environment.'

'Nothing clairvoyant, from the astropaths?' asked Maven.

'Hello? Hello! I say, excuse me!'

Primus swung his bullish head around. A timid-looking magos on the middle balcony lifted his hand, almost dropping the bundle of scrollcases he carried. Primus didn't recognise him. Though the ark was operating on a reduced crew, there were still tens of thousands of people aboard the *Zar Quaesitor*, so that wouldn't have been strange, only Primus did know everyone involved with the military aspect of the ship, and this fellow was not among them.

'Madam marshal, lord baron, if I may?' said the man.

'Who speaks?' said Primus. 'Who invited you to this meeting?'

'I am cartophraser to the Fourth Clade, my lord. My name is Oswen. And, er, well, I invited myself.'

'You have one more sentence to tell me why you think your attendance is appropriate,' said Primus. 'If I am unsatisfied, I shall eject you.'

'I have a map!' His voice squeaked. 'Here, somewhere, no, not this...' He almost dropped his bundle of cases and maps, lunging forward to catch them, before completing an undignified little juggling motion that saw him snatch one up, half crumpling it. 'Aha! Here it is, um, yes.' He held it out to no one in particular, and blinked, looking a little confused.

'Come down here,' Primus commanded. 'Now.'

The man hurried to obey, nearly dropping his maps for a third time as he banged into the massive Myrmidon cult bodyguard of the Cohort Three dominus. His hurried apologies preceded him onto the lower deck. Amalgams of men and machines stepped aside to let him pass. He came holding out his rolled-out map to Primus like an offering.

Primus took it, unrolled it, frowned at it.

'Any good?' Maven asked.

Iota gestured. Primus handed the map over. Iota's arms spread unnaturally far to pull it taut. A scan laser from her left eye passed over it twice, and she handed it back, then her right eye flickered, and projected a hololithic reproduction on the air.

The map was drawn by hand, on parchment, but well executed. It showed a flat landscape. Geometric edges suggested tessellated hexagons underpinning the construction. Neat handwriting gave the dimensions as two thousand miles across exactly, in all directions, with the width of each hexagon at fifty miles. As Primus had said, there was a range of small mountains surrounded by hills with wooded valleys in between, as well as an area of lakes, one of which was large, and a forest, but the majority biome appeared to be a moorland or wet prairie type. The landscape features were regular, if blurred by the spread of natural vegetations. Iota zoomed in, and they saw on the map, at each junction of the hexagonal plates, structures. One of these had been drawn at the side in cross section, a ziggurat of some sort.

'That is most useful,' said Maven, and finished his recaff.

'How did you come by this?' asked Primus.

'Well, um, I, er, I collect maps,' said Oswen. He was a nervous little man, hardly augmented, although an oversized intelligence core protruded from the top of his skull in a lopsided fin, the edges frilled with cooling vanes. One of his eyes was a boxy bionic with a yellow lens. A small pseudo-spider perched on his shoulder and repeated his words in binharic. 'Knowledge is power. Understanding is the true path. You know all that. Each of us has our own way to enlightenment. For me, it's maps.' He nodded, as if making a very pertinent point.

'That does not answer my question,' said Primus.

'Um, I purchased it from a data-merchant some years ago. He'd got it from someone who'd acquired it from the original explorator expedition. It was a good find. Very rare. But there you are. I had it, I thought you might need it, so I brought it.'

'I see,' said Primus. This was most suspicious.

'These are nodal field generators,' said Iota, pointing at the pyramids. 'Energy shields and atmospheric retention. Possible void shields.'

'What a fine representation this is!' said X99. 'You are to be congratulated, magos.'

'I didn't draw it, and I'm not a magos yet,' said Oswen modestly.

'I can see why,' said Alpha Primus sternly.

'Are we then to escort our glorious master onto the field, so that the Prime Conduit of the Omnissiah may make a show of force?' asked Iota. 'You seem to know our lord's will better than any of us, Primus, even though I am his field commander.'

'No. He wishes to meet the magi with minimal display of force. We are to prepare for battle and remain ready to deploy from the *Zar Quaesitor* if required. All attack craft are to be crewed and ready for launch. Baron Maven, your Knights are to embark onto their drop-keep now. You will establish a beachhead and possible evacuation point, should it be needed. Marshal, make your skitarii clades ready to deploy from bulk landers.'

'It shall be done.'

'X99,' Primus went on, 'make ready your cybernetic cohort. You will accompany the archmagos.'

'Send the map maker too,' said Iota.

Primus pivoted to look at her.

'Come now, you can't think him a security risk,' Iota said. 'Send him. He may prove useful.'

'I am honoured to serve,' said Oswen.

'If you wish,' said Primus. 'Very well.'

'Who are we expected to fight, just out of interest?' Maven asked. 'The Great Enemy, or the servants of our own god?'

Primus looked down upon the baron. He was so small.

'Either. Both. It does not matter, so long as Archmagos Dominus Cawl is safe. Be ready.'

CHAPTER THIRTEEN

A WARM WELCOME

With the faintest of electrical shivers, Cawl's lander passed through
Pontus Avernes' atmospheric shielding into clear air. A plain of
golden grasses extended in all directions, dotted with identical
ziggurats that had become spectacularly individuated by the flora
growing upon them. The roar of the lander as it descended scared
up flocks of pastel-coloured aviforms, and large ruminants heaved
themselves out of the mud to lumber away in slow-motion panic.

The lander set down. The hull had barely sunk into its landing
gear when the ramp opened and Cawl strode out, timing his
debarkation so that his mechanical claws hit the ground the
exact moment the ramp's toothed edge did. In order to appear
diplomatic, Cawl was unarmoured and unarmed. His war panoply of armour, shield generator, massive Omnissian axe and
solar atomiser were aboard the *Zar Quaesitor*. The eight-legged
buprestis drone hard-linked to his lower torso input array took

a few further steps onto the ground, its serrated head sucking in samples of dirt through its proboscis. It sensed something it didn't like and gave a warning trill.

'Hush now,' Cawl soothed. He breathed deeply through his facial cowling. The air was sweet. The landscape was well constructed, but there was something off about it, a weight to the atmosphere. He had the sense of powerful machine spirits offended by his trespass.

Daylight was glaring and omnidirectional. Cawl cast a shadow for each sun. All were pale phantoms in competition with the others. The aurorae streaming off the shields foxed sensors and pushed an annoying squeal over the vox. He could practically taste the energy, and the air was fuzzy with static. He moved a subsidiary limb out to more directly sample the soil, and a spark leapt from his robes to earth in the ground.

'Curious place,' he said.

The gang ramp clanked and groaned as four Kastelan robots walked out of the hold with the ponderous deliberateness of their kind. They spread out into a box around the archmagos. Sigma Fidelis followed, X99 behind him, busy with a satchel full of data-wafers. Oswen came next, eyes bulging.

'This is quite something,' he whispered. Nobody paid him any attention.

Next Qvo stepped out on clumsy legs. He was having difficulty with his robes, as if wearing clothes were a novel concept to him. When he got to the bottom he tripped and went down into grass. Motile lilac flowers shrank back from him, and he froze.

'They are just flowers, they won't bite! Up now.' Cawl helped his friend with a supplementary limb. He changed his mood from pensive to bright; Qvo needed buoying up. 'Look, Qvo. Pontus Avernes! The bridge between the stars. What a beautiful landscape, eh?'

'If you say so,' said Qvo. He looked out over the homogenous plain. Mountains far out to the edge offered the sole variation. On all other sides the landscape stopped at glaring walls of aurorae. 'It's muddy.' He lifted and planted his foot experimentally. The earth squelched.

'Don't look at the dirt, look at the construction!' Cawl said. 'This is a work of fine artifice.'

'Will it remain so?' said Qvo. He pointed. Between the regularly spaced pyramids, heaps dotted the plains, spoil from the delvings of tech-priests. Giant earth-moving machines, silent for the moment, waited to chew up virgin environment.

'I did not think you so sensitive to archaeology, my dear friend.'

'Eighty-seven deaths changes a man,' Qvo said. 'This is appalling. Do we not risk wrecking the very things that we seek? And what of the life we destroy? Do you ever ask yourself that?'

Cawl waved the destruction away. 'I am sure that they will not despoil it all. It is too big.'

The landscape reflected in the Kastelans' mirrored scoptic plates: they remained silent, watchful. Cawl looked skywards. The atmospheric envelope was thin, and the blackness of the void visible behind the shimmer of the shields. In that darkness, Avernes' tumultuous suns ran amok.

'Reminds me a little of Trisolian, don't you think, Qvo?' said Cawl. 'Such an awful ion wash. I can barely hear a thing. Vox is out, augurs restricted to sight range. Hmph, a nasty blindness. Trisolian had a little of that, but not so potent. That blue sun shouts loudly.'

'Where and when was Trisolian?' asked Qvo.

'Do you not remember?' said Cawl disappointedly. 'That's a shame, I thought those some of your best-preserved memories.'

'I do not recall.'

Cawl sighed. It came out harshly through the voxmitter mounted on his shoulder. 'It was the place where events began that led, alas, to your first demise, and to me becoming what I am now.' Cawl took on a thoughtful tone. 'Actually, I myself do not remember exactly. I've lost my memory too many times – mind wipes, tortures, arcane attack. Who knows what I have endured? I only know of our time together at Trisolian because the information is preserved in the holographic record of Friedisch's mind. So I suppose, seeing even I do not recall myself, I should allow you some latitude.'

'How very generous,' said Qvo drily.

'Nice cutting tone. You really are like him,' remarked Cawl.

'You're a monster. Making me die so many times. It's inhuman.'

'Yes. I am. But I am also your friend. Eventually, you shall become a real boy, to cite the ancient legend! Once your elements are reintegrated with the pan-dimensional etheric substrate of destiny, and the particles of your soul realigned, then you will once more be the Machine God's creation, and not mine.'

'You're talking about the warp.'

'Of course, of course. The Machine God moves in both materium and immaterium. Even I cannot improve on His work in that regard.' Cawl cast his eyes heavenwards and made a circle with his hands in the place his heart had once been. 'I can try though.'

'You are insufferable,' said Qvo.

'Don't let on to the scale of my ego, I've a lot of people to impress today. We're over there.' He jabbed a pincer at the nearest of the pyramids. 'Atmospheric field resonators of a superior make!' Cawl said. 'Such marvels we have here. No wonder our brethren dig, dig, dig.'

'Why did we set down so far away?' moaned Qvo. Curious, he had not seemed this… *whiny* since his original death. 'Isn't it dangerous to come here without your army?'

'My army is coming.' Cawl pointed up and behind him without looking. Qvo followed the outstretched claw to a point of light approaching the shields. 'Knights.'

'They're not here now, are they? You're vulnerable.'

'Tish-tosh, my not-Friedisch companion. I'm much too important to kill, even if they all hate me.' He became reflective. 'I don't think they all hate me.' He shook his head. 'Onwards!'

Cawl's hugely augmented body rose up with the sigh of pistons, and he moved forward. The robots set off a fraction of a second after the archmagos. They walked in eerie lockstep, huge feet squelching in the soft ground.

'Just try not to step on me,' Qvo muttered in the direction of the nearest machine.

Oswen brought up the rear, staring at everything in awe, jotting notes in a large leather-bound book he carried.

The landscape seemed completely natural: a spongy bog of coarse plants, mosses and treacherous hollows, dotted with open patches of water. But after a time a pattern emerged, a grid of blocked canals, scraps of walls and raised humps that hinted at buildings. A causeway lifted itself from the muck. Cawl swerved onto it and the others followed. Qvo took a few auspex soundings. There was a road surface beneath the peat, perfectly preserved.

'Does this look like it might have been a garden to you?' Cawl didn't wait for an answer. Conversation with him was notoriously one-sided. 'I see flora from seven different worlds. Fascinating. Do you see how they've formed their own ecosystem? I imagine this was formally laid out, that would explain the canal network and diversity of plants. I expect there were many more, but only those best suited to survival would have persisted. The level of detail and cunning the Machine God put into His creation for man to harness. Life is a marvellous thing! Look what mankind achieved here. Once all the secrets of the ancients are in our hands, then the old days of glory will come again.'

'No they won't,' said Qvo blackly. 'The Cult is debased, obsessed with the past. We've become blinkered.'

'True, true,' said Cawl. 'But I'm not them, am I?'

'Yes,' said Qvo, which sounded not so much an agreement, but a word said for the sake of feeling an active part in the conversation.

As they approached the pyramid, the garden's original layout became clearer, as if the pyramid acted to keep back the tides of nature's disorder. The pools took on straighter edges. Ancient masonry poked up from the ground. The soil was firmer, and the signs of ancient cultivation stood out. Flowerbeds, paths, statuary, all but lost beneath rattling rushes and sedge.

The horizon on Pontus Avernes was close. It tricked the eye. The pyramid was smaller and nearer than it had seemed from the ship. They saw now that the four corners were pronounced, with recessed stairways in the centre of each face. There were large, some might say bold, architectural flourishes at the edges that resembled rearing snakes. The augmented eyes of Cawl and Qvo saw energy patterns, as visible to them as iron filings sketching out the lines of force around a magnet. In the sky these projections intersected with those of the other pyramids, overlapping and reinforcing one another, thus forming the fields that protected the place. Closer still, they could feel the projections in their bodies. They shifted the fluids in their hydraulics. They tugged at their artificial hearts. They agitated the alloys of their limbs.

'Tangy,' said Cawl, smacking leathery lips. 'You know, I can get no readings past twenty feet below the ground. Uniformly so. One must ask what is down there. It's exciting, isn't it?'

The magi reached a neat moat surrounding the pyramid. Fish darted away as their shadows fell on the water. They turned the corner of the face furthest from their landing site, and were presented with an immense flagged area, big as a landing zone, for which purpose it was currently being used by three Mechanicus ships. Hulls in the colours of Tigrus, Accatran and Metallica steamed with dispersing heat. Groups of skitarii in uniforms to match moved towards Cawl. Query and danger signifiers flashed across informational space. Cawl's small party stopped. The robots raised their weapons fists, and gave out sorrowful bleeps.

'Belisarius, they are coming for us,' said Qvo uneasily.

'Of course they are coming for us. It is their job to come for us.' Cawl looked down on Qvo-89 and smiled. 'I do like it when you call me Belisarius.'

The skitarii raised their guns. Radiation flares were noted in Qvo's internal processors. As they passed the ships, Kataphron heavy-combat servitors rumbled down ramps from the Accatran lander.

'They don't look pleased to see us,' said Qvo.

Cawl scuttled forward so that he was fully on the flagged area, and then turned around to face his friend.

'You think we are at risk.'

'I do.'

'And why did we come here, you might be thinking. A very good question, which I shall now answer.'

'I didn't ask you anything, Belisarius.'

'Well, I'm answering anyway. You might think that I am here to display my free agency and lack of subservience to Mars, which knowing you inside and out, Qvo, you are thinking, because you are a clever fellow.'

'I am not thinking that,' said Qvo. 'I am thinking I am not ready to die again.'

Cawl continued his lecture.

'I like Mars to know what I am doing. The Synod approved my designation as Prime Conduit by a hefty margin. Even if Oud Oudia Raskian, that hab-sized rascal, hates my mechanical guts, I have a lot of support at home. I may need to call upon it at some point. However, if I tell them where I am and what I am doing all the time, it would prompt some of them, or worse, a lot them, to commit to assist me. That would lead to civil division on Mars, and potential internal conflict across the forge worlds. I'd much rather they got on with sending armies to Guilliman, because if I was being trailed by some foolish crusade of my own, it would look like I was trying to inveigle my way into some sort of power, which I really don't want, but which is exactly what Raskian fears. He fears I've gone rogue. Me being here, on this platform claimed by Mars, is a way of letting them know what I am doing without provoking such foolish actions. It's a way of me saying I have clout. They couldn't say no, you see. Being *here* is a way of doing a lot of things. Don't worry. There is no danger.'

The Kataphrons outpaced the skitarii, their butchered brains lacking the infantry's caution. Heavy treads broke ancient flagstones as they came to a jerking stop and trained their weapons on the tech-priests. The Kastelan robots returned the favour. Phosphor blasters and heavy stubbers pointed at heavy plasma cannons.

'We come in peace!' Qvo shouted. Oswen half hid behind him, but continued to write quickly.

'X99, stand down your automata!' Cawl commanded. The robots' arms dropped back to their sides, and they stood to attention. Cawl gave the approaching skitarii a regal wave. It did not stop the coils on the servitors' culverins glowing bright with accumulating charge. 'Three troops of three forge worlds acting in unison,' said Cawl. 'What a fine sight. Makes you proud to be Martian.'

In the way of the Cult when multiple forge worlds worked towards a common goal, the skitarii had quickly selected one of their number to lead. It was hard to imagine Terran troops finding an accord so soon. The Accatran Alpha was designated prime, and he stepped forward, his order transmitter bleeping melodically. He shouldered his weapon, and got down on his knee.

'Greetings to you, Archmagos Dominus Belisarius Cawl, great sapient, Prime Conduit of the Omnissiah. The lords of our worlds await you within the artefact, and humbly request your presence.'

The others knelt. The servitors dipped their weapons and their heads.

Cawl raised his many arms high.

'No need to bow and scrape on my account! Please, get up, get up! We are brothers in the steel. Let us behave like friends.' He said this with a great humility, but shot Qvo a grin and a wink.

Qvo did not need to draw on the accumulated experiences of four score lives to know it would be a trying day.

'Come on, everyone,' Cawl said to his party. 'Let's go inside!'

CHAPTER FOURTEEN

OLD VOICES

Half a hundred miles away, the lander Cawl had pointed out to Qvo punched through the shielding of Pontus Avernes. It hurtled towards the ground until, when it appeared it would crash into the plain, retro-rockets fired, slowing it, and it sank down. Blades of fire touched upon the sodden moss, calling up steam in huge rolling clouds.

The engines cut off. A vast shadow loomed over the earth. Mechanical noises sounded from the bank of hot fog. Lights appeared deep in the pluming white; red, predatory. Whining motors sounded, the soft hum of plasma reactors swelled.

War-horns announced a pair of Knight Armiger Helverins striding out of the vapour, condensation streaming down their red-and-white livery. One stopped, swinging its beetle's head back and forth over the plain, while the other turned on nimble feet and broke into a run, the twin spears of its autocannons locked forward. Mud splashed up its legs. A foot plunged deep into soft ground. The Knight stumbled, righted itself, and galloped on.

The other Knight remained still and watchful, sensorium whirring. Faint chirrs of active scanning devices sounded from under its chin.

Satisfied there were no hostiles present, the scout sent back the all clear, and moved on.

The fog blew away, revealing an immense drop-keep of House Taranis, one hundred and seventy yards long, one hundred wide, big enough to land two full lances of Knights. Open posterns, the egress for the small Armigers, let out a flood of yellow light. Crenellations bit at the sky. Automated weapons extruded themselves from gun-ports. It would have been more impressive still if it were not listing gently in the mud. Down one side, outstretched landing claws lengthened their pistons, pushing at the surface to arrest the tilt. Retrorockets fired intermittently. Neither succeeded in making the craft upright.

Heavy bolters and lascannons in sponson turrets tracked back and forth across the drop zone. Flagpoles whined up from housings, and pennants bearing the arrow and cog of Taranis unfurled. The pistons of the slipping claws hissed. Rocket stabilisers woofed exhaust. The keep continued to list, slowly, slowly, until it came to rest, ten degrees or so out of true. A klaxon gave out two harsh notes.

The posterns closed and the great gates they were set into opened, revealing the silhouettes of giants. War-horns ripped out across the moor. Heavy treads sounded from within, and a Cerastus Knight of the Acheron pattern bowed its lofty head to pass beneath the arch of the keep, moving awkwardly on the tilt of the deck. It stretched up to its full height upon leaving, like a man long confined loosening his muscles, before its lead foot lifted, and plunged down, sinking into the ground. The machine swayed, shifted around. It hauled the foot out, black water streaming from its limb, and stumbled forward.

'Emerge at cautious speed,' Scion Magnus Baron Roosev Maven Taranis voxed his Knights. 'The footing is worse than the soundings suggested.'

Iurgium's machine spirit flared with hot anger, but Roosev did not let it affect his judgement. Adjusting his pace and posture to suit the terrain, he moved away from the lander.

'Knights Armiger, fall in before me, test the way for the heavier engines, proceed at three-quarter speed. Do not outpace us. The rest of you, move in behind. Sacristans, prepare the uplink, and right the ship, for the love of the Omnissiah. I will not suffer the indignity of our keep toppling into this filth. We have our honour to uphold.'

The replies the sacristans gave were so garbled by static he was concerned their transmissions would not reach the *Zar Quaesitor*.

Roosev was a different man mounted. Less flippant, less gentle, harder, more forthright. He was *Iurgium*. And yet, a cloud of spiritual disapproval hung over him. The ghosts of his ancestors hovered around at the back of his awareness, appearing from the depths of shared consciousness like pale fish to scowl and tut before darting away. They did not like this battleground.

The Armigers were running ahead, picking out a firmer route for the larger Knights. More war machines came out from the keep. *Danubia*, *Vanitas* and *Foebreaker* first, all Questoris. A pair of close-range Armiger Warglaives followed. The Warglaives' armoured heads swung around warily, scanning for threats, sonar sounders pinging the ground to find the firmest route. They were to escort *Salutatia*, Scion Waldemar's machine, a Dominus-class Castellan that was the biggest of them all. When the Armiger pathfinders were satisfied, the great machine came out slowly, carefully, the gates only just large enough to permit

Salutatia to exit the keep. He paused outside the gates to activate his weapons systems, which came to life all at once, targeting lenses burning, turrets tracking back and forth. Letting out a deafening blare of his war-horn, Waldemar walked, shaking the ground with his tread.

Another Cerastus, this one a Lancer, came out last. *Contegeris* was its name. It ignited its shield. Disruption gleam shone around the tip of its lance. The heraldry on its pennants, tabard and armoured plates declared its pilot to be First Knight Allacer Maven Taranis, younger brother to the baron.

'This looks like a good place to fight – flat, open, good jousting ground.' He pressed his Knight's foot into the soft earth. 'Until you step on it.'

'We shall manage, First Knight,' said Roosev, testy with *Iurgium*'s wrath. 'Best foot forward.'

'Very funny,' Allacer said. He moved his head within his cockpit, and his mechanical steed mirrored him, sweeping its electric gaze across the land. 'To where do we ride?'

'The pyramid where the Prime Conduit holds his meeting.'

'Isn't that against our orders, brother?' According to etiquette, Allacer should have called Roosev by his title while in the field, but *Contegeris* had an overly familiar machine spirit, jubilant, almost, and it infected Allacer's soul with a forgetfulness of authority. 'Our orders are to patrol.'

'Patrol we shall. We shall scout the lands around the meeting pyramid first, passing these three structures in a wide arc.' Roosev highlighted other ziggurats on their shared tactical network. He frowned at the lines of interference skipping all over the screens. The particle wind and magnetic fields generated by the four stars were enough to make their house noosphere stutter, but there was another source to this disruption, emanating from the world itself, some power source deep underground. 'Then

GENEFATHER

we move on to march past the meeting place, to make our presence known.'

'We were told making ourselves known was not our mission,' said Allacer, bringing his Knight alongside his brother's. 'Readings say the other delegates have put down in front of the pyramid. Why has Prime Conduit Cawl landed so far away? It would be better if we were to escort him, to show these lords of lesser forge worlds that House Taranis walks at his side.'

'We were told to patrol, so we are patrolling,' said Roosev. He tried to keep the irritation out of his voice. *Iurgium*'s machine spirit veered between anger and misery out of combat, and his mood tugged Roosev's down. 'Although we shall do so in a directed and purposeful manner.'

'House Taranis does not skulk. Even if the living voice of the Machine God asks it to do so.'

'Indeed it does not, Allacer. Cawl knows all things, he would have anticipated that we would not like these orders. Having us... adapt them might have been the archmagos' intention all along.'

'Inscrutable are his words.'

'Ave Omnissiah.'

The Knights moved into their formations. *Iurgium*, *Contegeris* and *Danubia* in the first lance, *Salutatia*, *Vanitas* and *Foebreaker* in the second behind a forward arrowhead comprised of all four Armigers. Roosev gave the signal, and they set out, the heat from their reactors making the air shimmer in their wake.

Upon the higher levels of the ziggurat, a figure swathed in shadow observed the keep landing.

Alixia-Dyos watched Belisarius Cawl and his servants arrive at the base of the building. She crouched low, a ripple on the surface. Cameleoline in her robes made her a distortion on the stone, nothing more. A combination of active augur baffles and the strong energy fields generated by the building hid her from all technological means of detection. A psyker might have suspected something amiss, but if they were to have looked, they would have encountered only a peculiar void in their witch-sight, for the spy was protected against clairvoyance by amulets of dubious provenance.

There would be one moment of vulnerability. A half-second when detection was possible, but only if someone were looking in the right place at the right time. That was unlikely to happen. Alixia often relied on the incompetence of others to keep her safe.

She kept low, watched the greeting performed to Cawl by the warriors of Accatran, Metallica and Tigrus in a state of perfect stillness. When they had gone within, she pulled out a bulky device from under her robes: a glass cylinder with a handle, covered switch and a dial on the side. Three prongs with stacked insulation discs of diminishing size were mounted on the jar's cap.

Within the jar was the half-solid form of a lesser Neverborn. It was mindless, biting at glass it could not breach, a tiny sliver of false consciousness harvested from the warp, perhaps an errant dream solidified in that hell-realm, or the accumulated envies of a nobody far away in space and time. No thought or feeling, no matter how insignificant, went into the immaterium without effect. It was the genius of the Dark Mechanicum to find a use for these things.

The spy pulled out a pin from the switch cover, and flipped it up with her thumb. A button, bright red and stamped with a warning skull, was beneath. The daemon in the bottle raged.

Alixia twisted a knob below the switch. The device had a limited message capacity. It would be enough.

A lumen blinked. She recorded her message.

'Belisarius Cawl has arrived at Pontus Avernes.'

She pressed her thumb down. Hexagrammatic wards in the glass fed by fine silver wires glowed with power. The device grew warm. The captive daemon went wild, scrabbling at the container and howling, loud enough to hear through the warded glass. The generator made the handle hot. The spy deactivated the sense of pain in her hand, and grasped tightly. Curls of corposant rose from the Neverborn. The wards grew brighter. There was a sucking pop, and the imp vanished. White vapour swirled around the blackened jar. Green lights blinked in sequence. The message had been delivered.

Alixia-Dyos took out her melta-pistol, put the device on the stone and vaporised it.

Holstering her weapon, Alixia withdrew, not hurrying. She had to go below and greet the archmagos.

A scorch mark and fading thermal signature were the only signs she had been there.

Iurgium loped across the plains as well as it could. Within his armoured cockpit, Roosev kept a representation of the land open in one of his hololithic informational panes, the sure, hand-drawn lines of Oswen's map overlaid by details culled from auspex soak returns. If one disregarded the unusual subsurface features, and the total lack of underground penetration past twenty feet, there was not much to the plains. The Taranis Knights were far away from Pontus Avernes' more interesting topography. Some thousand miles in the direction Cawl's men had nominated as east, the hills began, and in their heart were the lakes. Beyond, small mountains. But where the Knights walked, all was rolling moor. It was dull land, yet deceptive. Black pools opened up without warning before the machines.

Deep banks of peat filled in lost irrigation channels, soft enough to mire *Iurgium*'s giant claws. He'd stagger through these, only to stumble again when his feet hit more solid ground where the metal substrate came close to the surface. A couple of times, Roosev heard *Iurgium*'s feet boom as if running over the hollow spaces, and his sensorium would crackle with the emissions of the hidden power sources far beneath them.

It was difficult to keep an even pace, and Roosev very much liked to canter smoothly. This place depressed him. The lurch of his machine as it encountered soft ground threw him about in his Throne Mechanicum with enough force to yank his spinal cables in an irksome way. The jolts of pain drew him out of his union with *Iurgium*'s spirit, making both pilot and machine sullen.

The spread of Armigers ahead helped find a path, but they were lighter, and despite their pilots' skill in scouting, the ground was so poor the routes they chose were not assured safe for the larger Knights. The Questors were neither as fast as the taller Cerastus, nor as nimble, and were less capable of freeing themselves when stuck. Sir Doldurun's Knight sank to the knee in one spot. If not for his lance comrade's quick actions in slipping his shoulder guard under *Foebreaker*'s, and half supporting, half slamming him back upright, he would have fallen. *Salutatia*, in particular, was at risk of foundering.

It was hard going. The multispectral vision of the Knight's ocular displays helped, but Roosev had to concentrate all the time to pick out potential pitfalls. The intense solar activity and the fields that protected the world from it made scrying difficult, and the noosphere was loud with headache-inducing noise.

Another bad step from *Iurgium* and another hot pain in Roosev's skull as a consequence. He hissed through his teeth. *Iurgium*'s spirit growled in his soul in response.

'Does something trouble you, my brother?' Allacer asked over the vox-net. 'You sound to be in pain.'

'Loose connection,' he snapped. 'The sacristans are getting lax. There are too many distractions for them aboard Cawl's ark. Too many wonders. It makes them sloppy.'

He tugged his restraint webbing tighter. Maybe that would help.

His ancestors swam closer to the forefront of his mind, drawn up from the depths by Roosev's irritable state of mind. Most were voiceless, psychic impressions of nobles from millennia past. A fragment of battle joy, a long regret. Fear. A memory of victory. There was nothing more to many of them than that. But a few had something to say for themselves, and none more than the ghost of Maven the Very Elder.

Who exactly he had been, Roosev did not know. He got the fleeting mental impression of a doleful face adorned with a large moustache and a nagging sense of disappointment. The stories of the house, which his tutors had regaled him with at tedious length back on Mars, maintained that this warrior had once been a baron, and was sufficiently old to have been born when the elderly Raf Maven was still lord, all those thousands of years ago. All other knowledge about him was lost, and the residual spirit himself did not seem to know who he had been.

Yet to say he'd been dead so long, he still had a lot of opinions, and most of those were disapproving. His ghost influenced *Iurgium*'s personality deeply, and Roosev blamed the Very Elder for making his steed only joyful in combat.

This is a poor place, a miserable place, beneath us, beneath the family of great Raf Maven. Beneath the glory of House Taranis. Maven the Very Elder's words haunted the hinterlands of Roosev's mind like whispers in a cathedrum. *No glory, no glory, no charge, no glory.*

Miserable miserable, moaned a host of other voices in chorus to the Very Elder's lead. *Miserable, miserable!*

Too much water, too much mud, no place for a charge, no place for honour. No glory, no place.

No place, no place. Too wet. No place.

Roosev gritted his teeth.

'Not now, honoured ancestors, not now.'

'Brother, you realise you are vox-casting this?' Allacer warned.

'Emperor save me. I have the old baron in my ear.'

Allacer chuckled. 'Delivering his usual helpful advice, is he?'

'You might say so.'

Allacer laughed again. 'My ghosts are quiet. I think they're enjoying the trip out.'

'Then aren't you the fortunate one,' grumbled Maven. He shut off his vox.

With the ghost of Maven the Very Elder nagging in his mind, and the treacherous earth beneath his feet threatening to foul his stride, Roosev almost missed the bright, silver note which sounded from a minor augury.

No honour, no glory. No honour.

'With the greatest respect, be quiet, old one,' Roosev murmured. He opened the vox again. 'I am getting an odd reading from the primary pyramid. Lance Iurgium, slow to walking pace, deviate path to meeting point. Lance Salutatia, maintain current course – continue patrol of outer perimeter.'

Iurgium and its two Armiger escorts cut away from the circular path they were following around the ziggurat, and curled inwards. *Contegeris* and the Questoris *Vanitas* and *Danubia* followed.

'We might endanger whatever peace Cawl has brokered here, Roosev,' Allacer warned.

'That is why we go slowly. We will not approach too close. Only so near that I can get a better reading.'

'What did you see?'

'Low-level psychic emanation, and a thermal spike.'

'I wouldn't put much trust in the readings. Those pyramids throw out all kinds of auspex alerts. I've had five junk echoes since we set out. We have no idea what sort of archeotech powers this place.'

'This one feels different.'

'I'm getting strong power emanations from around the pyramid. Distorted, but I am certain they're Mechanicus. We've got to assume the other magi have troops there,' said Allacer. 'Cawl's vulnerable. This whole thing is badly conceived.'

'We follow the orders of our chosen lord,' said Roosev. 'I am sure he has his reasons.' He was only paying half his attention to his brother. The rest was focused on his auspexes and augury arrays. Grids tracked across his displays. Waveforms peaked and hit troughs. There were several anomalous returns, from all around him. 'Lance Iurgium, halt,' he commanded.

The huge war machines came to a stop. Their feet were mired up to the ankles in the bog, their livery, pristine minutes ago, spattered with orange and black mud.

'Anything?' Allacer asked.

'Nothing,' he said reluctantly. 'It must be an auspex phantom coming off the devices inside the pyramids, or maybe a lensing effect, distorting the readings off the delegations' guards. Besides all this archeotech, there are a lot of tech-priests within. The Machine God knows the extent and types of their blessings. We do not.'

'You've achieved your wish,' said Allacer. 'We've made our presence known. Ident queries are coming in from all three transports on the ground.'

Roosev glanced over at his external vox and data arrays. He'd muted them to concentrate on the scan. Transliterations of the requests hung on the air in angry reds.

'So they are. Withdraw.' Roosev swung his Knight around, heading back away from the pyramid; his Armiger squires raced ahead, throwing up plumes of water. 'Let's not throw promethium on this particular fire – the archmagos is more than skilled at that himself.'

'So then?'

Iurgium pivoted easily at the waist to look at Allacer's Knight.

'Move back to original patrol pattern. Respond to our allies with messages of full amity, inform them we commend the Prime Conduit to their protection, and that we are patrolling for threats to the combined lords of the Adeptus Mechanicus, under the eye of the Machine God, Ave Omnissiah. Ensure they know that we mean no harm, and that any assistance in securing this world would be gratefully received.'

Allacer snorted. 'We don't need any help.'

'Humility can be an effective tool of diplomacy when properly employed, brother. Send it with all the proper forms and move out.'

CHAPTER FIFTEEN

THE TRIAL OF BELISARIUS CAWL

Cawl's robots joined with the delegations' warriors, and together they took Cawl, Qvo, Oswen and X99 Bolus inside in a manner that was more triumphal procession than escort. The skitarii struck up a marching cant across informational space. Its trilling peaks and troughs of binharic were full of complex skirls of code to blind opposing systems. The Kastelans joined in, adding a baritone hum. Qvo was surprised by that, but he jumped even more when the Kataphrons began to warble hideously from their desiccated throats. X99 was looking somewhat alarmed at his charges' sudden singing, if Qvo read the blinking LEDs in his face rightly.

'Are you doing this?' Qvo asked, raising a perfectly made eyebrow at the robots and the servitors. Both devices lacked sufficient agency to spontaneously burst into song.

'Mm-hmm,' said Cawl. 'Don't tell. Let everyone think it is the Machine God Himself showering us with blessings.'

'You're reprehensible,' said Qvo.

'A touch,' said Cawl.

The parade went through the pyramid's thick walls, and the perspective changed. They came into a cavernous space, a single room, with stepped pools descending to a plaza some way below. The volume within seemed bigger than what the exterior should be able to hold. For a moment, Qvo was taken aback, until his generous suite of sensors told him that it was an optical illusion, and not dimensional engineering. The builders had built this space deep into their planet's surface, with the lower half being a mirroring of the upper parts. Together they formed a roughly diamond-shaped cavern. Many polished surfaces expanded the sense of space.

The walls were a mass of blocky, fractal expressions. The air within was alive with surging currents of power, drawn up from deeper underground and projected skywards. The Motive Force was so strong in there, the Machine God seemed immanent, as if He would step out from a fold in space, and lift high the curtains of ignorance, so they could see the workings of reality for themselves.

The sensation passed. The pyramid's hall was not so impressive when one looked closely. The walls were cracked. Primitive lichens crowded joints in the inner surfaces. The pools were either dry or full of a dark, brackish water from which rose an unpleasant smell. And yet it was an appropriate place for the great believers of the machine to meet. An artefact of humankind's lost powers, which all the faithful spent their lives in toil to reattain. This was a holy space to them. Machine-priests of many different specialisations stood on eminences projecting from the walls, and they added their voxes to the procession's hymn.

Stairs led down around the sides, wide enough for the war

robots, shallow enough for the Kataphron to pitch down and descend on their clanking tracks. Qvo supposed the place must be silent most of the time, had been silent for thousands upon thousands of years since its makers fled. But for a moment it lived again, and it was glorious, the cavern reverberating to manifold widecast, and the temporary noosphere established by so many minds of the Mechanicus brought together thrummed with the cross-calls of data exchange.

They reached the plaza at the bottom of the pyramid. There, the delegations of Metallica, Accatran and Tigrus awaited Belisarius Cawl in a crowd a few dozen strong. The white and red of Metallica predominated, their magi forming more than half the crowd, with Accatran's steel and black and Tigrus' orange making up equal parts of the rest. Going by the variety of augmentations on display they were all mechasapients of the highest order, many of them having abandoned the human form entirely. Cawl came to a halt, and his escort did likewise, the robots looming behind him, the soldiers of the forge worlds peeling off to stand guard over their respective masters. Flocks of cyber-constructs buzzed overhead.

A barrage of identity signifiers cut the procession's hymn short.

'I am High Cognomaster Golophex Archimedius, third-lord of causal integrations, of Accatran,' one blurted.

'I am Archmagos 18561-op-Dephinius, lord of the data-tyrants of the Lysaon Temples, of Metallica,' canted another.

'I am Savant Ultimus Plucio-Trinarius-Slare, logis-arcanis of Tigrus,' said another.

Then another. 'A#01b23q1201011001.'

And another. 'Archmagos Logis Magnacomptroller Covarix Sestertius.'

And more, and more. Until the noosphere was thick with name-codes. Archmagos… Archmagos… Archmagos… On and on it went, until Qvo was faint with it.

All of a sudden, they were done, and the information cut out. The loss of data was traumatic, and Qvo almost fell.

Cawl took a little bow. 'I am Archmagos Dominus Belisarius Cawl,' he data-cast like the others, for all communication was conducted in the holy numerical language of binharic where so many tech-priests gathered.

It appeared the archmagi too had selected a leader to speak for them all: a giant, serpentine creature who moved in a manner that suggested a propensity for violence. He came forward, turning a silver mask of motile metal that smiled daggers more than diplomacy on Cawl and Qvo.

'Archmagos Belisarius Cawl, Prime Conduit of the Omnissiah. I am Archmagos Macroteknika Hryonalis Anaxerxes of Accatran, war leader and cognoscenti belligerus. It is a privilege to meet one so near to the state of true comprehension. I have been chosen as voice of this convocation, to interface with you directly for the purpose of efficiency. On behalf of us all, I welcome you to Pontus Avernes.'

The machine – even Qvo struggled to see him as a man – bowed and spread arms wide enough to embrace a battle tank. Empty heavy-weapon hard points gleamed on his shoulders.

'I know you, I know of your work, the great general of Accatran, yes!' said Cawl. 'I must say, this is a good turnout. Very flattering! I am humbled by your welcome. These are perilous days for our species, and we all have a great many things to do. You may be wondering if all this is not a monumental waste of your time. However, I promise that once I have revealed my plans, you shall regard your decision to come here as sound.' He gave a diffident laugh. 'Even if you find me a little audacious.'

The sense of unity between forge worlds was beautiful while it lasted. It fell apart round about then.

<8123ab12A112... 0110101010110!> blurted a thing that looked like

a small generatorum balanced on a bunch of thick, tentacular mechadendrites. Qvo's lexical decoder was slow in catching its meaning, but it was not happy. <I damn you as a heretek!>

Another figure pushed his way to the front, causing angry words and blurts from those he displaced. He, too, was far from worshipful.

'Archmagos dominus,' said the magos. Qvo initially took him for a member of the Accatranian delegation, for his robes were black, but then Qvo saw he could not be, for he favoured gold as his secondary colour, not iron grey, and then Qvo noticed about his neck an amulet displaying an altogether different allegiance.

The barred 'I' of the Imperial Inquisition.

'Who might you be?' said Cawl. 'You broadcast no identity. Quite rude, really. And what is that?' He pointed at the Inquisitorial badge.

There was something a little crazed about this magos; the eyes above his bonded respirator seemed triumphant, manically so.

'I am Frenk Gamma-87-Nu-3-Psi, of Zeran.'

'Zeran. Zeran?' said Cawl. 'That's a name I've not heard for a long time. I sent no messages to Zeran, though I have the greatest respect for their savants. Alas, it is in Imperium Nihilus, far away, and cut off from the galactic south. How did you come to be here?'

'Not because you summoned me, apostate!'

'Ah, you're one of those,' said Cawl. 'Have we met? You're not on some misguided quest for revenge, are you? I do have a habit of accumulating enemies.'

'Not misguided, no,' said Frenk. 'You interrupted the work of my associate.' He held up the pendant around his neck, brandishing it like a holy symbol to ward off malign spirits. 'Inquisitor Cehen-qui!'

'Ah, hmm, no. Have I met him?' asked Cawl. 'I have offended

more than a few members of the Imperial Inquisition down the centuries. Is there something particularly special about this one?'

'You stole from him, not five years ago!' Frenk said. He turned to face the crowd of magi. 'This innovator liberated a dangerous xenos organism and spirited it away from a maximum-security incarceration facility!'

'Now we're getting somewhere,' said Cawl in recognition. 'Lords archmagi, consider that this facility can't have been that secure if I got in. The creature he speaks of is actually safer with me, and useful to our efforts.'

Some of the magi gave amusement signifiers. It only encouraged Frenk to greater efforts, and he yelled with the vehemence of a preacher sending sinners to the pyre.

'From his own mouth he condemns himself! Guilty!'

'I'm only guilty of saving humanity. If that's the charge, I accept full responsibility.'

'There are many charges, worse charges.'

Cawl looked about the assembly of Adeptus Mechanicus lords and ladies.

'Do we really have to do this now?'

'You seek to avoid justice then?'

'I seek to avoid wasting everybody's time.'

<2ato1110101110111. Heretek accusation=suspicion. We have time,> canted the thing on the mechadendrites. Qvo caught its name floating on the noosphere. Kalisperis, a lector dogmis. Female, once. Odd that she carried no additional tags or had not replaced her original gender denominative, given the extent of modification. But there was no telling with tech-priests.

'Excuse me a moment,' said Cawl to Frenk. 'It may be better to get this out of the way. I am aware that my actions have led to some lingering concerns about my motivations. I know that some among you have doubts. I had intended to address these during my presentation to you, but perhaps we should seize this serendipity the Machine God provides us, and go over these misunderstandings now?'

A chitter of conversation bleeped over the crowd.

'We are in agreement. You may proceed,' data-cast Anaxerxes. 'Perhaps your investigative instincts will bring perfidy to light, Frenk Gamma-87-Nu-3-Psi. It could be valuable to have you question Lord Cawl. If you have not forgotten how to question one of your own kind.'

A murmur of amusement.

'I assure you that–'

'You will be silent until I say otherwise,' canted Anaxerxes, his never-changing expression staring down on the magos. 'I shall adjudicate. If your arguments are convincing, then we shall depart, and Archmagos Cawl shall receive no aid from us.'

'I demand that Cawl is turned over to me once I have presented the list of charges,' said Frenk.

'Negative. We shall depart. Cawl will go free. Consider that a victory. It is the fullest extent of indulgence you shall have. Remember, this will be a debate. This is not the trial of Belisarius Cawl!'

'We shall see,' said Frenk. 'I insist that I be allowed to record these proceedings, so that your agreement with my charges can form part of the greater case that my master shall make against Cawl.'

There was another rapid data exchange.

'Agreeable,' said Anaxerxes.

Frenk nodded. A black-and-gold servo-skull dropped from the flocks over the convocation. When it was in place opposite Cawl, Frenk laced his hands behind his back and pushed out his chest.

'Let us begin! The charges are as follows! The death of a Space Marine Chapter. Modus unbecoming–'

'Hang on a moment.' Cawl held up a mechanical hand. 'Do you wish to list them all, or may I answer them individually, as we proceed?'

Frenk Gamma-87-Nu-3-Psi's eyes narrowed. 'You may not answer them at all!'

'Negative,' interjected Anaxerxes. 'He may answer them. Consider this a chance for you both to state your cases, not a listing of heresies prior to burning, Frenk Gamma-87-Nu-3-Psi. Did I not make myself clear? A debate, not a condemnation.'

'Individually then,' said Cawl smugly.

Frenk looked about for more input from the crowd before beginning again.

'Charge the first! The death of a Space–'

'Sorry, sorry,' said Cawl. 'I have a further question, if I may?' He looked around for objections; seeing none, he continued. 'Magos Frenk, is there any structure to the order of your accusations?'

'What do you mean?'

'I mean, do you have a structure?' he said, with exaggerated puzzlement. 'Are you listing them in order of seriousness, or chronology, or are you just throwing them out there as they occur to you? I did wonder if...'

Frenk's eyes were hard. Cawl trailed off.

'Never mind. Please continue.'

'Charge the first. The destruction of the Space Marine Chapter the Scythes of the Emperor!'

Cawl nodded, as if Frenk had landed on a particularly pertinent point. 'Ah, a good one. Not too abstract, everyone can understand how serious that is. The death of an entire Space Marine Chapter! A fine opening blast. Well done you.'

'Aha!' blurted Frenk. 'So you admit it?'

'No, I do not. If you were going to be strictly accurate, the truth is that I was the cause of the *rebirth* of a Space Marine Chapter, and indeed of many Space Marine Chapters, but you speak of the Scythes of the Emperor, no? My lords of Mars!' said Cawl. 'Before they came to me, the Scythes of the Emperor were on the brink of extinction owing to infiltration of their attendant serfs by xenos agents and the subsequent loss of their home world to Hive Fleet Kraken. I admit that all the remaining, original Scythes of the Emperor fell in battle, but I say that this was at their own will. Since that day, not only have the Scythes of the Emperor been reinforced to full strength, and once more watch over the world of Sotha, a world I must add that my acolytes are in the process of returning to life at my own expense, but our joint expedition enabled the last of their Firstborn Space Marines to die with honour, expunging their guilt, purging the most pernicious xenos influence from the Chapter in the process and saving a noble organisation from being lost for all time. Take it up with Tetrarch Decimus Felix of Ultramar if you want corroboration.'

'Do you admit that during the course of this supposed salvation, you destroyed their fortress-monastery?' said Frenk.

'I did no such thing,' said Cawl. 'The xenos technology within the mountain that they had unwisely built their fortress-monastery upon destroyed their fortress-monastery. They have a new home now, again furnished at my expense.'

'Is this true, Cawl?' asked Anaxerxes.

'The Scythes of the Emperor have occupied the Aegida Orbital over Sotha, which my servants are upgrading for them. Their oaths are unbroken, their duties continue to be performed. All thanks to me.'

'The Scythes are now comprised entirely of your Primaris Space Marines, is that not the case?'

'Halt!' called Anaxerxes. 'I follow the course of your argument, and predict its ultimate point,' he said. 'You will suggest that these Space Marines are beholden to Archmagos Cawl and not to the Imperium. It seems everyone has a theory as to whom the Space Marines of the Ultima Founding owe their loyalty.' A weird, electronic bird chorus of digital laughter signatures rippled across the assembly.

'Machine God bless you, Frenk, but this really isn't a sympathetic audience for your accusations,' said Cawl.

'Pray be silent, Archmagos Cawl,' said Anaxerxes. 'Frenk is entitled to his moment. Proceed on to another point, Magos Frenk.'

'This is not a genuine court,' said Frenk. 'You cannot overrule me.'

'I can, and you are only able to put these charges because we allow it. Now continue under those conditions, or do not continue at all.'

Frenk pointed a finger at Cawl.

'One day, you will answer to these crimes in front of a real court of the Lex Imperialis.'

'I didn't realise that the Inquisition extended such courtesies as trials to their victims,' said Cawl. 'Times really are changing.'

'A man of your influence must be seen judged for his crimes,' snarled Frenk. 'Then he must pay for them in full.'

'Deary me, such spleen over one necron.'

'I said continue!' data-blurted Anaxerxes. 'Time is a finite resource. You both test our patience.'

'Very well,' said Frenk. 'The next charge. Do you deny that there are those who agitate for your installation as Fabricator General?'

'What a ridiculous accusation,' said Cawl, and tutted very loudly, breaking his informational stream. 'Of course people agitate for my installation. But it means nothing to me, and it is certainly not at my bidding. There are probably people agitating for the noble Anaxerxes' installation as Fabricator General. There are people who would put a servitor forward if it would serve their political goals.' Cawl faced the assembly. 'Listen, all of you. This does need addressing. I am aware of the rumours. But I have no wish to take up the office. I despise obligation. It limits freedom. I do not even aspire to your ranks, oh exalted magi. Oud Oudia Raskian is safe from any design of mine. He can keep his throne.'

'You behave as if it is within your gift to grant or remove power,' said Frenk. 'As if the Fabricator General rules only by your permission.'

'Do I? Really?' said Cawl. 'I thought I was being flippant. Very well, I shall clarify. I could not take Raskian's throne even if I wished to, and I assure you that I do not wish to, for the reasons I gave before and for a whole host more.'

'Your protestations of innocence do not convince me–'

'He cannot prove he does not wish to become Fabricator General. You cannot prove he does. The next point, please,' said Anaxerxes.

Frenk took a deep sucking breath through his bonded mask before continuing his data-cast. 'Do you deny that you are guilty of modus unbecoming, Archmagos Cawl?'

'No. I am guilty of that. Frequently. But we all have our foibles, don't we?'

'More flippancy?' said Frenk. 'More flippancy to conceal the most heinous form of modus unbecoming, one that will have greater resonance, perhaps, with this sympathetic audience of yours?' he added.

'And that would be…?' Cawl inquired.

'Tech-heresy! Heretical works. Innovation. Experimentation. The creation of novel technologies.' He pointed at Qvo, making him take a step back. 'You know exactly of what I speak. Do you deny that you are an innovator? That you are…' Frenk took a dramatic pause. 'An *empiricist*?'

Cawl looked to all those present.

'I do not deny it. Why would I deny that?'

'Then you are guilty of heresy! Heretek!'

'This unit is satisfied,' said Kalisperis the box, preceding general data-canted uproar.

Cawl looked around them all with a mild expression – he'd kept that strand of personality for today – until they had ceased their racket.

'Is this true, Cawl? Do you admit to being a heretek?' asked Anaxerxes. Frenk was practically rubbing his mechadendrites with glee, Qvo noted.

'I do not.'

'So then, what are you admitting? Empiricism is heresy.'

'This is where our opinions deviate, or rather, where the actual facts deviate from generally held option. Investigative, iterative experimentation is not heresy.'

'The Cult holds it to be so,' said Anaxerxes.

'Some sects within the Cult hold it to be so, and I admit they are currently in the ascendancy, but that doesn't stop them from being wrong,' said Cawl. 'Empirical exploration of the Great Work was once the driving principle of everything that we of Mars did. We have never recovered from the loss of our ancient knowledge. We obsess over the past, because that is where we see our greatness to be, and we do not see that we cannot relearn everything from the remains of our ancient civilisation, because so much of it has been lost.'

'Do you state that the quest for knowledge is fruitless?' someone interjected with a rattle of binharic so hysterical it was close to a scream.

'I state no such thing,' said Cawl. 'Allow me to explain. We cannot reconstruct the knowledge-base of our forebears through techno-archaeology alone.' More uproar. The cybernetic constructs in attendance began swooping back and forth in high agitation. 'But we can,' continued Cawl, at the same volume, because data-transfer was unaffected by sonic hubbub, 'reconstruct it by following the same paths of inquiry that our ancestors pursued. All I am guilty of is using the same techniques that they did in order to uncover what they uncovered.'

'So then! You openly admit to innovation,' said Frenk.

Cawl snorted, an organic, very human noise. 'Please!' he said in pure, simple sound before switching back to digital communion. 'Illogical! The flaw in your argument is that if that is so, you think me capable of exceeding the wisdom of the ancients.'

'Certainly not. You disrespect the wisdom of those who came before if you believe I believe you of all people are capable of such a thing!' crowed Frenk. To Qvo's eyes, and he'd faced more than a few such inquiries at Cawl's side over the aeons, he looked triumphant.

'I do not,' canted Cawl calmly. 'Like every being in this room, I long for nothing more than to rebuild the knowledge of our forebears. Taking under consideration my avowed motives, and your own assertion that I cannot hope to exceed the glories of the Dark Age of Technology, then how can I be guilty of innovation, if I am merely rediscovering what our ancestors already knew?'

'That is not the nature of innovation. Innovation is the combination of known techniques to create new artefacts and...' Frenk too dropped into standard human speech, not wishing to blemish the sacred binharic with the word, '*Sciences*.'

'Is that so? I would argue that innovation is the creation of entirely novel things. I make nothing new. I combine what is known to recreate that which was lost. My Primaris Space Marines are based upon the work of the Emperor, which was based upon the work of the ancients. The weapons I conceived of for their arming are all extrapolations from existing technologies...'

'Extrapolations are innovations!' squealed Frenk.

'...which were based upon rediscoveries of ancient technologies applied to existing knowledge! They are refinements, not innovation, and therefore not heretical. Ancient technologies, ancient techniques, ancient knowledge. I do nothing new.'

'You play with words. You lock yourself away for thousands of years, and you experiment. I put it to you that you are an experimentalist! Do you deny that you are an experimentalist?'

'I am an experimentalist. I experiment some of the time,' canted Cawl equably.

'Then you are guilty of–'

Cawl interrupted, lacing his transmission with a dominant data-blurt. 'I experiment with the wisdom of our forebears, within the confines of their sciences, sciences that you have said yourself I cannot improve upon, only attempt to comprehend. In fact, I can back this assertion up. I have performed verifiable tests. Is it not on record – and this is no boast but solely cold, hard fact expressed in the pure language of numbers – that I have uncovered more STC patterns than any other magos, living or dead, according to the archives of most holy and infallible Mars? You will know this, through your connections with the Omnissiah's Inquisition, of course.'

'Your undoubted achievements are beside the point of heresy,' said Frenk.

'Anaxerxes?' Cawl asked.

'Answer him,' said the general. The hubbub in the room was dying down.

'It is on record, yes,' said Frenk warily.

'So, I have conducted experiments to follow the logic paths of our ancestors. They did not have the benefit of their own remains to dig up, did they? I wished to recreate their methods so I might relearn what they knew. I set myself a test, once, having recovered an unknown STC archive. All that I knew of the contents was that it provided templates, among others, for a large form of contra-grav engine designed for heavy use. Low-altitude orbital plates, that kind of thing. I knew what its purpose was, I knew the rough principles of its operation, but without opening the STC, I did not know how it worked.'

'Do you have a point to make?' said Frenk. 'Surely you simply activated the STC.'

'On this occasion, no, I did not,' said Cawl. 'I wished to test my theorem. Using my developing understanding of the methods of the ancients, I set out to experiment, and recreate the device within the STC. It took fifteen years, but once I had a working prototype, I opened that STC. Do you know what I found?'

'Enlighten us,' said Frenk. It sounded like he was gritting his teeth behind his respirator, if he had teeth.

'My device was almost exactly the same as theirs. So I did it again, and again, and again, until I matched the precise designs of seven STCs I had uncovered, not opening them until I had pursued the same results using the same techniques. Therefore, I put it to you that I am no innovator. The use of the techniques of the ancestors to rediscover the knowledge of the ancestors cannot possibly be regarded as a crime.'

A strangled hush fell over the chamber. Servo-skulls hissed back and forth, searching for a threat they could feel but could not comprehend.

'After that,' said Cawl, 'I applied the same techniques to incomplete STCs or devices from that wondrous age. Then to concepts we know the ancients knew, but have few records of. Then machines and knowledge fields we have only the scantest archaeological records of. In each case, I was successful. In each case, I was not innovating, but merely rediscovering that which our illustrious forebears took for granted.'

'I suppose you will apply this same black reasoning to your illegal and blasphemous experimentation with xenos technology, or will you try to deny that?'

'I will not deny it,' said Cawl. By now, the other magi were too invested in his words and their implications to make a sound. 'I have experimented with xenos technology, but before you denounce me as a heretek once more, I will ask, are you proposing that the xenos are in possession of technologies that were beyond the comprehension of our holy forebears?'

'That's not what I'm saying,' said Frenk. 'That is blasphemy. Human technology is perfection itself.'

'It sounds like that's exactly what you are saying,' said Cawl. 'As we all know, the Machine God gave His knowledge of technology to mankind alone, and that makes all we have produced holy, and superior. But we do not exist alone in isolation as a species. By examining xenos technology, I may rediscover the routes to success that our ancestors enjoyed, even though xenos technology is of course inferior to anything our own people once created, as we all know,' canted Cawl disingenuously.

A few of the more radical attendees made liquid burbles of amusement code.

'Everything I do is to further the professed goals of the Cult Mechanicus,' Cawl went on. 'I admit, some of it may seem beyond the pale to more conservative members of the Cult, but we have lost so much, even since the Days of Wonder, when the Omnissiah walked among us as a living, breathing god. I can provide sound theological arguments for all I have said. It is there, in the scriptures of Mars. Do you see, my dear fellow Frenk Gamma-87-Nu-3-Psi, I am a scientist. It is an old term, and I follow old ways, but in doing so, I commit no heresy. I only strive to unlock the mysteries that the Machine God has placed before me, as He placed them before us all. His challenges. His progressions of knowledge that lead us by the hand to enlightenment. I explore His gifts that raised up our ancestors to heights of comprehension we are only dimly aware of, using His methods that He shared with us before through the magic of human ingenuity, and which now we foolishly spurn. In doing so, my explorations have led to the salvaging of scores of technologies that we did not previously understand. By returning to first principles, and relearning what our ancestors knew, rather than unearthing it from the cold ground, we do not dishonour them, we honour them. We follow the paths they trod in aeons past. We are not traitors to their memory! We are pilgrims, upon the greatest pilgrimage imaginable, the pilgrimage of knowledge.' He laced his binharic cant with subtle musics, and raised his arms. 'You cannot see the cathedra I visit. You cannot touch the tombs I seek. But the relics I uncover within these halls of thought are the holiest of all. Knowledge! Pure, honest, human knowledge that I freely share with you all. I have proven, time and again, that it is possible to be saintly by following the abstract path.'

'You are no saint! You are a heretek!' shouted Frenk in the slow and cumbersome organic speech. 'This is against the creed of the Cult!'

'It is against one version of a creed that has changed many times over the last fifteen thousand years,' said Cawl. 'I do nothing that goes against it.'

'Enough!' Anaxerxes canted. 'This is over. Cawl wins the debate.'

'This is a farce. If I ever get you in front of a real court or inquisitor, you are finished,' said Frenk, still speaking Gothic.

'Perhaps. But that won't ever happen, will it?' said Cawl.

'My associate will see that it does,' said Frenk.

'I believe when you say associate, you mean master,' said Anaxerxes.

A chirrup of binharic amusement signifiers went around the assembly again.

'I assert my authority. You should arrest him!' Frenk canted.

'No,' said Anaxerxes. 'Cawl operates at the fringes of modus becoming, but he is no heretek by our reckoning. Magos Frenk, I remind you that nobody prevented you from attending this conclave. We have allowed you to question the archmagos, but you have no authority here. This is sovereign Adeptus Mechanicus ground.'

'This is the symbol of the Inquisition,' said Frenk dangerously, brandishing his amulet once more. 'Imbued with the ultimate authority by the Omnissiah Himself.'

'If you were an inquisitor, then we might pay more heed to your demands, and maybe we would not,' said Anaxerxes. 'The truth is, most of us here are intrigued by what exactly Cawl intends to propose. You reveal yourself, Frenk Gamma-87-Nu-3-Psi, with the emotional usage of the organic speech. Your motives are impure. They are personal. As nominated representative of all here present, I say you have had your turn. If you cant again, or if you *speak* again,' he blurted, 'you shall be removed. You have been warned.'

Frenk looked like he would speak anyway, but he clenched an impotent fist.

'Archmagos Cawl,' Anaxerxes data-blurted, 'you have the floor. What is your purpose in calling us all here?'

'A good question,' said Cawl. 'If I told you we shall dub this conclave the Conclave Chronalis, would it intrigue you more?'

It did.

CHAPTER SIXTEEN

THE CONCLAVE CHRONALIS

Cawl was in his element. He enjoyed grandstanding, and there were few better opportunities to do so than before a group of tech-hungry machine-priests.

'My esteemed brothers and sisters,' he intoned. 'You will be aware of my recent adventure in the heart of the Pharos of Sotha.'

Some were, some weren't, but it never paid to patronise your audience.

'You may also be aware of my latest project.'

The lights plunged dramatically. Cawl had tasked a submind of his to infiltrate the pyramid's systems, no easy thing given their age and complexity, but accomplishable nonetheless. He gave the sliver of his consciousness the noospheric equivalent of a pat on the head – one of that size was an idiot thing, and easily pleased – while the greater part of his consciousness resisted the temptation to dive into the informational world it had discovered. There were wonders there, wrought in the exquisite machine tongue of the ancients. They would have to wait.

From a compact hololithic projector embedded in one of Cawl's attendant servo-skulls, a tri-D image of the galaxy burst, depicted in full-spectrum colour. He'd recreated it exactly, incorporating all its glorious noise and hue. To a standard human, it would have appeared pretty, a turning whorl of stars, bluish, purplish, ethereal as smoke yet weighty as all life. The yolk of stars at the centre blazed with cold white light. Its arms trailed lazily from this centre, growing dimmer to the edges, attenuating into a milky haze at the furthest bounds where intergalactic space began. The great work of the Machine God, perfect but for those places where the blunders of His children had injured it; warp-realspace interfaces a sickening colour with no real analogue in the mundane spectrum, but closest to a veinous purple.

To the tech-priests, the projection was more vivid, singing with radiation of wave and particle, and blazing with every colour from deepest infrared to furthest ultraviolet. It filled the space above the convocation, drawing delighted gasps and little burbles of approval. The projection was quite impressive: rarely were such things so comprehensively done, but fitting a full hololithic device into so small a space as a skull was really remarkable. They were impressed.

'The galaxy, some years ago,' he said. 'Until this happened.' The image shook. Streamers of sickly light raced away from warp storms large and small. The Eye of Terror and the Maelstrom swelled like metastasising cancers, reaching for each other with corruptive limbs. They joined, spread, dividing the glorious whole of the galaxy in twain, and flooded the stars with supernatural fallout.

'We can surmise that if this is not the ultimate goal of the

Warmaster Abaddon, it at least plays a crucial role in his plans,' said Cawl. 'For this event was foreseen by the most ancient of races, and they took steps to prevent it.'

Green speckled lights ignited along the course of the Rift.

'Many of us here have an inkling of the War in Heaven between the most enigmatic Old Ones and their arch-foes, the necrons, many millions of years ago. I surmise that their conflict fundamentally weakened the fabric of reality, causing this fault line that Abaddon has exploited. My researches have revealed that the necrons sought to stabilise the fault by the construction of their pylon worlds along what is now the route of the Rift. These green points represent those we knew of.' He waved a magician's hand; yellow lights sprang into being alongside them. Hundreds more. 'These yellow points we did not know of, until now. The Pharos was a superluminal beacon, one of a network of relay centres that facilitated instantaneous communication and transport between the worlds of the ancient necron kingdoms. I have visited several of these places. The Pharos was, until its destruction, the most intact. From its archives, I have learned all this and more.'

'I hear that you accidentally released a powerful C'tan shard during your investigations,' Anaxerxes interrupted him.

'Oh. Where did you hear that?'

'I have my sources,' said Anaxerxes.

Frenk made a choked noise at the revelation of this adventure. He evidently hadn't known about it. He looked like he was about to speak, but Anaxerxes silenced him with a stern signal.

'You have had your turn. Inload this data for your master, if you like, but do not interrupt,' the general said. 'If anyone is to question Belisarius Cawl, it shall be me.'

'It is true,' said Cawl, 'although I stress that I sent this being far, far away from the Imperium. It was a price worth paying. The data I retrieved from the Pharos enabled me to recreate an exact map of the ancient necron holdings. Every tomb world. Every pylon world.' He paused for effect. 'Every deposit of noctilith in the galaxy.'

There was a hushed silence. Cawl could practically hear the tech-priests salivating. He let it hang a moment.

'If you agree to help me,' Cawl said beguilingly, 'I shall pay you with this knowledge.'

'That is data of an incalculable worth!' said someone, out loud, in verbal Lingua Technis.

'We have not heard what he wants of us yet,' said another, more cynical voice.

'True,' said Cawl. 'You have not.' He paused again. 'What I want you to do is help me save the Great Work of our god. I want you to help me save the Imperium.'

<Query – forceful – HOW?> blurted another.

'Good question. Since I finished my work on the Primaris Space Marines, I have occupied myself with one thing – understanding and unlocking the secrets of the necron pylons. These devices held the great wound across the galaxy shut for millions of years. I wish to replicate their technology, improve it, and use it to restore what remains of the original network, while adding to it with our own. If I do this, I shall be able to close the Cicatrix Maledictum.'

Uproar greeted that. Variations on 'Impossible!' and 'Arrogance!' in the main. Cawl waited for it to die down.

'Not impossible,' he said, 'merely very difficult.'

'I have heard hypotheses that the necrons are attempting similar efforts with their null zones. Reports from within these areas suggest that this technology is vile, unclean xenos work, deadly to humanity!' one of the magi cried.

'Which is why we should perhaps do this ourselves, rather

than allowing the necrons to do so,' Cawl suggested pleasantly. 'I can do this. I have working prototypes based upon the original archeo-xenotech that do not adversely affect sentient beings. I am in a position to begin manufacturing them immediately. If we set aside my grand ambition, even the limited use of these devices will greatly enhance the Imperial war effort. Neverborn will cease to be. The incidence of psychic births will fall. The sorcery of the enemy will lose its power. Surely you must see, that any forge world that willingly aids me will be rewarded by the Lord Commander himself.'

'Do you have a test scheduled?' one asked.

'I do,' said Cawl. 'But there is one more thing I require before it can be activated. I require a fully integrated control system for these devices.'

'I see. Now we come to the meat of the matter,' said Anaxerxes. 'You need help to create such a system. Help of what kind?'

'Not create a system,' said Cawl. 'I could, given sufficient time, create my own. But we do not have time. Lord Guilliman, returned to life largely thanks to my efforts, has driven back the enemy, but the fate of the galaxy hangs in the balance. Even now, the forces of the Dark Gods move against us on every front. We must expedite this process. Recreate the restraint upon the warp and bring balance back between the materium and immaterium. This is my quest. I ask for your help. Here.'

A point on the map far to the south of Imperium Sanctus flashed brightly. The projection zoomed inwards, coming to rest on a black hole. It turned with menacing slowness, the centre a bulging pearl of uttermost dark sheened with a skin of fleeing energy. A glaring toroid of ionised matter ringed it. Space-time twisted around it. To the tech-priests, the electromagnetic scream of annihilated matter rang loud, yet the centre was completely unknowable, silent, its existence inferred and forever uncertain.

'This is Calligan's Maw,' he said. 'Named so by someone called Calligan, we must suppose. That is what it is marked down as upon the charts of the Astra Cartographica, anyway. All unimportant detail. What is important, is this.'

He zoomed in again. As the view dropped vertiginously towards the black hole, the toroid of energy around it got very large. Marking its glaring, colourful surface was a dark spiral turning towards the hole. At the very head of this track of doom was the pale, pinhead dot of a planet. It was some way from destruction yet, but that destruction was assured.

'This world has no name,' he said. 'At least, no human name. I only know of its existence because of what I learned from the Pharos. This black hole is not natural.' He pointed at it. 'It is a star collapsed by weapons of near-unimaginable power in ancient war. This world was caught upon the fringes of catastrophe when its sun was killed.'

'Why is this important?' Anaxerxes asked.

'This world is marked upon the ancient charts of the Pharos with numerous, significant annotations,' said Cawl. 'I have decoded these. Upon this planet, which the necrons called Irtanathep, was a pylon control nexus, a little like the Pharos, perhaps, but with a different purpose. I believe that at some point it was attacked in order to stop its operation, and in the process the star was destroyed.'

'Then what is the use of telling us this?' asked Archimedius. 'Surely the planet will have been devastated. We will find nothing there.'

'Not so,' spoke up Hierophant Temporalis Ikthin of the Chronalis Brotherhood. 'You are aware of the effects of gravity upon time.'

'Temporal dilation,' intoned another.

'Time slows under conditions of extreme gravity,' Ikthin said.

'This world was caught on the cusp of this black hole's event horizon.' A series of electronic screeches whooped out of his abdomen. 'For any inhabitants, a second would last an aeon. On this planet, at this moment, beings who lived before mankind's precursor species ever evolved will be looking to the sky in horror as their sun is swallowed, and they will be doing so for thousands of years after we have died. For them, it is millions of years ago. They are living in the past.' Ikthin turned his lidless silver eyes upon Cawl. 'This is why you want us. This is why you have requested so many magi who are hierophants in the ars chronometrica. You wish to go there.'

'I do,' said Cawl. He upped his data-cant broadcast strength to counter the rush of query requests that filled the noospheric spaces of the pyramid. 'For upon this world, the pylon network control centre will still be working, untouched by time. Pristine!' he said.

'This is insanity!' roared Kalisperis, in binharic, Gothic and Lingua Technis, all at once. 'To defy the nature of time! Chronaxic manipulation is one of the prime bans!'

More uproar, more heated this time. A split in the argument rapidly emerged, with some temporal experts insisting that no fundamental laws of either the Cult or of material science would be broken, as they were dealing with a natural effect. Others, a minority, to Cawl's relief, said it did not matter, because what Cawl proposed was de facto voyaging through time, no matter how cleverly it was dressed up, and that was clearly forbidden.

'How?' demanded Ikthin. 'How will you do it?' He repeated the question until the convocation quietened once more.

'Temporal manipulation, on a grand scale,' said Cawl. 'A tunnel through time and space to this frame of existence. We go in, we retrieve what we need, we leave along the same vector.'

'That would require great effort to stabilise frame shifting across several chronic time zones, both to get in and in order to extract within real-time relative parameters, so that you do not emerge thousands of years later,' said Ikthin. 'If you emerge.'

'It would,' said Cawl.

'Can it be done?' asked Archmagos Logis Magnacomptroller Covarix Sestertius. 'If so, at what cost?'

'It is theoretically possible, if one had the total output of a sun to employ,' said Ikthin. 'Such feats were possible in the Age of Technology, but now? Doubtful. The outlay in resources would be gargantuan.'

'I can do it,' said Cawl. 'With your help. The races who dominated the galaxy after the great war were sensible enough to leave the pylons alone. Even our own ancestors, whose ascendancy was, in cosmic terms, an eye-blink ago, let them be. We of the forge worlds have not been so wise.' He waved a hand. 'These time-lapse simulations show the loss of pylon worlds to Abaddon's thirteen Black Crusades.'

An Imperial date stamp appeared in the air, changing with each successive wave of attacks that came forth from the Eye of Terror after Horus' great betrayal. In the early days, no pylon worlds were affected, the Chaos fleets engaged on other errands, but as Abaddon's strategy evolved, and the millennia rolled unstoppably by, the pylon worlds of the necrons began to blink out, one or two at first, then handfuls of them, then dozens, until by the time Cadia fell, only a few hundred remained. Cawl waved his hand, the projection stopped.

'These are the worlds that we of the Imperium have destroyed, not knowing what we tampered with.'

More than half the remainder flared and died.

'We have undone the safeguards of epochs in a few millennia. Because of this the future of mankind is at stake. We of the Empire of Mars are partly culpable. Through our quest for knowledge and through the blind hatred of all things xenos, we have brought all the devils of the warp to our door. It is fortunate that nobody beyond this room has fully grasped that fact, for the wrath of the Adeptus Terra would surely be great.'

'That is obtuse, for a threat,' said Anaxerxes. 'But it is still a threat.'

'It is not a threat,' said Cawl. 'I am as guilty as many here. Guilty of ignorance! There is no greater sin in the eyes of the Machine God. Think of what I say as a moral imperative. What we put wrong, we must now put right.

'I am Belisarius Cawl, and it is often said that I can do anything.' He bowed his head in humility. 'But I cannot do this alone.'

Another round of data-cast and shouting was brought to a sudden stop by Anaxerxes. No words this time, but an unearthly, polyfrequency howl emitted from the perfect silver of his war mask. It blared as loudly as a Titan's war-horn, silencing everyone.

'You have given us much to discuss, Archmagos Cawl,' said Anaxerxes. 'A discussion we must have without you.'

'Then I shall await your decision with impatience,' Cawl said.

CHAPTER SEVENTEEN

BENEATH THE SURFACE OF THINGS

Primus breathed deep, extending his senses past the pain that dogged him always, past the ache of his muscles and the itchy, nervous energy that coursed through him at all times, out through his poorly anchored soul. Past the physical, past the mental, into the spiritual realms beyond life. The warp spread before him. Endless possibilities beckoned. Endless power. Temptation dragged at his heart, whispering the forbidden word in his ear.

Freedom.

He was not free, and would never be. He doubted anyone or anything truly was. He rejected power, and yet it was thrust on him. His dream bothered him. He must know more, and that meant going deeper. A mortal mind could not look upon the warp as it truly was. An order must be imposed, a cypher through which the mysteries of eternity might be safely interpreted.

Primus drew in his consciousness, preventing it from dilution in the raw soul stuff of the immaterium. From his own memories he forged a sub-realm he could traverse, a place of personal truths.

The methods were common to psykers. Throughout history those with a connection to the otherworld sought to impose humanity upon it, lest it strip their humanity from them. The symbolism varied. The Fenrisians had their Underverse, the Blood Angels their angelic visions, the Navigators their zodiacal allegories, the astropaths their verses and obfuscatory imagery, but the goal was the same: the protection of the soul against the inimical gods of the warp, and the ability to look upon that which could not be looked upon.

So it was Primus opened his eyes upon a hell of his own making, and yet it was a safer hell than the one it hid.

He came into himself already walking, his bare feet hitting the ice-cold decks of Cawl's laboratorium levels. Though the place reeked of strong chemicals, the smell of blood was everywhere beneath it. Lights flickered, illuminating frozen, screaming faces only half obscured by the frost covering their suspension caskets.

These were his brothers, stillborn all.

This was the place he was made.

Primus breathed deeply of the toxic airs. They burned his lungs the way they had the first time he had drawn breath. The cold was so intense it felt like fire. There was nothing good here, only horror, enough pain to drive a hundred men mad. Yet not only did he allow himself to feel this memory of pain, but he allowed himself to feel the pain of his meditating physical body, to which he was linked by a tenuous strand of thought. He welcomed it all. Pain was what he was. Comfort was the most pernicious freedom of all.

He walked down the long avenue of caskets, stuffed full of Cawl's abortive attempts to fashion him, each one identical to the smallest, subatomic detail. They were him, in the most fundamental sense. Cawl had told him many times that the pain he felt should not exist, that he was perfect in every way. He was dismissive of his offspring's suffering, as all fathers who have too much to do are. But Primus knew that the pain was real. How many brothers Cawl had made before he finally succeeded, Primus did not know, only that his name, designating him as first, was a mockery of fact, and that he bore the agonies of all those others.

In the distance there was screaming – raw, agonised, drawn from a well of pain that went down to the roots of time itself.

It was his voice.

Primus walked on. The screaming abruptly cut off.

The landscape distorted, becoming more bizarre, the methalon pods growing huge, so that he was small as an ant. The ceiling turned into a sky of blood. From surfaces of metal and of glass Primus' body was reflected, massive, powerful, heavy with muscle, yet knotted all over with rope-thick scars, accentuating the subtle mismatches in his skin tone. Cawl told Primus his base genetic coding was drawn from several sources, but that he was grown as a piece.

Primus did not believe him.

The landscape bent around on itself. Primus paddled through blood and spilled fluid. Broken machines fizzled dying sparks. Ahead was a pulsing sphere, swirled with oily patterns, that expanded to twice its size before contracting again.

Primus examined it. There. He could feel it now, the shape he had sensed in his dreams. Dreams were strolls through the hinterlands of the warp, but the tales they told were hard to interpret. Focused, conscious, he could see the truth, a distortion on the surface of the sphere, as if something inside was pulling that portion of the oily skin inwards. It was unmistakeable, the mass wake of something solid sailing the sea of souls.

Ships were approaching.

Primus opened his eyes. He left the vision. He summoned a servo-skull down from its roost.

'Establish communication with Archmagos Cawl,' he commanded.

Cawl and Qvo left the Kastelans, Oswen and X99 at the pyramid entrance and went for a walk around the upper levels. They paced in quiet companionship while Cawl took ambient field measurements of the pyramid's emissions, making little noises of interest at what he found. Qvo enjoyed the interplay of variable energies coursing through his body, and became quite lost in it, to the extent that he didn't realise that Cawl had started talking to him.

'Of course, some suggest a certain amount of understanding between the old empires.'

'I'm sorry, you were saying?' said Qvo dazedly. He came back into himself close to the low parapet marking the edge of the tier they were roaming. Cawl laid a gentle metal claw on his shoulder.

'Weren't you listening?'

Qvo thought about trying to cover his inattention, but instead opted for honesty.

'No,' he admitted.

Cawl looked at him curiously. 'You're owning up? Why not simply rerun the last few moments of our interaction?'

'I… I don't think I can,' said Qvo. 'I was lost in thought, you know, wandering off.'

'Daydreaming?' said Cawl.

'I suppose so,' said Qvo.

Cawl gave him a most peculiar look, then erupted into laughter, surprising Qvo. 'That's wonderful!'

'It is?'

'Yes! It shows you're becoming more… human.' He made a snort of amusement. 'And to think we spend so much time extolling the virtue of the machine, here I am trying to bring you back to life.'

'I appreciate it,' said Qvo, mostly because he felt he had to. He remained somewhat ambivalent about his repeated resurrections.

'I'm sure you do. Anyway, I was saying, I don't think this place is just a garden. I've always wanted to come here, you know, always good to turn two screws with one driver.'

'What is it then? This place, in your opinion.'

'I believe it to be some sort of neutral ground,' said Cawl. 'Consider the readings I have taken.'

'I don't know what they are.'

'I'm about to tell you,' said Cawl. 'They're fairly standard, if highly advanced, cohesive proton waveforms, exactly as you'd expect.'

Qvo wouldn't have expected that, but kept his silence.

'There's a webway gate somewhere here,' Cawl said. 'Don't you see? Look at this place. Look at how it is laid out. Look at its location. It is dramatic, peaceful, a garden surrounded by stellar fire!'

'It is unusual.'

'Yes, but this place was not made to impress men. The aeldari, for example, would simply lap all this stuff up.'

'True,' said Qvo. 'But we are a long way from the cores of both the old Terran and the ancient aeldari realms.'

'That is only supposition. There have been human colonies in this part of the galaxy for millennia,' said Cawl. 'The aeldari always were more lightly spread, but they are everywhere, even now. Imagine! We speak so often of the ancient days of the Age of Technology, and the might of the empire of Old Earth. We also speak, you and I, of the aeldari.'

'We do?'

'We do. We have. We speak of how powerful they were, just like the people of Old Earth. These two empires may have existed at the same time. One wonders what their relations could have been like. Peaceful? Belligerent? How might the aeldari have viewed us, they who had been masters of the stars for millions of years, when we came strutting onto the galactic scene? Would they patronise us? Help us? Were we a threat to them or they to us? And what about the other creatures who swarmed across the void? Even in the days of the xenocides, there was not always war between sentients.' Cawl gave a long, satisfied sigh. 'History, my dear Qvo! It is fascinating. In those days there must have been dealings between species. I think this place was made precisely for that. What manner of beings walked this world? What embassies were made? What secrets exchanged? If there's a webway gate here, I wonder what else they will find, our questing brethren, as they dig down deeper? Wonders, I'll wager.'

'Maybe,' said Qvo. He lacked Cawl's enthusiasm for speculation. 'If I may, Belisarius. You must not let yourself be distracted. I am concerned by this Magos Frenk.'

'He's an inquisitor's pet,' said Cawl. 'Nothing to worry about. He blew his chance.'

'I'm not sure he did,' said Qvo uneasily. 'What if this is just the beginning? What if he's just the first? They could be trying to flush you out.'

Cawl gave a pleased smile.

'Did I say something funny?'

'Something nice.' Cawl patted Qvo's back again. 'It's good to have friends to watch out for you.'

'But, Belisarius…' said Qvo. The distant cough and rumble of voidship motors firing up interrupted him. 'Our lander. It's taking off,' said Qvo. He watched the ship rise a few tens of feet into the air and then angle itself towards the pyramid.

'Yes,' said Cawl. 'While we were talking, I summoned it. I've had a communique from Primus.'

'We're going back then.' The lander roared over the plains, flattening grasses with its backwash as it came.

'I'm going back. Primus is in a snit about something. Shadows in the warp, all that. I need to go and calm him down.'

'What about me?'

'You're going to stay here and conduct a little field research. We can't pass up an opportunity like this. I have wanted to come here for a long time.'

'You did say.'

'Ah, but why? Because it's important, that's why.'

The lander swung around the pyramid, shaking its ancient bones, and set down alongside the craft of the other delegates. It dwarfed them, naturally.

Cawl led Qvo around to the front, to one of the flights of steep stairs that ran up the pyramid. From there they could see the ramp dropping, and figures coming out.

'X99 Bolus and his robotic friends will remain here with you, to protect you.'

'Why will I need protecting, Belisarius?' Qvo asked uneasily.

'That fellow, Oswen. He's staying here too. He's a collector of maps. I didn't even know I had him, if I'm truthful, but apparently, he's got a map of Pontus Avernes, and on that map, there are secret routes.'

'Oh no, you want me to use it?'

'I do!' said Cawl. He lowered his voice conspiratorially. 'There is a way into the interior right here, under this pyramid. I do love a secret route, don't you?'

'No,' said Qvo.

'Find that gate. See what else you can turn up. I recommend you head down as fast as you can into the inner levels, that's where all the interesting things will be, before the others catch on.' Cawl smiled as if Qvo had not said a thing. 'Serendipity plays such a role in all things. I wonder sometimes if the Machine God is spinning the cogs of reality just for me. Do you know, it was Alixia Kalisperis who suggested this place to meet? A fine idea.'

'The box on tentacles?' asked Qvo.

'That's the one,' said Cawl. 'Her idea, my great profit.'

'If the magi agree to help you. She doesn't seem to like you much.'

'She's a lector dogmis, they never do. She almost certainly brought me here to condemn me, but the others will come around,' said Cawl.

A soft tinkling, like a randomly strummed harp, sounded from everywhere at once.

'Ah,' said Cawl. 'It's time for the weather to turn. I'm going to get off before I get wet. Stay well, Qvo-89. I expect a full report!' Cawl surged off down the steps towards his ship, his multiple metal feet clattering. His flock of aerial constructs stayed where they were a moment, scanning the area with dead glass eyes, then turned all at once and flew after him.

Qvo lifted up a hand and feebly waved off his friend. If indeed they were friends, and Qvo wasn't just a mechanism that believed itself to be human enough to have friends. Less than twelve hours alive, and he had to deal with all this philosophy. It made him tired, and he didn't even know if he had to sleep.

Cawl boarded his ship. As if a powerful hose had been turned on in the sky, it suddenly, torrentially, began to rain. The ramp shut. The lander rose up through the sheeting water, falls of it rushing off the flight surfaces.

Qvo got soaked watching Cawl go.

* * *

'All is ready,' said Kolumbari-Enas. 'The trap will soon be sprung.'

Bile surveyed the army of servitors standing in silent, inactive ranks in the hold. The webway gate plundered from the nameless world was held against the wall by a mess of pins and brackets. It was in even worse shape than it had been upon its plinth, for Kolumbari-Enas' servants had not been gentle in removal, but Enas was true to his boasts. He did have webway craft. He could relocate and open a gate, even one so damaged. In proof, the gate's worn runes were lambent with power, a minimal glow at the moment, but ready to increase at Kolumbari-Enas' word. This gate would function.

'In my experience, people who say that usually fall first,' said Bile.

'Irritation expression curtailed,' squealed Kolumbari-Enas. 'Despite your cynicism, we are ready, Lord Bile. Lord Thrule's men will sweep the artificial world of the False Omnissiah's slaves. My servitors will plunder it for its secrets. You take what is aboard Cawl's ship while they are distracted.'

'So there is more in this for you than my payment. I thought when you declined to raid the *Zar Quaesitor*, the android was enough.'

'Supplementary expression of annoyance – cancelled/curtailed. The search for the truth of all things never ceases,' said Kolumbari-Enas. 'Disregarding opportunity is unwise. This is an ancient place. Much archeotech. Much xenotech. All shall be mine additional to payment due. Neither is greater than the other. Both are of value.'

Bile nodded. 'A sentiment after my own heart,' he said.

'Sentiment is nothing. Victory is all. *Zar Quaesitor* risk factors are too high to justify expenditure of men and machines.' The cloth of Kolumbari-Enas' hood rasped on the metal of his head as he turned to glare at Bile with hard, artificial eyes. 'We are in position. Advisory – go to your ship to begin your attack.'

'The *Zar Quaesitor* will be unable to respond. You are sure?'

'External defences will be taken offline. Enginarium will be taken offline. Shields will be taken offline. This equals certainty.'

'But you are still too frightened to go inside.'

'Realism is not fear. I must survive. Cawl is formidable. He has many powerful servants. I cannot deal with them all. Your chance of mission success is higher than mine, you have a singular goal.'

'Then I will succeed.'

'Your chances are still low.'

'You will be paid, in either case,' said Bile.

'Expression surprise – Bile retains honour.'

'I never lost it,' growled Bile. 'Nor did I lose my talent for battle. I will prevail, and I shall bring you something worthwhile back from Cawl's hoard to prove it. A little extra gift.'

'Gratitude expressed, even if result unlikely.'

Bile took a step closer. 'Doubt me again, and I will kill you.'

Bile departed. Kolumbari-Enas waited for his heavy footfalls to fade to nothing, and for the far door out of the hold to slide shut. Even then, he checked via his ship's internal vid-feeds to make sure the Chief Apothecary had gone.

When the corridor leading away from the hold was empty, he spread his arms and supplementary limbs wide. His jaw cracked as it dislocated, and a powerful data-caster pushed its way out of his face.

Singing a song of corrupted code, he called the stolen gate into life. Blue threaded with red veins swirled in the centre, awaiting the opening of the far side. The broken wraithbone shuddered, spitting sparks over the cyborgs waiting to use it. With a second cry of binharic, Kolumbari-Enas awakened his army. In unison, the eyes of a thousand servitors ignited with baleful warp fires, and their mechanical limbs clanked into action.

The time for victory was approaching.

* * *

'Why does it always have to be underground?' Qvo grumbled. He, Oswen, X99 Bolus and the five-strong cohort of Kastelans were following a wide corridor down from a door in the pyramid. It shut with a hiss and a quiet clack that belied its size, sealing them in the lower levels. They'd never have found it without the map, and from the look of the place they were in, nobody else had been there for a very long time.

'If it were lying around on the surface, magos, there'd be no archeotech to see,' said X99 Bolus. His synthesised chuckle reverberated strangely off the subterranean architecture. Subterranean was probably the wrong word, Qvo corrected himself. Pontus Avernes' artificial nature was entirely apparent beneath its sodden moors.

'It is even more entrancing than I imagined,' said Oswen excitedly. He had his precious map gripped in his hands. A thick plastek cover protected the parchment, and a good job too, for long trails of water drops pattered noisily from the ceiling. Every time one of X99's immense companions strode through one of these waterfalls, it struck up a loud drumming.

A servo-skull, whose fleshless face somehow managed to project an aura of utmost solemnity, cruised at Oswen's head height. It bore a large cold-plasma screen in manipulators hanging from beneath its jaw, which depicted a three-dimensional line map constantly updated by mapping skulls roving ahead.

Oswen was craning his head in every direction, eyes widening with each new wonder. 'Intersecting field generation technologies of Dark Age make,' he gabbled in excitement. 'Seamless crystal construction. Grown! It's all grown! It's amazing! The data is pouring in!'

'Like the water is pouring from this ceiling,' said Qvo, pulling his hood up over his head. Even though being wet or cold didn't really discomfort him, old habits died hard.

'Exactly!' said Oswen.

A stairwell opened at the side of the corridor. Steps went down in a series of perfectly right-angled flights. Qvo put his foot on them doubtfully, because they coursed with water and he expected corrosion, but despite his machine weight, they budged not a micron. Very well built, if disappointingly utilitarian.

Oswen paused, eyes flicking between parchment map and plasma map. The magnetically contained gas streams displaying the complex shivered every time water dropped through them.

'Do you have any idea where we're going?' Qvo asked Oswen.

'Definitely down. There's a marker on here that speaks of some significant location, and the returns the cartographic skulls are giving suggests a phenomenal amount of energy.'

'Great, that'll be this gate,' said Qvo without enthusiasm. In his experience, large amounts of energy usually meant large amounts of danger. He looked down into the dark and wondered when he had become so timid. Was it before he died? Was it because he had? He wondered if all the other Qvos were like this, because he had no real access to their emotional states. Remembering fear was like remembering being hurt, he thought. You recalled the incident, but not the pain. Some of his earlier selves had done some remarkably brave things, but he was not feeling very brave. Cawl said that he was moving closer to Friedisch's original personality, and if that were true, did that mean that Friedisch was a coward, and if so, did it mean that *he* was a coward?

He looked down the stairs again, into the unknown. There could be a wealth of knowledge down there, but it failed to excite him. When had the urge to fulfil his sacred duty left him? Only, in a certain sense, it hadn't left him, because this iteration had never had it in the first place.

He wished that Cawl would just leave him dead.

The floor shook with a heavy, robotic step. Qvo got out of

the way as X99's favoured automaton, Sigma Fidelis, reached the stairs and stopped. Its fellows came to a synchronised halt. Sigma Fidelis leaned forward. Lights pulsed behind its viewing plate. It made a grinding noise and stood up. It rotated its torso precisely, the feet followed, and it strode off. One by one, the other robots lurched after it.

'Where's he going?' Qvo asked.

'The stairs will not take Sigma Fidelis' mass. We should be grateful we have him, a lesser Kastelan would have carried on to its doom, but I do not need to watch him so closely, oh no,' X99 said happily. He pivoted on his heels in a poor imitation of his robots, and followed them down the corridor.

'I guessed that, and it's not what I asked,' said Qvo. 'Where is he going? Where are you going?' he shouted after X99 Bolus.

The datasmith's head turned one hundred and eighty degrees. 'To find an alternative route. I must accompany them. There will be a grav-well or lifter hereabouts. We will rejoin you in the lower levels.'

'What do we do about protection?!'

'We are all magi here, the Machine God watches over us,' X99 called. His head swivelled back, and he vanished into the dark.

'Easy for him to say, he's got five war machines at his beck and call,' said Qvo. 'All I've got is this.' He pulled out a small phosphor pistol.

'I don't even have that,' said Oswen. 'I'm not even a magos.'

'Neither am I,' said Qvo.

'I am sure we shall be fine,' said Oswen. 'We are about the Omnissiah's business. He shall watch over us.' With confidence Qvo did not share, Oswen headed down.

'Is this your first archeotech expedition?' Qvo asked.

'As a matter of fact, yes, it is,' said Oswen, looking back up, all innocence. 'What makes you ask that?'

'Nothing,' said Qvo. 'Nothing at all.'

CHAPTER EIGHTEEN

AN OFFER TO TALK

Primus found Cawl upon the command deck of the *Zar Quaesitor*. It was big, even for a ship of Imperial design. Three enormous oculus windows, each round and supported by complicated arrangements of ornate, armoured mullions fronted the deck. At the back, choirs of servitors drenched in red light ascended the walls in stepped tiers, permanently wired in place. Magi of the transmechanic and enginseer knowledge-castes strode about, all high ranking, all bearing heavy augmentation. Other tech-priests occupied crucial nexuses about major operations centres, also either partially or completely wired in place. Bands of lesser adepts of the Machine Cult roamed in solemn packs, sprinkling oils and wafting incense. Cawl had very little time for that sort of thing, but even his most radical followers needed to see the basic rites of the Cult upheld.

The *Zar Quaesitor* had no shipmaster. Cawl insisted he did not need one, for it was his ship, although Primus thought that egotism on his maker's part. Every ship needed a captain, and Cawl could not be everywhere at once. It was true that the ship possessed a formidable personality of its own, and the networked minds of its tech-priests provided strong problem-solving capabilities. It was not enough in Primus' mind, so he often took on the role of shipmaster himself.

Not then, though. For once, the archmagos dominus' station was occupied. Cawl himself stood upon the circular platform he used to oversee the work of his crew. It was extended to full height, the whole thing being a giant column floating in a cylinder of pressurised liquid. Atop it there was no command throne as one might expect on a more usual sort of vessel, only clamps for Cawl's feet, and a multiplicity of sockets for Cawl's bewildering array of appendages. He was up there surrounded by a dozen floating screens projected by servo-skulls, vat-angels and other cybernetic constructs, his close aide Wocolos the Integerarian at his side, his chromium head glinting, his thousand limbs hidden beneath a poncho that reached the floor.

Primus smothered a stab of jealousy at the sight of the second tech-priest so close to his creator and strode straight to the platform.

'My lord archmagos,' Primus called up dolefully. He got down on one knee and bowed his head.

'Ah! Primus! There you are.' Cawl lowered the level of the station, turning it from tower to dais. It reached its lowest setting with a soft hiss. Stairs clicked themselves out from the side. 'No need for that!' said Cawl. 'Get up, get up! Please.'

He extended one of many metal hands. Primus ignored it.

'My lord.' Primus was tall, even for a Space Marine. When he got to his feet his bald head was almost level with Cawl's.

'No need to be so stuffy. Now, you wanted to see me, and here I am.'

Primus looked past Cawl at Wocolos.

'What is it?'

'We should go somewhere private.'

Cawl started to laugh, but the look Primus gave him was an especially miserable one, and his mirth died in his throat.

'Very well. Let us walk. I shall activate a privacy field.'

Something hummed within the mechanisms Cawl wore on his back, and the sounds of the ship were deadened to nothing.

'Come on then,' said Cawl. 'Let's walk and talk.'

Primus nodded, but he put his helmet on to prevent his lips being read, and cut his vox, and the voxmitter incorporated into his helm's mask. His voice was muffled, but he spoke loudly so Cawl could hear him. Nobody else would be able to.

'My dream worried me, so I undertook to look into the warp. I found that there are several ships approaching. They will be here within a few hours. We do not have much time to prepare.'

'Ah, so someone was looking for me,' said Cawl. 'You were right, but it is to be expected.' He waved a mechadendrite, playing the pedagogue as always. 'We are fortunate we have not been directly challenged for so long. War is never far away.'

'I do not need reminding of that, my lord.'

They reached the back wall of the command deck, where a five-storey stack of servitors mouthed idiot words while their lobotomised brains worked to keep the *Zar Quaesitor* in position.

'I am assuming the subterfuge is due to a certain paranoia on your part?'

'Someone must have told them where we are,' said Primus. They turned and walked down the rear of the deck, passing into a cloister whose back wall was crammed with chattering cogitators. A junior transmechanic bowed and stepped out of their way to let them pass.

'You suspect a spy aboard the *Zar Quaesitor.*'

'Maybe,' said Primus. 'But it is more likely to be someone among the delegation. Everyone on board this ship has been mind-swept multiple times. They are loyal to you.'

'This is not a good place to fight,' said Cawl. 'One of the reasons I agreed to it, in point of fact. Too risky for those members of the Adeptus Mechanicus who disagree with my standpoint to attempt to, ah, correct it with violence. Any idea who is approaching? It could be an Imperial delegation, or other friendly parties.'

'We have had no notification by astropath,' said Primus. 'And it feels wrong.'

'I trust your seer's instincts,' said Cawl. 'I gave them to you for a reason, after all. Best put everyone on alert – quietly though, we do not want our foes to know they have been detected.'

They came out of the cloister, emerging into one of the more obscure corners of the deck. There was a minor oculus there, and it let in a flood of hard stellar light unmediated by atmosphere. Pontus Avernes' energy shielding shimmered brilliantly a few thousand miles away.

'I advise leaving,' said Primus.

'We can't leave!' said Cawl. 'I need the aid of these forge worlds. If we depart now, Frenk will only use it as proof of my treachery.'

'There is the question of the void shields. They are barely functional in this environment.'

'Take us closer in to Pontus Avernes,' said Cawl. 'If we are attacked, it will give us the option of taking shelter within its protection. I've performed many measurements, and its particle shields will be proof against most weapons.'

Primus nodded. 'It shall be done. Shall I contact the delegates?'

'Not yet,' said Cawl.

The eyes on one of Cawl's attendant skulls began to pulse.

'An incoming message, hmmm, source unknown,' Cawl explained to Primus. 'Drop privacy field. Give me the message.'

'Negatory,' a flat, electronic voice said through the skull.

'Expand,' said Cawl.

'Message delivered by hololithic tight beam. Targeted reception point, point unknown. Decoding impossible outside of target zone.'

'That could be from a friendly or a hostile,' Cawl said. 'Secret messages, eh? My ears only, I expect. Give the approximate location. Aboard the ship?'

'Affirmative.'

'Where?'

'Unknown.'

'Then find out. Machine God rust it all!' Cawl cursed. 'Primus, put us on pre-battle alert. Begin manoeuvres to bring us in to the flat world.' He began to move away quickly. He could gallop as fast as an equid should occasion demand.

'Where are you going?' Primus asked.

'To find out who wants to talk to me!' Cawl shouted back, then was gone.

The deeper Qvo and his party went, the stranger the interior of Pontus Avernes became. The stairs deposited them in an open level supported by a forest of pillars. Qvo thought them to be metal, but when he went to them and put his hand upon them, the sensors implanted in his palm shocked his core cogitator. He snatched his hand back.

'What?' said Oswen.

'They're alive,' said Qvo in hushed tones. He felt the stirring of awe in himself at the Machine God's bounty. He turned back to Oswen. 'They're all alive.'

Oswen let the map hang from his hands. 'How?'

Qvo put his hand back on the pillar. Oswen had been right. These things had not been forged in a foundry, but grown somehow from something that was like silica to touch, but possessing an entirely artificial atomic arrangement. He closed his eyes.

'There are channels within. Energy moves sluggishly through them. I get the impression that it is...' He opened his eyes, and smiled with delight. 'Dreaming!'

A suspicious frown lowered Oswen's eyebrows. 'Are you sure this is human technology? Have we been tricked? Is this instead the unclean work of the xenos?' He looked fearful and disappointed.

'No, this is not xenotech,' said Qvo. 'At least, I don't think so.'

'It doesn't conform to any kind of STC artefact I've read about or any of the ancients' construction protocols.'

'Cawl always tells me that we have become overly focused on the standard template construct system.'

'But it is sacred!'

'It is,' said Qvo, 'but the archmagos' point is that the STC system was only one thing our ancestors could do. The system was deliberately simple. It was a colonist's tool. Would you base all your opinions of the Imperium on what you would find on a frontier world?'

'I suppose not.'

'We do not know what else our ancestors could truly achieve. Look at this place.' Qvo turned around. The columns seemed to go on forever. 'How big is it? Can you perform an augur soak?'

'I... I... don't know,' said Oswen, who was looking nervously at his servo-skull's map. 'My mapping skulls have stopped moving.'

Qvo squinted into the gloom. Red lights glinted off the pillars several yards away. He took a few slow steps, then a few quicker ones as the lights got brighter. Oswen's skulls were hanging in a perfect circle, tilted down so that their eyes shone off the smooth floor. The one accompanying Oswen was still functional, but as the cartographer moved on, the edges of the map no longer filled themselves in, but stayed blank.

Qvo turned to look back, half expecting to see the stairs gone, but they were still there.

'That's something,' he said. He looked up at the ceiling, and across, taking in the moulded ribbing reinforcing the floor above. 'I'm surprised the Martian Synod haven't discovered this yet. I'm surprised they're digging.' He shuddered at the primitive approach. So brutal. So much would be lost that way.

'They didn't have this, did they?' said Oswen, slapping his map so that water bounced off the plastek coating. 'Auspex returns don't show anything, so they're digging blind.'

'The power of the ancients.'

'The power of the ancients,' agreed Oswen.

'We're lucky someone got in,' said Qvo. 'Otherwise we'd have no map.'

There was a noise from deep in the forest of columns, metal clashing on stone. Qvo squinted into the distance, then realised Cawl had probably given him a slew of ocular enhancements. Activating a thermal trace, he caught plumes of heated gas, exhaust perhaps, thinning into the air.

'We're not alone down here,' said Qvo. 'And I don't think it is Datasmith X99 Bolus.'

'If someone got in here before to make this map, then someone could get in again,' said Oswen.

'We'll have to be careful,' said Qvo. 'Something about this isn't right.'

Cawl followed the signal track high into the upper levels of the ship, far from the foundry levels and the command deck, and into a complex of vast warehouses and museums. These were his personal quarters, in a sense, part palace, part cathedrum to the self. It was not a place Cawl went often.

Servo-skulls swooped ahead of him, impellers buzzing, flat-sweep laser scanners painting the walls in bright red slices, making it seem that they cut the ship so it bled. More skulls kept their electronic vigilance on all frequencies, mundane and psykana. A hololith blended material and immaterial sciences, enabling instantaneous, medium-range communication without the comms lag that pure electromagnetic technology suffered from, being constrained by such annoyances as the speed of light. Their usage was generally limited to the same star system. Any greater range necessitated the use of astrotelepathy, as the psychic signal-to-noise ratio increased by the numerical square past a light hour's distance.

Of course, nobody but the priests of Mars had any inkling how this all worked, and even their knowledge was incomplete. It was dependent on superstition and rote learning. Cawl was one of the very few men alive who knew exactly how it worked, and it worried him greatly that whoever was wandering incorporeally around his domain was able to do so with impunity.

He hurried into a corridor thick with dust that he had not been down for decades. He passed a dead servitor slumped against a wall, its organic components long since having desiccated to a steely hardness in the ship's dry air. His flock of skulls swooped by a high arch. Cawl could feel the broadcast focus around here somewhere, but the closer he came to it, the more diffuse it seemed to become, and his skulls darted about uncertainly, unable to triangulate.

'I am not entirely happy with this situation,' he muttered to himself.

One skull braked hard in the air, let out a quacking noise of alarm, reversed, and spun around. Its laser rangefinder narrowed, broadened, swept over the arch it had so nearly passed, then it burbled a cascade of frightened data and darted down and under into the chamber beyond.

Cawl switched a larger part of his attention to its sensorium, gave out his own surprised yelp and hurried after it, summoning all skulls to follow. They chirred as they swept around, others coming up from behind, converging on the hololith locus.

'I've got it! Primus, I've got it! The focal point is within the Museum Omnis!'

He raced into the dark. The main lumens did not come on when he commanded, giving him further cause for concern. Was this lithocast a ruse, a means of seizing control of his ship?

A part of his mind raced through the circuits of the museum. A further command lit up the exhibits, though the main lights remained off.

The Museum Omnis was huge, and unlike many of Cawl's personal spaces, meticulously arranged. He made sure only to go there when he was wearing the right set of characteristics, the most diligent and organised parts of himself. He had to be sombre to go within. As he did not favour such personality traits, he had not visited for a very long time.

Even so, the Museum Omnis was important to him, and he called up what shreds of dignity he had within himself, and slowed his pace. Statues leaned out from pillars supporting the roof, their bowed faces grave. As he entered, mournful little cyber-constructs came out of suspended animation in their roosts and flapped drunkenly over the exhibits, their systems slow to awaken. The museum was full of Cawl's life, literally where the specimen jars of dead organs and discarded limbs were concerned. It was a memorial to himself, to times he no longer recalled. To the people he had once been and who were now no more.

He peered around the room, trying to catch the intruding light ghost. He saw nothing but unremembered moments from distant days. But then a pulse flashed down the frequency path, and the hololith cohered. Subordination codes flooded the near noospheric spaces. He immediately slapped them back, but not before three of his servo-skulls equipped with lithic ribbon generators were snared by whoever this intruder was, dropped out of formation, gathered into a rotating triangle, and switched mode to projection.

A misty figure formed in the middle of the room, already walking towards Cawl. Formless for the first steps, it became more real, almost solid, as the skulls adjusted their focal lengths to enable full coherence.

Then the figure came properly into being. Tall, transhuman, a Space Marine of the oldest sort, from the highest and mightiest of days, and he was a singular example. A machine akin to a mechanical arachnid squatted malevolently on his reactor pack. He had long, wispy hair. A manskin cloak spoke of cruelty. He grasped a cane with a skull-head handle which he swung forward briskly with each step. Cawl's extensive memory core immediately matched the cane. Not only a support, but Torment, a weapon once owned by a daemon.

Only one man carried that weapon.

The Space Marine stopped before him, amusement wrinkling his face. He grasped the cane in both hands and gave a little bow from the waist that was as much respectful as it was mocking.

'Belisarius Cawl, I presume?' said Fabius Bile.

CHAPTER NINETEEN

THE LABOURS OF LESSER MEN

Bile stood in a pool of hololithic light. The glow of it reflected off the artefacts in the Museum Omnis, lending them the semblance of movement, as if he were surrounded by an attentive audience. Cawl didn't like the effect, and with a forceful thought finally managed to activate the main lumens on the high ceiling. They came on loudly.

Bile faded a little, losing his illusion of solidity. A skull was hovering directly behind his head, presenting Bile, wherever he actually was, with a line of sight as if he had been there.

'This is a very fine collection,' said Bile, looking around. The skull circled, tracking his movements. 'Eclectic. I approve.'

'It is very personal to me,' said Cawl.

'I had gathered,' said Bile. 'Curious, I had not chosen this place to meet with you. The technology I have been loaned is precise, but not that precise. Perhaps the hand of serendipity is at work here?' He bent down to examine an artefact held in the soft glow of a stasis field.

'You are Fabius Bile, if I am not mistaken,' said Cawl.

Bile turned from the object. The servo-skull's eyes lit up Bile's with a red, infernal glow.

'My reputation precedes me.' He stood and moved on to something else that caught his eye, passing through a fragment of an Indrani null-field generator mounted on a block. How Cawl had come across the artefact and what significance it had once held for him, he had no idea.

'You are the original, the genuine Pater Mutatis, not one of his clones?'

Bile shrugged. 'Does it matter? They are me, and I am them. Geniuses all.'

Cawl let out a bark of laughter that boomed through his maxillary shield. 'They say I am arrogant, not unfairly I suppose, but I think I may have met my match in that regard.'

As Cawl talked, he tasked one of his subminds to put a trace on the incoming hololith. Even though the signal had now come to a focal point, tracking it was surprisingly difficult. The feed was thin, weak, still scattered by the Avernes siblings' endless stellar bickering. Only clever modulation of the frequency allowed it to carry enough information to transmit Bile's semblance into the museum. One thing was sure, if Bile was using hololithic means of communication, he must be close. For a moment, Cawl considered activating a ship-wide alert, but decided that might well cause his unexpected guest to withdraw. Despite his misgivings, Cawl found himself wanting to hear what this notorious Heretic Astartes had to say.

Bile smiled. 'I am arrogant. What genius is not? I am a genius, like you. A wise man acknowledges what he is good at. You will find no false modesty in this room, I think. But he also acknowledges his failings. Acknowledgement of one's talents cannot be accompanied by blindness to one's shortcomings, otherwise the wise man is not wise at all.'

'How very humble,' said Cawl.

'Humility is a virtue most of those born in our era neglect, arch-magos. I would venture that you have little time for it yourself.'

'Little,' Cawl said. 'I find humility gets in the way of my self-belief.'

Bile pulled a thoughtful face. 'Take my friendly advice, as one scientist to another. You should embrace humility. You should look within yourself with complete honesty. You will be better for acknowledging your fallibility.'

'I never said I was infallible.'

'You believe you are, though,' said Bile, reaching out with a phantom hand and speculatively passing it through a glassite case, and the broken skull inside. 'Take your great work, your Primaris Space Marines.' Bile bent low, peering into the skull's empty eyes. 'I admit that I was excited to see the work of this supposed genius. You, I mean.'

'I got that, thank you.' Cawl had enough of a handle on the trans-mission now to begin to follow it, but it was heavily encrypted. He set to work breaking the codes. 'What did you think of my work, as one scientist to another?' said Cawl, mocking Bile's words.

'I found it disappointing,' Bile said. He had a hard face, with nothing of kindness to it. 'I found little of interest, Cawl. I have examined your work exhaustively. It is nothing revolutionary, merely variations on the same, tired old theme. Muscle-swollen super soldiers, bigger, stronger, more annoyingly self-righteous...' He gave a sneer and moved on to a crystal claw thrusting up from a plinth. The light of his projection glittered through the transparent material. 'Calling the Primaris Space Marines an improvement might be technically true, but you cannot truly improve upon a flawed design.' Bile continued to pace around, his phantom passing through cabinets and display plinths.

'I did what was required,' said Cawl. He was irked at Bile's criticism. The Primaris Marines were a masterwork! Could he not see? He pushed the emotion aside. Why should he feel stung by the words of this monster? His wounded pride was disrupting the work of his subminds tracing the lithocast.

'You probably did. That stiff old bastard Guilliman probably loved them. But you and I' – Bile dropped his voice to a conspiratorial whisper – 'we are genetors of rare repute, we both know you could have done better.'

'Perhaps.'

'Come now!' Bile stood up straight. 'It is a poor craftsman who only delivers what is expected of him. An artist aims to exceed. Always.'

'You understand, I only had ten thousand years.'

'Are you mocking me?'

'More myself,' said Cawl. 'I had to design a whole new suite of weaponry, armour, vehicles, and equipment to go with them, if we're going to be fair to me, which I think we should be. The lord primarch wanted an improvement upon the designs of his creator. That is what I gave him. I think, under the circumstances of my commission, that last request rather trumped any benefit to me showing off any supposed artistry I may or may not have, don't you? I have seen the results of your art, Bile. You're not a scientist. You're a torturer.'

Bile turned glowing, doubled eyes upon the archmagos, suddenly angry. 'You are naive. You believe I have turned to Chaos?' He shrugged, his temper just as suddenly gone, or at least hidden. 'I suppose that is understandable. It is also not true. These gods my old brothers talk endlessly of, they are a sickness, a discordant note that destroys the harmony of the music of the spheres.

There are no gods, archmagos. There is only time, and being, and thinking things that brew themselves up out of the two.'

'That's a way of looking at it,' said Cawl.

'I am sure it would surprise you to learn that all I wish to do is what you wish to do.'

'Which would be?'

'Come now,' said Bile, shaking his head. 'I want to save humanity.'

'A fine sentiment for the man in the manskin leathers,' said Cawl. 'Most of the time, when people want to save people, it's not to add them to their wardrobe. If I'm not mistaken, you have been associating with the traitors that threaten to plunge our entire reality into an endless hell for the last ten millennia.' Cawl stalked around Bile, rising up over him on his motive carriage. 'You have bolstered their armies. You have aided their schemes. When you have not contented yourself with only abetting them, you have led them yourself in war against humanity. Your name is a byword for terror across hundreds of worlds. Wherever you go your surgeon's knife is red with the blood of blameless folk. I have files of the things you have made from the living tissue of Imperial citizens. Slaughtered civilians. Populations tortured into new, grotesque forms. I have this sickening feeling that you are pleading innocence with me. I am astounded.' Cawl leaned in. 'Yes, yes! Astounded. You are a monster.'

Bile looked up with a condescending smile. 'I have been called monster before, and by people that would surprise you. Look at yourself, do you think you would not give any child nightmares?'

'I may not be pretty, but I am nothing like you,' said Cawl.

'No, you are not. You are not as *good* as I am.' Bile began to pace again, gesturing with Torment. 'I vivisected one of your creations. More than one, actually. But this one sticks in the mind. He was ancient, almost as old as you or I. He was taken from a world far from Terra.' He made a show of musing. 'Kidnapped, that is the word for what happened to him. Ripped from his family without his permission. Experimented on for millennia. Thousands of years of pain to be turned into a living weapon. Ha! You call me a monster? We are both monsters, the pair of us.'

'If I am a monster, then I am a monster on the right side of history,' said Cawl.

'I say the same!' Bile laughed loudly. 'There is no right side! There is no good and bad, only two forces, equally bad as the other, locked in a death spiral. The Imperium is as rotten and degenerate as the followers of Abaddon are.'

'Then why do you help them rather than us? You could have used your talents for good.'

'What do you think I am trying to do?' Bile scoffed. 'What do you think would have happened if I had come back to Terra after Fulgrim fell? Would they have been there to welcome me with open arms? To hail my genius, my contribution to humanity? They would have shot me. If I had come back later, after Horus' failure, then they would have burned me alive instead. There's progress for you.'

'If I have my history correct, and please note this is a rhetorical question, then I would say balderdash,' said Cawl. 'You spent hundreds of years leading the fallen Children of the Emperor willingly.'

'And? You serve a moribund empire ruled by a corpse that feasts upon the souls of His subjects. There is no justice. There is no kindness. We are at the mercy of false gods on all sides.'

Bile moved on to another exhibit.

'Oh, I can see where this is going now,' said Cawl. 'This is the part where you tell me you wish to free us from all gods. By what? Replacing them with yourself?'

'I have been worshipped as a god,' said Bile evenly. 'I found I have no taste for it.'

'I have heard this song before.'

'I have had enough in my life with those who speak in nothing but dramatic metaphor,' snapped Bile. 'Songs, legends! No more! Will, Cawl. It is will that will save us, not stories.' He held up his hand and clenched it. 'My will. Your will. I know you want to stop all this, to drive Chaos out. As do I.'

'Now the evil genius declaims his plan. You are a cliche in a horrifying coat.'

Bile bared thin grey teeth. 'I have nothing to lose by telling you what I need, Cawl, or what I wish to achieve. I have every-thing to gain. Humanity is weak and imperfect. As we exist now as a species, we are finished. Don't argue with me on this point. You machine-priests spend your lives trying to mitigate the frailties of our kind. Many people, the Emperor included, have invested their time in creating superior strains of humanity. None of them had any success.'

'Until now?' offered Cawl. 'There's a surprise.'

'I laboured long to create a better race, one that would not fall to Chaos, that would not prey endlessly upon its own. For centuries I attempted this, until, weary, I became tired of it. I, Fabius Bile, became bored.'

'Well,' said Cawl. 'You have my sympathy there.'

'I became bored because I made a fundamental mistake. I believed that I must control everything, that only I could save the galaxy. I became dis-illusioned, knowing that was impos-sible. I abandoned my children. Cruelly. Some of what you say is right about me. By good fortune, it was the best thing I could have done. Since my reawakening I have become aware of my New Men again, and they have changed!' He began to speak quickly, enthusiastically. 'You should see them, Cawl. They are perfect. They are resistant to the lure of the powers in the warp, physically mighty, invulnerable to age and disease. Their societies are egalitarian and just. All know their place and are satisfied to fulfil their role. I have seen what they have made of themselves and I am humbled. I know now that the greatest creations must be like children, moulded by their maker but not finished. The greatest creations finish themselves.

'I have cloned every primarch, Cawl. They have all failed. If I were a more arrogant man, I would say that this is certainly the fault of the original material, and not my methods. But I must accept the possibility that I did not have all I needed to create a primarch successfully. The error lay with me.'

'You still want to recreate the Emperor's sons?' Cawl said. He wished to keep Bile talking. The algorithms employed by his subminds were steadily chewing through Bile's encryption. Deep in his core, he witnessed their unlocking as streams of numbers that turned green, and thereafter gave up their secrets. He was homing in on Bile's location, somewhere within the Avernes System, in the direction of the galactic core. He would not be far, could not be.

'I did,' Bile answered. 'It doesn't work. The first I made were mewling imbeciles, but I got better. I, like you, am still a believer in the ancient methods of discovery, and through observation and elimination refined my experiments. It got to a point that the last few I made were perfect copies in every way, so perfect they had all the flaws of their originals, including being attracted to the bright flame of damnation. I've come to believe the Emperor's creations are irredeemably touched by the warp, even your beloved lord and master.'

'Then you don't mean to repeat the exercise. You wish...' Cawl thought a moment. 'What do you wish?' He held up a finger. 'Aha! That's it. You wish to change the direction of your researches, not make your own primarch, but make something better. A being of your own design yet similar potential?'

'You have insight,' said Bile with a small bow of his head. 'I am human, I am imperfect. The Emperor's mistakes rot my body still. As many times as I have cheated death, I will not live forever. My New Men require leadership if they are to take the human race into the future. They need help to survive. I wish to make a king worthy of them. Something that avoids all the errors the Emperor committed.'

'That is an intriguing plan,' said Cawl gravely. An impish feeling was rising in his gut, not helped by Bile's increasing earnestness.

'Despite the simplicity of what you have achieved with the Primaris Marines, I admire the elegance of your solutions. You are undoubtedly a genius, Cawl, but you are a generalist. I am a specialist. I have knowledge and experience that you never will.'

'Possibly,' said Cawl. Bile still did not perceive the growing twinkle in Cawl's eyes.

'Definitely,' said Bile. 'No one is limitless in ability. If you give me what I desire, you will have played your part in saving mankind. Think, Cawl. The necrons, the tyranids, the orks… Chaos is not the only existential threat this galaxy faces. We are too weak as we are to survive. Do not let humanity perish at the hands of its myriad foes. Aid me. Let us put an end to these wars. All these Space Marines and temples to uncaring gods, these empires…' Bile swept his hand dismissively through the air. 'These are the labours of lesser men. True scientists like you and I know the value of the great celestial machine, the variety of life and purpose to be found in the stars, even if you believe your god is behind it and I do not. Mankind can and should be the pinnacle of existence! Let us rise above it all. Help me bring peace. Give me the Sangprimus Portum, and you will be remembered as a benefactor of a new era. Your name will live forever, enshrined in memory, a great hero to our species.'

Cawl looked at Bile, eyes round with surprise. Bile's hololith looked back at him expectantly.

'Well? What do you say? As one scientist to another,' said Bile again, and he held out his hand. 'Let us cooperate.'

CHAPTER TWENTY

QVO'S KEY

Following the trail of warmer air, Qvo picked up the pace, and though Oswen seemed more reluctant to do so, he stayed close enough to Qvo to tap him on the shoulder.

'We're getting near to the main energy source. Can you feel it?'

Qvo nodded. The air was full of liberated particles. The hair on his head rose with the static. His magi's senses registered non-trivial amounts of ionising radiation lancing the air. 'I don't have a fix on the machine itself yet, though. It's well shielded.'

'If it is a machine,' said Oswen.

'It's a machine,' said Qvo. The stairs were out of sight. All around them, the columns marched on as if to infinity, their relentless regularity causing peculiar optical effects that his visual cogitators struggled to correct.

Soon, the sound of a regular scraping reached them. Qvo picked up the pace, until he caught sight of what was ahead, stopped and ducked into the shelter of a pillar, waving at Oswen to do the same. He tried vox to communicate, but the storm of radiation coming off the central power source blasted his transmission to nothing.

'It's one of the magi!' he mouthed and pointed. The lector dogmis, Kalisperis. Oswen took in the lurching thing making its way through the underworld propelled by a clutch of tentacles, frowned, and crept up to Qvo's side.

'The theologian? What's she doing down here on her own?'

'I don't know, it's suspicious. Come on,' he said, 'let's see where she's going.'

'Are you sure it's safe?' said Oswen.

'No,' said Qvo. 'But I don't think she'll spot us. This place is unkind to auguries.' By way of example, he pointed out Oswen's map skull. The map projected by it was blank, and the skull's higher function inactive. It followed along solely by dint of the hardline plugging it into Oswen's head. 'Do you have adequate radiation shielding?'

Oswen gave a tight nod. 'I'm more enhanced than I look.'

Qvo gave him a questioning stare.

'My love of maps takes me into all sorts of toxic zones,' he said. 'I have to see they're accurate.'

'You are full of surprises, Oswen.'

They proceeded.

The sense of power built, its might now overwhelming some of their more prosaic senses. Qvo's internal enhancements fizzed with new and unwelcome electrical bridges. He shut down all he could, for the effect was painful, although he was reassured that they would not be detected. He checked over his uplink to the *Zar Quaesitor*, fearful he would lose connection to his data-looms and whatever he learned down here would be lost, but Cawl had equipped him with the highest technologies, and the entanglement transfer signal remained inviolate.

Kalisperis' manner of walking was slow, clumsy and seemed apt to end in disaster at any moment. They soon caught up to her, and their fear lessened. Although big, she looked incapable of combat. They grew bolder, getting closer, watching her erratic progress with curiosity.

After several minutes, the grand hall became lighter, and they saw ahead the source of the fresh illumination. A glow akin to the rising of a sun was shining up from the ground, bright enough to turn Magos Kalisperis into a silhouette. They felt the flow of magnificent energies deep inside themselves, and were so distracted by the power that they almost missed Kalisperis begin her descent down some unseen declivity.

'I'll bet the gate is down there,' said Qvo.

The columns came to an end. Though they were expecting the floor to dip, it did so much more suddenly than they had guessed, and they were so giddy with the raw energy washing around that Qvo nearly fell into a deep, circular pit.

Kalisperis was tottering down a flight of stairs leading to the centre. At the bottom was a rotating archway. Within its aperture shone the light.

'A webway gate,' Qvo said. 'It's not like any I've seen before.'

'Hey! Look at these,' said Oswen. He was pointing to one of dozens of steles about three feet high ringing the rim of the pit.

Qvo watched Kalisperis carefully. The tech-priests were now in the open, but she still didn't seem to have seen them.

'Hey, Magos Qvo! An inscription,' said Oswen again, when Qvo did not respond. 'I can't read it.'

'I'm coming,' said Qvo, annoyed by Oswen's naive joy at discovery. Like too many Cult members he forgot the peril they were in. 'Let me have a look.' Qvo went over to the stele, and looked over the writing. There were many scripts; one was obviously human, utilising the universal alphabet mankind had employed since the dawn of time. The meaning, however, was lost on him. He could see echoes of Imperial Gothic in some of the words, but beyond that it was gibberish. He guessed it to be the Ur-tongue of Old Earth, ancestor to any number of current languages, but now known to very few. The others didn't look human at all.

'Maybe Cawl was right,' Qvo said.

'Right about what?'

'He hypothesised that this place was some sort of diplomatic venue.'

Oswen's eyes widened. 'Blessed are the human conduits of the Omnissiah, for through them doth He dispense His wisdom.'

'Don't get too excited. Cawl's usually right about everything. It gets very wearing. Come on.' He grabbed Oswen's arm and dragged him back towards the columns. 'We'd best hide.'

'Shouldn't we do something?'

'Like what?' said Qvo. 'We don't know why she's down here. Her purpose could be completely legitimate. This place is an open archaeosite, remember?'

Oswen gave Qvo a look that surprised him; condescending almost, as if Qvo were a young acolyte who'd wired two positive terminals together.

'Legitimate? That's not very likely, is it?'

'Probably not,' said Qvo. 'But I've been doing this sort of thing for a long time.' Which was true and untrue, he reflected, seeing as he'd been literally born yesterday. 'If we act now, we will definitely cause some kind of incident.'

'Rely not upon the treacheries of probability,' quoted Oswen.

'Do you always spout so much scripture?' said Qvo.

'Only when I'm nervous,' said Oswen. 'We should act now.'

'I prefer to err on the side of caution,' said Qvo, 'especially when I might have to shoot someone innocent.' He had his phosphor pistol ready, regardless.

'Hold back no strike for fear of smiting the innocent, for they are outnumbered untold times by the gui–'

'Can we just stop that?' said Qvo.

Kalisperis had come to a halt by the gateway. The box fussily came down upon its coiled tentacles, then, to their surprise, the whole front half hinged open.

'By the Omnissiah,' breathed Qvo. 'She's all artifice!'

A slender, altogether more human figure dropped out of the front and approached the gate. It shimmered with the obscuring effect of cameleoline, until it threw off the outer layer, revealing a female form beneath. Whoever she was, she was a tech-priest – two mechadendrites extended from her shoulders. She produced some sort of device and depressed a button. The arch came to a stop, and sank to the ground, re-forming at the molecular level, solid metal running, and by doing so becoming more like entrances to the webway Qvo had seen elsewhere. Her mechadendrites darted forward, one plugging in to an unseen interface, the other confidently touching various spaces on the arch, activating indecipherable runes that seemed neither human nor aeldari.

Once the third number was active, a tremor passed through the floor, heading out from the gate. The nearest columns sang cleanly as struck tuning forks, each one emitting a harmonious note. This music emanated out in rings, each pillar joining the song, until the whole level was ringing with insistent music.

The world of Pontus Avernes shook.

The gate's brightness dimmed.

'This isn't good,' said Qvo. 'Not good at all.' He armed his weapon.

'What about erring on the side of caution?'

'I've erred. Opening secret, subterranean gates is never a good sign. You never know what might come through. She's had her chance.' He surprised himself by advancing confidently forward, gun out. Thank the Machine God he'd got used to his new legs finally. 'Excuse me!' he called over the singing of the columns. 'Excuse me, madame magos!'

A sixth rune flared. Another tremor rolled out from the glaring epicentre, sending forth a new round of notes to overlay the first, fading chorus. He reached the floor, and pointed his gun at her head.

'Stop right there,' he said.

She barely deigned to look at him. He caught a glimpse of a mostly human face, minimal augmetics, though her eyes were artificial, totally black orbs flickering with internal data cascades. They were well made, small enough to occupy only her natural sockets.

'Cawl's pet,' she said disinterestedly, and turned away. She continued to activate the controls of the gate. Now he was closer, Qvo saw that it was some sort of hybrid archeotech. He suspected unclean xenos influences. 'Go away,' she said.

'No,' he said.

He shot her, the blast from the phosphor pistol searing his visual input sensors. It met the invisible barrier of a protective field, and smeared itself to nothing. There was no light output as one would expect from a personal refractor, ion or conversion field. The shot just stopped dead.

'A personal power field?' he said. That was a rare artefact indeed.

She nodded, still continuing her work. 'The true followers of the Machine God are privy to many blessings you deniers of His glory could only dream about.'

'True followers?' He was beginning to understand. Qvo's gaze slid down to the hem of her robe. The edge was decorated with symbols of devotion to the machine: the sacred cog track, words in Lingua Technis and binharic number strings, but there were darker symbols there. 'You're Dark Mechanicum,' he said.

'*True* Mechanicum,' she said. 'Or New Mechanicum. Which-ever. Either is a preferred term for those who do not worship the False Omnissiah but follow the one, true, unpolluted Machine God. From my perspective, you're the Dark Mechanicum.'

He fired again, and again; each time his phosphor shots splashed harmlessly off her unidirectional energy barrier. His shooting inconvenienced her not one whit, and she worked on with not so much as a flinch until she was finished. The gate gave out a last tremor, and the light died back. A few dozen Qvos had been in the webway, and although it was often varied in form, he recognised the soft luminance you found in certain parts of it, and the undulating walls that appeared both an arm's reach and an infinity away. Qvo found himself staring down a tunnel short enough that he could see the end. He was look-ing into a ship's hold, he thought, and it was crammed with ranks of waiting servitors.

Kalisperis, if that was her real name, turned around, her mecha-dendrites detaching themselves from the gate and curling over her shoulders like snakes ready to strike.

'Now I can deal with you,' she said calmly.

Qvo backed up. He fired again. Again, the shot vanished against her power field.

'Let me help you with that,' she said. Her mechadendrite darted out and slapped Qvo's pistol from his hand. It whirled away and clattered against the silicon architecture. Qvo clutched his wrist.

She was more enhanced than she had at first appeared. Exposed supplementary metal muscles glinted in her hood, and the back of her neck was protected by an armoured cowling.

'You lapdogs of Terra have dragged us away from the true path of enlightenment. You damn humanity with your heresy.'

'You're the ones consorting with daemons!' Qvo said. He

banged his foot hard on the bottom step leading back up to the forest of columns. He fell, and looked up.

The top seemed so far away. There was no sign of Oswen. Kalisperis did not mention him. A flicker of hope kindled that she assumed Qvo was alone. He had a chance, if Oswen could get to X99 in time. Not much could stand in the way of a cohort of Kastelans. If, if, if, though.

'We do not consort. We use. You do not consort with steel, do you? You master it. You mould it. You beat it until it takes the form you decree. The stuff of the warp is a material like any other, a blessed part of the Machine God's Great Work. You are unwise to deny it.'

Qvo rolled over, began to crawl up the stairs, trying to get back to his feet, so he could run far from that place. He made it up three steps. Her dendrites whipped forward. One grabbed him by the throat and plucked him up high into the air. She turned him around so he faced her.

'Your time is done,' she said.

'You won't be able to strangle me,' he said. 'I don't breathe.'

'I know,' she said. 'I'm not trying to strangle you.' With a metallic rasp a data-spike sprang out of the palm of her second dendrite. Its three thick digits spread wide. 'I'm going to use you.' She grinned nastily. 'How terribly ironic that Cawl's love for his friend shall be his undoing. The uplink Cawl installs in all his versions of you is so strong, and pure. Subatomic entanglement communications arrays rendered at the finest scale.' She tutted. 'Technology of the ancients employed for such sentimental reasons.'

'I'm afraid I'm not following, Kalisperis,' said Qvo.

'I'm not Kalisperis. I am Alixia-Dyos of the Disciples of Nul. How limited you are, like those fools who allowed me to infiltrate their church on Accatran. You are a fine mechanism, but just a toy. I lured you down here. You are the key to Cawl's ship, and when I am done with you, I shall take everything you are, break it into components, and keep the pieces for myself.'

Right about now would be a good moment for Oswen to appear with X99's robots, Qvo thought, just as Alixia-Dyos' data-spike plunged into and through his eye, into the electronic brain behind it, and through his perpetual, memory-gathering uplink to the ship, right into the heart of the *Zar Quaesitor.*

Cawl looked at Bile's extended hand, then to his face, and he could not help himself any longer. He tried to hold back the flood of amusement, but the dam broke within, and his primary hands flew up to his mouth. Cawl snorted. Bile frowned as Cawl erupted into a fit of giggles that escalated in intensity until he was hooting with mirth.

'Now you are mocking me,' said Bile. 'I come here to speak with you as a respected equal, and you laugh at me?'

'I'm sorry! I'm sorry!' tittered Cawl. 'But that's just the most precious thing I've heard in three thousand years!' His voice and voxmitters hicced together. 'You want me to hand over the Sangprimus Portum? *To you?* You want me to give the sum total of all that remains of the Emperor's own work to a *Chaos Space Marine?* Oh by the Omnissiah, that is a good one! That's your *plan?* That I'd just hand it over. You'll be the architect?' said Cawl. 'I'll be your facilitator? So you can fill the universe with Chaos Primaris Space Marines?'

'I do not need your archive to do that. Your work is simplistic in the extreme.'

'Well then, so you can take the place of the Emperor and of the Warmaster and rule us all for our benefit instead.'

To Cawl's amazement, Bile actually looked hurt.

'I knew you would disappoint me,' he said. His outstretched hand clenched and withdrew.

'It doesn't matter what you wish. Every tyrant starts that way, Fabius Bile. I've crossed your trail before. I've met things that worship you. Godhood is not a choice. Even if you desire to avoid that burden, think about what you are saying! You are standing here, talking to me, a Prime Conduit of the Omnissiah, suggesting that your design alone should replace the sacred form of humanity? That you, alone, can improve upon His great design. That you are the sole man to save us all?' Cawl clapped metal fingers together with a harsh, dismissive noise. 'Bravo to you. I mean that with an enormous amount of withering sarcasm, in case your ego encourages you to misinterpret my scorn as praise.'

'Is it not the belief of your Cult that you are to improve upon the work of your god?' snarled Bile.

'Now you employ theological arguments when you run out of rationality,' said Cawl. 'Improve, yes, supplant, no. To burn everything down and start again is the urge of the megalomaniac. It was the urge of Horus, of Abaddon, of every messianic warlord since the dawn of time. It is the desire of these gods that you purport to despise.'

'Very well. Spurn me. That is your choice. You will come to admit that my improvements to the human stock are superior to any other,' said Bile. 'You will acknowledge the rectitude of my plan and you will regret that you turned down a part in it before the end.'

'Millions of tormented mutants suggest otherwise, Bile. Honestly! And I thought myself stricken by hubris.'

The skull behind Bile's head looked Cawl deep in the eye.

'If you will not give me what I require to save humanity, let it be on your head. I shall instead take it by force.'

'I knew you were going to say that,' said Cawl. 'I have had enough of offers I have no interest in. Begone from my sight.'

'A pity,' said Bile. He seemed to mean it. Then he smiled. 'But I anticipated this.'

GENEFATHER

'Then why try to persuade me?'

'I am not trying to persuade you.'

'No?' A sudden thrill of understanding hit Cawl.

'I was trying to distract you, Cawl. Now I have what I need. My associate is beside himself with excitement. You have so many wonders here. Perhaps it is time for you to get to know some of them better?'

Bile's hololith winked out. The servo-skulls he'd suborned for the visit crashed down onto the floor.

The lights flickered. The constant background hum of the ship at work subtly changed.

'Oh no,' Cawl said. 'Oh no.'

The lights went out. Thrusters fired with no warning, exerting huge forces on Cawl's body. He clamped his feet hard to the deck.

Klaxons began to howl all over the place. Red emergency lumens came on.

Cawl's mind plunged into the noosphere. All over the ship, systems were going offline. The manoeuvring jets were pushing it wide of its anchorage, towards Pontus Avernes. He expected daemonic scrapcode, the enemy's preferred method of attack. Virulent, but inherently unstable and therefore easy to deal with. What he found was far more formidable – non-contaminated, genuine binharic subversion programming. Semi-aware machine spirits were quickly locking him out of his own voidship. It was impressive, but whoever had given it to Bile had no idea of Cawl's capabilities.

'Tricky, tricky Fabius Bile,' said Cawl. 'We'll have this out in a moment, you'll see. I just need to find where it came from. It wasn't on that lithocast. That's far too obvious.'

Cawl found the source fast, and what passed for a heart in his augmetic chest cavity skipped a beat.

'Friedisch!'

The enemy were in Qvo's data-loom, using it to launch the informational attack on the *Zar Quaesitor*, not only highly inconvenient, but putting his entire Qvo archive in danger in the process.

Cawl was moving before he'd consciously registered the desire to do so. Deep, animal instincts propelled him, overpowering millennia of intricate cerebral enhancements with his need to protect his friend. His cyber-constructs were going crazy, dropping dead from the air or accelerating directly into the walls and exploding into their component parts. Gravity wavered in the deck plating. Lights turned off and on randomly. Snatches of music, playing at a sinister slowness, blasted out of voxmitters. All the while he could feel the ship heeling towards the artefact world.

He'd quite forgotten Bile's last words to him, until he got halfway to the door back into the corridor, whence came a soft flare of green light. Extradimensional energies registered on his augurs. The kind employed by the necrons.

A shadow fell across him, and he realised then another great error: that it had been foolish to come here without arming himself first.

'Hello, insect. I told you I'd get out, didn't I?' said AsanethAyu.

Within half a minute, the command deck of the *Zar Quaesitor* went from a state of serene operation to one of total chaos. The first sign Primus had was the servitors, whose normal behaviour suddenly ceased, and who all started howling.

Heads turned all over the deck in surprise.

'We're losing control!' shouted a transmechanic at the helm.

Primus had rarely heard so much panic in the voice of a machine-priest. Most of those who served on the bridge had their emotions cauterised. Cawl insisted that those that didn't had emotional vaults fitted to contain their feelings. Evidently, they were insufficiently large to hold that much fear.

Primus tried his communications, and was rewarded with an ear-splitting blast of noise from his helm.

'Find the archmagos!' Primus shouted.

'I cannot, my lord,' the nearest lexmechanic slurred. His vox-mitter slid up and down some unpleasant electronic scale.

Primus marched over to his vox-station and shoved him out of the way. He punched buttons, and adjusted settings, but each attempt only brought the same awful roaring that his helm had provided.

'Our... Our systems are being flooded with junk data!' the lexmechanic burbled.

'Not junk if they are piloting us into Pontus Avernes,' said Primus grimly. 'We're under attack. Someone's taken control. Find out who! Purge all systems. Quarantine all affected cogitators and data-looms,' he shouted.

Screens blinked off everywhere. Lumens went out. Random machine noises squealed out of apparatus in every corner.

'It's in everything!' reported another crewman. He stabbed at buttons. Flame shot out from his work desk.

Wocolos the Integerarian took charge.

'Shut down all noospheric connections between the *Zar Quaesitor* and subsidiary systems,' he ordered.

<INADVISABLE...> droned the magos-datalord. <PROGNOSTICATION... permanent damage to wider noosphere. Probability of damage to associated networks ninety-four per cent.>

'Override. By the will of the Machine God, make it be,' Wocolos commanded. 'Cut the data-roads at source. Save what we can.'

Primus felt helpless. He was no fool, but the technical skills needed to help the *Zar Quaesitor* were not his to command. Pontus Avernes was tilting up to them like an exquisite relief map, its perfect features laid out clear to see. Primus did a quick mental calculation of what would happen should a ship the mass of the *Zar Quaesitor* impact something that was essentially an oversized orbital plate.

For a few moments, there would be a fifth sun in the Avernes System, and then they would all be dead.

The lumens were out, leaving the bridge harshly lit by the system's fratricidal suns and the blizzards of nonsense occupying every hololith and screen. Primus turned in a circle, taking in the disorder of the Adeptus Mechanicus, realising as he watched them perform their bizarre tasks that they were already in battle, though no foe had presented itself. Priests were chanting all over the deck, sprinkling sacred oils which hissed in acrid clouds from overheated machinery. A racket of audible data exchange between the adepts filled the air, like the buzzing of bees disturbed in their nest. The servitors continued to wail and thrash. Half the cyber helpmeets were behaving erratically, racing around, or burbling loudly. Some were actively aggressive, and the noise on the electromagnetic spectrum grew and grew.

'Get me status reports!' Primus roared.

Someone, somewhere, with their emotions completely in check, began a litany of woe in a flat, robotic voice.

'Void shields – offline.'

'Main drive – offline.'

'Primary defences – offline.'

'Secondary defences – offline.'

'Augury systems – compromised.'

'Life support – compromised.'

'Vox-systems – compromised.'

On it went: all the ship's principal systems were either entirely non-functional or under external command. Primus grabbed the lexmechanic, hauling his heavy, cyborg body out of his seat until they were eye to eye.

'Can you get me an external vox-line?'

'All ship systems are locked. But non-core systems are still functional. Skitarii vox-nets. Fleet assets.'

'Is that a yes?' Primus said, very slowly, into his face.

'It is a yes,' said the lexmechanic.

Primus dropped him back into his chair.

'Then open communications with the rest of the Adeptus Mechanicus fleet here. Inform the delegates' voidships to take evasive action. Tell them we're not about to attack them. The last thing we need is them to interpret this as an act of aggression! Get me an internal vox-system activated, now. Summon Marshal Iota to the command deck.'

'It is done, Lord Primus,' said the lexmechanic. 'You have active subsidiary vox-link to the ship.'

'Personnel of the *Zar Quaesitor*, this is Alpha Primus. We are subjected to data assault. All hands to battle stations. Prepare for immediate physical attack.'

Query responses instantly came by return.

'Respond with a repetition of my orders in binharic and text,' he told the lexmechanic.

'My lord?' The query was broadcast from a still obedient servo-skull that swooped down to Primus' eye level, but came from the augury section. 'We have limited scanning, and there is nothing on the augur.'

'Ignore your scopes. They are coming! All hands to battle stations! Keep an eye on the void around us. Watch out for ships with occlusion devices and for in-system warp translation.'

Klaxons stuttered on, then ceased, then started again as the enginseer responsible for them wrestled them back under control. Their wailing was a sign of normal functions being restored, and it stiffened the resolve of the crew.

'They will attack. This assault is a precursor.'

'Responses are coming in from the Metallican and Accatranian delegations, my lord,' the lexmechanic relayed. 'They question your statements.'

'Give them a full situation report. Recommend they close down any means the enemy might use to infiltrate their systems.'

'They will say it is impossible for their data-fortresses to be breached.'

'It's happening here. Do we yet have any contact from the archmagos?'

'None, my lord.'

'Send out parties to look for him at his last known location. Activate crisis enginseer crews and get them down to the enginarium to aid the transmechanics there. Cut off the guidance systems from the main cogitator networks if you have to, and fly manually. I want this ship back under control!'

'My lord! There is a…'

Primus didn't listen to the rest of the warning. What he had feared was happening, in his line of sight through the oculus. Right in front of the *Zar Quaesitor*, a warp breach was forming. It rippled, unstable, bubbling like burning plastek, showing first the void then the hell-light of the warp in uneven patches.

Whoever was coming through into that stellar maelstrom was even more reckless than Cawl. He didn't need the ship's crew yammering on about probabilities of destruction. Bypassing the Mandeville points to arrive deep in any system was dangerous. Arriving in one full of gravity rip-tides like Avernes was suicidal. The forming breach was already failing, rippling in and out of existence. Any ship that attempted such an egress should, by rights, have been torn to pieces by material-immaterial gravitic shear exerted by the four dancing suns.

It was not a day for fairness.

The warp breach briefly stabilised and a heavily modified Gladius-class frigate arrowed out of the breach. As soon as it was clear, the rift collapsed with a sickly flash of light. How the vessel had managed such a feat, Primus could not begin to guess, but that was unimportant, for it was coming straight at them, using the confusion of the other Mechanicus vessels and the shelter of the *Zar Quaesitor* to approach unmolested by weapons fire. A Gladius frigate was of no danger to an Ark Mechanicus under normal circumstances, but at that moment the *Zar Quaesitor* was a sitting target.

Primus peered at the ship.

'Get me a name,' he said to a magos-logis.

'Data-looms are operating at less than fifteen per cent efficiency.'

'A name!'

The lexmechanic bent to his task.

'Name, signum and silhouette match the *Vesalius*, my lord. It is the ship of the arch-traitor Fabius Bile,' the logis responded.

Primus stood up and looked out of the grand oculus. Pricks of light flashed all along the frigate's flanks.

'Boarding craft incoming,' reported a magos-augurum.

Swarms of black specks ran ahead of the *Vesalius*. Primus narrowed his eyes.

'Magos prognosticans, give me a model of where those boarding craft will most likely hit.'

The prognosticans, a hugely augmented man who was more cogitator than person, chirruped with data, and cast the results to Primus' battle plate systems. Primus looked them over. He and the magos were in agreement about where the attack would come.

'Wocolos, you have command.'

'Where are you going, son of Cawl?' the Integerarian asked.

'To somewhere I shall be of use. Knowing Bile's history and particular interests, he can only be here to take the Sangprimus Portum.' A flash of his vision filled his mind, his stillborn brothers floating in their tanks. Bile would do far worse if he got the material in the vault.

'I shall not let that happen,' he swore, and strode from the bridge.

CHAPTER TWENTY-ONE

MECHANICUM WAR

Pontus Avernes shook with sudden, shocking fury.

Iurgium lurched as the ground liquified beneath its feet, sucking them down. Roosev slowed the Knight, preventing a stumble that would certainly have turned into a fall. The Knights following him split wide to avoid crashing into his mount, drawing themselves up to a halt nearby. Their sensorium heads panned across the plains, eyes glowing with heightened activity. Weapons activations chimed across the House Taranis noosphere.

'What by the Omnissiah was that?' Allacer asked. His lance was dancing with disruptive energies. His shield flared with his mount's nervousness.

'Unclear,' said Roosev.

'I have massive energy spikes on my augur,' said Allacer.

Lance Salutatia continued on, its machines wobbling as another, stronger earthquake ripped through the ground.

'Waldemar, bring your Knights to a halt immediately!' commanded Roosev angrily. 'Hold fast! I should not have to command you to protect yourself.'

'There is no sign of any threat,' Waldemar's voice crackled back.

'Steady, brother,' Allacer voxed privately. 'You insult his honour.'

'He dishonours himself,' Roosev said. The spirits of his ancestors moaned their interminable chorus of misery, led by that accursed phantom, Maven the Very Elder. *Iurgium* bridled, lifting and placing its feet like a skittish equid. It could smell approaching violence and was eager to partake.

Lightning crackled across the ground. Even through the armour plating of his cockpit, Roosev felt the air grow heavy.

'Scutum amalgam!' he commanded. 'Power all weapons.' *Iurgium's* growing excitement filled him, and he had to fight to retain control.

'What is it?' Allacer asked. 'Are we being attacked, brother?' The lances joined, and the Knights stomped around into a wide circle where they could cover one another's backs, each showing the wariness of its pilot in its motions. Ion shields flashed as they swung about to the forward aspect and touched, layering together into a shield wall.

'Better to be on guard than regretful,' Roosev said. 'Something is about to happen. *Iurgium* can sense it.'

He opened channels to the other Mechanicus assets on Pontus Avernes, but got only howling static in return. 'Communications are inoperative.'

'Brother!' Allacer called. An augur ping directed Roosev to the nominal east, where the lightning racing over the ground was drawing itself up into a flaring column of power. It was only the first. Other similar towers of lightning appeared. According to *Iurgium's* failing auguries, they were forming at regular intervals between the pyramids. Scores of them, leaping high, until they formed a current with the energy shields sheltering the planet, and stabilised into surging columns of light.

'By the three in one...' Allacer breathed. He was close to Roosev. His transmissions were at full gain, but his voice was faint, overwhelmed by the roar of energy.

A deep tone tolled across the land. Fractured, martial music followed, a fragment played stutteringly four times, then trailed into screeching oblivion. A few seconds of tri-D images ran a little after in the sky, so distorted they barely made sense. Beneath layers of ruinous data decay, Roosev thought he saw strangely dressed people, a flypast of void craft, but it was gone as soon as it started.

The columns of energy flexed in their middles, bowing out into lens-shapes. A silvery light poured from them, steady amid the flickering chaos of the power cascades. The columns of light broadened, becoming circles, becoming gates...

Things came through. They were amorphous to begin with, as picters and the human eye were dazzled by the glare. But they resolved into shapes that cantered eagerly onto the plains. Roosev thought them animals at first, but quickly revised his opinion when he noticed engine stacks and heavy weapons. Then he saw that though bestial, they were not beasts. He knew their kind, warp-spawned daemon machines, an unholy union of forbidden knowledge and the arcane sorceries of the warp. Smaller figures came with them, and their silhouettes were instantly recognisable.

Heretic Astartes. They were suddenly everywhere.

The traitors opened fire with man-portable heavy weapons as they came through the gates, moving in the power-assisted lope characteristic of their kind. They split into squads and fanned out, giving support to the unholy machines they accompanied. The beasts broke into a run. Already the Knights' ion shields were flaring as Roosev gave the order to return fire. Rockets streaked from the carapaces of *Vanitas* and *Danubia*. *Vanitas'* repeater battlecannon pumped, spitting shells at the foe. Mud and water fountained high where they hit. Heretic Astartes were lofted skywards or knocked off their feet, but it took more than mere explosives to fell a man blessed by the Emperor and the Dark Gods, and most of them hauled themselves back onto their feet. *Iurgium* stamped, impatient to fight. It was all Roosev could do to hold the Knight back and stop it breaking the shield wall to race into range with its flame cannon.

From behind him he heard the ferocious roar of *Salutatia's* volcano lance.

The battle for Pontus Avernes had begun.

Qvo was adrift in a place of shadows. They moved around him in featureless and sinister crowds. They seemed familiar, and then he realised that they were all him, or iterations of Qvo, more accurately. When he concentrated on one, it would resolve into a hazy image of some past moment, though he never saw more than the versions of himself, performing actions in isolation, or engaged in conversation with people he could not see.

When he looked away, they vanished into obscurity.

'To see oneself from outside so is disorienting, especially when one is not entirely sure if the person being observed is truly you.' Alixia-Dyos' mocking sympathy echoed through his mind. He looked for her, but couldn't see anything but the shadows acting out his past.

'You won't find me,' she said. 'It's interesting watching you watch yourself. How must it feel to be half-animated, brought back from the dead so many times, but never completely. I almost feel sorry for you. Belisarius Cawl must hate you.'

Qvo took a few steps. Though he knew this place was only a

mental construct, he felt he had to do something. He moved with treacly slowness, like a dreamer in a nightmare. The analogy struck him. He hadn't dreamed since he'd died.

Qvo was aware of a sort of hole high up above him. Data was being drawn in from all over his mindscape, so he went nearer, and he found himself looking at a visualisation of the tether joining him to the Qvo data-looms aboard the *Zar Quaesitor*. It looked like a void singularity, where the fabric of space-time turned itself inside out. A kind of whirlpool of reality. His thoughts were pulled unerringly to it, as he supposed they must always be, but he was not the only user of this gateway. A huge stream of data was roaring into the hole from Alixia.

'You're using me against Cawl,' he said.

'That's what I said, isn't it?' said Alixia. 'Be silent.'

'You can't make me,' he said quietly.

There was no reply, so he assumed he was right. And he was still alive, leading him to believe that in order for Alixia-Dyos to use his tether, he had to be whole. That was something.

Qvo had been made by Belisarius Cawl. His body was of superior build, and although his attacker was skilful, she could not shut down all his awareness. He had access enough to his sensors to gain an impression, not an image exactly, but a sense that dozens and dozens of servitors were marching out of the webway gate into the forest of columns. Tech-priests in Dark Mechanicum black came with them. It was strange to perceive these most traitorous beings behaving exactly like the Adeptus Mechanicus did in a place of technological wonder, excited as they set to work cataloguing, measuring and scanning the arte-fact world.

Qvo withdrew into the core of himself, hiding from Alixia. There was nothing he could do on the outside, either with his limbs or with his eternal connection to the ship. But he was not completely helpless. He could feel the spike transfixing his head. From there came the interface with his mind. The spike was physical, immovable. The data was not. He was the ghost in the machine.

Qvo had had plenty of practice at being a ghost.

He set his eyes on the data-pipe high overhead, and began to rise towards it.

CHAPTER TWENTY-TWO

ZAR QUAESITOR INVADED

Butcher-Bird led a flight of landing craft hurtling towards the *Zar Quaesitor*. Not so much as a single bullet came its way. Bile watched the Ark Mechanicus grow in the gunship's cockpit canopy. It was dead in space. Its weapons either hung limply in their mounts or tracked manically. Commandeering the thrusters and pushing it towards the flat world was a nice touch. The machine worshippers would be concentrating on wresting control of the engines back for fear of crashing. A dilemma that would keep efforts on restoring gunnery control to a minimum. Nobody would be firing anything from the *Zar Quaesitor*'s arsenal until he had been and gone.

'Kolumbari-Enas has done well,' said Bile.

'Yes, my maker,' said Porter, who was as always his constant shadow.

Cawl's ship was immense. Although it was classed an Ark

Mechanicus, it was much bigger than those he'd seen in the past. Most Imperial ships were built to a similar pattern, and that included the *Vesalius*. They were long and narrow, with heavily armoured prows, large engine blocks to the rear, and command-and-control centres housed in superstructures roughly two-thirds of the way down the spine towards the engines. The *Zar Quaesitor* looked nothing like that. It was fat, round, pregnant with the promise of plunder. The foremost part was made up of a lander of some size, currently locked into place. The underside was a mass of cranes and piers; the vessel was so big it possessed its own shipyard. No doubt this grand utility was replicated within, by laboratorium decks and manufactory complexes. It was truly a forge world in miniature. Its defences were extensive. Had they been active, it would have taken a battlefleet to deal with them. Hangar slots were stacked high, like the hives of insects. First-Among-Equals' servant had been thorough, and not one interception craft issued out to challenge them. He doubted they could even see him. Though it was a sign of unusual success, he suffered a touch of regret. His plans could have been more ambitious, had he known how helpless the Dark Mechanicum would make the target.

'A prize like this would be worth taking, if I had the troops to seize it,' said Bile. The things he could do with a ship like this... But in the transit hold was no millennial of warriors, only mutants, more beasts than men. His days as a lord of Space Marines were behind him.

He drew in a hissing breath.

'Maker?'

'Nothing, Porter. One mustn't wallow in might-have-beens. They burn the spirit.'

'You refer to the ship. You want it.'

Bile nodded. 'I cannot have it. We have a plan. We have a goal.

I fully expect us to succeed. You will learn one day that you must not be tempted to overstretch yourself. We have only rabble at our disposal, and though they are adequate for our intentions, to attempt anything grander without proper consideration would be far too risky. So instead, we shall make a virtue of our mutants, and our information. Cawl has proven himself as arrogant and blind as Sedayne was. We can expect victory.'

'I will serve you well in achieving it.'

'No doubt. First you shall hide yourself.'

'Am I not to fight?'

'You most assuredly are, but our success depends on surprise. Do not reveal yourself at the beginning of the battle. You are my secret weapon. Let them see my reduction in status. Once they understand that I have few legionaries at my back, it will draw the enemy on, for they will wish to finish me. This is what Sedayne would have done, and this is what Cawl will do. When they have overcommitted themselves, you shall strike and we shall seize our objective.'

The gunship raced alongside the high flanks of Cawl's home. Bile watched carefully, scrutinising the *Zar Quaesitor* by eye and by the gunship's sensorium, until he saw what he sought, a hangar with an active air shield near the top of the landing decks.

'There,' he said, pointing. 'Put us down there.' Despite himself, he was enjoying this. 'It is good to be going to war again.'

Butcher-Bird roared into the hangar bay under fire. The ship's weapons had been neutralised, but little could be done about the crew, and Cawl had a substantial contingent of warriors aboard. The gunship reared, blasting back hard on its jets to come to a stop, landing claws extended. The moment its shield bubble passed over the defenders, radium bullets began rattling off the underside, no hope of penetrating its thick armour. A caliver was brought up, its lance of plasma scoring a track across *Butcher-Bird*'s plating. Guns on the wings responded quickly, blasting the luckless skitarius into a scattering of bloodied electronic components.

The ship thumped down. Its arsenal opened up, scouring the area near it of warriors, but they were numerous. Cawl had evidently designed his hangars with defence in mind. They were one of the most vulnerable parts of a ship, after all. Retractable blast barriers sheltered further units of skitarii, while more occupied shooting galleries set into the ten-storey-high walls at the rear.

'We shall have to do this the old-fashioned way,' said Bile. 'Prepare to board! Release the frenzon.'

There was a whooshing as stimm mist flooded *Butcher-Bird*. A bloodthirsty bellow sounded up the stairs from the lower level. The animal stink of the beastmen intensified, beating even the chemical sharpness of the stimms, rich with adrenaline, excitement and terror.

'Stay on board until I say,' he told Porter. 'Do not reveal yourself.'

'Maker. I can protect you.'

Bile put his helmet on. 'I am Fabius Bile, once lord lieutenant of the Emperor's Children. I have been waging war for ten thousand years.' The helm seals hissed as they locked. 'I can protect myself.'

Bile went down the steps. The ramp slammed down. Bile's monsters screamed incoherent battle cries and raced out into a storm of bullets, wisps of frenzon curling after them. Bile's sensorium buzzed with rad-warnings from the skitarii's weaponry, but he paid no attention to them, and marched fearlessly into battle.

Several of his mutants were downed. Others were hit, and

would certainly die of rad poisoning later, but they were strong, engineered to be hardy, and fought on full of bullet wounds. Many were much larger than normal men, hulking brutes bulging with muscle. Quite possibly the exertions of this battle would kill many of them, overtaxing their inadequate hearts, their bodies overwhelmed by the frenzon. This was unimportant. They were cannon fodder. It amused him that some thought these genetic misshapes were his New Men. The very thought! They were largely natural, in their own fashion. Bile had allowed his mutant crew to breed freely, as natural selection would make them strong without effort on his part. Occasionally he stepped in to tweak genes and cull the weak, and a few among the horde had been specially made for this battle, but the real stiffening to the mix was the stimulant racing round the systems of each and every one.

More ships flew through the hangar slot. It was a big space, not as impressive as the embarkation decks of the old warships, but it was large enough. There was space for thirty or more medium craft, but only twelve of the berths were occupied, all by unarmed utility skiffs and personnel lighters. One of them was already burning on its pad.

Bile shot a skitarius down with his boltgun without thinking about it. His attention was always on his creations, not the foe. The foe died easily. His vid-corders ran constantly, in case any of his warrior-beasts did anything interesting. Brutus held his eye the most. He was magnificent, mighty as the Monster of Knossos from ancient tales, bull-headed, furious, indefatigable, the sole worthwhile beast among his sorry cavalcade. Brutus' physical armour was restricted to primitive plates of iron he had fashioned himself, but the refractor field Bile had given him offered more substantial protection. Radium bullets dropped from the air around him, their momentum stolen by the energy field and dispersed as blazing displays of light. The minotaur charged through rainbows of dispersed energy to end his attackers, hitting one of the barriers so hard it crumpled under his hooves when he leapt over and into the skitarii. He dipped his head, and tossed one of the enemy high into the air with a flick of his horns, blasting others apart with his modified ripper gun. The brutal axe he carried in his left hand swatted others off their feet, their limbs coming off as they were flung away.

Elsewhere, the battle hung in the balance. Mutants raced from Bile's craft, baying with a mix of exhilaration and fear. The skitarii were firing in disciplined volleys, timing each to inflict maximum devastation and psychological shock. Whoever had provided their combat programming knew what they were doing. An entire rank of mutants went down, but they were just a shield to the row behind, and these were comprised of Bile's largest. They roared and continued the attack. Bile followed, shooting another skitarius who leaned a little too far over the blast barriers. He fell back, his cyborg head emptied of brains and components by a single bolt.

A shot impacted Bile with punishing force, shattering ceramite at the top of his right pauldron. He looked up, his helm's optics zeroing in on his attacker. Up in a shooting gallery, snipers with transuranic arquebuses were firing on him.

'Ship gunnery, remove that threat,' he commanded, linking his helm feed directly to the gunners' stations. *Butcher-Bird* had such an aggressive, self-aware machine spirit that Bile was never sure if he was speaking to the crew or to the ship itself. It didn't matter, as long as his commands were obeyed. The ship's battle cannon coughed, slamming a high-explosive shell into the gallery. It punched through the armoured facing and went off inside, blasting a shower of smoking meat and machine parts out through the firing slits.

The wave of mutants poured over the barriers, trampling their own dead in their frenzy. The disciplined fusillades of the Adeptus Mechanicus broke down into scattered, uncoordinated fire. Bile strode forward and crossed the barrier himself. A radium carbine fired at point-blank range at his head was fended off with a swipe of Torment, the bullet going wide. He ended the existence of the cyborg with a shot from his bolt pistol, already moving to counter the attack of a skitarius prime who darted at him, power maul crackling. He was trying to exploit Bile's blind spot, coming in from the side. A combination of Bile's hyper-advanced sensorium and millennia-honed instincts anticipated the move. Bile turned easily, dropping his pistol, catching the arc-maul's shaft in his hand. Lightning crawled off the weapon's heavy head, danced around his fist, sending tingling agonies up his muscles. He disregarded the pain, enjoyed it, even.

Through gritted teeth he snarled.

'A pointless attempt at glory,' he said, and jammed the skull handle of Torment under the skitarius' chin. The cyborg let out a shrill cry of agony. The pain it felt was so intense, circuits burned out behind the vision slit of its sallet. The warrior jerked, and went limp.

Bile dropped the smoking corpse on the ground, already pivoting to his next target. He fought his way through an entire subclade of troopers in this way, ripping them apart with brutal economy, each death flowing into the next. No movement was wasted. Nothing could stand against him. He was done with them quickly, feet crunching on broken machine components, his long coat spattered with blood and oil. Bile had his eyes on the main access corridor to the hangar, a gangway wide enough to accommodate a heavy cargo hauler, and a ready route for reinforcements.

'Take the corridor,' he ordered, sweeping Torment round to point.

His mutants threw down their dying foes and surged up the access tunnel into the ship. Kolumbari-Enas had done his work well. Emplaced weapons that should have reaped a bloody toll on the boarders hung uselessly from their mountings.

Brutus came to his side.

'They are dead, Lord Bile,' he grunted. 'All dead.'

'Then find and kill more.' Bile pointed past the hulking beast-man, to where a vid-eye glared. 'And make sure we are not observed.'

'As you wish,' said Brutus. He turned, and opened fire, the heavy ripper gun shaking his arm as he shot the vid-unit to pieces. He grunted commands to his lesser kin to search out the ship's inward auguries.

'Porter, join me,' Bile voxed. 'Your moment is coming.'

Bile went to retrieve his bolt pistol, smiling at the howls of his beastmen echoing down the cargo corridor as their wave of violence spread deeper into the ship.

All was proceeding to plan.

Primus was forced to run through the ship. Internal transportation systems were behaving erratically. Lifters plummeted without warning. Bridges refused to extend. The transports that conveyed crew from one end of the vast craft to the other were locked hard to their monorails.

In places, fires were burning as circuits overloaded with surges of power. Cogitator brains cooked in their housings from want of cooling. Bedlam reigned.

Primus ignored the chaos and ran hard. The denizens of the ship stayed well clear.

'Marshal Iota, Marshal Iota.' He called and called again as he ran. He was going so fast he was panting by the time he secured a link to her.

'*Alpha Primus, I hear you. What by the sands of Mars is happening? I have limited data connection. Strategic situation unknown. I have not been able to reach the command deck.*'

'Belay my last order,' said Primus. 'We are under attack by Fabius Bile. Get all available personnel to the Vault Magnificans. Bile must be after the Sangprimus Portum. We cannot let it fall into his hands.'

Iota's voice buzzed out, and faded back in.

'*...have my compliance. We will strengthen defensive positions immediately. Where are you?*'

'Heading to the outer bounds. I have identified the most likely points of assault. I shall meet them head-on.'

A static-heavy vox message filled his helm.

'*Boarders assaulting deck seventy-three, quadrant delta-five.*'

Primus switched his feed to vid-capt systems on the deck. Nothing seemed amiss in the images, an internal view of a service access corridor running close to the outer hull skin. Then the image shook. Boarding torpedoes, he guessed. Moments later, the image whited out as melta-cutters burned their way into the corridor.

He turned to head them off, but a second message had him change direction again.

'*Lord Primus,*' Wocolos the Integerarian's deep voice reached him, remarkably stable. '*We are holding the infiltration code at bay within our comms systems. Time until–*'

A raucous buzzing drowned out his next words.

'Any contact with the archmagos dominus?'

'*None.*'

'Weapons and shields?'

'*All defensive systems remain offline, within and without. By the Omnissiah's grace, crucial life-sustaining systems remain active. For now, our priority is the drives. But listen, my lord, I have urgent*' news. *Fabius Bile is already aboard. A major attack is underway on hangar Epsilon-Zero.'*

'Can you give me visuals?' Primus demanded.

'Affirmative.'

Primus' sensorium painted a scene of violence. Gunfire was flashing everywhere across the deck. One of the ship's Arvus lighters had been hit and was burning fiercely. Skitarii Vanguard traded fire with the foe. Primus noted the enemy's fire seemed ineffective, then he saw the boarders were nothing but mutants, shambling monstrosities. Primus saw Bile for only a moment, radium rounds sparking off his power armour. An enormous, bull-headed beastman lumbered in front of Bile, shooting from an oversized hand cannon. The monster turned towards the vid-eye, raised his gun, and the feed cut out. Primus switched to other views, but these were also disabled rapidly. He saw a final clade of Vanguard fall beneath a thicket of bludgeons, and the last view was gone.

'I have eyes on Fabius Bile, moving to engage. Hangar Epsilon-Zero.' He widecast this message, partly in the hope any troops nearby would hear and divert there, but mainly so that the invaders heard him. A little pressure could lead to mistakes.

'What about deck seventy-three?' Wocolos voxed. *'We have boarders approaching multiple other sites.'*

'Marshal Iota will divert skitarii assets to intercept. I'm moving on Bile.'

'Do you require reinforcement? I can join you personally,' Iota voxed.

'No. I shall handle this myself,' Primus said. 'I doubt a single ancient Space Marine and his herd of gene-taints will pose much of a challenge to me.'

He upped his speed, racing the half a mile to where the arch-traitor was running amok.

CHAPTER TWENTY-THREE

HOUSE TARANIS SURROUNDED

Ion shields flared in a constant, blinding strobe. Weapons hammered the Knights from all sides. The Traitor Space Marines didn't have anything big enough to pose a real problem to the war engines. They kept back out of reach of the Knights' close-combat weapons, but they were an annoyance that was hard to ignore.

The daemon beasts were where the real danger lay.

Though they were an eclectic mix, Roosev recognised certain common patterns. Forgefiends kept up distance fire on House Taranis, sending dirty streams of corrupted plasma crashing into their ion shields. Defilers ran sideways, battlecannons booming, drawing closer with each pass. Roosev flagged them up for his men to prioritise, as they were even more dangerous up close. *Salutatia* engaged the longer-ranged machines in an artillery duel, the streams of its plasma pure blue to the forgefiends' dirty red. Its weapons kept them back, but its guns were Titan kill-ers, designed to bring down the largest machines. Although they annihilated whatever they hit, they were cumbersome, slow to fire. The forgefiends were nimble for things so heavily armed, and though three of them were burning wrecks, putting out columns of oily smoke, more often they danced aside from the volcano lance's laser beams, and dodged the splashes of super-heated matter sent forth by the plasma decimator.

To the Knights' advantage, very little of the enemy's fire got through their overlapping ion shields, and so far, they were holding their ground. Their relentless firing was keeping back the Space Marines, who had emerged onto a plain where they found few places to hide, and were being shot at from above thanks to the Knights' height. Otherwise the situation was dire. They were half blind, and they could not move out. In this matter, their ion shielding was a big disadvantage. As the lances were surrounded on all sides, they could not make use of their speed and mobility without exposing their unshielded and less well-armoured rear aspects. Large Knights like *Salutatia* excelled as firebases, solid pivots upon which a Knightly charge could turn. But not the others. It was not their role. Mobility was key to Imperial Knights, and it was denied to them.

Move, move, move, Maven the Very Elder wailed.

'I cannot, old man,' Roosev snarled angrily. *Iurgium* was furious, pulling at Roosev's mental reins. It was all Roosev could do to restrain it. He diverted the machine's fury towards an approach-ing Maulerfiend, a hobbling, doglike close-combat variant. He could not tell if it were he or *Iurgium* who loosed the stream of fire from the flame cannon, hot enough to melt plasteel and sear daemonic flesh.

A pack of smaller daemon-things took their chance, racing through the firestorm, evading detection thanks to the endless flaring of the ion shields. Roosev's first inkling was a moan from the chorus of his ancestors.

Beware! wailed the Very Elder, drawing Roosev's attention to a subtle ripple in his field harmonics as the pack passed through. He had a split second to react. A less experienced Knight would have missed it, but Roosev turned in time to see a skull-faced quadruped leaping at him.

Iurgium reeled backwards under the impact of the pouncing daemon machine. It gripped onto the housing of the reaper chainfist, hanging from the Knight's arm. Claws fashioned from a mixture of keratin and iron raked at plasteel. Such a limb, where sinew blended seamlessly with metal, should not exist, let alone function, nor should the burning light of hateful sentience in the skull-faced thing's eyes be possible, but it was there, trying to kill *Iurgium*, yet another horror born of Chaos unleashed upon the galaxy. Its talons ripped the Knight's loin banner to shreds, scratched at its paintwork, scouring free honour markings with vile, warp-corrupted steel. Jaws snapped at *Iurgium*'s face. Roosev twisted his own head back, and the Knight mimicked the move- ment, trying to keep the vital sensorium cluster out of harm's way. His reaper was pinned hard to his Knight's chest. He pushed at the daemon machine, meaning to free up the space to acti- vate the blade, but he could not. The daemon machine was too strong, too heavy. He felt a burst of sympathetic pain as another beast-thing closed its jaws around *Iurgium*'s shin plate, and then the burn of acidic venom eating into the Knight's machinery.

There was a thundering of feet, a heavy impact. The beast at his chest was impaled on a crackling shock lance. Roosev twisted with the hit, preventing the tip of the weapon carrying through into *Iurgium*'s own shoulder. *Contegeris* flashed past, taking the impaled daemon machine with it. Allacer overloaded the spear's disruption field, blasting the machine to pieces, and brought his gallop into check, swinging back round, small-arms fire spanking off the rear of his Knight ineffectually.

His reaper blade freed, Roosev sliced down into the monster savaging his leg. The chain track roared into life as it descended, not quite up to full speed when it hit. He more swatted away than cut the machine. It flipped, twisting its spine, to land neatly on all fours, showing the same agility as any flesh-and-blood felid. When it came at him again, Roosev was ready, the now roaring chainblade cutting through the creature in a welter of ichor, blood and oil.

A third member of the daemon pack was engaged in a delicate dance with *Vanitas*. Sir Mandus' chainsword blows hit only glancingly, his gatling cannon blasting up fountains of mud as the beast pranced away from it. He was breaking line, though thank the Omnissiah he had swung his ion aspect to the rear to cover his back.

'Mandus!' Roosev voxed.

Vanitas' sensors locked with his own ersatz eyes. Mandus understood, stepping *Vanitas* back to give Roosev a clear shot with his flame cannon.

Fire engulfed the daemon beast. It screamed loudly enough to be heard over the din of battle. Mandus riddled it with holes from his gatling cannon. As it tried to limp away, *Vanitas'* foot stamped the creature's head deep into the mud, stopping it dead.

'We can't stay here!' Allacer said, drawing himself level with Roosev, his shield front coming to rest a few feet from Roosev's. 'We are not made for standing in line. We have to charge.'

Attack, or perish! said the Very Elder.

Allacer was right. They could not maintain position. Though their ion shields were holding, it was only a matter of time before they would break, and they would be lost. Roosev surveyed the field. The enemy were bunched up now, attacking from all sides.

If they charged out, they might break through their lines and disrupt the attack. Then their mobility could come into play.

'Very well,' said Roosev. '*Danubia*, *Vanitas*, stay with *Salutatia*. Armigers too. Keep him free of melee. *Foebreaker*, *Contegeris*, charge on my mark. All other Knights, give covering fire when we break, then lap shields.'

He cast about for a suitable target. His sensors passed over the forgefiend packs.

Those, said the Very Elder, deep into the caverns of Roosev's mind.

'The forgefiends,' he voxed the others. 'They pose the greatest risk to the Knight Castellan.' *Iurgium*'s spirits lifted at the prospect of a charge, carrying Roosev's mood to giddying heights. 'Sir Doldurun!'

'Yes, lord scion?'

'Try to keep up.'

Blaring war-horns, Roosev set *Iurgium* into a charge. It needed little urging.

CHAPTER TWENTY-FOUR

FEAR THE MACHINE

If AsanethAyu hadn't announced herself, Cawl would have died. Properly died. She was a cryptek – she could have downed him from behind, and while he was helpless, she could have cracked his mental ciphers, and poured all manner of xenos filth into his systems. He doubted even he could have survived that.

Thank the Omnissiah for the all-too-human nature of these inhuman androids, he thought. She had to let him know who was going to kill him. That gave him time – picoseconds only, but that was enough – to reconfigure his energy shielding to absorb the gauss-bolt she flung from her hand at his head.

She was about to learn that even unarmed, Belisarius Cawl was far from harmless.

The discharge from the impact was spectacular. Her gauss stream was fragmented into a dozen arcs of crawling green lightning that crashed into the exhibits of the Museum Omnis, making them explode, and lighting up the hall with actinic starkness. Some were reflected back at her. His ocular systems were overloaded by the display, but so were hers. AsanethAyu screamed metallically as power raced through her metal frame, enough of a distraction for Cawl to charge at the cryptek. He was gratified at the sensation of shock she projected. She'd clearly expected him to die right then.

'Not dead!' he bellowed, amplifying the shout by a factor of ten and projecting it aggressively from the voxmitter bolted to his shoulder, turning his words into a sonic assault. Glass behind the cryptek exploded. Carefully curated pieces that had withstood aeons were sent toppling to the floor. And Cawl was still not done.

He threw himself at her. A dozen mechadendrites whipped forward. The lesser delivered bursts of debilitating power. The bigger ones he used to pick her up bodily, heft her over his head, and toss her across the room. Six hundred and ninety-eight pounds, his senses informed him she weighed, yet he threw her quite easily, his dendrite hive being made for industrial work. She let out a cry of anger as she slammed into the wall.

She was back on her feet instantly, her metal body undamaged.

'Do you intend to wrestle me into submission?' she scoffed. 'Brute force will not work.'

'I couldn't agree more,' said Cawl, and dove into his museum with stunning speed, his giant, mechanical body scattering exhibits everywhere. AsanethAyu chased the fleeing magos with a beam of buzzing gauss-fire which disintegrated layers off everything it touched. The ray cut out. Smoke drifted over smashed treasures.

From his hiding place a hundred yards away, Cawl dared a short scan pulse. It returned an image of AsanethAyu peering uncertainly around the hall.

She could not see him.

'I will find you!' she cried. 'I will kill you!'

'Oh no you won't,' said Cawl to himself, and set to work.

Iurgium and Roosev ceased to be two separate entities. By the will of the Omnissiah, the machine spirit of the venerable machine merged completely with the soul of Roosev and the echoes of previous Knights, creating a gestalt sentience imbued with the experience of centuries.

This was what true worship was. This was where the veil between the mundane and the sublime parted. Let others in the Cult modify their bodies with machinery. It was as nothing compared to this communion, the ultimate synthesis of man and machine. Roosev exalted in his new state, seeing out of *Iurgium*'s ocular sensors not at one remove, but as if they were truly his own. The Knight's limbs moved in perfect synchronicity with his thoughts. No longer was *Iurgium*'s rage a thing to be checked, but a part of him, a source of power and of righteous strength with which to smite the enemies of his god.

Fire roared from his cannon. He felt it as a warming in his limb. After combat, it was difficult to describe these sensations to those who had not experienced the soul-joining of warrior with war engine. His body was of metal, surging with the Motive Force. His arms were mighty weapons. It was more natural to sport heavy bolters, chainblade and flame cannon than it was to have fragile bone and muscle, tipped with feeble fingers. *Iurgium*'s contempt for flesh was clear to him. He accepted it, unequivocally, for the flesh was weak, and *Iurgium* was not.

The jet of flame engulfed a daemon engine. The unearthly powers of the warp held back the torrent but briefly. The daemon seemed to flicker and jump, not anchored fully to the material realm, and therefore not subject to its laws. But *Iurgium* plunged on, wielding its flame cannon like a lance, the conjoined wills animating the Knight pushing the jet of fire through to the creature as much as the momentum of a mounted man pushes a spear tip through the body of his foe.

False flesh ran like wax. Mechanical components gave out under the fierce heat. The daemon engine collapsed, screaming, its body dying. Warded chains on hatches burst, and out raced the spirit trapped within, shouting its hatred to the world before it was expelled back into the empyrean.

Iurgium was already past, trailing its fire as a pennant behind its mighty form. Reticules spun across Roosev-*Iurgium*'s vision, locking onto the things racing across the battlefield and dismissing them as unworthy of his attention.

He killed as he ran. Heavy bolters chattered death, blasting Heretic Astartes back. Short blasts from his flame cannon roasted traitors in their armour. The moor was ablaze. Thick white smoke obscured the melee, but still he ran on, sure of the path laid for him by his god. A Defiler turned to face him, claws raised in crablike threat. *Iurgium* was the larger and fiercer predator, its reach the greater. No matter that the thing piloting the Defiler was a daemon of the warp, *Iurgium*'s soul was given by the Machine God and driven by the righteous wrath of humanity.

Roosev-*Iurgium* swung his blade arm as he crossed paths with the Defiler, avoiding its clumsy flailing, and smashed the boxy torso from its legged carriage. Folded in by the force of the impact, chewed and rent by the great teeth of the blade, the torso bounced across the field, coming to rest in a black pool. Another furious cry, and another daemon was sent back to the warp.

In the name of the Omnissiah, he gave voice to his glory, blaring binharic songs of praise through his war-horn.

A dim apprehension of the overall battle was all the strategic picture Roosev had, not that he cared overly much. To pilot a Cerastus Acheron was to be blessed with ancient technology few possessed. The price for this honour was union with a fell and dolorous spirit, one which demanded surrender. Yet Roosev was also a prime scion of Taranis, a leader of men, and part of him, suppressed now in its turn as *Iurgium*'s rage had been before, noted the convergence of enemy assets on the pyramid designated as the meeting ground.

The traitors meant to slaughter as many of the magi as they could, of that he was sure.

Wailing songs of warning, he changed course, leaning his tall, beautiful mechanical body into the turn, elegant as a sprinter in a race. Again he sounded his horn, and *Iurgium* rejoiced to hear the answering songs of its brother Knights.

Fires were burning everywhere now, as *Salutatia* bombarded the plain, the potency of its plasma weaponry flash-drying sodden peat and setting it ablaze. Each shot from the Knight Castellan's main weapons left a burning trench in the ground. Small danger to creatures either made of metal or encased in it, but confusing to sensoria, and *Iurgium*'s view of the battlescape shrank. The part of *Iurgium* that was still Roosev could see no tactical sense to this conflict. It seemed a melee for the sake of fighting. It was not the first time he had seen the servants of the Great Enemy behave this way.

These thoughts were small, and quickly flooded out by *Iurgium*'s great wrath. Of far more import to the machine was that he find a worthy enemy.

He slowed a moment, scanning hard, then let out a joyous fanfare. Ahead was the perfect foe. A Space Marine, riding a machine beast spawned by unclean forges. He could feel the vile miasma of tainted noosphere around it, hear the corrupt strings of data directing the daemon engines into battle. Though his mount was small and puny compared to the great *Iurgium*, here was the lord of the machines, a disgraceful reflection of the Machine God's purity. For that he had to die.

Roosev-*Iurgium* did not hesitate, but accelerated to full charge, shield angled forward.

This was his first mistake.

The Space Marine turned in his saddle. The Helstrider beast he rode turned with him. A pathway was opened upon the surging rush of the higher spectra, and the Lord Discordant called out. A spear of polluted data slammed into *Iurgium*. There was no way to avoid it, for to hear it was to be infected, and *Iurgium* heard.

Together, *Iurgium* and Roosev felt pain. Chaotic impulses jammed cogitator commands, causing a critical failure cascade to race through the Knight's systems. Sensors whited out. Roosev's link to the noosphere disintegrated in a flurry of red-hot sparks. All over the great machine, motivator units went into spasm. *Iurgium* tripped, barely staying upright, leaning forward ever more as its momentum ran away with it. Its left foot landed badly, plunging far into the soft ground of the false world. Its right foot was slow in responding, too late to come up and push down, thrusting the Knight free of the mire. Instead its huge toes snagged, ripping up a furrow in the ground as *Iurgium* toppled.

The Knight hit the ground at speed, skidding several yards towards their now triumphant target. The impact jolted Roosev hard in his Throne Mechanicum, ripping at his spinal plugs. The pain was intense, and both he and *Iurgium* screamed as their soul bond was ruptured, and their personalities once more forced apart.

Roosev must have blacked out for a moment. When he came round, he was hanging from his throne restraints. Sparks fizzled in one corner of the cramped cockpit, filling the space with the eye-watering smoke of burning plasteks. Alarms peeped from every quarter. A detailed, tri-D model of *Iurgium* fizzed in the upper left of his hololithic display, multiple points flashing red with warnings. He breathed with difficulty. At least one of his ribs was broken, and his back was sticky with blood.

Shame, shame, shame, intoned the doleful voice of Maven the Very Elder.

'Allacer, brother...' Roosev coughed. The vox was inactive. The noosphere was a jumble of nonsense data. He could no longer see out of *Iurgium*'s eyes directly, and the small screens that his auguries fed into showed a much-narrowed view, the bottom half obscured with mud, most of the top blanked off by the Knight's carapace lip, which was jammed hard into the earth. *Iurgium*'s face was bent sideways on the ground at a dangerous angle. The strain on his neck connection would be near terminal.

The small field of vision the screens afforded showed nothing useful. Curls of smoke. Blades of grass twitching in the wind. A transhuman running by, boltgun trained on a target he deemed more pressing than the downed Knight.

Roosev craned his neck. His helm jammed on the back of his throne and the neck plugs pulled deep within his spine, making both him and his mount jerk with the pain.

To fall is ignoble, moaned his ancestor damningly.

'With all the respect due to you, sir, be silent!' said Roosev. He lifted a shaking hand and wrenched off his helm, dropping it onto the cockpit instrument board.

Removing it granted him enough space to crane his neck and look up through the cockpit glass, enough to see the Lord Discordant's mount stalking forward. Roosev blinked blood from his eyes. His enemy was an imposing warrior, twisted by mutation, bearing a chainbladed glaive in one massively swollen hand. His Helstrider mount was a hideous thing to behold – mostly mechanical, save for the nest of organics squirming around the foreparts in place of a head. These were half-fused to a mechanical proboscis that dripped iridescent liquors. The daemon machine scuttled unevenly towards him, taking half-steps sideways at random points, as if anxious of attack. The Chaos Space Marine mastered its nervousness with flicks of his reins. He, in contrast, projected an air of immense satisfaction.

The noosphere recoiled at the Chaos lord's presence. As he drew closer, more systems began to fail in the Knight. The secondary targeting displays went out.

Then came his voice, fell and full of triumph, hissing over the vox. Not broadcasted, this voice. Its words were fashioned directly from the buzz of static.

'You are bested, Knight,' he said. 'I am Lord Dandimus Thrule, master of machines and daemons both. Acknowledge your defeat at my hand and submit to me. Such things I could show you. Such uses I could put you to. Such power could be yours.'

Though Thrule's mutated head was twisted upon his neck, his eyes were so arresting, his helm-lenses glowing with an inner light, looking deep into Roosev's soul. A soothing hiss came out of the vox. Roosev felt the data-cant embedded within it, alive with unnatural energies. He felt *Iurgium*'s furious spirit tremble, and calm.

The Helstrider came closer. The liquids ran freely from its mouthparts, salivating in anticipation of the feast to come.

'Throne of the Omnissiah, damn you,' Roosev said. 'You will not take us.' He took his eyes from the enemy, refusing to be mesmerised. His head swam with concussion, but years of training and an intimate bond with his machine had his hands moving quickly over the banks of switches in front of him, disengaging his mind from the Throne Mechanicum and shifting its operation to emergency manual controls. 'Come, my faithful partner in war. Rouse yourself. Do not listen to him, o *Iurgium*!' He sang quick benedictions to smooth this most desperate of operations, and was rewarded by the shifting of his display lights from blue to red.

'There is a universe of opportunity for those who embrace the true *gods. For those who will not, there is only death,'* Thrule said, and now the voice sounded not from the vox, but within Roosev's head. Several mechadendrites rose above the lord's back, and curled forward.

Roosev grasped the levers set at the side of his throne. The pressure from the pedals changed subtly. It was impossible to pilot a Knight without a neural link, but it was possible to alter the balance between mental and physical input. As his union with *Iurgium* diminished further, he experienced great sadness, but also relief, for the powers of the Lord Discordant afflicted the Knight suit, not its pilot.

'For the love of Mars, my bold steed, move!' he pleaded, and pushed upon his controls.

Nothing happened. Roosev gave a cry, ramming the levers back and forth, but they might as well have been the wooden training rig he had spent much of his infancy within, playing at his future life.

'That's it, that's it.' Thrule reached *Iurgium*, speaking as if to an injured animal. He reined in his salivating beast, turning it sideways. The side of it filled the cockpit window, rippled flesh and metal stamped with thousands of tiny, glowing runes. Thrule slid his chainglaive into a holster welded to his monstrous mount's side, reached out, and placed his hand flat upon the top of the war engine.

A fizz of power surged through *Iurgium* and into Roosev. It hit him fully with the might of the unbridled Motive Force, but this was no clean source of life, but a black current from the wellsprings of the warp.

Roosev's vision flashed, and he found himself facing Thrule upon a plain of bones and steel. A red sky above raced with tortured, phantom faces. The Chaos lord was free of armour, clad in furs like a barbarian king, fully revealing the horror of his twisted body. His oversized hand rested upon the hilt of an upturned axe. It was toothed, like a cog, like the axes of the magi, but where the Machina Opus should be, as a boss in the centre of the blade, was a leering daemonic face. Gore caked it all.

Thrule's malformed features gloated at him.

'Oh,' Thrule said. *'So many pretty machines. So many vessels for my slaves from the warp to dwell within. You shall be their plaything.'*

Faint jabs in his skin. Roosev looked at his hands, and saw that his body in that place was a disgusting fusion of man and machine, part human, part *Iurgium*. Not in the pure manner of joining the Throne Mechanicum permitted, but a haphazard melding. He felt *Iurgium* in him, caged. Something was intruding into his veins, and he knew that subversive scrapcodes were racing for *Iurgium*'s cogitator brain, to rework it in a darker image.

No.

The voice was overwhelming. Mighty beyond bearing, but he knew it. Maven the Very Elder's voice, as he had never heard it before. A sheet of pure lightning cut the sky, and it bled, and more light fell in blessed streams of numeric data-code, hissing upon the ground where they touched.

No.

The old man materialised in front of Roosev, huge as a giant, dressed in archaic knight's armour. The holy cables of union dangled from his spinal rig, shining silver.

No! We deny you! Begone!

Maven the Very Elder held up his hand. Roosev felt the hot fever of Thrule's intrusion withdraw from his veins. The Chaos lord gave a frustrated shout, and Roosev was tumbling away from that awful landscape, back into the hell of the now.

He awoke with bleeding eyes. There was movement. *Iurgium* was stirring.

Now, scion, now! Maven the Very Elder intoned in his mind.

Iurgium let out a noise through its war-horn that sounded much like a moan of pain. Roosev grasped the controls once more and drew a shuddering breath.

'By the will of the Omnissiah,' he said, 'let mechanism move and gear mesh. Let oil flow and fuel burn. By the gift of the Motive Force, let servo catch and joint swivel. Let cogitator think and augur see.' He pushed upon the pedals. They were tense with potential.

Iurgium moved. Light fell into the cockpit as Thrule pulled back from the stricken Knight, and drew once more his ugly glaive.

'By the might of the Machine God, let reactor kindle and weapons engage! By the command of the three in one, let the enemies of mankind fall!'

Iurgium let out a blaring war-horn call. He felt the great Knight's spirit meshing with his own again, its fear gone. Clumsily, for the manuals gave only graceless control, Roosev moved the flame cannon forward and pushed upon it as a fallen man might push upon his palm to regain his feet. The great weight of the war machine bent the barrels then broke them with a rending squeal, rupturing the feed seals in the process, so that promethium emptied rapidly from the twin tanks set upon *Iurgium*'s back, and pooled in rainbow slicks upon the ground. The sacrifice of the weapon got the Knight up enough that he could drag one foot forward, and with another push the torso out of the sucking mud. *Iurgium* was on its knees, but upright nonetheless.

The Lord Discordant wheeled around on his beast, still trying his infernal tricks, slow to realise his technomagic no longer had any hold over the machine's noble spirit. The displays on Roosev's instrument board ignited with soft, holy lights, but Roosev had less and less need of them. The mind bridge between him and the machine was reconnecting, becoming stronger by the second. More fluidly now, he raised the reaper blade and its heavy bolters, the guns aimed squarely at his enemy.

They regarded each other a moment. Smoke billowed around them. From every quarter came the roar of war. Yet in their shared space was a moment of calm.

'You choose death. I must respect that.' The fallen lord's voice oozed over the airwaves with malevolent sincerity. *'In honour of your courage, I shall make sure it hurts.'*

The Helstrider pounced. Before Roosev could restrain the soul of his enraged mount, *Iurgium* opened up with the ruptured flame cannon, and the world exploded in fire.

CHAPTER TWENTY-FIVE

A CONUNDRUM

Cawl allowed himself another short scan pulse. The cryptek had come after him poorly prepared. She'd hit him with gauss technology, powerful compared to Imperial baseline stuff, but entirely quotidian by necron standards. He wondered why. She was a chronomancer, a being who could wield time as a weapon. Her own wargear was long lost, but Cawl had examples of the tools of her caste in his archive, some fine ones not far from where her prison was, in actual fact. His plan had always been to turn her and have her help him.

He could only surmise that she'd been too bent on revenge to have a proper look around. Or perhaps she'd found the paraphernalia – necrons did have a sense for their own tech – but could not get at it, which meant his crypto-locks on their vault had held. He'd based them on the necrons' own tesseract technology, with his own improvements, naturally; the intention being that even the necrons themselves wouldn't be able open them.

Yes, he thought. *That must be it.* Neither Bile's allies nor the captive had been able to outwit him. Not fortune then, but his own genius had saved him!

His spirits lifted somewhat as he considered his brilliance. There was no better test than a live test, and this was a test that was livelier than most. He judged he had passed with flying colours.

Auspex returns were sketchy, but he could not allow himself a full augur soak. She would track him down immediately, tracing the particle waves right back to his hiding place. But it was enough for him to ascertain that she had two of the scarabs that had guarded her tomb fused together in her hand, their feeder arrays reconfigured to make a workable pistol. He would never cease to be impressed by the adaptability of the necrons' technology.

Two could play at that game. He needed to make something to take her down, but what? That was the conundrum. He searched his memory for a catalogue of the museum's contents. It was, predictably, lacking, the victim of an impulsive data-purge or one of the incidents when hostile agents had messed with his mind.

He needed time. To get it, he needed to make her talk.

Cawl was good at talking. He patched into the ship's systems via the main info-structure of the chamber. Hardwired, so to speak. Harder to catch him that way. Through multiple data-casters he took control of the still-dazed cyber-cherubs flapping about the room. Though he was alarmed by the amount of subversive code coursing through the *Zar Quaesitor*'s systems, he forced himself to concentrate on the task in hand. One problem at a time.

'My dear AsanethAyu!' he said, projecting his voice through one of the cherubs. AsanethAyu locked onto it and blasted it out of the air. Fizzing chunks of flesh, feather and metal rained down, disintegrating greenly before they hit the floor, like a fall of digital snow.

'Shall we try that again?' he said, bringing forward another disposable drone. He watched her through the eyes of the cyborg. She was alert in her hunt, but she did not shoot this one from the air.

'There is no merit to discussion,' she said. 'There is only merit in your death.'

'I disagree,' said Cawl. He felt her alien, informatic senses reach out for him across the noosphere. 'You won't find me easily,' he said. 'And every minute that passes returns a higher probability of defeat for you.'

She swung her long metal skull face around the room. The sole eye glinted balefully. Unbound, her long, thin skeletal form seemed frailer somehow. Lacking the eerie glow of the tesseract bonds, the alloys that made her were dull with corrosion from her aeons-long sleep. Cawl had the impression of something weary that needed to complete one last task, and the will to do so was all that was keeping it alive.

She was dangerous yet.

'It also gives me greater opportunity to find you,' she said. 'You are unarmed. You were foolish not to don your war panoply. Did you fear to upset the other insects you went to converse with? Another sign of weakness. You should show strength, always!'

Cawl snagged the slave signal of one of the downed servo-skulls Fabius Bile had suborned. *Bile!* he thought; so much had happened. Very carefully, he reset its cogitator and coaxed it back to life.

'Diplomatic techniques have moved on a little in the last million years or so. You should try being friendly. It reaps great reward,' he said.

'Necrons have no need for friends,' she said. 'There is only the vanquished, and the vanquisher.' She turned suddenly, loosing a shot from her improvised pistol at a large display case holding the mounted exoskeleton of an insectoid being – something else Cawl could not recall the name of, but he winced anyway as the gauss-beam stripped away the atoms of case, creature and armature, causing the whole thing to collapse in shards of chitin and glass. It had no doubt been priceless.

He maintained his bravado nevertheless. 'You'll have to try harder than that!'

'Goading me will not distract me,' she said. She moved, her heavy metal feet crunching Cawl's shattered memories. Cawl now had the servo-skull up, sweeping low through the endless rows of glass cases.

'Will you not just hear me out?' he said. There. Ahead. Something he could use. A humanoid machine carriage, mounted on a stand. A chunky brass plaque read *Qvo-02*.

There wasn't much left. He'd favoured more organics back then, and they had long since decayed to dust. But the metal skeleton upon which he had moulded the likeness of his friend might still be functional. He had the skull approach and extend a tiny mechadendrite to a socket in the back of Qvo-02's skull. Danger increased, as the servo-skull had risen to head height to do so, where there was less cover. He bit back a breath of relief as the input spike mated with the socket, and the skull returned a thread of data from the machinery inside. It was at least nine thousand years old, but he built to last.

'What have you to say to me that you have not bored me with before? You want us to work together,' AsanethAyu said in a sing-song, mocking tone. 'You want to use my superior sciences to win glory for yourself in the eyes of the other primates who gambol through the ruins of my empire. I refuse again.'

'You always put such a negative spin on things,' said Cawl. 'I want to save the galaxy. Seeing as you live in it, that means saving you too.'

Qvo-02 was empty of life and mind. The butchered clone brain that Cawl had used to start his reconstruction of Friedisch was long gone. But the electronic architecture necessary to drive the thing was still in place. Cawl slipped into it as if stepping into a comfortable pair of shoes. Not that he'd worn shoes for several millennia.

AsanethAyu came to a stop, casting about again, still unsure.

'Do you wish to see all this reality fall to Chaos?' Cawl's drones said to her. He had three of them descend, and circle her, each speaking fragments of his message in turn. 'You necrons seemed to put a lot of effort into ensuring that would never happen.'

Now, he needed a weapon. Fortunately for him, there were a lot of weapons in the Museum Omnis. It was just a question of finding one that worked.

He risked a peek, and spotted one not too far away. A short carbine utilising plasma tech. No power source, but he could provide that from his own reactor. He just had to reach it.

'Have you figured that out all by yourself?' AsanethAyu said. 'How clever your species is, not yet out of second stage intelligence, and making such wise and solemn judgement.'

'It is true,' said Cawl. 'We are stronger as allies.'

'We defeated the Old Ones. We devoured our gods. We have no need of allies. We have no need of friends. Only slaves and prey. Nothing else.'

'Quite,' said Cawl. He flung his cyber-constructs at AsanethAyu and set Qvo-02's ragged old body into motion. It staggered off its stand, crashed into a man-sized clay tablet, sending it to fragments on the ground. AsanethAyu was firing already as Qvo-02 broke into a madcap sprint. His limbs were barely functional. He had not been lubricated for tens of centuries. Cawl was surprised he got as far as he did.

AsanethAyu downed the ancient facsimile with a triumphant shout. It exploded into pieces being eaten at by gauss discharge. She broke into a run, shoving Cawl's possessions aside, but when she reached the downed Qvo-02, she reared back, and made a noise of frustration.

'A mechanism!' She spun around, to find Cawl rising up behind her.

'My dear alien monster, you underestimate the utility of friendship,' Cawl said, the xenos plasma carbine grasped in his manipulators. 'Friedisch will do anything for me, even when he's dead.'

She was fast. They opened fire at the same time.

Cawl's plasma stream took her in the top of the chest. She was weakened without her equipment. The shot vaporised the top of her torso and her neck, and her head fell off, cracking the marble floor with a loud and undignified clang.

Her shot hit Cawl in the side. He yelped as corrosive energies ate into his body. There was no impact to speak of, just acidic, searing agony. It was the first pain he had experienced for a long time.

He had time to shut down his pain receptors, but the residual discharge corroded through something important before finally dissipating, and his control over his lower carriage vanished. His multiple legs folded into themselves, suddenly powerless. Cawl collapsed heavily onto the ground.

He lay sprawled, paralysed on the shattered glass and broken artefacts of his museum. He had no communication with his crew. His ship was being driven into a catastrophic collision, and one of the worst beings in the galaxy had his eyes on the Emperor's secrets.

'Well, this is sub-optimal,' he grumbled.

* * *

Qvo passed his eyes over the data-stream. Such noospheric constructs were always difficult to comprehend. It was his mind that had pasted a sort of understandable reality over the pure mathematics that made up informational space, and there was no way of knowing how representative it really was. He floated around it as a man in a dream. Awareness of what was happening outside came and went, all rather overshadowed by the crushing discomfort of having a data-spike poked into his brain.

Whatever Alixia was doing seemed to keep her mind off Qvo, either that or she didn't think him a threat. Her mistake, Qvo told himself. The sentiment fell flat. He'd always lacked Cawl's confidence, even when he'd been a real person.

'Don't question it, just get on with it,' Qvo said to himself.

He rose up through layers of shadow-selves, each of them trapped in their own individual slice of the past. Which iteration they were, he could not say. Did it really matter? He wondered if it did. He worried if it did. His thoughts turned briefly to Qvo-88, off on his way to Imperium Nihilus. It was unusual to have two of them abroad at once. What would it be like to meet himself? He supposed that was moot. It would never happen, because he was pretty certain once he severed the link with the data-looms back upon the ship, that would be it for Qvo-89, and the next time he thought these things he'd be Qvo-90.

'If the next Qvo would actually be me,' he said, then grew irritated by the whole thing.

The interface was before him as a throbbing ball of possibility. Within, the motes of creation held in superpositional states, not the yes/no simplicity of ones and zeroes, but a collection of infinite maybes.

Because he was looking at them, some of them would be collapsing into a determined state, and it would be as if they had always been so, and in that way every sentient being was totally free and completely enslaved.

Hesitantly, he extended his hand into the flow.

It tickled weirdly. He supposed in that space he was data too, and the subordination commands Alixia was pumping into the Ark Mechanicus flowed through the very stuff of his being. Was this his soul, he wondered, a simple stream of decisions taken? Was that what everyone's soul was? Collapsing particle states, making certainty from nothing?

He closed his eyes and followed the flow, finding it rushing into his data-looms and from there into the *Zar Quaesitor*'s informational spaces, suborning the ship's systems and filling its noosphere. Qvo was taken aback a moment at how much access Cawl had given him; he who was nothing more than a half-man, the dream of someone who used to be. His life was worth nothing, because his was no life.

Still, Cawl's efforts were touching. He was really trying.

'I'm doing this for you, Belisarius,' he said.

Gritting imaginary teeth, he plunged his nominal hand deeper into the light, and squeezed all those maybes into a definite, solitary negative.

He went with them into blackness.

Cawl groaned and opened his eyes. His fingers twitched. His auto-repair systems were going into overdrive. Metal nerves re-formed. His components were coming back under his control. He thought he might move his head, and when he tried it worked, so he looked down his side. His mechadendrite hive was hard at work, patching up the worst of the damage. *Give it five minutes*, he thought with a grin, *and I'll be back on my feet*.

There was another groan, this time from the ship, and a subtle yet detectable change in motion.

'The thrusters. They're off!' He pushed himself up on his hands. Various bits of himself protested. He was still paralysed from the waist down, but whereas a normal man might drag useless legs behind himself, Cawl was attached to something close in weight to a battle tank. He was going nowhere.

The lumens clunked on decisively, buzzing as they came up to full brightness.

'Lumens!' he said. He had a much clearer view of the mess AsanethAyu had made of his museum. 'Are we back in control?' He tried a noospheric link, got nothing. With a mechadendrite he scrabbled through the wrack on the floor. It found a port, plugged in, and Cawl pushed his consciousness out into the ship.

Sure enough, the *Zar Quaesitor* was free of invasive machine spirits. Its network was stuttering, as multiple systems attempted to reactivate themselves, but the situation had improved.

'Vox!' he said, and put through a line to the command deck. 'Hello, hello, this is your archmagos speaking. I would like a brief situation report, if you please.'

'Archmagos Cawl? You're alive!'

'Of course I am, Wocolos. It's not like you to be so melodramatic,' said Cawl. 'I've had some difficulties but they have been resolved. Report now, please.'

'We have regained control. However they got in, that route has been closed. Shields are coming online. We will have weapons control within five minutes. I assume you wish us to remove Bile's ship from the void?'

'Ah, so you know about him.'

'The Sangprimus Portum is secure. Magos Iota has the vault locked down. A macroclade stands at guard. There is no conceivable way Bile can get through with the resources he has at hand.'

A sudden thrill of disquiet gripped Cawl. Here was a puzzle.

It did seem rather foolish, all this. Bile announcing himself and his intentions, attacking so openly. Neither asking for the material nor attempting to take it had any chance of success whatsoever. Unless, of course…

'Oh no. Where's Primus?' Cawl asked urgently.

'He left the command deck to me, my lord,' said Wocolos, sensing Cawl's unease and switching into binharic to speed their dialogue. *'He has gone to repel the boarders. Bile himself has come aboard. It would be a great victory for the Imperium if he were to be slain.'*

'No, no, no! The Machine God curse my circuits,' said Cawl. He pushed at the ground. His massive carriage remained inert. He strained hard, grunting. 'I will guess right now that he went alone.'

'Yes, Primus was insistent that the majority of the effort be put into defending the Sangprimus Portum. Many boarding parties were sent aboard. It looks like Bile planned a multi-front attack. They are all contained.'

'And I would also say you cannot raise Primus via the noosphere or the vox.'

'No my lord. The area of the ship he has gone into is still lacking communication.'

'That's because Bile is jamming it.'

'Archmagos?'

'Bile told me that he was going to take the Sangprimus Portum. Primus guessed that, didn't he? It's obvious, after all. *Too* obvious. Bile told me what he was doing, because that's not what he's going to do!' He strained again. This time, one of his larger feet moved, scraping loudly on the marble floor. 'It's a trap, Wocolos! Bile is not after the Sangprimus Portum, because he knew he would not be able to get to it. It's too heavily defended.'

Another heave. He cried out with the effort, then something snapped into place, the spinal interface finally engaged, and his feet burst into activity, twisting him painfully. There was a tearing in his uninjured side where fibre bundles parted from ancient nerves, forcing him to reroute his bio-signals, but in a moment he was back up, leaning awkwardly, hand pressed to the gauss wound while mechadendrites continued to work on the damage. A supplementary limb lifted the plasma carbine up from the ground. A number of tentacular limbs welded it into place upon one of the archmagos' weapons mounts.

'But Primus… In Primus is everything I have done to make the Primaris Space Marines, and more. Every secret, every trick is encoded in his gene-seed. Omnissiah save us!' He lurched forward, grimacing at the pain and his pitiful pace, going over to the cryptek's head. Already, AsanethAyu's body showed signs of regenerating. Cawl plucked up the head and moved it away from the body. 'Fabius Bile is not interested in the original material,' he continued, 'because he does not need the original material.

'He is going to take Primus instead.'

CHAPTER TWENTY-SIX

PRIMUS ATTACKS

Primus encountered the first of Bile's mutants in a stairwell leading down to the main cargo routes. Three small beastmen, starved scrawny, bloodied hands clutching shiny things pillaged from the dead. The worth of this loot was dubious, and it was thoroughly smirched with gore, yet they seemed well pleased by it. They did not get to enjoy it for long.

When they heard Primus thundering down the stairs like an avalanche of ceramite, they turned to see. It was the last thing they ever did. They had enough time to appear frightened, not enough to react.

Primus needed no weapons to deal with pathetic abhumans like these. He leapt down one flight of steps, taking one in the chest with his foot, bearing the creature down to the ground and crushing him flat under his enormous armoured weight. As he landed, he turned, his right fist punching forward and connecting with the head of the second creature. It flew away from him, coming off the neck, the body spraying filthy blood. The shattered remains hadn't even hit the wall before Primus' left elbow connected with the shoulder of the last, cowering beast, snapping its collarbone and powering down into the ribcage. The wizened thing folded into itself, bones shattered, insides jellied.

<Aggressional episode, three point two seconds,> his armour reported. Threat detectors activated, numbers scrolling at the edge of the eyeline. They returned green signifiers. Readouts of his blood chemistry ran across his vision.

<No threat in range,> the armour's machine spirit stated.

A moment of quiet stole up on him. His pharmacopoeia rebalanced his systems. Blood dripped loudly.

Primus upped the gain on his auto-senses to maximum. Now he could hear the boarders rampaging through the vessel in many directions. They must have dispersed, seeking violence and flesh to devour. What was the traitor thinking? Taking an objective on a ship the size of the *Zar Quaesitor* required careful planning, an exact application of force, and a clear extraction route. From what he'd seen so far, Bile had none of that. All of his followers were going to die for nothing.

With luck, the old monster would be joining them.

The lumens in the stairwell flickered. The motion of the ship changed. The binary assault had been thwarted, one way or another.

Primus opened his vox.

'Wocolos. Do you have control? Do you have Bile's location?'

A blank, soundless return. Not even static.

'Wocolos, respond.'

Nothing. Still no communications then.

Trusting to Iota to keep the Sangprimus Portum safe, he continued towards the primary target.

* * *

If Qvo thought his time was done, he was about to be disappointed. The first hint that he was still alive was the thunderous rattle of heavy stubber fire. It was a rather poor show, all things considered.

He reactivated – came round didn't really seem an appropriate term for him – lying on his back, looking up into a gun barrel. Instinctively, he raised his hands.

'Don't shoot?' he ventured. His visual centres were compromised. All he could see was the gun.

'I knew it! I knew you were in league with the enemy!'

'Magos Frenk?' Qvo said. He blinked. His sensors recalibrated, and he saw Frenk leaning over him. There was a lot of shooting going on nearby. He could smell blood and spilled lubricants.

Frenk's gun did not waver. Qvo refocused on Frenk's eyes, which seemed even more insane than before.

'I shall be taking you into custody. You shall provide evidence against your master if you do not wish to suffer torments unimaginable!'

'I'm sorry, but is that shooting? What's going on?' Qvo got up. Frenk brandished the gun, but did not shoot. 'Do stop that,' said Qvo. 'Either shoot me or put it away.'

'I am an agent of the...'

'Shush. Please,' said Qvo. 'I'm past caring.' Though he kept his hands in the air, out of habit.

There was a dead servitor on the floor. Qvo followed a trail of blood to another, and another, then he realised that the whole of the depression around the webway gate was full of shattered corpses. Among them were a couple of dead Dark Mechanicum tech-priests. He could not see Alixia-Dyos.

The noise of gunfire was coming from above. A Kastelan robot stomped past the lip of the pit, gunfists held out in front of it spitting phosphor-bright rounds. It stopped, set its feet, and swung its cognis flamer in an arc, targeting something Qvo could not see.

'Magos! You have recovered!' Oswen shouted down from the hall of pillars. He had a pistol in his hand. For such a bookish little man, he seemed unduly excited by the battle.

'Yes, well. I am made of sterner stuff than most,' shouted Qvo. He did not correct Oswen's misuse of the title magos. Giving Frenk an inkling of what he actually was really would lead them into all manner of problems. Oswen waved and moved off.

'I take it the Dark Mechanicum's attempt to take this facility is going to be unsuccessful?'

'Get up there,' Frenk said, waving his gun.

'I'm not on their side!' said Qvo. 'Don't you think we should do something about that rather than worrying about me?' He waved his head at the gate.

Frenk looked at it then at Qvo.

'That is an open gate into an enemy ship. The very least I'd do is shut it. Unless you have a large bomb we could send through there? That would be even better. And the columns up there. They're all resonating. I'll bet this isn't the sole opening this machine has made into the webway. We should deal with this here, at source, right now.'

Frenk looked up to where the battle was petering out.

'Get X99 down here and let him decide, if you don't trust me.'

'You're right, I don't. I don't trust him either. He's another servant of Cawl.'

'Deal with the gate. Let's argue later. What happened to the female magos?'

'I don't know. Escaped back through the gate, I imagine. When we arrived, we saw many of them retreat into there. They left their servitors behind.'

'Well then, shut it up now before they come back with rein-forcements, maybe?'

Frenk gave him a hard look, then tapped a vox-link set into his arm. 'Don't think this means I'll let you go.'

'Of course.'

They waited a few minutes. There were rather a lot of servitors up in the column forest, and the Kastelans went about destroy-ing them with mechanical thoroughness.

When X99 arrived, there was a short debate about the solution to be employed regarding the gate. In the end, the Mechanicus dealt with the problem in the time-honoured manner of having their robots smash it to pieces. It transpired that even hybrid alloys could not withstand a pummelling from half a dozen power fists. Nor, for that matter, could the mechanisms con-trolling the pillars.

The gate collapsed with a disappointing fizzle. The columns ceased singing.

After that was accomplished, they headed upwards.

Primus roared as he entered the main cargoway to the port-side hangar decks, his vox-caster amplifying his war cries into shocking blasts of sound, scattering beastmen back into the rooms they had been looting. The braver ones Primus employed his chainsword upon. The diamond-edged teeth sheared through their feeble weapons and limbs alike. Blood and gobbets of flesh sprayed up the walls in dripping arcs.

A larger example, taller by a horned head than his brethren and heavily muscled, caught Primus' weapon with the polearm he carried. This was entirely of metal, with a vibroblade head fashioned like an axe. Primus' chainsword skated down the metal, leaving bright tracks upon it. The beastman stepped back and around, overbalancing the Space Marine, swinging his weapon in for the kill, but his follow-up strike rang off Primus' forearm, and the Space Marine backhanded the mutant, snapping its muzzle round so hard its neck broke.

A few others stood their ground. Among them were creatures armed with lasguns and autoguns, and they took shelter behind a rank of their fellows carrying swords and metal-hafted spears.

Primus charged at them headlong. Bullets ricocheted off his armour. Las-beams scored molten tracks into ceramite. Nothing they had could breach his war plate easily, and he hit them full pelt and unharmed, knocking them aside like skittles. Those around his impact site went down as if he'd tossed a grenade among them, bones shattered, bleating horribly as he trampled over them. Threat alarms wailed in his helm as the remaining beastmen shot at him at point-blank range. They died for their troubles.

The swift slaughter he inflicted was too much for the remainder's morale, and they too broke and ran, following their kin deeper into the Ark Mechanicus.

Primus marked the positions of the routes they had taken on his armour's cartograph. They would need hunting down later. The last thing they needed were tribes of mutants establishing themselves somewhere in the massive vessel.

He went on, more cautiously now, paying close attention to his armour's auto-senses. The corridor was poorly lit by emergency lumens. Most of the ship's systems were still offline. Lacking active atmosphere-recycling, the air was growing hot and stuffy. He passed sentry guns inactive in their turrets in the wall.

There was a junction up ahead, where a transverse route crossed the principal cargo corridor. One of the trolleys that carried containers had stopped halfway across the main way. It was a good place for an ambush.

Primus slowed, took out his bolt pistol. He felt ahead with

his psychic senses. Sure enough, there were several ambushers waiting for him.

The corridor echoed with feedback as he activated his voxmitter.

'Come out. I know you are there. Cease hiding and get on with it,' he said. His voice boomed down the corridor.

A huge creature stepped out, taller than Primus, more massive than an ogryn. It was the mutant he had seen in the vid-feed from the hangar. In form it was part human, part bovine, an uncanny match for the Minoan hybrid of ancient legend. It was so heavily muscled its bull's head seemed to sprout from its shoulders without the intervention of a neck. A wide baldrick, primitive iron armour plates, belt and loincloth were its only garments. In one hand it carried a massive, double-bladed axe, wide as Primus' torso, that crackled with disruption lightning. In the other it bore a custom ripper gun, supplied by a large circular magazine. The shoulder strap dangling beneath it carried several more rounds in loops, each as large as a heavy grenade. It wore a brooch that looked like it carried a refraction field and the entirety of the forearm was covered in a vambrace set with noctilith crystals. Primus felt their anti-psychic field from all the way up the corridor.

'You are looking for me?' it said. It spoke thickly, with difficulty, its tongue too big for its mouth, yet it managed somehow to convey its amusement at the man coming for it. 'You find me. Now I, Brutus, will kill you.'

'If you say so,' said Primus. The creature's cohorts were getting into position. He charged anyway.

He opened fire as he ran, five bolts that raced ahead of him on bright points of fire. The air around the beastman flared with the reaction of the refractor field a couple of feet short of the thing's chest. Slow ripples spread from each impact point, and the bolts blew, the energy released diverted around it in leaping patterns.

The beastman did not so much as flinch at the explosions. His own gun was already swinging up to draw a bead upon Alpha Primus. His brutish finger squeezed on the trigger.

A ripper gun was little more sophisticated than a rapid-fire shotgun, a sturdy weapon that could withstand the ungentle attentions of the ogryns they were issued to. The rounds it fired, however, were large, and hammered into Primus' armour. It took him a moment to realise that unlike an ogryn, the beast was a passable shot, and was managing to train the notoriously inaccurate gun on Primus' left side, trying to upset his stride, even break the armour. The impacts staggered him, shaking his vision and provoking a wary peep of alarm from the machine spirit. He clenched his jaw to stop his teeth breaking, but still he came on.

The gun ran through its fifteen rounds in a single burst. By then Primus was within ten feet of the beastman. His cohorts lumbered out of the cross tunnel from both sides, around the stranded cargo conveyor. They were big, not as tall or broad as Brutus but still massive with genetically enhanced strength. Their veins strained close to bursting. Their eyes bulged out of their heads. Tall glass injector units clustered around the tops of their backs, the thick, luminous liquids in them rapidly draining as they were pumped into the creatures' bodies.

These were men, all but one of standard baseline type, granted momentary power by their wicked lord. Bile's famed New Men, Primus supposed. They did not look so daunting, coming together and then forward in a mob. The beastman Brutus stepped back with a bestial smile, calmly reloading his magazine from the bandolier swinging from the gun.

Primus slew the first of the enhanced with a downward slash of his chainsword. Guts unravelled from its torn belly, but it was unimpaired by this mortal wound, and its twitching hands raked at Primus' armour. Primus had intended to knock through them, and tackle their bull-headed leader, but he was slowed by them, their bulked-up bodies arresting him, and they leapt on his back, forcing him to his knees. His chainsword chewed through another of the warriors, spattering them all with a slurry of ground-up flesh, but then the tooth track encountered metal implants, caught, and stalled.

Primus disappeared under a heaving mass of limbs. In a frenzy, the drugged warriors ripped at him until their hands bled.

'Too easy,' Primus heard Brutus say, followed by the crisp snap of the refilled magazine slotting back into place.

Fingers pulled at Primus' armour; they were strong enough to rip it away, but the enhanced had put themselves at a disadvantage in their lust for his destruction. They could not get the leverage to breach his battle plate. Still, Primus remained trapped, and so he switched tactics. He closed his eyes, breathed deep, and reached out past the bodies writhing on top of him, out past the ship, out past the void.

Out into the warp.

A flash of lilac announced the birth of a force dome that flung the enhanced humans aside even as it blasted them to pieces. They disintegrated, bits of muscle and scraps of skin plastering the walls. Primus stood, steaming with power and evaporating blood, surrounded by a perfect circle of scorched floor.

'Now you,' said Primus.

'You are a witch,' said Brutus. 'You look at me with hate. But we are the same. Your twist is inside, is all.'

'I look upon you with the hatred I feel for all evil men, no matter their form,' said Primus.

'We are better than men,' said Brutus, 'our masters make us so. They should be brothers.'

'Cawl is nothing like Bile,' Primus said.

Brutus fired his ripper gun.

Primus stood, enclosing himself in a shining skin of psychic energy, stopping ripper slugs dead. Two got through, but they were so spent they did little more than plink off his armour.

Brutus threw his gun aside, and touched the amulet. A crackle of energy sped up his arm, and the sense of psychic dimming grew more intense. 'I prefer blade to blade anyway,' he said, setting his axe in front of himself.

Primus attacked. The beast's amulet disrupted his psychic powers, but it made no difference. He wanted to finish this thing with his hands, not his mind. Only then would he prove himself the creation of a better man.

He came in hard. The beast responded, swinging his axe over his head and down in a punishing arc. Primus moved aside at the last instant. The axe thumped into the deck with a deafening explosion as its disruptor field annihilated a patch of metal two feet across. Primus punched with his bolt pistol, hitting the beast on the jaw. He staggered back, but was not sufficiently dazed to succumb to Primus' follow-up cut with his chainsword. Brutus recovered quickly, and slammed hard with the haft of his weapon – an unsubtle parry, but effective, forcing Primus back.

Brutus shook his head. Blood trickled from one of his wide nostrils.

'We both strong!' he said. 'Good, I wish for real challenge. I keep your head as trophy.'

They moved away from the stranded cargo truck, deeper into the wide, dark corridor heading out to the hangars. In the dimness, Brutus and Primus circled each other. Primus had only a few rounds left in his pistol, and was not willing to expend them against the monster's shield. His head ached from the effect of the blackstone.

'Good fight, yes. Between two made things. Two new things. Our masters are lords of creation! It is good we battle, to see who is strong.'

'We are not the same!' said Primus. Though he was. That was why he had to kill this thing, to make that true.

'You are,' said Brutus. He threw out his axe, letting the shaft slide right out, until he had it gripped at the very end, and swung at Primus, forcing the Space Marine to lean back out of the way. He stepped forward as Primus dodged, running his hand up the shaft of the axe as it finished its swing and then bringing it down again.

Primus did not move. Brutus lowed in anticipation of Primus' demise, but the giant Astartes dropped his chainsword, put out his hand and grabbed the axe beneath the twin beards, stopping it dead. He absorbed the force of the swing, then he pushed back.

The two gene-wrought beings struggled against each other, strength against strength.

Disruption lightning crackled around them. Primus clenched his jaw. Brutus grunted, pushing on the axe, shifting his weight to drive the blades down towards Primus' helm. There was no momentum to the blade, but the touch of the disruption field alone would kill him, shattering the atoms of his helm and then his head.

'You are strong,' said Brutus.

'Stronger than you,' said Primus. He raised his pistol in his other hand, and put a single bolt into Brutus' throat.

The round barely had time to ignite its rocket motor before it smacked into the creature's body. Still accelerating as it penetrated, the mass-reactive tripped on the way out, blasting a crater in the back of Brutus' neck and taking the beastman's spine with it.

Primus stepped aside as Brutus went limp and toppled forward.

He landed hard on the deck, already dead, a pool of blood spreading rapidly over the metal.

'Much stronger than you,' Primus said. He retrieved his sword and cut the head free with a single swing, grasped a horn and lifted it. 'And now I have your head.'

Blood ran down his plain grey armour as he set out again.

Fabius Bile was nearby.

The door from the lower levels swung inwards into the pyramid. Qvo, Oswen, Frenk, X99 and the Kastelans emerged into the bottom-most level of the stepped inner chamber. Battle raged there. From the centre of the room the lords of the Mechanicus were holding at bay a number of Heretic Astartes who were trying to force their way inwards from outside, down the steps. Powerful energy screens deflected a hail of bolt-shots. Heavy weapons fire dispersed harmlessly. As Qvo came into the room behind Sigma Fidelis, a traitor took a caliver shot in the chest, and fell from the ledge he occupied with a gurgling cry, trailing fire, until he hit one of the stagnant pools with an almighty splash. There were many corpses lying upon the prominences of the room, armour broken, but the heretics were making headway. Dozens of shattered skitarii were scattered around, and the hulking forms of heavy combat servitors burned with oily smoke. The magi were alone now, and soon the traitors would be present in enough numbers to overwhelm their conclave.

'In the nick of time!' X99 proclaimed. 'Sigma Fidelis, forward!'

'Compliance,' the war-robot droned, and stomped into the fray, phosphor guns blazing. Its less-free-thinking kin followed obediently, fanning out into a V formation of ceramite.

'I don't really think they need our help,' Qvo said, watching Anaxerxes of Accatran eviscerate a pair of Space Marines with flashing energy claws.

'Silence, traitor,' Frenk hissed in his ear.

The Heretic Astartes realised their plan had failed when the quintet of powerful war automata and not the expected Chaos reinforcements came up from below. The Space Marines began to fall back.

'By the grace of the Omnissiah, the enemy run!' X99 proclaimed. 'Cohort forward!' One of the robots jolted as a missile got through its energy field and blew on its shoulder. Its back-mounted phosphor blaster rotated round and fired back, and the Kastelan just kept on walking through the flames. They were imperturbable, these warriors of plasteel.

Qvo and the party from below sheltered in their formidable lee. Shots rebounded from their repulsor grid.

'Magnificent, aren't they?' X99 canted to him conversationally. 'I would consider swapping their data-wafers for something a little more belligerent, but I refrain. This aegis protocol serves us admirably.'

Qvo, whose core personality hailed from a less superstitious age, found himself in agreement. The robots were magnificent.

'They are enough to make my faith circuits sing with praise for the Machine God,' he replied to X99, and found that he meant it.

The Space Marines were running now, their previously carefully laid fire patterns falling apart.

'It's not just us. Something else has spooked them,' said Qvo. 'I have never seen Space Marines of any sort flee like this.'

They found out what as they exited the pyramid onto the plains. An hour of battle had transformed the place from swamp to blasted wasteland. The ruined hulks of war machines raised new features over the grassland, which now burned in dozens of places. There appeared to be a number of portals of some kind opened across the facility, and it was to these the Space Marines were running. They were in full flight not for lack of courage, but to avoid being left behind. Qvo realised he had been right thinking there would be other portals connected to the gate in the lower levels of Pontus Avernes, and now that was gone, these others were shutting.

One by one, the gates diminished in size to unsteady points, flickered, and went out. The Space Marines ran towards them, their power armour propelling them at superhuman speeds. They jumped into the light, swerving to new destinations as each gate collapsed in turn, until there was only one escape route left, and then none.

A handful of Space Marines were left behind. As war-horns blared from Cawl's surviving Knights, they prepared to sell themselves dearly.

'It looks like it is all over,' said Qvo. 'What a peculiar little battle.'

'It's not over for you,' said Frenk.

'I think you will find that it is.' A tall shadow fell over them.

'Archmagos Macroteknika Anaxerxes,' said Frenk.

'Let him go, magos. Now. I won't ask again.'

Primus found Bile squatting in the wide entryway into the hangar. With the chirurgeon's arms moving jerkily around him, and silhouetted by the ferocious light of Avernes' suns, his appearance lived up to his name of Spider.

Two of the chirurgeon's arms were suturing bits of dead flesh together, a gruesome, nervous habit, while Bile pushed the ferrule of his war-cane, Torment, through the detritus left by skitarii dead, left to right and right to left, doodling in the debris. Long, ratty white-blond hair fell from his scalp. He looked unhealthy, if unaccountably pleased with himself.

'Now,' said Bile loudly. He got to his feet, and peered critically at Primus. 'You are the being Cawl calls Alpha Primus, correct? My, my, here you are at last.' He was the kind of man that declaimed rather than spoke. 'There is true mastery of the genetor's art! Are you not magnificent? Such design. Such puissance crammed into one body. It is rare I praise the genecraft of others, but you… You are a masterpiece!'

'Silence,' said Primus. Bile declined to obey.

'I see the work of the Emperor Himself born anew in you.'

Primus tossed Brutus' head at Bile. It sailed in a precise arc and thumped down right in front of him, tongue lolling.

'You will lay down your arms and give your surrender now to the Archmagos Dominus Belisarius Cawl,' Primus said. 'He will treat you mercifully.'

Bile lifted Brutus' long tongue with the tip of Torment and let it fall back. 'You really are asking me to surrender?'

'You have penetrated barely three hundred yards into the ship. Your creatures on these levels are scattered or dead. We have purged most of our systems of your attempts at infiltration. Your other boarding parties have been contained. Within minutes, the magi who serve the archmagos dominus will have returned our weapons to our control. Your ship will be destroyed. Your most powerful warrior is dead. There is no way that you can prevail against me.' Primus let the light of the warp shine in his helm-lenses. 'You have lost, Fabius Bile.'

Bile stabbed Torment into Brutus' cooling flesh and ground it about. Then he began to laugh, a dry chuckle that became a loud expression of mirth so forceful it brought on a violent cough. Primus waited while it subsided. Bile wiped his mouth upon the back of his gauntlet.

'Does Cawl make all his creatures as arrogant as himself?'

'I speak truth. It is not arrogance. Surrender now or your life, long as it has been, is over.'

'No,' said Bile, suddenly vicious. 'You are not *seeing*. You assume I am old and addle-brained. I commanded the Third Legion into battle, boy. I pitted wits against the Emperor Himself. Do you think this strategy the best I could do? I have you right where I want you.'

'Is that so?' Primus gunned his chainsword to free its teeth of gore.

'It is so,' said Bile. 'You will see when you meet my most powerful warrior.' He smiled nastily. 'Poor Brutus was not.'

Primus came on guard. 'We are alone here. I feel no one.'

'You wouldn't, by design,' said Bile. 'Your master is not the only man gifted in the creation of exceptional children.'

There was no movement in the warp. Not the slightest betrayal of thought, not the least glow of an incarnate soul, but he heard them, coming up behind him, light footsteps running at what must have been close to forty miles an hour, and the whistle of an approaching projectile.

He ducked, unwilling to turn his back on Bile, as a javelin speared out of the dark behind him. It scraped past the tip of his helm, as if the thrower had almost perfectly predicted where he would move to, hurtled into the hangar and embedded itself in a cargo skiff. It came fast as a bullet, an impossible speed for a human to bestow upon a cast weapon, and Primus expected some sort of dart launcher, not the slender woman who came after, armed only with an unpowered sword. She leapt high as she approached him, and drove her blade down at his head. He parried with his chainsword, and was shocked by the strength of the blow. It staggered him, as surely as a hit from a power-armoured Adeptus Astartes would.

She bore down on him, landed feet apart on his shoulders, backflipped off and swung again. He parried once more, and they leaned into one another, weapons locked. Dark eyes glared at him from an inhuman face, but human still. Another of Bile's genetic abominations, but different. It was not a gene-twist, it was not malformed. It had been designed.

'Shall we see what he can do, Porter?' said Bile, backing into the hangar. 'I for one am keen to witness how Cawl's chimera fares against you.'

Porter stepped back, breaking the contact suddenly. Primus saw it coming and didn't follow and overbalance, but kept his feet, squeezed his chainsword trigger and struck with the track running at full speed, aiming to rip the blade from the woman's hands with the whirring teeth. Porter did an elegant dodge before the chain track could bite, and spun around on the heel of one foot, coming into position in guard at his left. He turned to face her.

She smiled coldly at him, blade held ready.

Their battle began in earnest.

CHAPTER TWENTY-SEVEN

SONS AND DAUGHTERS

Primus and Porter fought through the wreckage of the hangar. Porter leapt nimbly over obstructions. Primus bulldozed his way through them, trampling the mixed organics and machinery of dead skitarii. Porter attacked relentlessly with a shockingly powerful strength. She rained blows down upon him, her speed incredible. The force of her blows took its toll on his chainsword, and soon it was bereft of teeth, and he cast it aside.

Through all this Bile watched. He did not engage. Nor did the great gunship add its fire to the battle.

Porter sensed the momentary distraction as Primus glanced at Bile, and aimed for Primus' vulnerable knee. He turned his leg just in time, her blade hitting within a fraction of an inch of the articulated metal of the joint back. Chips of ceramite exploded from the blow. Primus countered with a backhand, a blow that would have shattered rockcrete, had it landed. But

Porter dove to the side, rolling away. Primus fired at her, his shot chasing empty space. The bolts slammed into the floor, into the bodies, into the ships sitting on their launchpads. Craters blew in everything. She wasn't tiring.

'Good, Porter. Good!' Bile called from the sidelines.

Primus' pistol ran dry. He dropped it, and pulled out his combat knife.

'Enough,' he said. 'Let us finish this.'

He turned. She circled him. There was a pattern to everyone's movements, no matter how skilled. Even a grandmaster favours certain tricks above others, and has their own way of performing them. He watched the way she swung her shoulders, the way she moved her feet, how a strange double musculature played under her skin.

There was a tense moment. She could sense he was about to lunge. Black post-human eyes locked with his transhuman gaze.

They moved together. Porter came in hard, sword swinging one way, then the other, anticipating where Primus would be.

Only Primus had changed his own patterns of movement. Within him, the genetic traits of the Emperor's sons burned bright.

Primus was where Porter did not expect. She recovered, bringing her sword up, but Primus blocked with his forearm. Steel sparked from ceramite. Their fight turned into a deadly flurry of blows, hands moving to attack, being countered, shifting position. She was too close to use her blade, so punched with its quillons. He held his sword-long knife reversed. Gradually, he forced her to retreat, following in too close to allow her to escape. For the first time, he saw a hint of dismay on her engineered face.

She made an error. He saw the opening. Primus feinted to her head, provoking a block that exposed her torso. Pivoting hard, he slammed her hard in the sternum with the flat of his left hand. A standard human would have died immediately from the blow, their ribcage shattered, heart burst. Her carapace broke under the heel of his palm. He had no idea how much punishment her dermal scutes would take, but he felt bone grind, and she was sent backwards. Her sword flew from her hand and clattered on the ground. When she landed, she lay still.

Judging her out of action, Primus turned on Bile.

'She is formidable,' he said as he advanced. 'What is she?'

'One of the beings who will replace *Homo sapiens* and rule the galaxy, saving our species in the process.'

'By wiping them out?'

'Evolution is a bloody game.'

Bile's bolt pistol came up preternaturally fast; for such a relic he could move. Primus waved his hand. A blow of telekinetic force sent it wide. A second wrenched it from the Primogenitor's grasp, and it slammed into the gutted wreck of a lighter.

Bile rubbed his wrist. 'I sense the seed of the cyclops in you. Cawl is rash. You should not be.'

'Be silent. You cannot save yourself,' said Primus. He drew deep on the warp, preparing to end the life of the most malevolent Spider. His eye-lenses glowed with power.

'I suppose I can't,' said Bile. 'Porter will, though.'

Primus heard a movement in the air. He turned too late. Against all odds, Bile's abomination was up and fighting again. She landed on his backpack. He staggered at the sudden change in weight. Her hands were all over his face, clawing at him. He could hear the bones grinding in her chest. He could smell her blood. Still she fought with an animal ferocity.

She got her fingers under his helmet, twisted, yanking it free, and threw it aside. Primus caught her about the shoulder, plucked her off his back and tossed her hard head over heels into the bullet-pocked defence barriers surrounding the hangar landing field. She leapt to her feet, and raced at him again, but Primus blasted her back with a telekine wave that sent debris crashing everywhere.

'She will die, you will die,' Primus said, turning back to Bile.

Bile shrugged. He had a strange pistol in his hand. The tall vessels of fluid on his back swirled.

'Then it is time to bring this to a close.'

There was a hissing of tiny, crystalline darts in the air. Primus felt them like fine rain on his face. He ignored them, and lifted his hand, using it to focus his power. Bile gave out a surprised choke when he was lifted up off the floor. His eyes were wide with shock as Primus strode towards him, as if he could not believe what he was seeing. He tried to raise his strange gun again, but Primus crushed it with a thought, shattering its armaglass barrel, bending metal to scrap.

He took another step, teeth gritted, intent on ridding the galaxy of this evil once and for all, ready to boil Bile's brains in his skull, but as he took another step, his foot dragged. He felt dizzy. His hold on the warp broke, and his psychic grip relaxed.

Bile dropped to the floor, and took in an enormous, whooping breath.

Primus' foot caught on the back of his heel. His fingers were limp. Before he knew it, he was falling, and lay stunned in the detritus of battle.

He could no longer move his limbs.

Bile pushed himself back to his feet. 'My, my, you are even more impressive than I suspected.' His voice was hoarse. His footsteps drew near. Primus was completely paralysed. 'I almost underestimated you. It is fortunate for me,' he said, bending down, gripping Primus' armour and heaving him over onto his back, 'that I am a cautious man.'

Primus blinked. Bile again looked surprised, as Primus clenched his fist and made to get up.

'Though perhaps not cautious enough,' Primus said through numb lips.

'Just enough,' said Bile, and jabbed Primus in the throat with Torment.

Even for a being used to living in constant pain, the agony Torment inflicted was unbearable. Primus screamed freely for the first time since he had been taken from his genesis capsule.

Bile dropped eagerly to his knees. A limb of his chirurgeon lowered, saw whirring.

'Let's see what we have in here, shall we?'

Bile stabbed down, the blade kissed ceramite, and bit deep into Primus' chest.

There were long periods of nothingness where Roosev thought he might be dead. No external sensory input, no sensation from his body, no communion with his throne.

Death, said Maven the Very Elder into his mind with deep and heartfelt relief. *Finally, death.*

Then the black came again, and the voice faded, and he thought that death was coming for certain, but it would depart and be replaced by...

Moments...

A daemon machine's mouth snapped inches from his Knight's failing ocular sensors, coating their cracked lenses with acid drool. His chainblade transfixed it, coring a huge hole through its belly, so that it surely should have burst into two pieces, and yet it did not, and would not yield, but was squirming around on the spinning teeth, desperate to sink fangs into the Knight Cerastus' helm.

Welcome, peaceful death.

Flames roared up *Iurgium*'s body, overheating its systems, causing its joints to seize. Promethium burned with an uncompromising fury. Metal softened, began to run.

So quiet, the end. Peace, I have yearned for you…

Lights in the sky failed. A panic in the enemy. Retreat. Still the beast – now riderless, where had its rider gone? – squirmed and snapped and roared.

Different light. Coherent, killing light cast by holy weaponry. The Machine God spoke unto the debased machine-beast, and His words were of death.

Now, the end, the end, the end…

The Very Elder's voice faded. Roosev prepared to follow him into the glittering halls of technology.

'Ave Omnissiah. I go to worship the lord of knowledge, and to learn at His feet,' he said. His voice was hoarse. He wheezed.

True blackness. He lost consciousness for a while.

Then noise. The sound of an angle grinder cutting. Sparks sprayed into his cockpit, there was the squeal of metal, and the cockpit hatch was torn away. Servitors stepped back. Allacer, a bandage across his hand, leaned in, peering up at Roosev in concern.

'Brother?'

Roosev groaned.

'Brother!' Allacer's face was transformed. He leaned out and shouted behind him. 'Thank the Omnissiah, the lord scion lives!'

Outside, there was the noise of jubilation, but it was distant. Of much greater volume was the Very Elder's voice once more in his mind.

That was a very fine battle, he said.

Cawl limped his way into the hangar. Amid the corpses and the wrecked void craft, he saw with horror Fabius Bile crouched over the body of Primus, his Apothecary's tools red with blood, and for a terrible moment he thought Primus was dead.

'Leave him be,' said Cawl. 'Get out.'

Bile continued his work, chirurgeon's blades flashing. Primus' breastplate was off, his undersuit sliced away and his chest and neck open.

'Archmagos Cawl. I wondered when you would join us,' said Bile, without looking up.

Bile pushed a long tube into the lower wound. There was a sucking pop, and a gobbet of matter was drawn up into a clear storage flask. It bobbed about in suspension fluid. Alpha Primus' gene-seed.

'Stop,' Cawl said. He levelled his plasma carbine at the ancient Apothecary.

Bile did not stop. Spidery limbs descended. Las-scalpels cut. The smell of freshly burned flesh hung on the air.

'Come one step closer and Porter here will kill you,' said Bile. He glanced up, and Cawl turned slightly, seeing a slender female figure stalking him. He had not noticed her before. She was limping, bleeding dark-coloured blood from breathing spiracles set in her neck, but she looked deadly. 'As wise as you are, and as wounded as she is, you are no match for her. You will be dead in moments, and your creation lost.' Click click click, went the chirurgeon's limbs, dipping in and out of Primus' wounds. 'If that is not enough disincentive, then I regret to say that, should you come any closer, I will end the life of this marvellous creation of yours.'

One of the chirurgeon's arms went down level with Primus' neck, swivelling to present a razor-edge circular saw to his throat. No matter how much Bile moved as he worked on the prone Space Marine, the limb stayed perfectly still.

'You might be thinking that you could kill me before this saw activates. That might be true, but I assure you that the chirurgeon has enough self-determination to kill Primus even if you were to kill me.' He looked up and smiled sympathetically. 'Neither of us wants that.'

'You did not want the Sangprimus Portum,' said Cawl. 'Primus was your target all along.'

Bile smiled wickedly. 'I wouldn't say I did not want it. I would be most glad to get my hands on it, but you are a considerable force in this galaxy, Cawl. There was little chance of my securing it with the poor assets I have at my disposal. But why bother, when everything I need is here, in the body of your creation? As I told you, I was disappointed when I examined your Primaris Marines, but then, a few years ago, I heard of a peculiar warrior who fought at your side, a warrior who was mighty in the arts of war, and of the warp. At first, I thought the reports exaggerated, as these things so often are. But they were not. Meeting him in person showed me they were, if anything, an understatement. I must say, there is artistry here that exceeds all my expectations of you. You have my respect, archmagos.'

Cawl was unsure of what to do. The noosphere had yet to be re-established in the hangar. He could call in no aid.

'I would guess you have not told Lord Guilliman exactly what you have made here.'

Cawl stared at him stonily.

Bile nodded in understanding. 'Wise. I guess you also have not told him either, have you?' Bile smiled fondly down at Primus. 'I can think of no other reason why he did not use the full extent of his abilities when he came against us. I was a little concerned, you know. I thought I might have bitten off more than I could chew.' Bile looked to Cawl again as his chirurgeon continued to work. 'But he doesn't know what he is, does he? Tell me, so I may hear it for myself, from out of the mouth of the man who is confident enough to attempt something like this. Something so audacious. I sense the unprecedented blending of many lines of gene-seed in this being. I see such potential, and yet I can only guess the half of what you have done. Tell me what he is, Archmagos Cawl. Do me this favour. Sate my curiosity.'

Cawl looked to Bile, then to Primus, then back again. What, indeed, was Primus? The first Primaris, which in a sense he was, though that was not strictly true? A great experiment? A deliberate provocation to the hidebound fools who ran the Martian empire? A demonstration of his own hubris? A death sentence, maybe, if his nature were revealed?

He was all those things and more, but none of them mattered. Only one thing mattered.

'He is my son,' Cawl said flatly. All lightness fled him. All his personality overlays, all his clever neurological tricks went. The weight of the moment pushed all that aside. He was exposed, open. The core of his being laid bare. For a few moments, he was no other person than Belisarius Cawl.

'I see,' said Bile. He looked at Porter. 'I understand. I too have affection for my creations. My progeny, almost.'

'I don't think you do understand,' said Cawl. 'He is not some thing whose elements were culled from whatever debased source I could get my hands on. He is far more. His genetic code is complex, but there are elements of myself in him.'

'Porter is just as finely designed…'

'He is not designed! Not completely. Do you not see? I made him from myself. In his genecode, I live on. I nurtured him. I…' He paused, unsure whether he could voice the words. 'I love him. He is my son.'

'Then I am sorry that I must do this,' said Bile, and pushed his hand deep into Primus' chest cavity. Cawl tensed, trapped. For the first time in a long time, he felt defeated. Bile's face twisted in concentration.

'Aha!' he said. 'There we have it.'

Carefully, he exposed Primus' lower progenoid gland. A deft

flick of a knife and he had it open. The tube went in. Gene-seed was sucked out into more suspension vials.

'Don't worry. All done now,' said Bile. He stowed the vials in his belt. 'If you are quick, when I am gone, you can save him.'

'You're… you're not going to kill him?' said Cawl.

'Nor you, archmagos,' said Bile. 'I would rather burn a dozen worlds than destroy so exquisite a masterpiece as your Alpha Primus. As for you, our goals are the same, though you do not admit it. I find it ironic that you spent so much time trying to convince that xenos monster of your common goals, and yet you cannot see ours. So I leave you alive in the hope that one day you will come to your senses. The thought of working with you is an enticing one.' He looked down at Primus and shook his head with respect. 'Remarkable.' He beckoned. 'Come along, Porter, we have what we need. We are leaving the arch-magos' company.'

The engines of Bile's gunship ignited. The ramp came down. Bile turned to walk towards it. His engineered companion followed backwards, limping heavily, but her face always turned to Cawl, sword up and steady.

Cawl stepped forward. 'I could kill you now. I could destroy your ship when you leave this hangar. Blast your *Vesalius* from the void.'

'Then what is stopping you?' said Bile, and stepped onto the ramp.

'That,' said Cawl. He pointed at a device like a tall syringe stabbed into Primus' exposed shoulder. The tube was topped with a small machine, whose exposed gears made it rotate round and round a toothed track. 'A booby trap?'

'Yes!' Bile shouted gleefully over the rising whine of *Butcher-Bird*'s engines. 'Once I am in the warp, it will deactivate itself. Should I die, or the signal fail before then, your precious child will be injected with mutagenic acid. He will die instantly, and there will be nothing left for you to salvage. I sincerely do not wish to terminally damage such a masterpiece, but one must guarantee one's own safety. Remember the mercy I showed you and him, Cawl. One day, I may come to collect the favour.' He turned to look around the hangar one last time. 'I apologise for the mess. If only you had listened to me, we could have avoided all this unpleasantness.'

Bile strode up the ramp. Porter followed. The ramp closed, the ship rose on screaming pillars of fire, turned, and powered out of the hangar.

The noosphere surged back into life.

'*My lord!*' Wocolos' voice sounded in his internal vox. '*You live!*'

'Allow Bile to depart. No fire upon his gunship or the *Vesalius*.'

'*Archmagos?*' said Wocolos. '*We have a firm target lock. One word, and he is dead.*'

'Do as I say!' shouted Cawl, and the anguish in his voice stopped all further comment from Wocolos. He scurried over to Primus. 'Get me a medicae team to my position. Immediately!'

CHAPTER TWENTY-EIGHT

PUZZLE PIECES

'Firstly, let's get one thing out of the way, Primus,' said Cawl, as they walked up the rows of skitarii lining the entrance into the pyramid. 'You were right. I should be more careful.'

'You should have heeded me,' said Primus with difficulty. Bile had cut deep. The great Space Marine was unusually quiet, and Qvo wondered if the wounds he had suffered were more than physical. Losing a progenoid gland must carry some sort of emotional cost.

Iota made a small noise in her voxmitter. Her war-body was burnished to a brilliant shine that caught the light of Pontus Avernes' endless day and reflected it back at the heavens.

'And the marshal,' added Primus. 'She said the same.'

'Yes, yes, apologies to the marshal too,' said Cawl. He affected a breezy air, but could not completely cover his disquiet.

'Then if I was correct, you also admit you were wrong?' said

Primus. The grafts covering the wounds where his glands had been torn out were swollen, and he marched stiffly.

Qvo made the last of the line of four at the head of Cawl's procession. The archmagos had turned out thousands of tech-priests from his ship, and they marched solemnly, droning prayers to the Machine God. A dense swarm of skulls, cherubs, angels, pseudo-arachnid mechabots, and every other kind of semi-autonomous drone dreamt up in the deeps of the forge worlds flew over them. The fumes of scented oil billowed white and strong amid long banners bearing the holy Machina Opus. It was an amazing sight, though rather diminished by Primus and Cawl's testy exchange, Qvo thought.

'I am not saying that, I am only saying that you might have had a point. Well done.'

'You are taking this disaster as an opportunity to patronise me?' said Primus.

Cawl looked peeved. 'You can look at it like that, if you wish. I mean well.'

'I know,' said Primus. He paused. He almost didn't speak his next words, but Qvo could tell they wanted to be said. They seemed heavy in his mouth, like ball bearings, and they rolled out almost of their own volition. 'Thank you,' he said. 'For saving me.'

Cawl looked down.

'Why would I not, my boy?' he said, quietly enough that his words were almost lost in the noise of the parade.

They passed into a pyramid now dazzlingly lit. Victory had brought out a jubilant mood among the Mechanicus, and they showed it by renovating the pyramid so that it looked how it must have done thousands of years ago. Mechanisms in the wall had been found and reactivated, and they projected a shifting array of light sculptures depicting ancient humans in bizarre modes of dress. Whole cadres of lesser tech-priests were around them, eagerly taking records of the sleek technology glimpsed within the recordings. Every time an artefact appeared they let out an excited chorus of binharic.

'I have one of those in the hold,' said Cawl to Qvo, pointing at an arrow-shaped void-fighter racing through a projection. 'Shh,' he said, with his finger to his lips.

And so down once more into the under halls of Pontus Avernes, whose secret door was now wide open and choked with conduits snaking below. The hall was filled with brilliant light, glorious choruses, and scented, burning oil. All the pomp of the Machine God.

Once more, the dignitaries of three forge worlds waited. Once more, Belisarius Cawl came to a stop behind them and gave a surprisingly delicate bow.

'My lords and ladies of the Machine God,' he proclaimed. 'Have you reached your decision?'

Anaxerxes was at the fore again. He seemed positively energised by the prior battle. Qvo was sure he would declare for Cawl.

'We have. Each world shall deliver its response by delegation, for is it not written that the domains of the Machine God are individual in all, if united in purpose?'

'It is so,' said Cawl.

'We of Accatran declare for you,' said Anaxerxes. 'We will provide the materials and expertise you require. Despite our misgivings...' He looked sideways at Frenk. 'We judge the potential gains to be made in terms of data gathered to be too important to be overlooked.'

'The hour is late. The Great Rift threatens to destroy the entirety of the Machine God's Great Work. No solution, no matter how extreme, no matter how *blasphemous*, should be disregarded,' said Magnacomptroller Sestertius. 'This treachery from within our own ranks has only served to convince us that the Prime Conduit's proposed course of action is valid.'

Frenk tensed.

Anaxerxes spoke again. 'We do this on the condition that any xenotech recovered be given over to whichever parties decide to take part in the expedition, and that its fate be decided by whichever forge world is judged senior in rank by the Codex Feodalis of Mars.'

Lord Datamage Kinzellian of Tigrus rolled forward upon his assault tracks, and spoke.

'We of Tigrus concur. The same offer of aid, contingent upon the same conditions.'

There was a tension on the air. Perhaps Anaxerxes did not expect the others to assent. Tigrus was a grade higher in Mars' estimation than Accatran, and would therefore be favoured in any tech-giving.

'This is what they're really after,' Cawl canted privately to Qvo. 'Their radicals wish to get their hands on alien technology, under the guise of keeping it safe, of course. Now we shall see what Metallica has to say.'

A white-robed lector dogmis of Metallica came forward.

'No,' he said. 'We judge this venture to be entirely contrary to the codes of the Cult. Abhor the alien, abhor the work of the alien! No good can come of disturbing this time-locked world. Who knows what horrors shall be unleashed?'

'And yet we and Tigrus stand in agreement,' said Anaxerxes.

'Then you shall be judged accordingly. In the spirit of this gathering we shall not attempt to detain you here.'

More likely because we outnumber and outgun you, thought Qvo.

'But we shall be sending another delegation to Mars to pursue your excommunication from the Cult Mechanicus,' the lector dogmis said. 'Let it be known, Magos Frenk, that your warnings have not fallen upon deaf ears. We shall ask for the ultimate sanction. Belisarius Cawl has gone too far.' The lector dogmis' eyes lingered on Qvo, giving him a very human shiver down his artificial spine. 'We depart now. Our business here is concluded.'

Frenk looked pleased as he followed the Metallicans out. They pointedly cut their cants of praise together, and their tech-priests examining the structure reluctantly departed with them.

It took three minutes of clattering bionics and humming engines for the whole Metallican delegation to leave.

'They didn't even contest ownership of the discoveries here,' canted Qvo.

'Oh, very serious,' replied Cawl. Then he clapped his hands together. 'Well, that's all sorted out then. When shall we start?'

Fabius Bile pored over the gene-seed taken from Alpha Primus with increasing respect.

'I was too hasty in dismissing his work,' he said. His breath plumed extravagantly from his mouth in the freezing air of the laboratory.

'Do you see genius in this sample?' asked Petros the Bezoar, Bile's only constant companion besides Porter. A Space Marine of the old orders, he was oath-bound to Slaanesh to try every intoxicant in the galaxy. Bile regarded his choice as imbecilic, but tolerated him.

'I do. I do! This goes much beyond what Cawl did in the Primaris Space Marines. There is an artist's hand at work here. At play, even.'

Petros belched into his clamped rebreather. His grey face glistened with sweat. 'I would not have thought a superstitious tinkerer like Cawl to be up to the task.'

Bile looked up at him testily. 'Are you well enough to assist me today, Petros? I have limited material. I do not want it to become contaminated.'

'I suffer the after-effects of my latest tasting, that is all.'

'Then you promise not to vomit on anything?'

'That is why I am wearing my respiration mask,' Petros said.

Bile nodded. 'Very well. Pay attention!'

He went back to filleting the gene-seed on the bench before him, teasing out the zygote clusters clinging to the inside, and carefully depositing them into test tubes.

'Yes,' he said, half to himself. 'Soon I shall have Abaddon off my back, and then we will be able to truly explore what wonders Cawl put into his son.'

They came aboard in pairs, or alone, heading for the great forge-fane, until eight figures clad in black were gathered there, around the sarcophagus granted to Kolumbari-Enas by Fabius Bile. They greeted one another with the secret codes of their order, then took up their appointed spots. Eight of them in a circle, the zero-position unoccupied. This was the way it had been since the days of their founding.

Their leader, the First-Among-Equals, Kolumbari-Enas, held wide his arms, and let out a long stream of binharic in praise of the Dark Gods. His fellows joined, and slowly, ponderously, the stasis casket opened.

Inside was an android of terrible aspect, skull-faced and grim, fashioned of black metal, not dissimilar to a necron, in fact, but entirely of human make.

'Behold, the form immaculate,' Kolumbari-Enas intoned. 'Behold, the android of Chaos!'

It was dead, inert. The Neverborn it had been made to house was long gone back into the warp, yet a hint of power clung to it, and as the Disciples of Nul discovered as they examined it, it was fully functional. Replete with forgotten technologies, made by hands unknown, for purposes long forgotten.

Now it was theirs, and by their arts of sorcery and science, would be restored.

'The vessel must be prepared!' Kolumbari-Enas called. 'Make it fit so that our master might live again!'

'I don't think you have quite grasped how much of a predicament you are in, my dear,' said Cawl. He looked down at the cryptek, whose disembodied head he held in his hands. Wires inserted into her neck fed her artificial brain with power, and she gave an angry growl.

Qvo took a step back. Cawl darted him an admonishing frown.

'Are you more amenable to working within my terms? With me, and not against me?' he said to his captive.

'Never!' said AsanethAyu.

'Your alternative option is not good,' said Cawl. 'To be shut down and kept within stasis until I get around to disassembling your marvellous alien brain. That might be some time. I can be forgetful.' They were once more in his Necron Archive, and he gestured threateningly at the piles of disassembled artefacts arrayed behind him. AsanethAyu's stasis casket yawned open, the interior adapted with clamps for the head.

'Eternal imprisonment or your bodiless servant. You offer no palatable option,' said the head. 'Therefore I decline.'

Cawl sighed. 'I refer you to our earlier conversation. Do you have a counter offer?'

She said nothing. Lights danced in her orbicular eye, then she spoke with restrained annoyance.

'Give me my body back, and I will aid you.'

'My issue with that, AsanethAyu, is that I do not trust you,' said Cawl. 'Prove yourself to me, be loyal, aid me first, and I will return your body to you.'

'I could kill you at any time,' said the necron.

'We both know that threat is not true. You are at my mercy. It is time to go to sleep for a while. I will return soon, and present your options again. Serve me willingly, help me save both our peoples, or suffer dissection.'

Cawl gently laid AsanethAyu's head into the casket, and undertook the rites of initiation. The door shut on her.

'That's that done, then,' said Cawl. 'A pity.'

She seemed inactive, should have been inactive, but an accusatory air clung to the giant eye staring through the viewing window. Qvo shuddered.

'Something bothering you?' said Cawl. 'She can't hurt us, even if it does look like she's glaring at us.'

'It does, doesn't it?' said Qvo. 'It's not that though. There is a lesson here for the Cult Mechanicus. The necrons are what lie at the end of the road should we go too far in pursuit of perfection.'

'Well said,' said Cawl. 'Though I prefer to look at it from a slightly more optimistic point of view.'

'How is that even remotely possible?'

'The similarity between us means there is space for common ground,' said Cawl.

'The necrons are evil!' said Qvo. 'They want to cut the souls from the bodies of every living creature in the galaxy. They harvest us, use us for sport and their weird sciences,' he protested.

'Are they evil?' said Cawl. 'I am not so sure. I prefer to see them as supremely rational, and it is through their rationality that we shall come to an accord.' AsanethAyu looked even angrier, though her face had not objectively changed. 'Call them soulless monsters if you will. I found Trazyn the Infinite to be a perfectly acceptable conversational partner. They might wish to dominate the universe, but they hold the key to defeating Chaos for good. Our goals are aligned.'

'To a point,' said Qvo.

'To a point,' agreed Cawl.

For Qvo, the issue went deeper. Both he and the cryptek were essentially mechanisms masquerading as life, but he wasn't willing to say. It was too personal, too frightening, to contemplate.

'Bile said the same to you.'

'He did,' admitted Cawl. 'The difference there is that I am right and he was wrong.'

Qvo held his peace.

'We still need her,' said Cawl, misinterpreting his friend's silence. 'However you look at it.'

Qvo nodded glumly. There was another death they needed to attend to. Best get it over with.

'I suppose this is it then,' said Qvo. It was harder to say than he had expected.

'What do you mean, my friend?' said Cawl, genuinely puzzled.

'I've been exposed as a weakness, archmagos.'

'Archmagos? Weakness? What's all this about?'

'You can't let me stay. I'm a liability,' Qvo explained. 'You must end your Qvo project. Put me back in the box like the cryptek here and blow the box to pieces.' He gave a weak smile. 'It's time to let me die. Please,' he added.

Cawl bent down, his insectoid carriage waddling back, and his long spine bending in such a way that he came face to face with his friend, and for a moment, an illusion existed that Cawl was still just a man.

'Why?'

'I'm your flaw, Belisarius,' said Qvo. 'The Machine God dictates that we must eliminate our flaws. Flesh is weak. Your affection for me...' He lifted his hands. 'It is weak.'

'Oh, my dear fellow...'

'Dyos said you must hate me, bringing me back all these times,' Qvo said in a small voice. Cawl looked embarrassed, but before he could speak, Qvo stopped him. 'I know it's not true,' he said. 'I know, if anything, it's the opposite. Belisarius, I make you vulnerable. Because of my existence, this ship was almost destroyed. Primus nearly died. The Omnissiah alone in His infinite wisdom could not have saved us if Alixia-Dyos had succeeded.'

Cawl smiled. 'She did fail though, didn't she? And she didn't just fail all on her own, she failed because of you.' He put his hands on Qvo's shoulders. 'These people who fall for the lies of the Dark Gods, they do it from despair. They fall into the trap of thinking that the gentler human emotions are worthless, that they leave us with vulnerabilities that can be exploited. All they have room for is hate and fear and horror. They neglect affection. They chase individual strength and forget that human beings only succeed together. No man is an island, a great thinker once said. A man is remembered for his deeds, but he is remembered by his companions. In short, we all need friends, and so I need you.'

'But, Belisarius!'

'My dear, dear Friedisch,' Cawl said 'We will speak no more about this. I could never shut you down. You and I have been through far too much together.'

'I'm not Friedisch, Belisarius,' said Qvo.

'No, not yet,' said Cawl, squeezing Qvo's shoulder gently and releasing him. 'But you will be one day.'

He rose up again, his metal claws clattering on the deck as his long, centaur's body rearranged itself. He frowned at Asane-thAyu's head in the box, then at the scarabs waiting on racks on the far side of the room. Then he smiled.

'Are you up for a game of regicide, Qvo?' he said. 'I appear to be lacking an opponent.'

ABOUT THE AUTHOR

Guy Haley is the author of the Siege of Terra novel
The Lost and the Damned, as well as the Horus Heresy
novels *Titandeath*, *Wolfsbane* and *Pharos*, and the
Primarchs novels *Konrad Curze: The Night Haunter*,
Corax: Lord of Shadows and *Perturabo: The Hammer
of Olympia*. He has also written many Warhammer
40,000 novels, including the Dawn of Fire books
Avenging Son and *Throne of Light*, as well as *Belisarius
Cawl: The Great Work*, *Genefather*, the Dark Imperium
trilogy, *The Devastation of Baal*, *Dante*, *Darkness in
the Blood* and *Astorath: Angel of Mercy*. For Age of
Sigmar he has penned the Drekki Flynt novels *The
Arkanaut's Oath* and *The Ghosts of Barak-Minoz* as
well as many other stories. He lives in Yorkshire with
his wife and son.

RENEGADES: HARROWMASTER
by Mike Brooks

Secrets and lies abound with the mysterious Alpha Legion, but as extinction becomes an ever-present reality for the Serpent's Teeth warband, Solomon Akurra seeks a new way of war…

An extract from
Renegades: Harrowmaster
by Mike Brooks

Jonn Brezik clutched his lasgun, muttered prayers under his breath, and hunkered further into the ditch in which he and seven others were crouching as the world shook around them. The weapon in his slightly trembling hands was an M35 M-Galaxy Short: solid, reliable and well maintained, with a fully charged clip, and a scrimshaw he had carved himself hanging off the barrel. He had another four ammo clips on his belt, along with the long, single-edged combat knife that had been his father's. He was not wearing the old man's flak vest – not a lot of point, given the state it had ended up in – and as enemy fire streaked overhead again, Jonn began to do the mental arithmetic of whether, right now, he would prefer to be in possession of a gun or functional body armour. The gun could kill the people shooting at him, that was for sure, but he would have to be accurate for that to work, and there didn't seem to be any shortage of the bastards. On the other hand, even the best armour would give out eventually, if he lacked any way of dissuading the other side from shooting at him–

'Brezik, you with us?'

Jonn jerked and blinked, then focused on the woman who had spoken. Suran Teeler, sixty years old at least, with a face that looked like a particularly hard rock had been hit repeatedly with another rock. She was staring at him with eyes like dark flint, and he forced himself to nod.

'Yeah. Yeah, I'm here.'

'You sure? Because you seem a bit distracted right now,' Teeler said. 'Which, given we're in the middle of a bastard *warzone*, is something of a feat.'

'I'll be fine, sarge,' Jonn replied. He closed his eyes for a moment, and sighed. 'It's just the dreams again. Feels like I haven't slept properly for a month.'

'You've been having them too?' Kanzad asked. He was a big man with a beard like a bush. 'The sky ripping open?'

Jonn looked over at him. He and Kanzad did not really get on – there was no enmity as such, no blood feud; they just rubbed each other the wrong way – but there was no mockery on the hairy face turned in his direction.

'Yeah,' he said slowly. 'The sky ripping open. Well, not just our sky. All the skies. What does that mean, if we're both having the same dream?'

'It means absolute jack-dung until we get out of here alive,' Teeler snapped. 'You want to compare dream notes after we're done, that's fine. Right now, I want your attention on the matter in hand! And Brezik?'

'Yes, sarge?' Jonn replied, clutching his lasgun a little tighter.

'Stop calling me "sarge".'

'Sorry, s– Sorry. Force of habit.'

A throaty drone grew in the air behind them, and Jonn looked up to see lights in the night sky, closing the distance at a tremendous speed. The drone grew into a whine, and then into a roar as the aircraft shot overhead: two Lightnings flanking an Avenger, all three heading further into the combat zone.

'That's the signal!' Teeler yelled, scrambling to her feet with a swiftness that belied her years. 'Go, go, go!'

Jonn leaped up and followed her, clambering out of the ditch and charging across the chewed-up ground beyond. He desperately tried to keep up some sort of speed without twisting an ankle in the great ruts and gouts torn into the earth by bombardments, and the repeated traversing of wheeled and tracked vehicles. He could see other groups just like his on either side, screaming their battle cries as they advanced on the enemy that were being savaged by aerial gunfire from their fighters. Jonn raised his voice to join in, adrenaline and fear squeezing his words until they came out as little more than a feral scream:

'FOR THE EMPEROR!'

Streams of fire began spewing skywards as the enemy finally got their anti-aircraft batteries online. Jonn heard the *thump-thump-thump* of Hydra quad autocannons, and one of the fighters – a Lightning, he thought, although it was hard to tell at this distance, and in the dark – came apart in a flower of flame, and scattered itself over the defenders below.

'Keep moving!' Teeler yelled as one or two in their group slowed slightly. 'We've got one shot at this!'

Jonn pressed on, despite the temptation to hang back and let others take the brunt of the enemy gunfire. Presenting the defenders with targets one at a time would only ensure they all died: this massed rush, so there were simply too many of them to kill in time, was the only way to close the distance and get into the enemy lines. Once there, the odds became far more even.

They passed through a line of metal posts, some no more than girders driven upright into the mud, and the fortifications ahead began to sparkle with ruby-red bolts of super-focused light. They had entered the kill-zone, the functional range of a lasgun, and the defenders now knew that their shots would not be wasted.

Kanzad jerked, then jerked again, then fell on his face. Jonn did not stop for him. He would not have stopped for anyone. Stopping meant dying. He charged onwards, his face contorted into a rictus of fear and hatred, daring the galaxy to come and take him.

The galaxy obliged.

The first las-bolt struck him in the right shoulder and burned straight through. It was a sharp pain, but a clean pain, and he staggered but kept moving. It was his trigger arm, and his lasgun was supported by a strap. So long as his left arm could aim the barrel and his right could pull the trigger, he was still in this fight.

The next shot hit him in the gut, puncturing the muscle wall of his stomach and doubling him over. He managed to retain his feet, just, but his momentum was gone. He began to curl up around the pain, and the stench of his own flash-cooked flesh. Eyes screwed up, face towards the ground, Jonn Brezik did not even see the last shot. It struck the top of his head, and killed him instantly.